Cottonwood Flowing

M. Marie Lewis

Copyright © 2019 M. Marie Lewis.

All rights reserved. No part of this book may be reproduced, stored, or transmitted by any means—whether auditory, graphic, mechanical, or electronic—without written permission of the author, except in the case of brief excerpts used in critical articles and reviews. Unauthorized reproduction of any part of this work is illegal and is punishable by law.

This is a work of fiction. All of the characters, names, incidents, organizations, and dialogue in this novel are either the products of the author's imagination or are used fictitiously.

ISBN: 978-1-6847-0793-5 (sc)
ISBN: 978-1-6847-0795-9 (hc)
ISBN: 978-1-6847-0794-2 (e)

Library of Congress Control Number: 2019911590

Because of the dynamic nature of the Internet, any web addresses or links contained in this book may have changed since publication and may no longer be valid. The views expressed in this work are solely those of the author and do not necessarily reflect the views of the publisher, and the publisher hereby disclaims any responsibility for them.

Any people depicted in stock imagery provided by Getty Images are models, and such images are being used for illustrative purposes only.
Certain stock imagery © Getty Images.

Lulu Publishing Services rev. date: 08/08/2019

TO MY FRIEND,
ARLYCE,
BECAUSE YOU INSPIRED ME.
I wish you'd gotten
a chance to see the final print.
Godspeed, my friend;

AND TO JANE,
because you are you.

Prologue

The u-boat was deadly quiet, fifty meters below the surface of the sea, silently waiting for a retreat of the enemy above. In the one hundred percent humidity, the stench in the air was putrid; the smell of rotten food, urine, and phosphorus was overwhelming. Crewmen, treading quietly in stockinged feet, with faces ghostly white and wild, scared eyes peering out of overgrown beards, winced at the sounds of the Asdic impulses pinging around them. Herr Oberleutnant, captain of the vessel, had earlier ordered the men to don the brown canvas life vests in preparation for a hasty retreat from the vessel, should the damages prove to be fatal.

As the noxious fumes from the batteries leaked into the compartments, many of the newer crew members gagged and vomited as the poisons seeped into their bodies. Two things were faced with certainty; within a very short time, the crew would face suicide within the confines of the iron coffin in which they were buried, or death above. A decision had to come swiftly, or all crew would suffocate in agony; the u-boat, a remarkably efficient war machine, had but one fatal flaw: its batteries required resurfacing every twenty to twenty-four hours.

The patrol of nine U-boats left Brest, at the tip of occupied France, in early 1943, attempting to break through the Allied-controlled Strait of Gibraltar. The u-boat Kreigsmarine were well aware that the calm waters of the Mediterranean were dangerous for boat and crew. Allied Forces controlled bases all around the Strait, and escape without easy detection was nearly impossible in its shallow, pristine waters.

The wolf pack, nine Atlantic Type VII unterseeboots, had swept into the Strait under cover of darkness, covertly shutting down radar equipment and running on battery power, deep below the surface by day, diesel power when they resurfaced at night. Rommel's forces in Tunisia were coming under heavy attack, and the wolf-pack had set out to keep the Allies from replenishing their weapons and supplies inland. Dodging patrols, the pack had reached Cape Bouharoun near Algiers in a raging storm and had been ambushed by a convoy of British destroyers.

Radar warning receivers were of little use against the Allied forces in the Mediterranean; even if undetected by radar, the u-boat could be easily visible in the shallow depth of the Strait. Tommies, attacking a fleet from every direction would surround the u-boat, forcing it to submerge, and finish it when, at its last breath, it was forced to resurface.

"A-l-a-a-r-m!"

Circling each other in the dark, the u-boats and the Allied convoy began a game of cat and mouse, with each vessel alternating between hunter and prey. Heavy seas had rendered the u-boat deck guns largely ineffective, and, desperate to escape a fatal blow, three of the nine u-boats hastily descended undersea.

Torpedoes ripped through the Portside of U-491, hitting directly into its saddle fuel tank and causing it to explode in a tremendous roar and list heavily before vanishing into the sea as water filled its control room. Communications from U-890 and U-685, both badly damaged, indicated dread: ATTACKED. BOMBS. SINKING. U-796, hunted by two vessels and under heavy fire, had fired and executed a crash dive, but seconds too late, and a depth charge pierced its bow. Fifty-six men served on U-796; all were flung forward like marionettes tossed across the stage. As the boat had descended, it lurched aft, uncontrollably and the Oberleutnant shouted orders from the control room.

"Everyone, to the stern!"

Crew ran down the narrow corridor to the stern, in hopes of stabilizing the vessel before it hit aground. The bombardment of heavy artillery had been deafening; depth charges shook the hull of the damaged boat, causing equipment and boxes of canned goods to scuttle about as men braced for the impact of their boat settling on the ocean floor.

Second Lieutenant Erich Gerhardt could hear the heavy breathing of the crewmen around him in the stifling air between depth charge shocks. Crew members worked together to assess damage to the boat and assist any injured; there were many. A midshipman, only nineteen years of age, had been impaled by a broken pipe, dying almost instantly. As the storm subsided and the wages of war from above diminished, the crew waited silently, in hopes that a resurface would bring escape.

Erich had not seen men die before. As a new soldier, having been conscripted into the German navy, he had volunteered for u-boat training. He had never seen hand-to-hand combat. As the boat began its slow ascent to the surface, and the Captain issued his final orders, Erich, a good Catholic boy, prayed for mercy on his soul.

The girl pressed her Arabian forward, locking her knees into the horse's flank. Golden red curls, pulling free from the tightly held braid at the nape of her neck, glistened like spun satin in the sunlight. The skirt she wore bunched between her legs, a pale lavender petticoat visible under the lace-trimmed hem of her dress. Capped sleeves encircled long arms tanned from the summer sun, above slender hands woven tightly into the mare's long, chestnut mane. In contrast to the formality of the dress, she wore no shoes; as the hem of her dress rode high in the wake of galloping wind, a glimmer of creamy white thigh could be glimpsed.

Bare of saddle, she handled the mare as if as an extension of the supple lines of the horse, running her through the clearing as though they were one, on a journey traveled a thousand times before. Her young face turned up into the heat of the sun, brow furrowed in concentration, eyes closed. Beads of perspiration clung to her full upper lip and sweat ran down into the nape of her neck; mid-summer humidity, stifling in its intensity, clung to her skin. Suddenly, her eyes flew open as she reined the mare abruptly, turning her in rapid circles in the clearing, back and forth, and a tiny cry swept through her lips. Just as abruptly, she stopped the pace, threw her face down into the mare's sweat-glistened neck, and wept, sobs wrenching from her body.

The wind carried the girl's sobs across the meadow, churning the sounds into a cavalcade of wails. Leaves in the trees rustled, grasses swept a lullaby with the breeze, and, when the last sobs quieted into tiny sniffles, the girl lay motionless, draped over the mare, who stood perfectly still. How long the girl sat in stillness she could not say, but as the wind slowly waned and the muffled sniffles faded, clouds passed over the afternoon sun, and the girl sat up and shuddered, rubbing her hands across her arms seeking warmth, and wiped her nose with the back of her hand.

She turned the horse swiftly in the direction she had ridden from, urgent once again, as the wind began to rip through the forest on all sides of her, pulling at her hair, her dress. She left the clearing as quickly as she had come into it, urging the horse to quicken as a hard rain started to fall in thick, heavy torrents.

Across the meadow, in the shadows of a glen of trees and tall grasses, propped lazily against the rough trunk of an old oak tree, he watched.

Chapter One

Spring in Champaign, Illinois can bring violent rain, and this day was no exception. As Claire Beaumont drove to work on Monday morning, sheets of rain drove into her windshield, making it nearly impossible to see. Impatiently clicking through radio stations while drinking her coffee, she narrowly missed hitting a pickup ahead of her traveling at about half the marked speed in the blinding rain. Slamming on her brakes and watching the coffee spill over her console, she decided to settle on the last station her fingers had managed to click while she swerved.

As strains of *China Grove* enveloped the car, Claire reflected on the day ahead. An assistant professor of anthropology at University of Illinois, Urbana-Champaign, she knew that one of the top items of the day would be the committee faculty meeting scheduled for 9:00 a.m. Given the visibility and traffic considerations, Claire was certain she would barely make the meeting in time, a fact that left her unsettled.

Pulling into the faculty parking lot, she was dismayed to discover that she had no umbrella. She pulled the hood of her hound's tooth jacket over her head and clumsily started across campus toward Davenport Hall, holding precariously to the books and trying desperately to keep from getting soaked through. She probably chose the wrong day to wear the vintage Jerry Gilden sheath dress, but she had been waiting all winter to be able to put it on, it was so sweet, and you can't wear a Jerry Gilden without the right shoes, which were definitely the wrong choice on a day like today.

Claire loved the old building, with its grand entrance and beautiful hardwood flooring. Built in early 1900, the old building offered up the aroma of old wood, old books and years of academia. Right now, however, Claire was only thinking of how far her car was parked from the building in the blinding rain and she stepped up her pace and raced up the steps to the third floor, entering the conference room just as the committee chairman entered the room.

"Good morning, Dr. Beaumont."

"Good morning, sir."

Breathing a sigh of relief, she sank into a chair at the far end of the table and opened a notepad.

An hour later the meeting was adjourned, and Claire made her way to her office. She squeezed into the tiny room and hung her jacket, still damp from the jaunt through the rain, and switched on her computer. The room was cramped, but she had a nice view of the main campus and, on a sunny spring day, would enjoy the warm sun coming in through the tiny window.

On this occasion, the rain cast a gloomy darkness to the room, and Claire switched on the lamp at her desk and searched in her desk drawer for a bottle of water and a hair clip; the rain had sent her chestnut hair into a wild mess, and she needed to get the wet mass off of her neck. Browsing emails, she found a note from Marcus Castigan, asking if the two were still on for their date for tomorrow evening. Dinner at Hibachi. Sushi. Beautiful sea bass with Saikyo miso. Decent wine list. "Yes", Claire typed, "I'll meet you at seven."

As she reached for her phone to check voicemail, she heard a knock on her door and her assistant popped her head around the corner without preamble. Shea Froeling, undergrad and Claire's research assistant for the last two years.

"Chad Everett is hoping you will have a few minutes to talk with him about his paper for Sociocultural," Shea's crisp, husky voice crossed the room before her petite frame did. She brushed punky black bangs out of stunningly blue eyes with black tipped nails. "He's hoping you'll take a glance through his intro."

"Hey, Shea," Claire replied, still holding the receiver between ear and graceful shoulder. "What's the paper on?"

"Umm, let me check..." Shea skimmed the clipboard she grabbed from the hook next to the door, and found the student's name and thesis information on the list. "Looks like evolution of Irish clan and gang power. The New York Draft riots."

"Sure."

"Okay, thanks Claire." Shea put the clipboard back on its hook and sauntered out the door, her Sumatra brown Birkenstock clogs, visible under low-rise jeans, clopping on the hardwood. "I'll let him know."

"Can you put it on my calendar?" Claire calls out to her retreating back.

"Okay!" Shea throws over her shoulder and shut the door behind her.

Thunder clapped outside of her window, making her jump. The telephone on her desk rang, and she jumped again, feeling the rush of adrenalin in the pit of her stomach. Chiding herself out loud, she picked up the phone.

"This is Claire Beaumont," she said into the mouthpiece.

"Claire?" A voice on the other end of the telephone. "This is Matt."

Puzzled, Claire's brow wrinkles to a frown. "Who?"

"Matt," The masculine voice was a bit amused. "Matt Hendricks."

"Oh, Matt!" She was shocked, and slightly embarrassed that she did not recognize the voice and could feel color suffuse her cheeks. How could she not remember the voice of the first boy she had ever kissed? Of course, she could have only been about eight at the time, visiting Grandma and Grandpa's farm in Minnesota. Still, the kiss was not the last time she had seen him, or kissed him, and his distinct voice, deep and caressing, was not one that a girl should easily forget. Claire was immediately unsettled.

Bemusement filled her voice as she spoke. "Oh, hello... I- I didn't recognize your voice. How are you?"

"I'm fine, Claire," He sounded serious and hesitant.

Silence. Matt, after all these years. Claire gulped, shocked at the voice on the other end of the line. Then she began to get a sinking feeling in the pit of her stomach; it was unlikely that Matt would be making a social call at 10 o'clock on a Monday morning to Illinois from Minnesota, or any morning, for that matter. "Eva..."

More hesitation and a slight intake of breath. "Claire—"

"What happened?"

"We think Eva had a stroke last night."

Claire could feel her heart pounding, and she put her hand to her mouth. She pictured Eva, her lovely grandmother, strong of spirit and prideful, and could not quite grasp the possibility that such a strong spirit could be vulnerable. "Is she all right?"

"We're not sure yet, Claire. I stopped over last night to check up on one of the mares, and I saw smoke coming from the kitchen." Matt was the town vet.

"What? There was a fire at the house?"

"Yes; apparently she had something cooking, and it caught fire."

"Oh, Matt," Claire could feel tears behind her closed eyes. She pictured the big old farmhouse with its simple craftsman design and large, flowing screen porch. "Where is she?"

"She's at the hospital in town." By town, Matt was referring to New Ulm, Minnesota, the place where Claire's grandparents had lived, and flourished, until her grandfather, Tom, had passed quietly in his sleep in the very hospital a few years before. "When I found her, she was lying on the floor. The fire must have just started, or the house would have been gone, I think. There's some damage to the kitchen."

Claire could picture the simple country kitchen where her silver-haired grandmother would cook baby red potatoes in the middle of summer, fresh from the garden, and slice succulent heirloom tomatoes, with cucumber salads and sweet, honey-dipped doughnuts, fresh from the hot skillet on the stove. She remembered setting the oak mission-style table with the bone china that Grandma had gotten as a wedding gift when she married Grandpa in the '40s.

"Grandma, why are we using the china? Is it a special day?" Ten-year-old Claire had asked.

"Oh, Claire, every day is special when my favorite little wee-one comes to visit me!" Eva's crystal voice, ever so slightly tinged with her Irish heritage, sounded like a bird song on a spring day.

"But it's so pretty," Claire remembered the dainty floral pattern of the china; the cup and saucer with the gold fluted rim and how Eva would let her drink coffee, laced heavily with cream and sugar, just like the grown-ups. "What if I drop it?"

"Sweetie, you must not worry about that! You are a princess, don't forget that..." Her thoughts drifted back from the memory to the present.

"Who's taking care of her there?" Claire asked.

"Dr. Johnson. Claire, they think it would be best if you came as quickly as you can. I don't have a lot of details, but she has suffered a pretty traumatic stroke; they're not saying much to me at this point, you'll want to check in..."

"Okay, Matt. Thank you for letting me know. I'll call the hospital right away and see what I can do with my schedule." Claire was already pulling up internet flight information on her computer.

"Claire, let me know when you've booked a flight, and I can come into the Cities to pick you up."

Claire paused, butterflies knotting her stomach. "No, that's fine."

"Claire," Matt hesitated, briefly, before continuing. "She's had some setbacks these last few months. Doc thinks that this is not the first stroke she's had."

"Few months?"

"Several months, actually. When was the last time you saw her?"

Guilt pulled at Claire. When was the last time? She had not gone home over Christmas; had, instead, chosen to take the period break from class work for research. She had gone to the Pacific and had phoned her grandmother from somewhere in Makati City to wish her a Happy New Year. Grandma had sounded tired, mistook Claire's voice for Isabelle, Claire's mother. When Claire corrected her, she had laughed it off, and claimed senility.

"I think it was last summer..."

Silence on the other end of the line. Claire, feeling defensive and not liking it, said crisply, "Matt, thanks for calling. I'd better call the hospital and make some arrangements."

"Okay. I'll see you later." He sounded amused and all-knowing. "Bye."

Claire sat back in her chair and stared out the window. Sheets of rain were hitting it with force; she could see the recurrent lightening beaming in the sky, flashes of light pulsing every few seconds before the momentary roar of thunder. She remembered clearly the day her parents were killed in the car accident. Isabelle, the head-strung beauty who, in her second year at Berkley, had begun a love affair with her history professor, Edward Beaumont. Edward, a distinguished looking figure even in his mid-forties, was indulgent of his beautiful wife, and doted on both of his girls.

During a drive through Oakland on the 980, after attending a fundraiser for a local woman's shelter, Edward's Mercedes had been struck from behind by a late model Ford being driven by twenty-three year old Michael Williams, who, having just beaten his eighteen year old girlfriend into a coma, had fled and was speeding down the freeway in a panic. Distracted momentarily by the sound of a siren, he had turned his head to look behind him, not seeing the dark sedan ahead. The crash had set off a chain reaction, and before the chain finally broke, six lives were ended. The fact that Marcus Williams survived was dubbed a bit of a miracle. The fact he had been fleeing the scene of a crime that would put his girlfriend into the very shelter system Claire's parents had so generously supported, did not go unnoticed by Claire, who was devastated by the loss of her parents. By the time the trial was over, Claire had been packed up and shipped off to farm country in Minnesota, a grieving, bitter spirit.

A million miles away, cocooned in a world known only to her, Eva lay still in her hospital bed; breathing tubes hooked to the respirator pull her mouth into a grimace and drool slides slowly down the side of her face. She is in a fetal position, under a warming blanket, her arms covered with bruises from the several attempts to insert the IV. Her stunning white hair is now partially shaved to make way for the pressure gauge that has been inserted into her skull, and her skin is loose from her bones, as though her body has shrunk from within. Outwardly, Eva Nielsen looks like a tiny, helpless old woman who does not have long for this earth.

Inwardly, enveloped in a warm and welcoming place, she has gone back in time. She can feel her mother's hands running through her hair, and hear her soothing voice whispering in her ear. "You are a princess, Aoife, born of royal blood, descendant of a countess in our mother land." She feels the warmth of her mother's arms enveloping her in their soft circle; hears her mother's heartbeat against her ear as her mother tells her the story of how she came to be, and she blissfully falls back into the darkness.

Chapter Two

'My God, my life must be worth more than this...' Lyneah Hamilton stood before the mirror in her bedroom, shaking, as she heard Hank gun the engine of his pickup and spew gravel across her home. She reached into her oversized handbag and found a pack of cigarettes, rummaging until she found an orange Bick buried in change she had collected waitressing at the Blue Moon. Trying to steady a shaky hand, she slipped a cigarette into her dusky rose-colored mouth and lit it, dragging deeply and closing her eyes to the smoke that filtered around her head. Sighing heavily, she sank onto the bed.

This one had been a bad one, leaving her spent and bruised around her upper arm where Hank had grabbed her, demanding to know where she put her tip money. He'd pushed her down on to the bed, twisting her arm around until the muscle in her shoulder burned, and held her with his knee behind her neck while he turned her purse upside down on the bed. Hank's behavior had become increasingly erratic. He'd become so secretive, and increasingly paranoid, losing weight and disappearing for days at a time.

In the bathroom mirror, hardened eyes stared out at her from the mirror, dark circles smudging her cheeks and fine lines deepening from the smoke and the alcohol. Always thin, she was now nearly gaunt, and her prominent cheekbones accentuated even further the hollows of her cheeks and the tight lines of her mouth.

The youngest daughter of Betty Lou and Gerald "Jerry" Hamilton,

Lyneah Marie Hamilton had been a quiet bookworm in school. Always tall for her age, she was awkward as a teen, always feeling a little out of place, trying to melt into the wall. She was sweet, and thoughtful, but painfully shy.

As adolescence gave way to puberty, Lyneah bloomed into a beautiful girl. Her full lips, sandy blonde hair and well-balanced figure caught more than one eye around town. She developed a bit of a wild streak, and a propensity toward running with the wrong type of man in the wrong types of places. She was a bright girl, and she managed to graduate from high school with honors, much to the relief of her very concerned parents. She enrolled in college at Mankato State, with dreams of someday being a lawyer or an engineer.

Not far into her sophomore year, Lyneah crashed her car into another in the parking lot outside of her dorm, and, drunk and incoherent, left the car running, found her room, and passed out. Lyneah's parents had made it clear they would not support her self-destructive behavior any further. She'd left school, gotten a job in the Cities as a cocktail waitress, and continued to dream that she would return to school when she figured herself out.

Long later, when Lyneah found herself with child after a brief affair, she packed up her meager belongings and headed back to New Ulm. Somewhere deep within, she knew that she wanted to keep this child growing inside of her and raise him or her up right. She also knew that, despite her ability to make dramatically poor decisions, her parents would help her support their grandchild.

She frowned; not a drop to drink, nor a man for years, until the beautiful, dark and brooding Hank Beaudine walked into the Blue Moon and caught her eye. He was so mysterious, so handsome, and so persistent. The more Lyneah resisted, the more persistent he had become, until, one night in October, when she locked up and ran through the frost tipped night to her old Malibu. She'd found him leaning lazily against the driver's side door, casually smoking a cigarette and watching her approach.

"'Lady like you shouldn't be out here alone so late at night," he drawled in a baritone voice so rich it could melt butter.

"Hi, Hank," Lyneah stood for a moment, shivering in her thin t-shirt. "What can I do for you?"

"You can stop being so stubborn and take a ride with me tonight."

Lyneah looked at his handsome, rugged face, under the Stetson he wore over brown curls that wisped around his ears. She wanted to reach out and curl one of those locks around her little finger so bad it sent a tiny thrill into her tummy. "It's late and I need to get home."

"Lyneah, you and I both know your little one is with your mama for the night."

She pondered that for a moment, suddenly nervous, fidgeting, and fumbled around in her purse for a pack of cigarettes, her eyes never leaving his. "Hank, you and I both know you're no good for me."

He laughed, a deep, belly laugh, and she melted even further. "Honey, I'm talking about having a cup a' coffee and some nice conversation."

She put the cigarette into her mouth, and he reached out and lit it for her. "What do you and I have to talk about?"

Suddenly serious, his tone softened. "How about if you come out to the diner for a cup of coffee and find out? You don't have to fear me, Lyneah," he continued softly. "I won't lay a hand on you unless you want me to. I just want to get to know you better."

She blinked hard, breathed deeply and, finally, relented. Stubbing out the cigarette with her toe, she nodded. "Fine, but just coffee. I'm not interested in anything else. And I'm tired, so let's not be out too long – I have to work tomorrow night, too."

She learned that Hank had grown up near Connersville, Indiana, and worked at the auto parts manufacturer for most of his life, along with his father and other kin. When the market dried up, he found himself calling his Minnesota cousin, and found work there.

Over the course of the evening, savoring the rich buttermilk cakes and mahogany coffee, Lyneah shared things with Hank she rarely shared with others. How it had been to be raised in the close-knit community with three older sisters. How it had been to compete with each of those sisters as they moved into successful lives; Diana, a corporate attorney in Minnetonka; Maxine, the wife of State Representative John Hess, and mother of three great kids. Jacqueline, five years Lyneah's senior and her youngest sister, who, with her husband Dave, were local teachers.

She also made it clear, she was no angel. "Hank, I've been around the block more times than I care to admit. I'm no saint--"

He'd held up his hand. "Lyneah, I don't care where you been." He'd said in his slow, Indiana drawl. "I care about where you go from here." She'd liked that.

After that, every night Lyneah worked, Hank showed up at closing. They sometimes went to the diner for coffee. Other nights they took cool walks down by the lake, autumn air biting at their noses and sounds of leaves rustling in the trees. They were walking in the park, under streetlights shining brightly in the sweet, chilly air, when the first snow of the season began to fall. The tiny, perfect snowflakes fluttered around Lyneah's face, dancing in the crisp breeze, and she reached her hands out to her sides, leaned her head back, closed her eyes, and stuck her tongue between her lips, to catch a flake.

Hank had stepped forward just she opened her eyes, the smile on her face slowly dying as realization dawned. She lifted her face as he leaned in, eyes now dusky with awakening, and felt his breath on her lips as he kissed her, his tongue playing with hers in a sweet dance.

The effect had about dropped her to her knees. Warning bells went off in her head as her body moved to meld with his. "Oh, shit," she thought as she let herself go.

He'd stayed that night, and most nights since. He hadn't technically moved in, she would not concede that, but he had brought over a toothbrush, and a pair of worn Ariat cowboy boots that she now tripped over as she stumbled out of the bathroom. She kicked them as hard as she could, and one flew into the wall and knocked down a picture mural of her son. As she picked it up, she felt sick; the last thing Travis needed was a man in his life who couldn't deal without booze.

As much as she wanted Hank, he had, as she predicted, not been good for her, and that could only mean bad things for her son. He'd lied, when he said he didn't care about where she'd been and did not hesitate to point out the flaws she'd shared earlier. The life she'd created seemed to be slowly ebbing away. Now, as she readied to leave, she heard voicemail pick up a call.

"Hi, honey," she recognized her mom's voice. "I just wanted to call you and let you know that Claire's coming in sometime tomorrow night, and I thought we should try to get together and stock the fridge for her. I'll talk with you more tomorrow." She paused, and this time when she spoke, there was a hint of worry in her voice. "Okay, then, sweetie; be careful tonight. 'Love you." Click.

Time to go to work. As she made her way there, she thought of her aunt Eva, and was deeply saddened. Of all the people in Lyneah's life, Eva had been the one who seemed to understand her the most. It was to Eva that Lyneah would turn in her times of trouble, and Eva who would know just how to mend the pain.

Investigator Chris Breuning glanced through the reports he had picked up from his mail slot as he made his way to his desk in the crowded office. The 6'4" detective walked through the maze of desks with a carefree gait, and he settled into his chair with ease. His boyish grin, slightly lopsided due to a scar on his upper left lip, a souvenir from a sucker punch landed by a thug with a propensity toward gaudy rings and teenage girls, flashed as he greeted his fellow coworkers. On the job for just a few months, he was fast becoming a favorite among the staff of the Brown County law enforcement center. Most of his coworkers were in awe of the flamboyant detective, and wondered why he had left Chicago's Bureau of Investigative Services Organized Crime Division for Brown County's considerably smaller law enforcement center.

He plopped the reports and his mail onto the desk in front of him and pulled up his chair. The desk was immaculate, as was Chris himself; always impeccably dressed in a suit and tie, he took a lot of good-natured ribbing from his coworkers about it.

Picking his way through the files, he scanned a few cases before opening the file for Eva Nielsen, an elderly woman who was found in her burning home in rural Brown County. A local veterinarian had stopped for a routine check, saw smoke coming through the windows and called 911. Brown County dispatched a uniformed patrol to the property, and Deputy Ben Lahr had been the first official to arrive on the scene. Ms. Nielsen was soon transported to the Medical Center while the fire department quickly defused the flame, which appeared to have started near a stove in the kitchen of the farmhouse.

Lahr wrote and submitted the report, theorizing that the victim, an elderly woman, had been cooking, had fallen ill and forgotten to turn off the stove. She went to lie down on the sofa, instead falling and hitting her head on the coffee table, where Matt Hendricks found her. Attached to the report was a separate memo containing follow up information regarding the victim. Staff at the Medical Center had contacted law enforcement this morning to report injuries that were found during the medical examination, and the Chief had assigned follow up to Investigator Chris Breuning.

Chris dialed the hospital, asking for Dr. Richard Johnson, the name listed in the memo.

After several minutes of being on hold while listening to advertisements for the various departmental specialties available at the hospital, a resonant voice came on the line. "This is Dick Johnson."

"Doctor Johnson, this is Detective Christopher Bruening," Chris replied. "I'm calling about some information that has been passed on to me regarding a patient of yours. Are you treating Eva Nielsen?"

"Yes, I am."

"I'd like to talk with you regarding the injuries that were reported after Mrs. Nielsen was brought into the hospital. Is this a good time?"

Doctor Johnson sounded hesitant, "I'm on rounds now. Can you come into my office later today? I can have my staff let you know my schedule and meet you in my office. Have you spoken with anyone in the family yet?"

"No, I have not. I just picked up the case this morning."

Dick Johnson's voice was concerned. "Eva's got a granddaughter flying in sometime today. I don't believe she is aware of the extent of the injuries Eva sustained."

What were the injuries?" Chris asked.

The doctor was quiet for a moment, contemplative. "At this point I'd rather talk with you in person. My concern is that nothing has been shared with the family as of this morning. Eva's sister-in-law, Betty Hamilton, was informed last evening, but they think that Eva had a stroke. I'd like to be able to share information with the family before this becomes too public."

Chris thought for a moment. "Doctor, I can work with that. However, if this is a crime, we really want to get moving on the investigation as quickly as possible. Tell me, Doc, do you think that Mrs. Nielsen was attacked? Is that what prompted the call to the PD?"

Dick Johnson's voice, gentle and resonant, with a slight German brogue, was firm. "Yes. Let's talk later. I'll put you through to my assistant, and they'll find time in my schedule. I'll be finished with rounds around 11:00 and back in my office shortly after that."

"Thanks." Chris made an appointment, and dropped the line, just as a young uniform approached his desk. Lean, with a shock of cropped red hair and a sprinkling of light freckles across the bridge of his nose, Officer Ben Lahr looked not a day over sixteen, but carried himself with military precision.

When he spoke, Chris heard quiet, youthful respect. "Detective Breuning?"

Chris stood, reached his hand out to the young officer. "Yes. You must be Ben Lahr?"

The young man had a firm handshake; his shockingly blue eyes gazed directly into Chris's. "Yes. It's a pleasure meeting you, sir."

"Thank you. Have a seat." Chris gestured to the chair opposite his desk. "I've been around for a few months but have not had a chance to meet all of the patrol officers. Have you been with the county long?"

Ben sat straight in the chair, his knees brushing the desk's metal trim. "I came on in '07, after a tour in Iraq, then signed for another in '09. I've haven't been home long.

Chris studied Ben, his regard for the younger man growing. "What Company were you with, Ben?"

"I was with the 1st Battalion, 141st Field Artillery, Sir."

"B Company?"

"Yes, sir."

Chris studied the young man. This was one of the moments where one knows that looks can be deceiving; while Ben Lahr looked like a kid, the experience he had overseas been notorious, and deadly. The Company had come under heavy artillery fire near Baghdad, losing three of its men. "What's your rank, son?"

"Staff Sergeant, sir."

"You had a rough time over there, huh?"

Ben nodded, a subtle shutter closing over his eyes.

A moment of silence followed. Taking the hint, Chris's gregarious personality worked to break the ice. "Hmm, 'you join the force when you were twelve?"

Ben's youthful face was impassive for a few seconds, then broke into a grin. "Actually, I was seventeen, sir."

"You don't look much older than that now…"

Ben laughed, easily. "I get that a lot."

Chris smiled, and hoped he would have more time to talk with this man later, perhaps over a few beers at a local place. They had more in common than Ben knew. Right now, it was time to get down to the business at hand. He leaned forward and opened the file. "You were the first responder to Eva Nielsen's place."

Over the next half hour or so, Ben recounted his call to the farmhouse, with Chris interjecting periodically for clarification, asking questions and taking notes. After the interview was over, the deputy handed over his card, offering his assistance at any time during his investigation. Chris thanked him; they stood and shook hands, and both headed out the door of the station into the cool morning rain.

Eva Nielsen is dreaming, although she is unaware that she is. The injury to her brain has detached her from her current surroundings. She is in a meadow; washes of light halo around the trees surrounding her meadow; glimmers of moonlight pierce through the waving trees. She lies in the tall grass, gazing up into the clear evening sky. It is Indian summer in late October, and she shivers as the coarse grass brushes her cheek. She turns her head as she hears the rustle of footsteps and smiles to herself, believing she is hidden within the tall meadow grass, and she waits.

The boy approaches; she sees the contours of his serious face in the gathering dusk and hears his urgent whisper. "Eva?" his German brogue is hesitant, accentuated with concern. She sits up quickly, and the boy sees her, startled momentarily, then he smiles. His silvery blonde hair flickers in the moonlight and moves with the slight breeze as he steps closer to her.

"Eva," he says again, and his voice is like a caress. She feels something stir, deep within her, something new, and the boy is aware of it, too. As he kneels beside her, her hand reaches out, touching his face, her forefinger moving slowly along his high cheekbone and strong Roman nose, coming to rest just beneath the collar of his tan gabardine work shirt. She can feel his heartbeat. The smile leaves her face, and her lips part. He gazes down at her for a moment, uncertain. From deep within her, the wiles of womanhood startle her innocent mind, and she reaches her other hand to grasp the collar of his shirt and draw his mouth to hers, their tongues dancing to a sweet melody as they lay back in the tall grass.

They are suddenly one. His body melds into hers in the meadow, like the liquid wax of a candle slowly burning, and then he is gone. Eva reaches for him, not wanting to leave this moment, and they are now both standing, the boy in the distance along a lane, bathed in light. His familiar face smiles a sad smile at her, and he shakes his head.

"Nein," he says softly, but his lips do not move, as if he is speaking in her head. It is not time.

Eva is confused. She feels no pain, but her body is fluid, detached. She looks down at her hands, and they are flickering, disappearing and reappearing as if in a mist. She looks up to the boy, frightened, and he is gone. She tears her gaze away from the light in which he had been standing and feels herself being drawn away from the meadow, and lets the respirator continue to sustain her life.

Chris Breuning's meeting with Doc Johnson yielded much information. He pondered the meeting as he drove, heading to the country house, he, along with his grandfather, called home.

Doctor Richard Johnson, "Dick" to his friends and colleagues had been practicing general medicine in the New Ulm area for over forty years. He was, quite clearly, devoted to his patients, and on the wall was a bulletin board covered with pictures of children. Patients, he explained; most of them delivered by the doc himself; he'd stopped doing deliveries in the

'90s. Nowadays, he limited his practice, leaving deliveries to the younger and more specialized. He often, however, continued to see those kids on the wall, who were now old enough to bring him their own children for care.

Dr. Johnson invited Chris to sit down at a table on the opposite wall, and, pulling Eva's chart, inserted a CT scan into the x-ray viewer. "Look here," he pointed to an area of dark tissue in the left portion of the screen. "Eva did suffer a stroke. See the darkening tissue here, around the lighter area? That is a stroke that occurs when a blood clot detaches or ruptures. Eva's been having some issues with smaller strokes, and we've been treating her for them with medications; not uncommon in a woman her age."

He pointed to another area on the outer edge of the brain. "See this? *This* is caused by some trauma to the head, a blow of some sort. 'Might even be a blow from a hand. For a woman of her age it wouldn't take much to cause this kind of trauma, given she's on blood thinning medications due to her recent history."

"What leads you to believe this is from a blow rather than damage from the fall?"

"Location of the wound; shape of the wound," the doctor pulled a diagram from the file on the table. "This shows a very specific pattern of bruising, and breakage of the skin behind her left ear. See the way it spiders out from the point of impact? He pointed to the middle of the wound diagram. "This is an unusual pattern, see the way the bruise pattern curves and deepens on the end? Can't make out what it is, but it's not consistent with any fall I've run across."

Chris frowned, trying to determine what could cause the injury. "Is this to scale?"

"Yes."

He peered over the diagram. "What else did you find, Doc? Other injuries?"

Dr. Johnson leaned back in his chair, fingering the pen between his fingers. "Eva had bruises on her forearm that appeared to be from the grip of a hand."

"Which arm?"

"The right. Also, on the same arm, a slight gash, almost like a cut with a knife or sharp instrument. I can't identify what it was, but it may have been caused when she fell. Some bruising on her back and right shoulder; those appear to be more consistent with a fall. And her knees were banged up."

Chris said. "The officer that responded thought she may have fallen on a knitting bag."

"Could be," the doctor countered. "She has several bruises on her legs, and a slight fracture in her hip, right side. Bruising on her cheekbone and eye on the left. If I were to speculate, I'd say she was slapped or hit on the left side of her face, in addition to the injury on her head. The blow caused the epidural bleeding, and dislodged a clot that was already present in her brain."

"Did you take any pictures of the patient?"

"Not yet."

"I'd like to take some."

Doc Johnson peered over his reading glasses at the detective. "Son, I am not one to get in the way of any criminal investigation, but my patient is not going to be photographed at this time. She's in critical care, and not in a position to be moved around for a photo shoot."

Chris swallowed. "Doctor Johnson, we really need to get photographs of the injuries…"

Dr. Johnson held up his hand. "Understood. But no one sees her, except close family, until she improves."

Chris thought for a moment. "I need to see her. Or have one of our female officers, if you prefer, come in and document the evidence, look for any further signs of injury or sexual crime. Can you document the injuries for me?

The doctor held up his hand. "We have individuals on staff here who are trained in victim admittance. We have done a rape kit; there are no indications of that. We also clipped her fingernails and bagged them." He handed an envelope to Chris. "We'll handle photographs when we can make sure she's stable enough."

"Thanks. How well do you know Ms. Nielsen?" Chris asked.

"Quite well, actually. She and her late husband, Tom, were upstanding pillars of the community. They both donated considerable time and money to charitable organizations in the area."

"What kind of organizations?"

"Many. Tom loved the kids. He was instrumental in organizing the Boys and Girls club, volunteer coached little league and hockey. Eva gave riding lessons to underprivileged kids for free and spent time volunteering at the crisis center. A lot of kids learned values from those two that stayed with them into their adult years. I credit Tom and Eva with turning some of their lives around."

"Any enemies?"

"None that I'm aware of. I doubt it, but you'd have to ask the family"

"What did Mr. Nielsen die from?"

"Cancer. Two years ago."

Chris turned the page of the notebook he was writing in. "What can you tell me about the family?"

"They had one daughter; she was killed in a car accident several years ago, in California, along with her husband. Tom and Eva raised their daughter, Claire. Good kid, heart-broken over her parents' death. She lives in Illinois."

Chris concluded the interview and stood to take his leave. The doctor reached out to shake his hand. "Damned shame what happened to Eva; if there's anything further I can do, let me know. Talk to the family; get ahold of Betty Hamilton; that's Eva's sister-in-law and her closest friend. She can help you."

Chris picked up the envelope that had been prepared for him and took his hand. "Thank you, Dr. Johnson. I'll be in touch."

Chapter Three

As Claire made her way to her hometown, she reflected on the life she had led with her extraordinary grandmother. She'd spent the remainder of her day, with the help of Shea, planning for her classes. The end of the semester was near, and most of the students were preparing for finals and packing to go home or to summer jobs.

The earliest she could fly out of Illinois put her in the Minneapolis airport after nine. She planned to pick up a rental car and drive the hour and a half to New Ulm. It was going to be a late night, and, according to her Auntie Betty, she would not be able to stay at the farm, due to the fire and smoke damage.

As Claire sat in her window seat above the cloud bank, she stared into the fading night. Worry gripped her; feeling exactly what she had felt when she got the news that her parents were dead. Dread, pure dread, and she felt it now. When the flight attendant came around, she accepted the sandwich, but she could only pick at it. Instead, she drank from the complimentary bottle of water, leaned her head back and closed her eyes, exhausted.

Unbidden, thoughts of Matt came into her head. She had no intention of calling him to pick her up, or even let him know when she got into town. Although he had shown a kindness in letting her know what happened to her grandmother, she and Matthew Hendricks had carefully avoided each other for several year.

She had known him most of her life, having met him in her eighth year when she had gone to the farm for summer vacation. On that 4th of July, Tom and Eva hosted a community picnic on the farm; neighbors and friends had appeared, bearing potluck and their young children. The children had gathered around the stables for pony rides, then, if they were old enough, they headed off down the beaten path to the meadow. On the edge of the meadow was an old, abandoned building site, where Eva's parents had first made their home in the early years of the 1920s.

The building site, long abandoned, sat on the edge of the woods. Down the hill, the river rippled where water bugs and crawfish made their way downstream. While the children were forbidden from going near the old pump house at the very edge of the river, the remaining ruins held all sorts of treasures. If you were careful, you could walk along the roof timbers toward the back of the old house, where a pine shelf had collapsed amid an array of ceramic dishes. Claire, taunted by a few of the kids for being a California baby, had taken young Eddie Gibbs' dare and started across the beams, eight feet above the dirt floor of the old cabin's basement.

Matt had been nearby, and turned to see Claire balancing halfway across the beam. He could hear Eddie, taunting her as she balanced, arms outstretched, moving slowly toward the back of the crumpled house. Matt raced up the hill and shouted at Eddie to shut his fat mouth.

Eddie laughed, and kept going. "Baby! Baby! California Baby!"

"Claire, you don't have to do it." She could hear Matt's voice across the clearing as he reached the group. "Come on. He's just being a jerk."

Eddie turned, his pudgy face contorted. "Screw you, Hendricks."

No, screw you, Eddie," Matt returned, facing off with the bigger kid, who was older by two years and outweighed him by a large margin. "She's just a kid. You're a bully, like your old man."

Eddie, enraged, turned on Matt, screwing up his face and his fist and hauled off with a right hook that would have done some damage if Matt, smarter and faster, had not ducked. Eddie's swing set him off balance, and he fell to the ground, only to jump to his feet and tackle Matt. The commotion and ensuing fight caused Claire to turn quickly, and she lost her footing. Screaming as she fell to the ground below, her leg had slammed into a tangle of thorny sumac that had overgrown the dwelling. The thorns ripped through her skin, leaving angry welts on her arms, tearing the little yellow shorts and tie-dyed t-shirt she was wearing. The leg twisted as she fell onto a large rock lying hidden within the gnarled sumac, and she felt something give.

Matt, on the ground under the weight of the bigger boy, and being pummeled, worked to get his bearings as he tried to roll Eddie over. Sweating and covered with dirt, he felt Eddie loosen his grasp and tried to extricate himself from the hold. Eddie used his free arm to land a punch onto Matt's face, and Matt could feel pain and blood spurt from his nose. He reached his hands up to grab Eddie's hair and yank hard. Hissing with pain, Eddie swung back, and Matt, shoving hard, pushed Eddie off him. He rolled in the dirt to his feet, spitting blood, and became aware of the commotion at the edge of the crumpled house.

Some of the kids were crying, and he realized, just as he heard her cries, that Claire was not on the beam anymore. His heart racing, he ran to the edge of the foundation, saw her lying there, and his stomach did a flip. Without further thought, Matt grabbed the beam with one hand, and the stone footings with the other, and climbed down to her, making his way carefully through the tangled brush.

Uncle Jerry and Auntie Betty's youngest daughter, Lyneah, had agreed to walk along with the group and watch over them while they played. But, Jess Gibbs, Eddie's brother, was also along, and the two had stolen away, a bit further into the woods. When they heard the screaming they ran back, just in time to see the young Hendricks boy lifting Claire out of the basement. When Lyneah reached down to take Claire, Matt refused; instead, he carried her all the way back to the house by himself.

Claire could feel his arms around her, cradling her close. She felt his heart, beating strong and fast against her cheek. So many years later, she can recall burying her face into his neck, seeking comfort, and tasting the sweat on his lips. She sighs, taking a long drink of water, and silently chides herself, thinking that was the moment she'd fallen in love with the then eleven-year-old Matthew Hendricks.

Claire's mother, the stunning Isabelle, was barefoot, in a lovely organza sundress, holding a glass of sun tea with lemon. She was loved in her hometown, and there were sure to be many gatherings of friends and family in their month-long sojourn from the city. Rarely had they flown home. Claire's father, Edward, so formal on most days, had been relaxed and casual on those road trips. They spent so much time laughing in the car, sometimes it made her tummy ache. Her parents would hold hands in the front seat, and Claire would watch them, see her daddy reach across the seat to run his hands through her mama's hair as its satin swirled around her face, and would feel a happiness in those moments she could not describe.

Isabelle as if with sixth sense turned, a frown on her face, and saw the group of children returning from the meadow. Seeing the young boy carrying her little wisp of a girl, she dropped her glass and ran across the vast lawn to the trail. She gathered Claire in her arms, oblivious to the dirt and blood that was now staining her lovely dress. Claire clung to Matt's neck for a fraction of a moment, reaching her little face up to kiss his cheek, her lips landing in the vicinity of the corner of his mouth, then turned to her mama. As she was carried away, she had stolen a last look at the boy who had saved her. Standing on the meadow road, his chest heaving from the long walk, his dark eyes had never left her face.

And so it began. Claire had broken an ankle and had required stitches on her left wrist. She ran her fingers absently across that scar and remembered the visit to the emergency room; the tetanus shot in her right arm, the brace on her ankle. Doc Johnson had personally attended her wounds himself. She had slept through the evening, into the night, waking in the dark to the sounds of distant fireworks. She knew that Eddie had gotten into trouble and hoped that Matt did not. As she had gazed out the window of her bedroom, linen curtains flowing in the breeze that swirled in, chasing the heat away, thoughts of the boy surrounded her.

Gazing out the window of the DC-10, as daylight faded into night, she recalled those times with surrealistic clarity. She had asked her grandmother if she could write a thank you to the boy who had saved her, and her grandmother had pulled out her personalized stationery, the one with the horses on it. Claire had written to the boy "Dear Matthew," in her large, childish block print. "Thank you for saving me. Love, Claire Beaumont." She asked her grandmother to mail it for her and included her own mailing address in California.

She had gone back home and waited. Because she had been unable to run and play with her friends, she had spent lot of time in the garden with her mother, hobbling behind her as Izzy tended to the flowers. Her mother had been such a lovely creature, so vibrant with color of her own. She had an aura of wisdom that surrounded her, a glow of sorts, and an intuition about others that gave her a level of sensitivity beyond the average. It was almost as if she had a *knowing*. Claire had been fascinated by this *knowing*; she had watched her mother assess people and be able to respond to them even *before* she knew what she was responding to. Isabelle could sense the growing restlessness in her daughter that summer, and the cause of it all.

"Claire, honey," she had said, on her knees in the dirt, hair pulled into a chignon at the nape of her neck, her fingers digging in the soil. "Maybe it's time to stop waiting for a letter, and just remember the kindness that Matthew showed you when he carried you back…"

"Mama, why won't he write to me?"

"Honey, he's only a young boy; young boys do not write letters very often these days."

Claire, sitting on the ground next to her and licking a blue raspberry freeze pop, had not been able to understand that. "But, mama, he *saved* me. That means we have a bond."

Izzy smiled with amusement, looking up at her daughter. "Who told you that?"

"Justine did. She said that, since he saved me, and I'm a princess, then he is my prince, and we have a bond."

"Well, that may be fun to think, and true in fairytales, but in real life, I think he may not feel quite the same way."

"Mo-om, I *am* a real princess. Grandma tells me that all the time."

Isabelle stood, and moved a few feet down to weed around the gardenias. "Well, since Grandma says it, it must be true, then, hey?"

Claire stayed put, stretched out on the blanket. She tilted her head back to drain the melted blue sweetness down her throat, feeling a droplet fall down her chin. "It is true, mama. Does that mean you're a queen then?"

"No, Claire, I'm not a queen."

"Then what are you?"

Laughingly, "I'm your mom. And it's time to go in and make dinner. Daddy will be home, soon."

She helped her little girl to her feet, caught the hat as it slid off Claire's head, and gave her a quick hug. "Claire, my little chickadee, just you wait and see. I think, if you're patient, you will get a letter from your prince very soon."

Claire felt the warmth of her mother's embrace and looked up into her pretty face. "You think so, mama?"

Her mama smiled. "I know so. Now, come on; we'll make Daddy's favorite shrimp, and you can cut the vegetables for a salad. Would you like that…?"

Claire, now closing her eyes, hearing the white noise around her, could still feel her mother. She could smell her, a mixture of linen, perfume and earth. Sometimes, in moments like this, she was convinced her mother was still there, watching over her, comforting her. The sense of Isabelle's presence had stayed with her since the crash that took her mother from her and was at its strongest when Claire was at her toughest points in life. Like now.

Within just a few days of that conversation in the garden, a letter came in the mail. They had become pen pals of sorts, she and Matthew Hendricks, the boy from Minnesota; each year, the letters getting longer, more frequent, pages filled with thoughts and dreams. Matt would write of life on the farm; chasing chickens and pulling eggs from the chicken coop; delivering calves, his love for the animals. Claire wrote of cocktail parties by the pool; walks along the wharf by the bay, eating trays of calamari and walking among the street vendors. Over the years, there had been hundreds of pages, innocence giving way to the throes of romance and young love. She had kept every letter, pages well-worn from being read repeatedly, until the day she had learned of Matt's betrayal.

On that day, she curled up on her bed, clutching the little red teddy bear Matt had won for her at the county fair, and wept inconsolably. Eva slid into the bed beside her, took her into her arms like she would a small child, caressing her damp head, until the tears had finally dissipated into sniffles, just as she had done each time she had heard her granddaughter weep for the loss of her mother in the years that followed the crash.

"Oh, honey, what happened?" Claire could hear sweet concern in her grandmother's voice. "Did you and Matt have a fight?"

"He's with someone else!" she said, tremulously, her voice shaking through her tears. "He's cheating, Grandma!"

Eva had been bewildered. "That doesn't sound like Matt. Are you sure, Claire? Have you talked with him yourself?"

"Yes, I'm sure." She had not wanted to tell her grandmother anymore.

The sounds of the plane lulled her and soon she is drifting back in time, driving down to the park to play basketball with her friends and have some lunch at the drive-in. Melinda Castigan, a snooty, well-endowed girl with pouty lips and skimpy clothes, is at the park, smoking a cigarette and talking with a group of people at a picnic table near the swing set. Melinda calls her name as she drops the cigarette in the grass and stomps it briefly with her foot.

Claire, puzzled, turns; she and Melinda are not friends, at least not anymore. For a time, when Claire came to town after her parents died, she had hung out with Melinda and her friends, but that had been short-lived. When Claire drifted away from the rough edges of the crowd, Melinda had seemed to harbor a resentment that had never gone away, even as they had grown older.

"Yeah?" Claire stops and turns toward her. "I'm going to the bathroom. Did you want something?"

Melinda walked by her side. "I'll walk with you."

Claire shrugged. "Okay."

"So, Claire, how is Matt doing?"

Claire doesn't like the snide tone in Melinda's voice, or the smell of smoke that clings to her skin. She is walking too close to Claire, and Claire can feel the heat of Melinda's arm as it brushes against hers. It makes her uncomfortable.

Moving slightly away, Claire shrugs. "He's fine."

"He comin' home this weekend?"

"No; he's studying for finals."

She picks up the pace, and, entering the public restroom. Melinda follows her and leans into a mirror, opening her vibrant red lips and brushing her tongue across her teeth. She is dressed in tight jeans, ripped at the knees, and her black hair is spiraled and tied up in a large black bow.

"You know, my sister, Kimber, lives in Mankato. She works at a bar down near campus." Melinda reaches in her pocket and pulls blood red lipstick out. Turning it in front of her, her black-lined eyes look into Claire's through the mirror. "She sees Matt quite a lot at the bar."

Claire, stomach sinking, feels her breath quicken a bit as she tries to quell the urge to turn away. "So?"

"So, she goes and hangs out at parties and stuff." Melinda, in no hurry, leans into the mirror and lines her already red lips with more of the lipstick. "You sure he's studying this weekend?"

Claire stares at the lipstick as it brushes the harsh color across Melinda's sultry mouth. "Why are you asking this, Mel?"

Melinda turns and leans back against the sink. She folds her arms and looks at Claire with a malicious gleam in her eyes, and a touch of saccharine in her voice. "I just thought you should know that he's got a girlfriend up there, in case he hasn't told you."

The air sucks out of Claire's lungs. "You're lying."

"I thought you'd say that, sweetie," Melinda, taller than Claire in her leather boots, looks down at her with mock sympathy. "He obviously hasn't told you anything yet."

"Told me what?"

"Claire, he's seeing someone; a girl from school. Some blonde named Jamie." Melinda reaches into the breast pocket of her vest and pulls out a pack of Marlboro lights, and lights up. "There's a party down at River Park this weekend, and a dance on the pier tonight. Sounds like everyone's going to be there." She eyes Claire's pale face through smoke. "Matt's going with this Jamie chick."

Claire stares down at the floor, feeling sickness spreading through her body; she feels like she's going to throw up. Melinda stands watching for a moment, then seems to soften. "Look, kid, I thought you should know. I mean, we're friends."

Claire looks into Melinda's eyes, and feels a surge of rage at this smug girl. "Fuck you, Melinda. You don't give a shit about me, and your sister's lying, or you are. Leave me alone."

She turned and walked quickly through the door, leaving Melinda standing there. She'd run across the park to her car.

Her friend, Sadie, had called out to her from the basketball court. "Claire? Are you okay? Where are you going?"

Claire had not stopped; with shaking fingers she had unlocked the door and sunk into the driver's seat. Sadie had run over to the car and stood in the open driver's side door.

"What's wrong?"

Claire slumped over the steering wheel. "It's Melinda. She says Matt is seeing someone at school."

"Oh, Claire," Sadie said with sympathy. "That can't be true. You guys love each other. You know that Melinda's just a gossipy bitch who can't stand it when someone is happy."

Claire, numb, looked up from the wheel. "I'm going to find out."

"What are you going to do?"

"I'm going to drive to Mankato; there's a dance on the pier tonight."

"Claire, you don't have to do that. I'm sure it's nothing."

Claire had stared hard into her best friend's eyes. "Sadie, he hasn't called much; we've been having problems, you know that. And he never mentioned the dance, Sadie, not once when we've talked this week. I just need to know."

Sadie stood there for a moment, looking down at her friend's face. "Okay, I'll go with you. Just let me grab my bag." She sprinted to the court, grabbed it, and ran back to the car. "Let me drive." For once, Claire relented, and they left the park and headed east.

Now jolted from her sleep, Claire hears the captain's voice, announcing the approach into MSP. After landing, she heads for baggage claim. She is still groggy; stress has made her tired, the trip has made her achy, and she is not looking forward to the long drive to New Ulm. She stops at the coffee shop and grabs their special brew of the day, adding cream and cane sugar before continuing toward the claim area. She stands around the carousel, and sees her luggage come down the chute. As it comes around the carousel, she reaches for one bag while holding her coffee with the other, drops it next to her and tries for the larger bag, which is rapidly moving beyond her reach, just as a strong arm reaches across her shoulder. She turns to thank the gentleman for his kindness and finds herself face to face with the notorious Matthew Hendricks.

Chapter Four

Late in the day, Chris drove to the Nielsen farm. The rain that had poured down on the Minnesota River Valley began to clear, leaving a deep purple hue across the horizon and turning everything a brilliant, earthy green. It had always amazed Chris, this emergence from the deep freeze of a Minnesota winter; the long winter days so entombing in their isolation. Snow gave way to the black dirt of turned fields, ready to be planted. Winter wheat, lush in its rich, yellow-green hue, emerging atop rolling hills where the water drained into the hollows.

Spring is a time to smell the grass, the damp, pungent scent of earth and cattle. It is time to see the bustle of activity as farmers work fields and natives emerge from the hibernation of their homes, breathing in the fresh cool air. Minnesotans relish springtime like no other human being, because such time is short lived; before long, spring gives way to the humidity of summer. Long hot, sticky days flow into nights when the mosquitoes swarm over the lakes and swamps, forcing many indoors once again. But this, this release from winter's bondage, is paradise.

Chris did not grow up in Minnesota; his father, William Breuning II, after graduating law school left Minnesota for a firm in Chicago. Chris's grandfather, Bill Breuning, was a second-generation Minnesotan, born and raised on the St. Croix. A large man, with rough hands, broad shoulders and an infectious grin, Bill had worked with his family, watching as the lumbering trade his father had built withered with the diminishing white pine forests as the trade moved northward toward the Superior shores. When the logging company closed, Bill moved his family to the lush Minnesota River Valley.

Will never fully embraced his father's regard for the working-class citizens who were his patrons at the car dealership. He used his ever-present wit and youthful good looks to marry the daughter of one of the senior-most attorneys in the firm. When Christopher W. Breuning was born, both Will and his lovely wife, Kate, had fully expected that their young son would grow up to follow his father's distinguished footsteps. They had not, however, anticipated how genetics and sheer will would distinguish their pugnacious child from others. Christopher grew strong, and solid, with his grandfather's broad shoulders and broad hands. When his parents pulled strings to get his application to Western Academy off the wait list, he joined the Marines.

Chris spent much of his youth rebelling against his father's arrogant attitude about their humble roots. In truth, Chris's resemblance to his grandfather, Bill, in both action and physique, was more than unsettling to Will, and he worked diligently to rein the boy in. Christopher loved Granddad even while Will despised him, and the more Will pushed his son, the more Chris resented him. Eventually he enrolled in U Chicago and took a degree in Criminology, ending up in organized crime.

After Chris returned from Iraq in '91 he tried to make amends with his parents. He'd even married a nice lawyer from the DA's office, a woman who could have been hand-picked by Julia. Gloria was lithe, like a dancer, toned and flexible, dark and exotic. In the bedroom, she could move like no other woman he'd known.

At home in the apartment they shared, after a dinner party at the Breuning house one evening, Chris watched his wife slip out of her Ferragamo heels and black scoop necked dinner dress from his position on the bed. "You and Will were pretty tight tonight."

She looked up at him demurely, sculpted eyebrows raised as she pulled hose off her fine legs. "Chris, you should give your father a chance. He's a good man and can do a lot for you, if you'd let him."

"What do you mean by that?"

"Frankly, he's got a lot of pull in this city. If you want to move up in the department, he can help you do that. He knows a lot of people."

Chris's hackles rose. "I'd rather do it on my own; I don't want his help."

She stood up, reached behind her to unsnap the bra and let it fall to the floor, small breasts thrust forward as she walked to the bed and leaned over him. "Darling, I don't mean you *need* his help, but he's there if you *want* his help. Why waste all that power and money?" She reached out a tongue and licked his lips. "Now stop talking and give me some action…" She laughed as he rolled her over onto her back.

He'd thought they would make a good team, the two of them, and for a while they had. But they wanted different things; when he talked kids, she'd said she was not ready for children, and may never be; she was on the fast track, and a woman on the fast track can't be tied down with children – it wouldn't look good. They spent more hours apart. Some days, their professional paths would cross, and Chris began to feel that the only time they talked was when they were working.

The end had been difficult. Chris, overwrought about the end of his marriage and its circumstances, began a descent into the bottle that nearly cost him his job. When he found out that his father was going to sell Bill's estate and put him in assisted living, Chris made the move, and ended up in the heartland, living with his grandfather, leaving the painful past behind.

Chris turned into the Nielsen drive, followed the curvy driveway through a tunnel of mature oak trees, and pulled in front of the house. Ben Lahr was leaning against a squad car in the sun, watching him approach. Chris grabbed his 35 mm camera and stuck a tiny recorder and an evidence kit into his pocket and greeted the Deputy.

"Hey," Chris said as he stepped up to where Ben was, reaching out to shake hands.

"Thanks for coming out."

Ben smiled. "No problem."

Both crawled under the police tape, and surveyed the house. There were no torn screens, no markings around the door handle, no broken glass to indicate forced entry. The kitchen, to the left of the main entrance, was in shambles, water pooled on the old hardwood floor, and he could see damage up into the ceiling of the room. Chris could smell smoke and wet fabric and damp wood.

Ms. Nielsen had several antique furniture pieces scattered around the rooms, including a built-in mission style cabinet full of rosewood and depression glass. Nothing appeared to be missing from the collection, although he would have a family member go through thee inventory with him. Late afternoon sun was peeking through the transom window above the cabinet, leaving a trail of light across the maple flooring and oak dining table. Two Victorian armchairs sat nestled in a bay area, with an oval empire writing table sitting between them.

There was extensive smoke damage in the kitchen, and they were careful to watch where they stepped, concerned that the floor may be unstable where the home had burned. The cabinets were original and had been painted a gleaming white at some point since the house was built. All upper cabinets near the stove were burned through; crushed glasses, dishes and cans littered the counter and floor, having fallen when the cabinets collapsed from flames licking through their wooden frames.

A compact mobile island, with a maple butcher block countertop, had been knocked into the refrigerator, directly opposite the window facing the drive. It overturned, knocking the contents of the drawers onto the floor. Chris kneeled to examine the island; the rollers on the bottom closest to the fire were melted, the top two dripped now hardened plastic. The bottom of the island was dimpled with blisters of polyurethane. The pattern of fire damage seemed to indicate that the cabinet was knocked over before the fire department got there.

He turned to Ben. "Any idea of this happened when the fire department was here, or if it happened before?"

Ben nodded, "I talked with the fire chief this afternoon. They found it like that."

"Seems heavy for an elderly woman to push over, doesn't it?"

"Yeah."

Chris shot pictures of the kitchen and the island, searching for clues. Too many people had traversed the kitchen; water likely diluted any evidence he could collect there. In the living room, oak bookshelves lined the far walls; a plush sofa sat in the middle of the room, with a sofa table behind it. Between the sofa and the table, now knocked askew, was a knitting bag; knitting needles protruding. Yarn had rolled from the bag across the floor, and Chris could see that the bag had been flattened, likely when Ms. Nielsen fell onto it. The end table nearest the hall that led to the kitchen was knocked over.

The stairs to the bedrooms circled to a landing that overlooked the stairwell, and in the corner of the landing was an antique divan next to a table that held a washbasin and pitcher from some era past. At the end of the hall was Eva's bedroom. The smell of smoke clung to every surface. The closet, situated directly above the kitchen stove, was open and clothing strewn about on the floor, trampled and muddied from wet feet. Soot arched in the back wall of the closet.

Ben carefully opened drawers and looked at the contents of the dresser and chest of drawers. "These have been rifled through." He turned to look at Chris, who was shining a flashlight into the closet.

Chris nodded, and kept searching through the closet. "How can you tell?"

"Everything else in the house is neat. Clean. The drawers are messed up, but just enough. Someone was careful, but not too careful."

"Anything obvious?"

"Not so far…"

Late in her shift, Lyneah stepped out back of the bar and stood in the alley around the corner from the entrance, smoking a cigarette. The cool air felt good on her skin. Bob Anderson, a supervisor from the plant, had come in with his wife for dinner. Carolyn, a perky little blonde with a flashy smile, worked as a teacher's aide part time at the school. When she saw Carolyn head to the restroom, she sat at their table and asked Bob about Hank losing his job.

"Now, Lyneah, you know I can't talk about what goes on down at the plant." He said.

She'd pleaded. "Bob, please. I just really need to know what happened."

"I can't, Lyn," Bob said, looking around the bar and taking a drink from his frosty beer mug. "I could lose my job if I talk about employee issues with other people."

"Bob, I don't want you to lose your job; I just want to know what's going on with Hank." She had looked at him searchingly. "Please."

He'd hesitated. "Look, I really can't say. But it wasn't good, Lyn." He leaned closer to her. "There's an investigation." He sighed, looking at her with kindness. "All I can tell you is he's bad news, Lyn. You need to take care of yourself and kick his ass out the door."

Reflecting on the conversation, she tossed the cigarette into the ash receptacle, stretching her back, and arching slightly, trying to work out a kink. Yawning, she closed her eyes for a moment, feeling the cool air caress her skin. It felt good to feel spring on her skin and she savored the moment before heading back into the bar. She turned to head back in, and suddenly found herself gripped from behind by arms of steel, pulling her hips back tightly. She froze, recognizing Hank's scent, his breath in her ear, and cringed. "Hello, darlin'," his voice said softly as he reached one of his hands up to grab a handful of gold tresses and breathe deeply.

"Jesus, Hank, you scared me to death..." She tried to move away from his grasp, but his arm just tightened further. She could feel the heat of his body against her back, smell liquor on his breath. "What are you doing here?"

She felt his hand run down her arm and tried not to shiver; she could feel the sickness of dread in her chest, anticipating *badness*. "I came to take you home."

She moved to disengage herself, trying to pull his arm from her waist, which stuck like glue. "I don't think so, Hank."

She felt the change, the stiffening of the body, the subtle tightening of his grip on her waist, and a tiny tinge of fear crept in. Her senses heightened. She had become familiar with his mood swings and tried to remain calm as she reasoned with him. "Hank, it's been a long day. I'm tired. I don't want to fight, I- I just want to sleep when I get home because I work early tomorrow, too."

He stood still for a moment, then continued to run his hand up and down her arm as the other one gripped her hair a little tighter. "Oh, I *do* think so, Lyneah," he breathed into her ear, making her cringe. "You're coming home with me."

Lyneah could feel the cold grip of fear deep inside of her. This time, however, she did not feel the resignation to submit, instead, she wrenched her arm away, catching him off guard and felt some hair pull from her head as she turned to face him.

"Look, Hank. I'm done. Finished. I'm not doing this anymore. You can come by in a couple of days and pick your stuff up. I'll put it in the garden shed."

His face darkened. "You're kidding me. You think you can walk away from me?"

"Yes, I can. I don't need any of this abusive shit anymore, Hank. You're a drunk, and when you drink, you're an asshole."

"Ah, you don't mean that; you're just pissed off because we had a little fight."

Lyneah could feel the anger boil up inside her and tried to remain calm. "What is wrong with you, Hank? You think you can treat people like that, and they'll just come crawling back and all is forgiven? *Every time?* You're crazy. I'm not putting up with that, anymore. Please leave me alone."

He laughed. "Come on, baby. Lighten up. You know you don't want me to go…"

"Yes, Hank, I do." She stared defiantly up into his eyes, quaking inside, but showing no fear. "Get your crap out of my house and stay away from me."

"What do you want? You want me to say I'm sorry?"

She turned to go and heard him snarl as he grabbed her by the neck, shoving her back into the wall of the bar, the brick digging into her back as she felt his rough hand squeeze her throat, She could feel panic welling up and instinct propelled her hands to his fingers, trying to pull them from her neck. He pressed his face into her forehead, and whispered, "You'll never have anyone else …"

Lyneah closed her eyes to fight back the tears that stung. Suddenly, his grip on her throat turned into a menacing caress. "This don't end until I say it ends."

"Lyneah? You need any help, there?" From down the dark alley, she heard the voice of Leo Christian, a thick, German gentleman and a father of a high school classmate.

Hank ran his arm casually around her shoulder and turned to Leo's voice. "Everything's fine. Go on into the bar."

"Lyn?"

Lyneah, gulped, then, as quickly as she could, disengaged herself from Hank's arm and ran toward the end of the alley. She ran her hand over her eyes, and smiled tremulously at Leo, seeing the concern on his face. "I'm fine, Leo," she said, shakily, tucking her hand into his arm. "I'll come in with you; just finishing my break…"

Hank watched her go. "You remember what I said, Lyneah."

She ignored him and kept walking. Leo opened the door for her and patted her gently on the arm as they walked in through the crowd. "You just let me know if there's anything I can do for you, Lyn. I got lots of friends around here, can help me take care of business, if you know what I mean."

"Thanks, Leo. I'll keep that in mind," she said, only half-jokingly. "You have a good time tonight and behave yourself!" she threw over her shoulder as she grabbed her tray from the station.

"Matt," Claire was breathless, her heart pounding in her throat. "What are you doing here?"

He stood over her, his familiar face more weather-worn than she'd seen him last, but still Matt. Leaner, older, hair still tousled so that she felt the hysterical impulse to reach out and touch it. His eyes, impossibly green as to be almost turquoise, searched her face, silently, as if looking for some sign. When he spoke, his penetrating voice radiated memory, flooding her senses. "I came to take you home, Claire."

"I – I," she paused, trying to think. "I've arranged for a car."

"No need. I told your aunt I'd drive you."

Still reeling from the shock of seeing this man whose boy image had just been dominating her thoughts, Claire tried hard to regain her composure. She drew in a breath, and breathed out, slowly. "Matt, I appreciate your concern; however, I am fully capable of finding my way back to New Ulm from here. I've done it many, many times since I grew up."

He stood, studying her for long enough to make her uncomfortable, then spoke again. "I'm aware of how much you've "grown up", Claire." Her name on his tongue made her breathless. "But I made a promise to Betty that I'd see you safely to her place. She's leaving the light on for you, and you are to sleep in Jacquie's old room, in case no one's up when you get in."

Betty had not mentioned any of this to Claire, only that the farmhouse was uninhabitable due to the fire. Claire bit her lip, not wanting to appear ungracious, but wanting desperately to extricate herself from having to spend two hours in a car with Matt.

She put on her best professional smile, she held up her hand. "Look, I appreciate your being here, but you don't have to stay. I'll find my way."

He stared down at her again. She saw the flicker of amusement, just a tiny flash, then the same impassive expression. "Nope. I made a promise; I aim to keep it." And with that, he picked up the two largest bags and headed toward the escalator.

Claire stood gaping for a moment, then grabbed her bags and started after him, awkwardly, still in the heels she had worn for classes that day. She felt her control unraveling as she followed him toward the parking ramp and called out to him. "Listen, what's the point of you coming here, anyway? We don't know each other anymore. Anyone from the family could have come, so I can't understand why *you* decided to show up. Please, wait!"

He kept walking, apparently heedless of her words behind him. "*Damn it*," she muttered under her breath.

"Fine. I'm not going anywhere with you. You can deliver my luggage…"

That stopped him. He turned to look back at her, and actually grinned. "You haven't changed a bit, have you?"

She bit her cheek, and felt the ire rising. What the hell was he trying to prove? "I don't want to go with you; I have no intention of riding in a car with you for any length of time, much less two hours. Just, - just let me go."

"'Can't do it, Claire. Be reasonable, here. How would it look if I showed up with two suitcases and no niece?"

"I could care less how it would look. Am I not making myself clear?" She ran a manicured finger through her tresses, trying to smooth them. "I am just too tired to argue with you, and we're wasting time…"

"Exactly," he said, and turned once more, stepping onto the escalator. "Come on, let's get you home."

She watched him descend, saw him turn to look up at her and smile a wry smile, shrugging a shoulder, and she relented. But she reminded herself, only for the moment. She intended to stay far, far away from the man who had always been like a drug to her. Far, far away.

In the warmth of the car, she found herself relaxing, and vowed to engage in minimal conversation. Matt, too, did not seem too inclined to say much. She kicked off her heels and, before they had reached the 169 interchange, she fell asleep, curling her long legs under her and leaning against the window, her linen jacket under her neck.

Matt had watched her approach the baggage claim area. He'd seen her long legs in those patent leather heels and vintage dress that clung to the curves of her body. The dress, a shimmer of pearl cream, had swayed with each move of her hips, and it had taken him a while to realize he wasn't breathing. She had been a pretty teenager; she was a beautiful woman. Sophisticated, and far out of reach.

He studied her profile; she still had that cute pixie nose, but the jawline was harder. Her eyebrows were perfectly coiffed, skin flawless. Fine lines had appeared around her mouth and eyes but did not mar the beauty. He saw the tiny mole, right under her left earlobe, and remembered touching it with his lips. He wanted to touch it now, but decided it was not a good idea. He had been a young, headstrong college kid the last time he'd seen her, and she had been hurt and defiant. He had been responsible for that and had not ever had the chance to make it right. He wasn't all that sure of why he was attempting to, now. Many years had passed since that summer; a lifetime stood between the two of them.

Claire dreamed she was underwater, encased in an iron box, her arms tangled in cables or wires. She was drowning. She could see the sunlight above, through the water, casting a brilliant shimmer across the water, but could not disentangle herself from shackles that held her in the box. As she looked up into the light, she saw someone, a stranger, blonde hair flowing with the current, shimmering in the light. He was in a white vest, and his hand reached down to her. As she reached back, she felt his hand, warm and strong, encircle hers, and woke with a start. She sat up quickly, felt Matt's hand over hers, and looked at him.

"You were dreaming," he said.

Claire licked dry lips and pushed her unruly hair from her eyes. "Yes." She quickly removed her hand from his grasp and reached up to redo the pin holding her hair back. "I was drowning."

She looks out into the darkness. "Where are we?"

"169," Matt replied. "We'll be there in a half hour or so."

"Thanks." Claire opened the visor mirror above her head, and ran her finger under eyes that looked strained. She felt tense sitting next to Matt, and wanted the ride to be over.

Matt, too, felt the tension building between them as the silence grew. Claire was the first to speak. "I want to see Eva."

"I don't think the hospital will allow that so late."

"They will."

"Claire, she's getting the best of care; you should rest and see her in the morning."

She turned to look at him in the glow of the dash lights. "Please, Matt. I just want to see her tonight." She looked away. "I'm afraid that tomorrow will be too late." The dream had left her confused and out of sorts. She felt a deep presence of her grandmother and it overwhelmed her.

She said. "Matt, you found her. What happened?"

He paused. "The horses were restless. I thought it was because of the storm, but when I walked to the far end of the stable, I saw smoke coming out of the kitchen."

Claire felt sick. "Go on," she said quietly.

"I found her on the floor in the living room. She wasn't conscious, Claire." He glanced at her; she could feel his eyes on her in the dark glow of the dash lights. "I picked her up and carried her outside." Matt could remember how light she had felt in his arms. "Called 911 and sat on the bench until they got there."

"She had a lump on her head, scratches, but, quite frankly, I thought she had a stroke and hit her head on the table when she fell." Matt replayed it again, in his head. "I thought she was cooking and forgot. I stop out there a lot after rounds, and she feeds me." He smiled, faintly. "She's a hell of a cook."

Claire stared at his profile, surprised by this twist of information. "She never mentioned that she saw you so much." Claire puzzled for a moment. "What about her mental state? You told me on the phone that you thought you'd seen some changes in her recently, some setbacks. What are you seeing?"

"She's just, well, she's just not quite as spry as she used to be."

"Spry?"

Matt pursed his lips for a moment. "She's been more absent-minded. She's become pretty frail, and sometimes talks about Tom as if he's still around. I'm not sure if that's because she thinks he is, or if she actually talks to him sometimes." Eva had always been eccentric, and talking to spirits would not necessarily be out of the realm of possibility for her. "I stopped out there a few months ago. She came to the door all dressed up, in a hat, and a long gown that looked like something she may have worn in high school or something. She said she'd been dancing."

"She invited me in, for dinner, and the dining room was lit with candles and she had the table set for two. 'Said she'd made my favorite. After that, we had a great dinner, and she seemed to snap out of it. I decided that night that I was going to check in on her more often, and now we have, sort of, a weekly standing date, most Sunday nights."

"Do you think someone was trying to steal from her, or something? Any ideas?"

"I think that it's possible. The county has had lots of changes since we were kids. More drugs, and people know she's out there alone a lot of the time."

"Is Dave still running the stable? With his boys?"

"Yes, he is, and then she's got a kid from town coming in on weekends to clean pens and feed. He seems like a decent kid, kinda rough around the edges, but, you know, she's got causes all over the place."

They were approaching her hometown; Claire could see lights in the distance. She reached into a bag in the backseat and grabbed a pair of sneakers, slipping them over her bare feet and tossed the heels back in the bag. "I meant what I said about seeing her tonight, even for just a few minutes. Celia, Sadie's sister, is on station tonight in ICU. I've already talked with her."

When Matt pulled into the entrance, Claire opened the door, climbed out, and then leaned into the car. "You're free to come in with me, if you'd like."

"Okay. I'll park the car. See you in a few minutes."

Claire made her way into ICU with familiarity; she'd spent summers as a nursing assistant. Reaching the quiet and darkened ICU, she found Celia Wollard, the sister of one of her closest friends, who came around the desk and hugged her briefly, then motioned her down the hall. "Claire, it's so good to see you," she whispered. "I'm so sorry about your grandmother. She's in ICU 3."

Claire felt her heart pounding in her chest as she quietly made her way to Eva's room. The anticipation was constricting her throat, and she felt suddenly frightened, uncertain of what she would find. She opened the door and froze, staring at the tiny figure lying on the hospital bed, tubes and wires and equipment attached to her. Tears sprang to her eyes as she tiptoed into the room. She touched the cool hand that was lying on the sheet, running her hand softly up and down the pale skin that was exposed and unobstructed by IV tubes. She seemed to have bruises everywhere on her arm.

"Gran, it's me, Claire," she whispered. "I love you."

Nothing. Just the sound of the respirator pushing sustenance into the form before her. Eva's hair, usually beautifully coifed, lay matted to her head. Claire brushed it from her forehead, where her skin seemed so translucent, paper thin.

She felt rather than heard Matt step behind her, and she leaned over to kiss her grandmother carefully on the forehead. "I will be here to see you tomorrow," Claire whispered closely to her ear. "Don't leave me, Gran. Please." A tear fell from her eye to her grandmother's cheek, and she gently brushed it away with her forefinger.

Eva was in a dreamland. She felt the boy's arms around her, blanketed in comfort, but was so cold, so very cold. She felt the boy's body, so strong, spooned around her own, under the blanket. She turned, eyes searching his, dim light caressing his face and playing across the strong jaw line. He looked down at her, just for a moment, and groaned, mumbling words she did not know, but understood in her soul.

"Meine schatzi…" He pulled her to him, and she opened her arms, meeting his kiss and tongue with a fervor of her own. His hands worked under her coat and sweater, brushing her breasts through her bra. She disengaged from him long enough to unclasp it and pull the sweater over her head. His lips found her breasts, tongue gently kneading, causing her to gasp and pull him onto her, her young body welcoming his.

Slowly, carefully, he removed their clothing, his fingers touching her velvet softness, caressing, opening her, working her to a feverish dampness, and then he carefully entered her. Her body resisted, just for a moment, and she cried out. He cupped her face with his strong, rough hands, and slowly began the dance. She ran her hands down his back, felt the swell of his lean buttocks, pushing him further inside of her, urging him. He pumped harder, faster, and she cried out as he came into her, taut and spent. He brushed a tear from her face, a tear shed with love and passion. She had never felt such bliss.

Chapter Five

Lyneah left the bar after her shift, feeling sick. *I will not do this anymore. I will not do this anymore...* She sat staring at her home, still feeling the adrenaline pumping her senses to a higher level, anticipating something ominous to sneak out of the darkness and clamp its fingers around her throat. She felt like a child, hunkered down as low as she could go into the blankets, peering into her closet for the boogey man. Lyneah wanted to crawl into the safety of her childhood room, where no boogey man was bigger than her daddy, and no one had made her feel safer.

She left the car running and pulled the house key from the keychain that dangled from the ignition. She wished she had left the porch light on, but it had been daylight and she had been upset and in a hurry. Tonight, it seemed especially dark. She darted toward the steps, tripped over one of Travis's toys lying in the grass, and fell hard on her hands; pain shot up her arm. "Shit," she mumbled and sat for a moment in the grass, holding her wrist. "This is ridiculous."

She ran her hand across the wet grass until she found the key she had dropped and stood awkwardly. The cold dampness of mud and grass seeped through her jeans. Sighing, she unlocked the door, and went inside. The house was still, and when she flicked the light on in the tiny entryway, she found nothing amiss. Breathing a sigh of relief, she removed her shoes and quickly gathered an overnight bag. Five minutes later she was on her way to her parents' home.

Claire spent the better part of the next day with her grandmother, whose condition remained the same. This news had been neither encouraging or discouraging; she is nearing 90, they told Claire. We do not know if she will recover, or what will recover. Have no expectations. Still, Claire clung to hope and prayed that she would not yet lose the one who had taken care of her for much of her life and felt more at ease knowing that she was near Eva.

The house had been off limits for a few days of police processing, so Claire had spent the time when she was not at the hospital at her aunt and uncle's place. Betty was an excellent cook, and Claire found herself enjoying the home cooking she had been brought up with; home-made stews, savory bread, pot roast with all the lovely garden trimmings. This was not the foodstuff of her usual diet, but it felt good to eat a meal that had been prepared with love and tradition.

Lyneah was also staying at the Hamiltons. When she had seen Lyneah, briefly, she was shocked at how much weight her older cousin had lost, and how tired and gaunt she looked. Claire wondered what was up but didn't want to pry.

The two were some years apart in age; Lyneah was Izzy's first cousin, the youngest born to Grandpa Tom's sister, Betty. She was always kind to Claire, stopping at the farm and playing with Claire, curling her hair and applying lipstick, dancing to the latest music and playing dress up. She had been so lively, long blonde hair and low-cut blouses, and Claire had been fascinated to watch her cousin apply eye shadow in front of the mirror, curling her hair, then Claire's tresses, and spraying hairspray until it stung Claire's nose and made her sneeze. They had giggled a lot.

Claire now stood and surveyed the old house, a twinge of regret seeping into her insides. She stepped over the police tape and into the house. Walking slowly through the house, she smelled the pungent scent of smoke and decaying food. She went up the stairs, glancing in each room, and found herself in her grandmother's room, which was the only room in the upper floor that appeared to be affected by the fire. Eva's clothes were lying on the floor, strewn out from the closet, and she began to pick them up, the colorful pantsuits and all the lovely dresses that Eva would wear.

When she had finished scooping up the dresses and laying them across the bed, she stepped into the large dark closet. She was not able to see far into it, so she found a flashlight she knew her grandmother kept in her night table, and shown it into the closet, a long, narrow corridor that ran the length of the room. Claire crawled tentatively toward the other end, keeping to the inside wall to avoid the clothing racks and shelving that were attached to the wall. She did not remember ever really being in here before; as a child, there were always so many things to do, and then, when she had moved here the year of her parents' death, she had not been terribly engaging or curious, just cloaked in grief.

Moving the flashlight to the back wall of the space, she was stunned to see, hanging from the rack, what she believed to be Eva's wedding dress. Ivory satin, shimmery in the flashlight's glow, with tulle around the tiny waist and delicate rosebud lace surrounding the v-line collar. Claire carefully pulled it from its rack and backed out of the closet. She ran her hands down the full-length sleeve to the v point at the end of it, imagining Eva in the dress. *Why have I never seen this before?*

Thankfully, there was no damage to the dress. She stepped back into the closet, and rummaged further into the back, spying vintage clothes and an old chest crammed into the corner. She pulled the boxes out and stacked them under the window, paused to open the window to let some fresh air into the stuffy room. She shuffled back into the closet and pulled the chest carefully out into the room, lifting it at the door so as not to scratch the maple flooring, and set it on the oriental rug that was centered in the room.

The chest was old, very old, shaped like a steamer chest, with straps of dyed leather running across the top, buckled at two places in the front. It had a lock with a tiny latch, and Claire moved to open it, just as she heard a knock and a call from the front door. The insurance guy, she sighed, and went down the stairs to greet him.

Lyneah rose to a quiet house, feeling achy and tired from a restless sleep. She grabbed a cup of coffee, this time in a "World's Greatest Dad" mug from the hodge podge of mugs in the cupboard, a memorial to every charity Jer attended in his spare time. She added a generous dollop of cream and stepped out onto the back deck. She lit a cigarette, smoked slowly while she drank her coffee. Lyneah had begun to cut back on the habit already, but the morning ritual was hard to break, and she savored the stimulating combination of nicotine and caffeine coursing through her body.

Her sister Diana was going to drive out and take care of business. Diana, a lawyer in St. Paul, of short stature, with cropped dark blonde curls and a stocky frame, had become the ad hoc advocate for the entire family, rendering legal advice, counsel and, most importantly, an absolutely unwavering backbone in times when someone she loved was in need. When she heard that Lyneah was having domestic problems with that no-good Hank Beaudine, she had damn near jumped out of her skin at the chance to get involved, because no man should ever treat her baby sister like that. He was no good, but she had, with difficulty, refrained from trying to persuade Lyneah to dump his ass, even when she had quietly had him investigated and found things that she didn't like.

Sighing, Lyneah stubbed her cigarette in the can full of sand she had discreetly hidden behind a large terra cotta pot filled with geraniums. *That* had been the conversation of last evening, when Diana, having been informed by one of the sisters of Lyneah's recent troubles, had called.

"Lynnie," Diana's sharp, husky voice spoke over the phone. "What's going on?"

"Nothing, really," Lyneah had replied into her cell phone, fumbling in her purse for a stick of gum to compensate for the nicotine she craved. "Why?"

"I heard that you have been having some problems with Hank."

"Yeah. Well, it's not a big deal," she tried to be nonchalant. "I just decided not to see him, anymore. And he's not happy about it."

"How much "not happy"?"

"Really, really pissed off, actually."

He hit you, or anything?"

Lyneah, absently stroking the bruises on her arm from Hank's earlier assault, stifled the urge to confess. "No. He did not hit me." Not really a lie, just an omission of the whole truth.

"Did he hurt you, in *any way*." Diana's business voice, which meant she was harnessing impatience.

"Well, he got pretty mad, and did get a bit physical, but nothing I couldn't handle."

Her sister was, if anything, brutally honest. "Look, any bit of physical is too much. I didn't want to tell you this, but he's got some bad stuff in his background, Lynnie—"

"What do you mean, Diana?" Lyneah demanded. "Did you go off and check into him when I specifically told you to mind your own business?"

"Of course, I did, kid." Diana sounded a bit smug. "I told you a long time ago to let me check him out, and you refused to listen. It's not that I think you would have listened anyway, but it's good information to have, especially now."

Lyneah could feel the tug of irritation that came with being the youngest in the family. "Geez, Diana, I'm not a teenager, anymore. I must make my own decisions. Right now, I've decided to cut Hank loose. It's just not going well."

"Humph, well, I'm coming out tomorrow; Mom said you don't work. We'll go over to your place and talk about what we should do." She paused, and her voice softened just a bit. "Look, I want to help. And I know you're not telling me everything, and that's okay, for now, but we need to talk. Okay?"

"Okay. Thanks, Diana. Love you."

"You, too, kiddo," Diana replied, and the call was abruptly ended.

Lyneah's thoughts drifted to the past. Diana Hamilton, nine years older than Lyneah, and the oldest child of the Hamilton girls, had been a sports fanatic in school, loving to play ball with the neighborhood boys, who tolerated her gender because she had a mean right hook and an equally mean fast pitch. She could skate like the wind, on the pond behind the house, and outrun any boy on the block, even with her short legs. Diana, with hair always snarled and knees perpetually skinned from sliding into base or recklessly racing her bicycle down the steep, rocky hill out by the old Moss millpond, always hated dressing like a girl. By the time she reached age ten, Betty had given up on trying to tame her oldest daughter's curls, or her tomboy behavior.

Diana was the only sister who did not treat her like she was a doll; rather, she encouraged Lyneah to spread her wings and experience life. She allowed Lyneah to tag along, sometimes, when Diana played ball at the Lions baseball diamond, where Lyneah would sit in the stands and watched her big sister play and cuss like a sailor. Then one evening at the dinner table, while her father sipped whiskey sour and watched the NBC Nightly news with John Chancellor, little Lyneah dropped a glob of gravy onto her new hot pink shorts, and piped out, "shit, god-damn."

The other Hamilton girls, chatting over their swiss steak, mashed potatoes and butter beans, were suddenly silent. Jerry looked at Betty, over his glasses, and Betty, astonishment written all over her face, dropped her fork, turned to her youngest daughter, and said, smartly, "Where did you learn language like that, young lady?"

Lyneah, sensing something was wrong, but uncertain just what it was, glanced around the table. "What do you mean, Mom?"

"I mean, "her mother replied sternly, "where did you hear the words you just said."

"'At the ball field." Lyneah, who had never really been in trouble for anything, looked to her older sister, who hastily stuck her fork into a butter bean and put it into her mouth, for support. "What's wrong with saying shit god damn? Diana says it all the time."

All eyes at the table, Maxine and Jacquie curious and amused, Betty Lou disgruntled and Jer looking like he wished he were anywhere but there, turned to Diana. She turned a deep beet red, gulped, and set down her fork, wiped her mouth with the quicker picker upper, and peeked tentatively at her mother through her choppy bangs. A lecture followed, and after a three-day grounding, Lyneah was not allowed to accompany Diana to ballgames anymore.

Later, Diana would return home for visits, bringing various classmates, in particular a dark-haired wisp of a girl named Sunny Carlisle. Sunny, a graduate of Philosophy, was as slight and waiflike as Diana was thick.

Cottonwood Flowing

In the summer before their senior year at Hamlin, they rented a cabin on Middleton Lake, and Diana worked for the Parks Department, while Sunny waited tables at a resort. Lyneah, a teenager then, went to spend a weekend with them in July, and the three girls tubed around the lake, sunbathed, and drank marguerites into the evening hours.

At dusk, tipsy with liquor, they started a bonfire and sat, switching to beer and a little cannabis. Lyneah, after getting her first taste of the potent weed, felt the buzz drifting through her body, and lay afloat on her blanket, staring into the night sky. Sunny and Diana giggled quietly, picked her up and tucked her into bed where she promptly dozed into oblivion.

Later, she awoke dazed, having to pee. She drank about a gallon of water, took two aspirins from the cabinet, and started back toward her bedroom, when she heard laughter outside. Curious, she slipped quietly to the window. The moon was full, glistening like diamonds across the lake. The fire in the pit was diminishing, but Lyneah could see, clearly, the silhouette of her sister, naked, standing in the moonlight. Sunny, long dark hair flowing down her back, was kneeling in the grass, suckling and kissing Diana's breasts, one hand kneading between Diana's legs. Lyneah, at once repulsed and fascinated, felt her heart pounding at this sight, but could not look away.

She watched in fascination, as her sister removed Sunny's tiny bikini top and rub her face into Sunny's breasts, kneading and caressing them as Sunny leaned back until her back was on the ground. As she watched the two make love in the moonlight, Lyneah, feeling like a betrayed voyeur, turned and tiptoed back to her room as quickly as she could, and lay wide awake, way into the night, her stomach in knots and her eyes full of tears.

It was near dawn when she fell asleep, and Diana woke her at noon on Sunday, teasing her about being hung over. Lyneah could not look her sister in the eye, and feigning illness, not too difficult because the booze had made her feel thick-headed and sick to her stomach, she stayed in bed for the rest of the afternoon. When dusk came, she could hear Sunny and Diana talking on the deck, and smelled the steaks they grilled, along with packets of potatoes and onions, smothered in butter, roasting on the grill in foil.

Years later, she reflected on that experience, and acknowledged that she had probably always known Diana was gay. Or, at least, different from the other sisters, who were always fawning over boys and mooning over the latest teen idol. She had always just attributed it to maturity rather than anything else. It could not have been easy for Diana, growing up in a conservative town in a time when being a lesbian was considered a social disease. During her young adulthood, building a practice for herself, Diana kept her private life separated from her family life. Jacquie married Dave, and Maxine, an airline stewardess, met and married an up and coming congressional candidate named John Hess. No one paid any particular attention to Diana's love life.

Diana never officially "came out"; it was just not proper protocol for a girl from mid-Minnesota to make such a statement. She settled into a relationship with Meredith Lincoln, a professor of law at UM. Meredith was a lovely woman, and the family adored her; she was bright, kind, and had a soft demeanor that seemed to temper Diana's hard edge. Although no one said a word, it would become common knowledge that the two were a couple, and Meredith was accepted into the Hamilton clan. Lyneah never told Diana what she'd seen years before; she knew that it would have mortified Diana, and she just didn't see any reason to open that door.

On the way to Lyneah's place, they talked about Hank. "Lynnie, I want to tell you what I found on Hank. It's something that's bugged me for a long time, but I want to make sure you're ready to hear what I have to say."

Lyneah signed. "I'm ready. I don't actually *feel* ready, but we might as well get it over with. I suppose he's got some type of criminal record." She sighed again and looked out the window. Her luck.

Diana looked over at her, then back to the road. "Hank Joshua Beaudine, age 43. Grew up in Connersville, Indiana. Played football for the local team. Worked as an assembly person for eighteen years."

"So, I know that stuff already."

"Lost his job because he was suspected of stealing."

Lyneah felt her breath quicken. Just like Bob had said the other night. "And?"

"He was told that charges would be dropped if he left voluntarily. Seems he disappeared shortly after that." Diana sought out her sister's eyes, but Lyneah was still staring out the window. "Lyneah, he left a wife and two kids behind."

Lyneah's heart pounded as she whipped her face around and searched her sister's face with wide, astonished eyes. "What?"

"He did. Apparently, he's been avoiding paying child support. Seems there was a domestic disturbance a few months before he left town, and he wasn't allowed in the house."

Lyneah leaned back in the seat and closed her eyes. "Oh, God." She felt the tears start behind her eyelids. "Kids?"

"Two, a boy and a girl."

"How old?"

"I don't know. I didn't dig that far."

Lyneah felt sick. Kids? A wife?? He'd never said a word. Never. "Shit, Diana. *This*, you should have told me."

"I didn't know about the child support order until yesterday. And, you may recall that I tried to talk with you about him a few times; you didn't want anything to do with it."

That was true; Lyneah had made it clear that she didn't need her lawyer sister digging up dirt and she wanted to let this relationship steer its own course. Hindsight is always 20/20. Now, here she sat, feeling like a fool. *Damned idiot*, she chided herself. *What did you expect, trusting a man like that? Remember, if he's attracted to you, he's trouble.*

Diana kept glancing at her sister, who looked beaten and vulnerable. She sure knew how to pick the wrong men. "Don't be so hard on yourself, Lyneah. You can only trust a man based on what he's saying and doing, not on what he's not disclosing."

They turned into the drive of Lyneah's lot and pulled up to the garage. The yard needed mowing, spring rains having left the grass a lush and thick green. She picked a bike off the sidewalk and leaned it against the railing before reaching for the door, key in hand. She turned back to say something to Diana, and felt the screen door give way, sending her falling down the narrow wooden steps to the ground.

The tempered glass cracked, but did not shatter across her shoulder, and she skinned her shin, falling off the steps onto her left side. She lay, stunned for a moment, and felt Diana move the door roughly off her, tipping it on its side and letting it fall to the ground. "Jesus, are you okay?"

Lyneah couldn't speak for a moment, then nodded. She felt something on the side of her head, and she reached her hand up to it feeling something wet. Blood, its warmth starting to run down above her ear.

"Here, let me take a look at you. Don't move yet. I'll go into the house and get a blanket."

Lyneah nodded again, and she saw Diana reach for the keys to the door. She leaned back in the dirt and soft grass, and closed her eyes, slowly stretching her legs straight and rubbing her hip. She heard Diana curse softly and looked back at the house. Diana was standing in the doorway, key in hand, staring inside. She turned quickly and shut the door, running to the car. "Stay put. I need my cell phone."

Lyneah sat up quickly but was disoriented enough to lay back down. "Wh-what?"

"Just stay put." Diana ordered as she pulled her phone from the console and reached into her glove compartment. Lyneah felt sick as she saw her sister pull the pistol out of the case with one hand as she dialed 911 with the other.

Lyneah could hear her talking on the cell. "We've had a break in. Someone came to the house broke in the door, and ransacked it..." She paused, then gave the address to Lyneah's house. "No- no one was here. No one has been here for a few days... Yes. My name is Diana Hamilton. No, I do not live here, my sister does. She is Lyneah Hamilton." A pause. "Yes."

Diana finished the call and kneeled next to her sister. "Listen, I'm going to walk around the house. We're not going inside until the police get here, okay?" Lyneah could not answer her; she could only stare at the gun, a small one, resting in her sister's hand. "Lynnie, look at me. Do you understand?"

"Bastard broke in." Diana stood. "I think he's gone, but I'll look around." Diana stepped to the car and grabbed a travel blanket from the backseat, laying it across Lyneah's shoulders as she gingerly tried to move. "I'll be back."

Lyneah stifled the hysterical urge to giggle at that quote from the movies. Seeing Diana, short and stocky, with her weapon raised and sneaking around the corner of the house had a surreal quality to it. There she was, like a Bond girl, traipsing through the hydrangeas and lilacs, looking for trouble. The thought that the trouble was Hank sobered

Lyneah up considerably, and she looked around anxiously. She could hear the distant wail of a siren and knew that the cops would be here soon. She tried to stand, thought better of it, and slithered over to the steps, climbing onto the bottom one just as an unmarked came to a halt behind the red beamer.

Chris Breuning had taken the call, because, by sheer coincidence, he happened to be driving out in that very direction to try to locate Hank Beaudine regarding some outstanding warrants and his fingerprints found at Eva Nielsen's house. The outstanding warrants could be readily explained, the fingerprints could not, although Eva's sister, Betty Lou Hamilton, had said that Hank had been to the house with her daughter, Lyneah, because they had done some odd jobs for her aunt.

He saw the woman sitting on the step, wrapped in a blanket. He saw blood running down the side of her head, and felt the adrenaline quicken his heartbeat. He cautiously exited the car, and saw a small woman come around the corner, carrying a weapon. He stood by the car, waiting for her to approach, his hand on his own holster.

"What's going on here?" he asked casually as the woman continued to walk across the lawn, now veering toward the girl on the steps, a weary look on her face. "I understand you've had some trouble."

He walked toward the woman on the steps, and, when she looked up, eyeing him warily, he was taken aback by the vivid violet blue of her eyes, and the beauty of her face. Like a model, only with eyes that lacked hope. She was older than he originally thought, and, judging by the guarded look in her eye, accustomed to being treated poorly by men. He'd seen the look a hundred times before.

The shorter woman spoke. "I'm Diana Hamilton, this is my sister Lyneah. She's been seeing a dirtbag named Hank Beaudine that broke in here when she was gone and messed up the place."

He surveyed her noncommittally. "You got a permit for that?" pointing to the Glock. Nice weapon. Compact, deadly.

"Yes, I do." Ms. Hamilton surveyed him, holstering the weapon. "And you are?"

"Detective Chris Breuning. Ma'am, are you alright? You look like you've had a little accident."

"Yes," Lyneah Hamilton replied, her sweet voice rippling like a cool stream on a hot day. She held the end of a travel blanket up to her head. "Just banged up a bit. The door fell on me when I tried to open it."

"You had a break in?"

Lyneah nodded, but her sister cut in. "The door was kicked in. Come on, I'll show you."

Chris ignored her for a moment, focusing on the girl on the steps. "Are you sure you're all right? Let me take a look at that wound." She looked down but removed the blanket from her head. It was a scrape where she'd hit pavement; needed cleaning, but not too deep. "I'll take a quick look at the house and we'll get you in and clean you up, okay?"

She nodded, still looking down, not saying anything. Chris was struck with the impulse to raise her face so he could look into those vivid eyes again but didn't.

The house was a mess. Chris could see floral sofa cushions and pillows slashed and flung on the floor. Books tossed off the mahogany bookshelf standing in the corner, strewn about carelessly, lying open and crumpled. Cabinet doors were standing open, and there were canisters of coffee, flour and sugar open on the counter, the contents strewn across the cabinets, on the floor and in the sink.

Chris frowned. "Tell me why you think Hank Beaudine did this."

Diana sighed. "Hank and Lyneah were dating, and he was damned near living here for a few months. She won't say much to me, but I did hear from a girl she works with, who said that she's been scared of the guy, and that he's been causing her some trouble. She's been staying with my parents since." Her voice softened. "I know she's scared, and I've seen that look on her face before. If he hasn't abused her yet, he's threatened to."

Chris's eyes swept the hallway. A man's pair of boots lay carelessly on the floor. "'Forgot his boots?"

Diana eyed them. "He's a dumbass. Probably pissed up and didn't notice what he was doing."

Chris didn't respond but continued into the bedroom area. Both rooms had been ransacked. Lyneah's room was soft, feminine. He eyed the paintings on the walls. Landscapes, in watercolor, strewn with vivid splashes of reds, greens, lavender; floral designs. Split Rock lighthouse, with a boy standing at the rail; Chris stepped closer, and noticed they were signed. "Lyneah's an artist?"

"Yes, she's always had talent. She's attending school for graphic design, in Mankato."

Every drawer from the oak chest was open, its contents dumped; Chris could see bottles of cologne, lingerie, bikini briefs in cotton, with tiny pansies on them, all spilled on the floor. In addition, there were some items, in a basket next to the closet, that were men's garments, socks, t-shirts. Not a lot, but definitely left behind.

"Those Beaudine's?"

"I think so," Diana was puzzled. "Why would he leave the things he came for? Unless he was after something else? Maybe it was just for some cash and a little warning," Chris could hear the disdain in her voice. "Asshole."

Lyneah Hamilton coming through the door; the look on her face was horrified. "Oh, my God," she said through a sob. She looked at him, tears filling her eyes, then at Diana, who quickly crossed through the chaos and embraced her sister.

Chris spoke. "Before you touch anything, I'm going to call in a BCA team. It's best if we step back outside. Do you have a first aid kit?"

Lyneah felt herself being led out the back patio, into a chair next to an old umbrella table. She hurt everywhere, mostly in her heart. "I screwed up again, Diana," she said quietly. "I was so good, for so long, and then I let that bastard in."

"Shh, little sister," Diana replied softly. "You've done a great job with Travis. You're doing all the right things. Don't beat yourself up. You've done the best you could, in getting rid of him; he just wasn't taking no for an answer."

"But I should have been prepared for something like this, Di. I should have been stronger. I knew he was a mistake, right from the very beginning, but I just let him talk me into so much."

"He's gone, kiddo. Each time we make a mistake, we learn from it. Just consider Hank one big mistake." Diana smiled. "Your last, by the way. And this time you're not going to hide. He's not going to get away with this."

"Yes," But inside, she was afraid. "Yes, you're right."

Chapter Six

Claire awoke in the darkness, disoriented. She was dreaming of Matt, a distorted dream of running away from the sight of him wrapped around a summer blonde, who was kissing him in the evening sun. She had run, but, as in dreams, had been paralyzed, as if running in position, and she could hear Matt breathing behind her, calling her name.

"Claire – Claire, wait!" She kept running.

Sitting up in the darkness, her thin cotton nightshirt clung to her with dampness. She could smell the pungent remnants of the fire, and felt slightly ill from the odor. She sipped from a tepid water bottle, and looked out into the moonlit night, remembering. After leaving the park that fateful day, Sadie drove them to her parents' house, to change. "You can't go there looking like that, Claire. Come on, let's clean up. The dance doesn't start until later, anyway."

The two of them had run the main highway all the way to Mankato, and down to the riverfront. The place was packed with people partying with their classmates and friends for the last time before summer break. Girls clad in bikinis and cut off shorts were dancing in groups in front of the bandstand, and Claire could smell food stands, which would have been delicious but for the growing knot in her stomach.

There must have been thousands of people along the parkway, and finding Matt would probably be impossible, but Claire was compelled to keep going. Sadie, trailing behind this girl on a mission, did not say much, until it became clear that they could not cover all the ground with such a crowd. "Claire, I'm not sure we're going to find him."

Sadie had taken hold of Claire's arm, and turned her around to face one another. "Claire, is this what you really want to do?" Her voice was concerned, and her eyes searched her friend's face. "It's just not a place where you want to talk about your relationship, ya' know? You should give him a chance to tell you what's going on when you see him. Give yourself a chance to calm down."

They were standing dead center in front of the amphitheater, surrounded by bodies and lawn chairs and coolers, when Claire saw Sadie's eyes widen. She turned to look, the knot growing tighter, and Sadie, recovering, held fast to her arm. "Claire, look at me," she demanded. "We need to get out of here."

Claire wrenched herself free and turned to look. Not twenty feet away, dressed in shorts and a white button-down shirt that looked eerily familiar, stood Matt, entangled in a hot, sexy dance move with a big-haired blonde in a neon pink bikini that spared nothing. Claire stood, transfixed, bile reaching her throat, as she saw the girl turn around and rub her bottom into Matt, who was laughing, and saw him put his arms around the girl's bare waist. Claire saw his beautiful hands, the hands that had touched and caressed her body, touch this girl's bare skin, and she nearly fainted.

Sadie, still holding one of her arms, tried to pull her away, but Claire could not budge. When the girl turned around and licked Matt's neck with erotic familiarity, Claire felt her knees begin to give way, and felt Sadie's arm around her, supporting her. Matt's eye's looking out into the crowd, suddenly locked with hers, and held there, briefly, widening with shock. She stood for just a moment and watched as he tried to untangled himself from the blonde beauty, who was not about to let him go, then she turned toward the parking area, walking fast, tears blurring her vision, Sadie right beside her.

She heard his voice, the voice she loved so well, calling her, "Claire, Claire, wait!" and she broke into a run, running hard, fast, as fast as her legs would carry her, through the crowds and around the food stands, the tears running down her pale cheeks.

Matt caught up with her in few short strides. "Claire, please stop-" She felt his hand grab her arm, the hand she had just seen around the other girl's waist, and felt absolute revulsion. "Get away from me!" she shouted at him, wresting her arm away.

"No. It's nothing, Claire. Nothing." She turned to face him, and his face was distraught, his eyes pleading with her. "Claire, we're all just saying good-bye for the summer."

"Bullshit, you jerk." She could not bear to look at him, her tear-stained, mascara streaked face was contorted in pain and rage. "I know all about your little girlfriend. Word spreads fast when you screw around."

"Claire, I'm not screwing around." Matt had returned. "It's not like that."

"Okay, then, how is 'it'?'

Matt hesitated, not sure what to say. Claire could see the pained look on his face, the doubt, the confusion, and she knew. "God, Matt, please, no. Please don't say you've been seeing her. Not that way…"

Matt stood, looking down at her. "Claire, it's just—"

"What were you thinking? Why? What happened to us?"

He just stood looking down at her, helplessly. "I don't know, Claire." He seemed to struggle to find words. "Nothing really happened."

She was dumbfounded. "What do you mean, 'nothing *really* happened?"

He just stood, shaking his head, getting defensive. "Claire, we need to talk about this, alone. Somewhere quiet."

"What is there to say? You've obviously been making time here while I waited around at home. If you have something to say, say it! But don't look at me like *I've* done something wrong. I haven't; I've been faithful to you since I was a little kid."

Matt was silent, looking down at her face, and then he said it, softly. "Claire, I think that it's best if we take a break, for a while. Just to clear our heads and think."

"Wh-what?"

Be apart from Matt? At the time, in that moment, it had been an inconceivable thought. "What about our future? I thought you loved me!"

"I do love you, Claire," Matt was nearly in tears himself. "But we can't get along, I'm up here, studying my ass off to keep the honors scholarship and then, when I get home, all we do is fight. You want to leave, I want to stay."

"There are ways to do this, you know. I don't have to go to California-"

"Claire, we're young. We both want things, different things…"

"As in, I want a life with you, and you want *her*?" Claire could hear her voice rising, bitterly. People in clusters, holding go cups and bottles of beer in can coolers, were glancing at them, some watching openly. The band had taken a break, and she could hear the hysteria in her own voice. "That's sweet, Matt. Real nice."

Matt glanced around, then took her by the arm to lead her somewhere quiet. "Let's get out of here. See, we can't even have a civil conversation."

"Civil! Did you say civil? You asshole, *you* cheat on me, and you want me to be civil?" Claire was incredulous.

"Geez, Claire, I mean we fight. We don't talk, anymore. And I didn't cheat. We've been talking, that's all. She's a nice girl, Claire. She's just a little drunk and wanted to dance."

"Oh, my God. I can't hear this right now…" Claire wrenched her arm away, one more time. "Are you crazy? How can you stand there and talk about how great she is?"

"Dammit, Claire, you know what I mean. I was not cheating with her, she was just dancing, fooling around. That's all."

"It didn't look like that was all, to me. I saw her kiss you." Claire stopped, and gulped back a sob, and suddenly, the fire went out of her. "Where I've kissed you, Matt. You're not supposed to let another girl touch you like that…"

Matt closed his eyes, then looked away, trying to avoid seeing Claire's pain. "I've been thinking about us. How we seem to want different things. I don't know how to say what I want to say, but it's not the same, anymore. I need time to think about what's right. For both of us. You know how I feel about you. It's not the same as how I feel about Jamie."

Hearing him call the girl by name sent a knife into Claire's heart. She looked away and then said, with finality, "None of that is an excuse for what you did with that, that, whatever you want to call her. You cheated on me. On us. This break is permanent." And with that, she turned and walked away.

Sadie, who had been standing nearby, watching the whole thing, threw Matt a look that would cut glass, said, "You're a stupid jerk, Matt Hendricks," and followed her friend across the grass, toward home. Matt let them go.

Sighing, Claire cleared the memory and tried to shake it off. She turned on the bedside lamp, slipped into her grandmother's bedroom, and pulled the trunk into her room and sat next to it on the floor. It was dome topped, with paper design, rather than leather, and looked to date back to the late 1800s. The lock was keyed, but, as she ran her fingers along the brass, she felt a clasp, and, using her thumb, pulled the clasp back from the lock, heard a click, and saw the lock shaft pop out from the keyhole. Feeling excitement, she lifted the dome lid, and peered inside.

The inside of the dome lid was lavishly papered, and, in the center, a lithograph of a lovely Victorian lady, laying erotically across a fainting chair, her curls tumbling out of a comb secured at the top of her head. Ah, a bridal chest; Claire felt like she'd found buried treasure. There were two sides to the compartment; one with a flat lid, the other with a domed top, likely a hat box. Atop the box lid, there was an insignia, and, peering closer in the dim light, she made out the word, "R.N. Woollett, with an address in Minneapolis.

She opened the hat box first; inside she found a long, tulle bridal veil. She touched it gently, and felt tears form in her eyes, picturing the veil on Eva's small frame, flowing down her back and around her shoulders, as it was in the picture above the mantle. White, satin gloves, and a blue kerchief were also in the box, along with a small jewelry box containing a pair of lovely clasp earrings, of teardrop pearl and faux crystal, tarnished silver. She placed the small box gently back in the tray.

Closing the hatbox lid, Claire opened the next compartment, and sat back in surprise. There, nestled among the remnants of Claire's own childhood, rocks, toys, school papers, sat a bundle of letters, addressed to her. She recognized the handwriting, immediately, would recognize the neat scribble, the way Matt had always snuck in a smiling face on the envelope, anywhere. "Oh, Gran," she now said softly. "Why did you keep these?" As she pulled the bundle from the box, her hands trembled and she sat back against the bed.

Claire had been inconsolable after the breakup. Every dream she had

had about her future, every hope, every thought, always included Matt. His deception had crushed her and she'd cried herself to sleep every night for weeks. On the eve of her departure to California for college, Eva had stepped into her room and said she had a phone call from Matt. Claire had refused to take the call. She had stood by the window, in this very room, looking out over the lawn to the horse barns below, and said, "I can't, Grandma. I just can't…."

He had tried several more calls that night, all refused. Claire had boxed all of the things that were to be shipped with her to college and had taken the bundle of letters that now lay in her lap and tossed them in the trash. When, in a last ditch effort to talk with her before she left, Matt showed up on the doorstep, she could hear Eva trying to soothe him from where she crouched, in the dark, near the window of her bedroom, her hand clenched over her own mouth to stifle the sobs that were building in her chest.

"Matt, dear," Claire heard her Grandmother's voice on the porch below her room. "She just won't see you. I'm sorry. Give her some time. Perhaps she will come around when she doesn't feel so wounded…"

That time never came. Claire left Minnesota; there had been other letters, other attempts to reach out to her, but she would not give in to the addiction that was Matt Hendricks. She had asked her grandmother to toss the letters and to not share her address with him, no matter what. Eva had abided, but reluctantly.

When Claire was a senior, studying anthropology and archaeology at Berkeley, she had called Eva to wish her a happy birthday one Sunday evening, and learned that Matthew was getting married. Claire had hung up the telephone and sat in her tiny studio apartment, one of several that were renovated in an old mansion overlooking the marina, and cried big, rolling tears.

The tears she had shed earlier over Eva's wedding veil threatened again, and she closed her eyes, brushing them away. He'd written over thirty letters, the last one as she entered her senior year in California, and Eva had kept every single one, including the lifelong bundle of dreams that Claire had tossed in the trash before she left the farm to start her new life.

Claire sat forward and carefully placed the letters back where they were, in the compartment, and shut the lid of the trunk. In the distance, she heard a car, slowing, as though it was going to turn into the drive. She heard the car stop, and quickly peaked out the window, peering through a crack in the lacy drapery. No headlights. The night was still, and she could hear, through the open window, the sounds of the horses whinnying in the fenced meadow south of the barns. She tiptoed back into Eva's room, which overlooked the front yard and drive, and thought she saw the flicker of a flashlight in the woods along the drive. Her heart skipped a beat, and, feeling very vulnerable, she ran back into her room to grab her cell phone. Throwing on a pair of sweats and grabbing her sandals, she moved as quickly and quietly as she could down the stairs, wincing at every creak she heard in the stark quiet of the night.

Pausing at the foot of the stairs, she tried to see through the paned windows overlooking the porch, but it was too dark. There! Claire was certain she saw a light in the distance, down by the road, but it was just a slight flicker, and she wondered if her imagination, already at a high level of anxiety, was getting the better of her. She walked past the living room and office, and, careful to avoid the kitchen area, she circled around the dining room table where she knew the floor was clear, and peered again through the panes out into the darkness. Now she saw nothing, but heard Simka, the most curious of Eva's mares, whinny again and trot toward the fence along the drive. In the moonlight, she could make out Simka's shape, her head bobbing as she whinnied across the drive toward the woods along the north side.

There were few hounds that were a better watchdog than a curious horse, and Claire stepped quietly out onto the porch, slipping into her sandals while she proceeded toward the outer screen door, still creeping as quietly as possible, her cell phone gripped in her hand. Speaking of hounds, where was Max? Max, the personable little border collie that had been at Eva's side for so many years it was hard to count. Curiously, Claire recalled that she had not seen him since her return to the farm.

She stepped out onto the stone steps, walking quickly to her right, into the shadows of one of the oak trees that adorned either side of the stone pathway leading to the drive and to the barns down the hill. The moonlight cast a sheen across the farm, and Claire caught her breath as she felt her first niggling of panic. Standing here with a cell phone and nothing else to use to defend herself seemed an absurd idea, and the more she thought about it, the more she decided she should have stayed put and called the police.

She turned to walk back to the house and jumped, stifling a scream. There, across the walk to the north, was a tall man, cloaked in black, stealthily walking toward the house, a dark figure casting an eerie shadow across the moonlit grass. True fear gripped her. Was he alone? She stood as still as she could under the oak, straining her eyes to see if there was anyone else with the ominous figure, and saw no one. The man was too close for her to get into the house without being seen, and uncertainty lingered in her racing brain as she tried to determine what to do.

He suddenly stopped, and Claire stopped breathing, straining back against the bark of the oak tree. She could not make out his face in the darkness, but she knew he looked up at the house, then, suddenly, turned and looked straight at her, startling her so she nearly cried out. She clamped her eyes shut and stood stock still; paralyzed, praying to God that he would go. When she finally opened her eyes in the darkness, the man was gone. Vanished.

Claire stood under the tree for what seemed like hours before she dared move, in case he was in the house, or around a dark corner, waiting for her. She stood still, lightheaded and breathed heavily, trying to steady herself, and heard a car start in the distance. Slowly, her eyes frantically searching, straining in the moonlight, she let herself into the porch, whipping her head from side to side to see if anyone was there, then flung herself through the front door and slammed it behind her, leaning on it as her fingers fumbled with the latch. Chest heaving, she stumbled to the back of the house, through the office around the stairs and tripped over an ottoman that was pushed into the middle of the room, falling heavily to the floor.

"Shit," Claire muttered as she felt pain in her ankle and right wrist. "Shit, shit, shit." She sat on the floor for a moment, holding her wrist and rocking back and forth, fighting back tears that sprang automatically to her eyes from the sudden pain. Then, wincing, she stood and hobbled to the back door, wryly thinking that, if the dude was coming, he'd have had plenty of time to get into the back door and rape and pillage her by now. She locked the door, and climbed the stairs to the bathroom, turned on the light and surveyed the damage. Her knee was rug burned, and she cleaned it carefully before applying an ointment and bandage. The wrist was swollen, but not too bad. Not bothering to take off her sweats, she curled up on the top of her bed, pondering. Should she call the cops? She decided to wait until the morning.

When Claire woke, it was with a start. Sunlight streamed into the window, and she could hear some nagging, repetitive sound creeping into her lethargic brain. Sitting up stiffly, it took her a moment before she was able to figure out that it was her cell phone, chirping somewhere in the folds of the Darling quilt that lay rumpled across her bed. She searched around, under the down pillows and finally found it near the foot of her bed, just as she missed the call. Peering at the number through sleepy eyes, she realized it was Matt's mother, Geneva. The voicemail was kind, friendly, as Geneva, herself, was. The voice, so soft, Claire could barely hear it, was rich and warm with southern honey. "Claire, it's Geneva." Matt's mother, Geneva, born and raised in Atlanta, was as proper a southern belle as one could find in the Minnesota River Valley, calling to invite her over.

They had not spoken for nearly twenty years, and yet, it was as if it was just yesterday; Geneva was as warm and sweet as she had always been.

The morning air was cool and crisp, and Claire was glad for the light lavender sweater she had draped over her shoulders as she looked out over the vast lawn. She could see Dave Gunderson, the farm manager in the skid steer, hauling bails with the grapple fork out to the east pasture where he kept cattle. Part of the deal with Dave and his fourteen year old twin boys, Bryce and Andrew, was that he would manage the horses and keep some of his own young stock in the old cattle pasture and cow barn, where, years before, Eva's parents had milked cows and raised steers for slaughter. The two boys, both hockey players, strong and muscular, were constantly with their father, but for the days, as in this one, where they were at school.

As she drove out the driveway, Claire spotted a young man she had not seen before. He was carrying a pail of grain to the mares, scooped from a hand-made trailer attached to a four wheeler on the side of the fence. He stopped and looked at the car as she drove slowly by and raised a gloved hand to wave abruptly at her. He was young, with shoulder length, shaggy black hair, and a narrow face, wearing worn levis and a black hooded sweatshirt sporting a skull and crossbones on the front, with a tear down the center from the hood to the center of his chest. Claire shivered, waving briefly as she turned the car out of the driveway. Matt was right; this kid looked like another of Eva's misfits, and she made a mental note to find out more about him; the kid gave her the creeps, even from a distance.

Chris Breuning started his day with a morning jog, running along the gravel road in front of the home he shared with his grandfather, Bill. The sun shown brightly, but Chris could make out, in the far western sky, the beginnings of a spring storm brewing, which would circle its typical path from the Dakota plains to fall southward as it travelled east. 'CCO radio predicted that this would be the first thunderstorm of the season and would hit the Minnesota River Valley sometime late in the day.

When he circled back into the driveway, he could see the kitchen light on, and, entering the house, was greeted with the fresh smell of coffee and peppery sausage and onion frying in a cast iron skillet. His stomach rumbled and he smiled a greeting at his old grandfather, who was just setting a carton of eggs next to the old gas stove. "You keep making me those big breakfasts and I won't be able to chase the bad guys, anymore." He laughed, patting his lean belly.

The old man nodded his greeting and grinned at his grandson. "Yah," he said with his slight German accent. "You need to keep up your strength."

The two sat down to eat at the old Formica table in the corner of the kitchen, right next to the window. They spoke mainly of the garden that Bill intended to plant this spring, and the sets he had started in the old shop; long rows of starter cups filled with dirt and seed, sprouting under heating lamps and carefully tended every day. Potatoes on the south side, onions, carrots, beets. The list grew as Bill drank his coffee, first stirring in two spoons of sugar and pouring small dashes onto a saucer plate and drinking from that until the cup had cooled.

Bill grunted his good-bye and waved absently as Chris headed out the door. Chris's first order of business as he approached the city was to stop at the hospital to check on Eva Nielsen. It would become his early morning ritual, with Dick Johnson's blessing, to stop in, and this morning, as he stepped into the room, he saw a young woman, thick hair braided down her back and a slight sprinkling of freckles across her pert nose, glance his way. He stepped quietly into the room and she assessed him with a veiled look as he approached.

"Ms. Beaumont?" he asked quietly. "Christopher Breuning. I'm investigating your grandmother's case."

The young woman stood and reached out to shake his hand with a cool, firm grip. "Hello," she said, also quietly. "I intended to give you a call today."

"How is she doing today?"

Claire turned and reached down to stroke her grandmother's frail hand. "There has been no change. Doc says she's as strong as an ox and has the body of a sixty year old..." she looked up and smiled tremulously at him. "I just wish she could tell me that herself."

Chris, seeing the pain in her eyes and hearing it in her voice, tried to be gentle. "I was hoping we could have a chance to talk this morning. I can fill you in and I have some questions you might be able to help answer."

"Sure," Claire answered. She settled the thin, veined hand back onto the bed, and covered it with a blanket, tenderly tucking her grandmother into its folds, and placing a hand-made patchwork quilt across the frail torso. "You want to go get a cup of coffee?"

Although Chris was still full from breakfast, he agreed. "Sure." He followed her out of the room, watching her take a last, wary glance toward her grandmother's still form. After grabbing two cups of coffee in the cafeteria, they settled at a small table in the far end of the room, amid orderlies and a few scrubbed nursing staff who were finishing breakfast before their shifts started.

As Chris went through the questions, Claire listened intently, and answered with quiet authority. No, she said, Gran did not have enemies; never has. She did, however, have a tendency toward taking in strays from the neighborhood, and sometimes those kids were not so savory. She told him about the young boy who was working at the stables that morning. "Look, I don't know anything about the kid, but he seemed out of place mucking around the stables, and I think I saw a tattoo on his neck, but I'm not sure; his hair was long and I was driving out the driveway. I'm going to stop and talk with Dave Gunderson, the stable manager, to see what he can tell me. I'd like him checked out."

Chris agreed, and was quiet for a moment. "You think he had anything to do with the robbery?"

"I really can't say. Matt told me a bit about him; said his dad is away in Afghanistan or something, and his mom has hooked up with some white trash," Claire stared straight into his eye as she said it, "and they live somewhere outside of town. Kid's name is Wayne. I don't know his last name, but Matt or Dave could help you."

"Mhmm. What can you tell me about the vet, Matt Hendricks?" Chris noted that Claire was taken aback by that question, and wondered why.

"Why do you ask that?"

"Because he was the gentleman who found your grandmother on the night of the fire."

Claire stared into her coffee for a moment, then said evenly, "There's really nothing to tell. Matt's been a friend of the family for years; neighbors, that sort of thing. He's tended to grandma's stables for years. After Doc Zimmerman retired from large animal medicine, Matt took over that part of the practice."

"Any reason to believe that Mr. Hendricks is not stable financially, or anything like that."

This time, Claire stared defiantly at the detective. "Surely, you don't think Matt is a suspect, do you?"

"Not really. Just trying to cover every base."

Chris sensed this mode of questioning was not going to go anywhere, so he switched. "Have you seen any pictures of the injury your grandmother sustained? It is unusual, and, quite frankly, we're still trying to sort out if it was caused by a fall, or if she was hit by someone."

"No, I have not," she replied. "Do you have them with you?"

"Yes." He reached into his breast pocket and pulled out an envelope that had been left at the nurse's station for him. "This may be a bit disturbing for you."

She swallowed and nodded. He fingered some photos, then laid two on the table for her to look at. The first was a photo of Eva's head, more from a distance, and a nurse, with gloved hands, was gently cradling her head and holding her white hair and a bandage away from her ear. The second was a close up of the wound itself, a puckered hole behind Eva's ear, with a circular pattern that ended in a narrow point on one side. The wound was clean of blood, and not stitched in anyway, leaving a clear view of how deep it was. Claire shuddered inwardly, closed her eyes, trying to picture what could have caused the injury and putting distance between picturing the wound and her grandmother's tiny form.

"I'll have to think about it." She said after opening her eyes and peering at the picture again, this time picking it up and holding it closer to her face. "It does look unusual."

Chris thanked her for her time and handed her his business card. "If you think of anything, can you give me a call?"

"Yes." She took the card and slid it into a side pocket of her designer bag. "By the way, you're the same guy who's working my cousin's case, right? Lyneah Hamilton?"

Chris looked steadily at her. "Yes."

"How is that going? Are you going to be able to find this Beaudine guy before he hurts her again? She has a son, you know."

He sighed. "He seems to have skipped town for now, but we're following it. You know anything about his relatives?"

"Seem like decent people, although a bit rough and tumble. It's a small town, you know; everyone knows most everyone. I think they're hard-working people; two boys work at the mill, just like their dad did before. I don't know anything about this Beaudine; I don't live here anymore, and rarely come to visit."

Claire stopped for a moment, trying to figure out how to proceed. "Do you have any idea if he was involved in hurting my grandmother?"

Chris's response was ambiguous. "I can't say. He's been in the house, according to your family. Apparently, he and Ms. Hamilton had done some work around there for your grandmother."

Gran is," Claire said, hesitantly, "non-judgmental and soft when it came to the black sheep in the world. It does not surprise me that she let Lyneah's boyfriend do some odd jobs around the place. It's just the way she is."

Chris thanked her, then crumpled his paper cup and napkin into a ball.

"One more thing," Clair said. "Last night, sometime after midnight, someone I don't know parked at the end of the driveway and walked into the yard. I think he was intending to come in the house but saw my car and took off."

Chapter Seven

Within a week, Claire had cleaned up much of the mess from the fire, washing walls and windows, hired professionals to clean the carpets, and rented a dumpster. She'd spent several hours going through everything, throwing out what was not salvageable. The foodstuff, canned goods, spices, home canned jars of fruit and vegetables were thrown out, the heat from the fire having damaged most of the items beyond repair.

Matthew had been deliberately distant, a fact which left Claire both relieved and unsettled. She chided herself in wishing he would reconnect, and then hoping like hell that he would not. She had also carefully avoided Geneva Hendricks, knowing their meeting was inevitable.

Claire set her coffee cup down on the desk in her old bedroom. Sitting on the rattan chair with the faded, powder blue cushion, she fingered the trinkets of a girl's youth; perfume bottles smelling of Love's Babysoft; the proverbial shiny lip gloss. Shuffling through the drawers she came upon the photo album, its cover a leopard pattern in mints and black.

The first pages filled with Mom and Dad, one with little Claire on Dad's bare shoulders on the beach near their home, taken with the new Polaroid camera that Claire had received for her seventh birthday. Grandpa Tom sitting in his favorite chair on the porch, smoking a pipe and looking so relaxed and debonair as he gazes down at his bride, Eva, who is watching something in the yard. His love for Eva was so clear in that gaze, it made Claire's heart ache.

She found pictures of herself, after the accident, her face unsmiling as she posed with Tom and Eva at Easter, standing in Jer and Betty Lou's living room by their large, picture window. Her hair is died jet black, cut to shoulder length, and she has pulled some of it to the side of and over the top of her head, with a black, lacy net headband holding it in place. Her clothes are dark, the jeans acid washed and full of holes, a sweatshirt with the collar and sleeves cut out, cropped over her midriff, a white tank top underneath. She remembered being angry that she had to be there that day and had refused to dress nicely. Grandma had simply smiled that morning, touched her hair lovingly, and said, "That's fine, Princess."

She had so missed the sound of her father's laughter lingering like the scent of his morning coffee, strong and robust, long after he had left the room. Or her mother's warm skin as Izzy carried her to bed, after her evening bath, not caring if she got a little water on her expensive and pretty dress, just wanting to tuck her princess into bed before she left Claire with the nanny for an evening out. She had smelled so good, sweet, like flowers and sunshine, and Claire used to bury her head in the pillow after her mama tucked her in, breathing in the touch of citrus and honey that was her mother.

On the next page, there she was, maybe a year later, and she can feel a pang in her chest. She sat on the tailgate of Matt's pickup in the sun, her swimsuit top over cutoff shorts, hair pulled back in a ponytail, now its natural color, and longer. She has dark, plastic sunglasses perched on her nose, and Matt's brother, Jeremy, sits next to her, with his arm around her shoulders. Rachel Mae, tiny, with short blonde hair and a red bandana over her head, the girl Jeremy should have married, sits on the other side of him, her face frozen in a toothy smile, leaning into Jeremy. He cocked his head to the side, and cops a lopsided grin, showing two thumbs up. Matt was the one behind the camera and the pickup was parked in Flandreau Park, for a tubing excursion down the Cottonwood River.

Jeremy Hendricks was always a wild one; a restless spirit. Claire, Jeremy, Rachel and Matt would ride their bikes down the gravel road between the Hendricks and Nielsen farms, hot and sweating in the humidity of a Midwestern summer day and run through the irrigation system that sent crystal clear and icy cold water shooting across the road. Sometimes they would try to beat the pounding water gushing from the end spouts, racing with their bikes in the muddy gravel. Other times they slowed to follow the water's path, feeling the water droplets pelting their skin as the irrigator's center pivot mechanisms moved it ever so slowly around the cornfield, knee high by the 4th of July.

"Ahh," she can still hear Jeremy's youthful voice, just beginning to change, in the mid-July sun as he stands under the spout. "That feels like freedom…"

They'd had a great time tubing that day the picture was taken. Laughing, sunburn, stolen moments in the shade along the banks of the river, trying to fight off mosquitoes if they ventured too far into the woods. Friends joined in, and someone brought a couple cases of beer. As the evening sun set in, and the mosquitoes forced them to call it an evening, the foursome had piled into the pickup and headed out.

Jeremy had been crazy drunk, leaning out the window of the pickup and shouting to the world, making the girls giggle in the cramped extended cab's backseat. Matt was sober, and tolerant, although, through his gruff exterior, "Jesus, Jeremy, settle down, will you?" He was trying not to laugh.

When they blew a tire just off the Highway 14 bridge, everyone had piled out of the truck. Jeremy stumbled and fell into the embankment backwards, sending Rachel and Claire into stitches of laughter. Matt had not been amused; rather, was perturbed that he'd had a flat, and scrounged around in the back of the pickup to find a jack, changing the tire as Jeremey scrambled through the ditch to the woods nearby, calling that he had to take a leak.

Rachel and Claire sat down in the grassy incline beyond the road ditch, watching Matt change the tire, both still buzzed up from the beer and the day in the sun. The sun was slowly setting in the west, still brilliant on the horizon, and Claire laid back, stretched her legs before her, and rested her head on her arms. Cumulus clouds, like great tufts of cotton, moved across the sky. She could hear a killdeer nearby, and robins singing a song in the trees beyond the road. Cars drove by; no one stopped, although occasionally someone honked.

There are times in one's life that are inexorable, defining moments. Claire heard Matt toss the old tire and tools into the back of the pickup, and she glanced lazily over to watch him take off his grey t-shirt; his tanned shoulder muscles flexing in the sun as he wiped grease from his hands into the shirt and turned to toss it into the cab of the pickup through the open window. Jeremy, having returned from the woods, wandered toward the bridge, singing. She could hear the words drifting behind him, "pour some sugar on me…"

She sat up as she heard Matt call Jeremy back to the pickup, only to hear Jeremy laugh. "Hold on, hold on! I'm gonna jump the bridge."

Claire heard Matt shout, "No, Jeremy! Stop!" and she scrambled to her feet, shielding her eyes from the sun with her hand, and watched as Jeremy climbed the wall of the bridge, precariously standing there. Matt started running, as did Rachel; Claire stood transfixed as, just yards from where she stood, she could make out Jeremy's face as he grinned in their direction, his beautiful mischievous grin, and his arms outstretched, then he disappeared off the bridge into the river below.

As if in slow motion, she could hear Matt's voice, "Jeremy….." as he ran to the bridge. Rachel screamed, and followed. They both called his name, over and over, and Claire ran down the embankment, tumbling over rocks and brush, ready to give him a piece of her mind for being so stupid and scaring everybody that way.

The moment never came; searchers found his body downriver, hours later. The water that year was high, and according to the coroner's report, Jeremy had hit his head, probably on the bridge on his way down, and was knocked out before he hit the water.

In the advent of time when cell phones were not yet common, Rachel had flagged down a passing car, a local on his way home from work; he had pulled into the next place and called the police. By the time the police were at the bridge, someone had called Geneva. She had been frantic, running across the road to where Rachel stood with her arms wrapped around her body, shivering and watching people searching below.

Matt was answering questions in a police car, having passed a field sobriety test, and Claire had continued along the embankment, frantically searching with the others for Jeremy. Geneva wrapped her arms around Rachel and they stood together, weeping, waiting.

And, there the two had kept their vigil, after twilight had settled over the bridge. Claire, scratched and dirtied from her searching, emerged from the darkness, barefoot and sweating, having gone as far as she dared go, afraid of being pulled into the heavy currents of the river; more afraid of what she would find in the dark waters if she continued. She stood, slightly separated from the woman and the girl who continued to hold each other, silent, and listening to the calls of the rescuers and the sound of the boat, trolling downriver.

The stillness in the air made every sound carry, and, when a call from one of the volunteers was heard, Claire held her breath, straining to hear the words. "Chief, we've got something!" the words echoed across darkness and water, drifting up the embankment.

Geneva turned to hold Rachel, who began to sob, and, over the tiny girl's head, turned sorrowful eyes toward Claire. Claire never forgot the look on this mother's face, pure anguish, as Geneva swayed and let go of Rachel, her knees buckled beneath her and she fell to the ground, a low keening sound coming from deep within her soul.

Claire could not stand to see Geneva's pain, and she turned and stumbled into Matt, who was approaching from behind. She clung to the shirt he had been given by one of the volunteers, its soft fabric curled tightly in her fists as she sobbed into his chest. He held her tightly, saying nothing, and watched Jack, his father, reach down to pick up his mother's crumpled form.

When the searchers carried the lifeless body of Jeremy Hendricks up the embankment, Geneva had been inconsolable, her screeches, "no, no, no…please, please, no--" carrying far into the night. Friends and neighbors had come to offer support, and they stood awkwardly in silence as they watched the crew carry the gurney to an ambulance parked nearby. Matt held Claire stiffly, unmoving as he watched the ambulance, deputies, neighbors and friends drove away in a procession of headlights away from the bridge.

As Claire touched the page of the photo album, she felt her eyes misting, and she shut them tight, closing the book in her lap.

Lyneah strapped her son, Travis, into the backseat of her old car, and set the picnic basket she'd prepared in the seat beside him. Her mom handed her another grocery bag, full to the brim with foodstuff she had stocked for Claire, as well, and as she reached to hug her mom, Lyneah thanks her for the offering.

He was excited to be going to see Auntie Eva's horses. As Lyneah pulled onto the road from the driveway, Travis chattered excitedly behind her. "Can we ride today, mom?"

"Not sure, honey. We'll have lunch with Claire, first."

Okay." Then, "is Claire my cousin?"

"Yep."

"Does she like to play with Legos?"

Lyneah smiles; Travis thinks anyone who is a cousin is his age. "I think she might be a bit old for that, sweetie."

"Oh." He looked out the window, staring. "Is Hank going to be there?"

Lyneah glanced in the rearview mirror. "No, he's not, Travis."

Why not?"

"Because he doesn't know Claire and was not invited today."

"Does he have his own family, mom?"

Ponder. "Yes."

"Who is his family?"

Ponder again. White lies, and the proverbial answer to protect the children. "I don't know Travis." Change the subject. "Hey, Grandma made your favorite cupcakes for dessert today! Cool, huh?"

It works, at least for the moment. "Goodie!"

Lyneah turns on the radio, trying to find some music. "Mom."

She sighs, glancing again into the mirror as she makes a turn. "What?"

"Is Hank going to come to my baseball game?"

"No."

"Why not?"

"Well," she begins, awkwardly. "Hank is moving away, and we're not going to see him, anymore. That's all. Sometimes, people move."

He thinks for a moment. "Like we moved to Grandma and Grandpa's house?"

"No, honey, we have not moved; we're just staying there for a little while, that's all."

"Why?"

"Because we have to get some things fixed at our house."

"What things?"

Tiny niggling of irritation; slight imperfections of character that come out when children get the best of us. "Just some things. Listen, I need to concentrate on driving; how about if you play your video game for a while?"

Travis seems content with that. "Okay, Mommy."

Lyneah smiles, still feels alight when she hears her little boy call her that. "Thank you, sweetie."

"You're welcome."

After lunch, the two women sat on the front porch, visiting.

Lyneah watching Travis play outside, asks "Where's Max?"

"I don't know." Claire frowned. "No one has seen him for some time, now."

"Hmmm. That's strange."

"Yes."

They were silent for a moment, then Lyneah speaks again, hesitant. "Claire, I'm so sorry about Eva. I honesty love her so much, and she has always treated me so well, no matter what. She just never judged." Her eyes are troubled. "I don't want to believe Hank had anything to do with this, but I don't know."

Claire waits, looking at her cousin kindly. Lyneah continues, "I feel so bad about it. Just please know that I would never, ever do anything to hurt Eva, or bring anyone into her house that would, either."

Claire puts her hand on Lyneah's thin shoulder. "I know that, Lyn."

Lyn held back tears that threaten to fall. "God, it's awful to think about."

"Yes, it is." Claire sits back. "But do not blame yourself. Have you seen him at all?"

"No." Lyneah leans back. "Not since the night he broke into my house."

"Where do you think he is?"

Lyneah snorts. "Who knows. He probably went back to his wife and kids."

Claire was sympathetic. "You can't blame yourself. Men sometimes lie." She pauses. "Maybe they lie more than they tell the truth?" She smiled. "They sure don't make them like Grandpa Tom and Uncle Jer, anymore, do they?"

Both heard the rumble of distant thunder. "Well, we'd better go inside," Claire says as she picks up paper plates and napkins to throw away. "Hey, Trav, you ready for dessert, yet?"

He runs up the steps and jumps through the door. "Yeah!"

Claire put the cupcakes on a plate and carried them into the living room, setting the tray on the table in front of the couch. "Here you go, Travis." She sets a pumpkin cupcake, ensconced with generous portions of butter creme frosting on top, in front of him as he sits on the floor by the table. "These look so good!"

He smiled and bites into one as his mom joined them from the kitchen, carrying a tray of drinks. "Is Auntie Eva going to come home from the hospital soon?"

"I hope so, Travis," Claire replies.

"Can I see her?"

"Soon, perhaps." Claire licked frosting from her fingers. "I'm sure she would like that."

"Where's Max?"

"I'm not sure, Travis. I have not seen him since I came home."

He took a bite of his cupcake, a dollop of sweet frosting touching the tip of his nose. "You came here on a airplane?"

"Yes, I did."

"What is it like on a airplane?"

"Hmmm. It's sometimes noisy, and sometimes not. It can be pretty crowded." Not sure how to answer that.

"You see birds in the sky?"

Claire smiled down at him. "Sometimes, but I think we are usually flying too high in the sky for birds."

He looks puzzled, and Lyneah steps in. "Let me wipe your nose; you have frosting all over your face, pumpkin."

He obediently cocked his head back so his mom can gently wipe his face. When he turns back to the table, he frowned. "Where is the horse?"

Lyneah also frowned. "What horse?"

"You know, mommy, the horse."

"The horses are out in the barn."

"No, mo-om, the *horse*." He is impatient, trying to get his point across.

Claire asked, "You're not talking about the horses outside?"

"Ung-huh."

Lyneah chides, "Travis, chew and swallow and don't talk with your mouth full."

He obeys, then points to the table. "The horse that stands right here."

Dawning hits both Lyneah and Claire's faces simultaneously. Eva's statue of a sleek and rearing stallion, an anniversary gift from Tom many years back, had always sat on the coffee table in the family room, and was now absent. Claire sat back and gazed around the room, trying to find it. "That's strange, isn't it?"

Lyneah nodded, and looked around, too. "It's always been right here."

Another thought strikes Claire as she stands up and searches around the room. The statue, a bronze and marble horse rearing up on its haunches, was about sixteen inches high and was usually within reach of the sofa where Matt had found Eva. Weighing in at around ten pounds, it was easy enough for someone to pick up and use as a weapon, and Claire's stomach lurched as she realized that the proud head of the statue, with its delicate, pointed ears, could have made the strange wound on the side of Eva's head. She quietly explains as much to Lyneah and excuses herself to find Detective Breuning's card in her handbag.

Evening settled with thunder showers and sweltering heat. After she'd left a message for the detective and Lyneah and Travis had gone back to the Hamiltons', Claire had taken a long, cool shower and had settled into the den for some work. She returned several calls, one of them to Marcus, who had called to see how things were, and wondered when she would be back. He did not pick up, so she left a message, and then spent a couple of hours working before she stood and stretched her back, making her way through the kitchen and dining area to a cooler she had stashed with bottles of water and food that Betty had sent over. She saw headlights pull into the drive and stepped out onto the porch just as Matt's truck pulled up to the house.

The rain had turned into a mist, but occasional thunder could be heard in the distance. She leaned back against the door frame of the house, watching him exit the vehicle and pull a couple of bags out of the back. He saw her standing in the shadows of the eaves, the light from the dining room behind her hallowing her form, and he hesitated for a fraction of a second before climbing the stairs and, transferring both bags to his left hand, opened the screen door with his right.

They stared at each other briefly, not moving; Claire spoke first. "Whatcha' doin' here, Matt?"

"Evenin'," he replied.

She simply gazed up at him, waiting, casually opening the bottle of water and taking a swallow.

It's Sunday," he finally said, holding up the bags. "Sunday is date night."

Claire pursed her lips slightly, shaking her head. "No, it's not."

Matt ignored that, and, slipped past her to open the door to the house. "We've both got to eat, Claire. And, by the looks of you, you haven't been eating enough."

Claire bit her tongue and followed him into the house. He set the bags on the dining table, and pulled out containers of foodstuff, and a bottle of wine from one package. She picked up the bottle, noted the vintage and a perfect eyebrow raised in approval.

He laughed. "Even us country folk know how to pick a bottle of wine."

She sighed. "Look, I'm busy tonight-"

"You don't look like you're going anywhere," he said dryly as his eyes swept over her light cotton dress and bare feet.

"That's not the point."

"Well, then what is the point, Claire?" he asked as he delved into the second bag, pulling out foil wrapped containers still warm to the touch.

She absently ran her fingers through her hair, a habit Matthew remembered well as one she did when she was nervous. Still, he admired how she was keeping her cool. "The point is that you and I do not have any reason to eat anything together, or talk to one another, or even be in the same room, okay? I mean, it's been many, many years, and I, for one, have moved on and do not need any reminders of some long, forgotten romance." She put her hands on her hips and looked at him defiantly.

Matt's heart fluttered a beat; he'd known she wouldn't be easy, but he knew if he let her win and bowed out, he would not have another chance, and he didn't want to blow it now. "Look, I know you've been working hard this week. I ran into Jerry in town and he said you didn't have anything to cook with, and you'd been refusing to go to their place for meals, so I thought I'd swing by with some dinner and see how things were going. You know, I care about Eva, too."

"I know that, but this isn't necessary, Matt. You could have just called."

"Why don't you go into the buffet and get a couple of wine glasses. I have plastic forks and plates for the rest of it."

He set a foil package on the table and opened it; and steam rose from the packet. "I picked up some pasta from Charlie's." he said, referring to a downtown eatery that served an eclectic variety. "Their seafood vermicelli is magnificent. There are salads, too."

She remained silent but acquiesced and pulled two wine glasses from the cabinet. The food did smell good, and she was hungry. Might as well get it over with and kick him out the door at the earliest opportunity.

The food was, indeed, magnificent. Seared scallops and shrimp nestled in a sauce of lemon and olive oil, with a touch of hot pepper and basil; green beans, perfectly cooked, salad and crusty bread with small saucers of olive oil and herbs to dip it in. Matt produced a wine corker from a drawer in the buffet, and she wondered at the familiarity of it; Sunday night dates must have included wine with Eva.

It was awkward at first, sitting at this table alone with each other after so many years, but, as Matt drew her out, and the wine loosened her tongue, she opened up a bit. They talked about work, and Eva. His practice. Her job.

She told him that she had found the old photo album in a drawer, and she ran upstairs to grab it. When she returned, he had produced a second bottle of wine from the bag, and she could feel it going to her head a bit. "You don't have to open that." She said and sat down next to him with the photos. "I think I've had enough!"

He opened it, anyway, and poured each of them a generous amount before opening the album. They laughed out loud at some of the pictures, and talked quietly for a while, sipping wine.

Things grew quiet for a moment, when the last page was viewed and the album closed, and suddenly, out of nowhere and possibly a bit too much wine, Claire wanted to know. "What became of Jamie?"

Matt appeared taken aback by the question, and took his time answering. "We dated a few months." He said vaguely.

Claire could feel her cheeks flushing, and she took another sip. "What happened?"

"She decided to move on; said she needed other things."

"Was it hard for you?" Where were these questions coming from? She asked herself but was not able to stop them.

"The truth? Not much. She needed someone to hold her hand and pay more attention to her, and I wasn't it."

Claire held up her hand. "No. I'm sorry; too much wine. It's none of my business."

"Nah, it's not a problem. She wound up with some lawyer in the Cities, think they moved out of state. Last I heard she was having babies and he was heading up a department in Raleigh, or something."

"How about you, Claire? What's your life like? You seeing anyone?"

She briefly described Marcus, describing his virtues, sounding flat.

"You love him, Claire?"

Rather than answer the question, she blurted out, "Why did you send me letters, Matt?"

He didn't say anything, and she rushed on, "I mean, I found a packet of letters you had written to me after I left, in Eva's closet, and I wondered why you would have sent those after what happened?"

"Did you read them?"

"No." Claire shook her head.

"None of them?"

She shook her head more firmly. "No."

He looked away, and took a gulp from his glass, dribbling a bit of the red down his chin and wiping it with the back of his hand. "I guess old habits die hard."

"You know, I never knew they were here. I told Grandma to get rid of everything."

He was thoughtful, staring out the window, before he turned to look at her. "I know. But it was what I did when I needed to talk. We used to do that, remember, when we were kids? I started writing things to you I never told anyone. I guess I was holding onto the past, or something." He adjusted in his seat. "Old habits." He said again.

She looked down at the glass in her hand, and pushed it away, wiping her damp palms on the dress in her lap. "You married." It was a statement.

"Yes."

"And?"

"She was kind, soft-hearted. She moved here and we lived in an apartment in town. She answered phones at the clinic. She really liked it here."

Claire felt a bit queasy as Matt talked about his ex-wife. "Where was she from?"

"North Dakota. 'Moved back there after the divorce. I don't know if she's remarried, I don't hear from her, anymore."

"What happened?"

He seemed uncomfortable, leaned back and rumpled his hair with his left hand. "You really want to know all this, Claire?"

"Sure." Dead on eye contact, trying to appear nonchalant. She took another sip of the wine and hoped her hand wasn't trembling too much.

"She was the baby of her family. Everyone loved her. She played basketball, and got a scholarship to UND. Studied psychology. Said she wanted to help people."

"Did she?"

He studied her face. "Sometimes."

"Why'd she leave?"

His eyes never left her face. "Because I couldn't give her what she deserved."

"What couldn't you give her, Matt?"

He paused, frowning. The next words shocked. "She wasn't you."

Dangerous ground and Claire needed to do some serious backtracking. "Well, umm, thanks for the food; it was really good." She stood too quickly and swayed ever so slightly. Matt reached out and caught her by the arm, and his touch sent ripples through her body. She pulled away, and grumbled, "I'm okay."

"Are you, Claire?" he asked. She could feel tension as he stepped forward, as though he was going to touch her, again, and somewhere in the den, her cell phone chirped. Relieved, she nearly stumbled as she ran to get it. "I've got to take that."

She found it on the desk, picked it up. Marcus. "Hello?"

"Hi, Claire. It's Marcus."

"Yes! How are you, Marcus?" She turned to peak around the corner at Matt, ran smack into the middle of his chest and dropped the telephone.

"Claire? Did I lose you? Claire??" she could hear his muffled voice calling into the rug.

"Shit," she mumbled under her breath as she reached down and retrieved it, glaring at Matt and apologizing to the man on the other end of the line. "I'm sorry, Marcus, I dropped the phone." She pointed a finger to the door, snapping it at Matt, who leaned against the wall, not budging. She frowned at him, then turned away. "What's up?"

"I hadn't heard from you. How's your grandmother?"

"There hasn't been much of a change." She could feel Matt's presence in the room, and deliberately moved past him, only to have him follow her to the living room. She plopped on the sofa, making small talk with Marcus. Matt left the room for a moment, then returned with the two glasses of wine coddled in his fingers. She shook her head and frowned again, but he ignored it, set her glass on the table in front of her, and settled into the loveseat.

Awkward. Try as she might, Claire could not block out the man, whose long legs were gracing her grandmother's antique table, one foot folded over the other and casually rocking back and forth. Although appearing to be hanging on every word, she was having problems concentrating, in part due to wine, but mostly, much to her chagrin, the man on her left.

"...so, the end of tri social is scheduled for the end of next week. Martinson and Altobelle are heading up the entertainment committee, so it should be fun. Are you going to be back?"

"What?"

"Are you going to be back for the social next Friday?'

"I don't think so; I've got my classes covered, and Shea is available. I think I'll be here for a few weeks, yet."

She could hear the disappointment in his pleasant voice. "'Too bad, Claire. I'd like to see you soon. Perhaps in a couple of weeks?"

"Perhaps." She knew she was being vague, not her typical style. "Will you check in with Shea to make sure she's getting what she needs? She's handling everything; I'll be reviewing final essays and she'll coordinate exams with Dr. Hall."

"Sure. Let me know if you need anything, Claire. I'll be in touch."

"Bye."

"See ya."

She sat for a moment, after disconnecting, then got up and left Matt in the chair, going out to clear the dishes and leftover food. She heard him come up behind her and handed him one of the bags. "Thank you for dinner. I'm tired."

He set the bag down and said, "You have a cooler for the food?"

Claire points to the corner. "Over there."

They put the food in the cooler and straightened at the same time. While she crumpled the bags and trash, he corked the wine with a glass cork he found in the pantry, and she tossed the trash.

"I'll talk with you soon, Claire," Matt said as he moved toward the door. "Lock the door, okay?"

"Of course," she followed him out onto the porch. The air felt cool on her skin, refreshing, and she stopped, closing her eyes and breathing in the essence of spring that had been brought on by the rains.

He watched her, caught his breath, then impulsively reached out, held her face with both of his hands, and kissed her hard and fast on the mouth. She was caught off guard, then stepped back, putting her hand to her lips. Before she could protest, he stepped off the porch, the screen door swinging behind him as he made his way down the steps. She watched him drive off, still standing in the same spot for a long time afterward.

When Lyneah stopped in to see her Aunt Eva before her lunch shift on Tuesday, she was surprised to see Detective Breuning standing at the hospital bed. The day started out damp and cold, with a storm cell dropping an abundance of rain over the area; the forecast called for yet more rain, and, according to the local radio station, the National Weather Service had issued flood warnings along the swollen Minnesota River, extending all the way from Granite Falls to Shakopee.

The darkness outside accentuated the dimness of Eva's room, and Chris Breuning's presence in the room startled Lyneah. Hearing her gasp, Chris turned, and instantly recognized her. He smiled and reached out his hand. "Good morning," he whispered. "How's it going today?"

Lyneah's cool fingers were enveloped in Chris's large, warm hand, and she nervously returned the smile. "Hello. I didn't expect to see you here."

He held her hand for a moment longer, then disengaged, looking sheepish. "No, I suppose not," he laughed, quietly. "I stop by every morning on my way in to work."

She was puzzled but did not ask why. "How is she today?" she asked instead, and reached down to touch her aunt's arm before arranging the blanket over her still form. Removing the afghan she recognized as one her own mother had made from the end of the bed, covered her aunt with it, as well.

"No real change; she had a rough night; I guess. Had a bit of a fever, but she's stabilized now."

Chris subtly glanced at Lyneah's profile, noting the bandage over the wound she had sustained in the fall at her house, and the bruise, now fading to yellow and green. In the dim room, shadows cast a glow across her features, making her pale skin reflect like perfected porcelain. 'Stunning,' he thought to himself. "'How about you?" He reached a hand over to push her blonde tresses away from the wound, and stopped when she flinched, wary. "Sshh," his voice caressed, as if comforting a small child, and he gently lifted her hair from the wound. "Healing?"

She nodded, not trusting herself to speak; the proximity of this big cop, with his gentle touch and manner, was disconcerting. She looked down. "It's fine."

"Are you?" he asked, lifting her face lightly by the chin, carefully, to meet her eyes.

"Am I what?" she replied.

"Fine."

She nodded, stepping slightly away from him, and he dropped his hand. "Yes."

"How's your boy? Travis, right?"

She nodded. "He's doing well. He wants to go back home, but I'm-I'm not ready yet."

He nodded. "You staying with your parents?"

"Yes. Travis loves it there, too, but we'd both like to get back home; sometime this week. Anything new?"

Chris frowned. "Nothing yet; seems Mr. Beaudine has disappeared." He said. "Has he contacted you?"

She shook her head vigorously. "No, I haven't seen him since before the break-in."

"Did you go down and file the restraining order, like we talked about?"

She shook her head. "Not yet."

He nodded, unwilling to push too much; happened all the time with battered women. "You should."

"Yes," she said, softly. "I know."

It wasn't that she didn't want to file, she just didn't think it would do any good. Nothing was going to keep a man like Hank Beaudine from getting to her if he chose; he just wasn't choosing, probably scared off by the police. Lyneah suspected that his cousins had gotten word to him that the police were looking for him, and he was on his merry way back to Indiana and the wife and kids he'd left behind. Good riddance to him. The restraining order was just another hassle to go through, when all she really wanted to do was forget the whole thing and get back to normal.

And stay as far away from any man who came within ten feet of her as possible. Like this one, for instance. Last thing she needed was to be attracted to a cop who was investigating her ex. And he certainly was attractive; rugged, tall, broad shoulders, chiseled features and strong, searing eyes.

She kept her eyes averted, but Chris missed nothing, knowing she was unaware of how open her face was, and how much he could see her struggling with herself.

"Probably not in the county, by now, but you never know."

She nodded in agreement. For the next few minutes, they talked quietly about the weather; the rain, the river. He told her about his grandfather's garden plans, and she told him about how much Travis wanted a garden, so she was going to build him a small, platform garden in her yard, where he could, quite literally, watch the radishes grow. When she kissed her aunt's forehead and turned to leave, Chris followed her out, and they walked together to the hospital entrance.

She pulled the hood of her jacket over her head, then looked up, crystal blue eyes staring into his, and she put her hand on his arm, before quickly withdrawing it. "Look, I want you to know I would never, ever have had Hank in my aunt's house if I suspected he would harm her. Never." She said. "Please, understand that. Never."

Chris looked down at her. "Do you think he had something to do with it?"

She turned away, gazing out at the rain. "I don't know. I'd like to believe he didn't, but, I really don't know." She looked up one more time. "I wish I could know for sure." She said, simply, and stepped out the door. "See ya!" he heard her call over her shoulder as she jogged toward her car in the parking lot.

The letters beckoned Claire. "Read us… read us…" she could almost hear their cacophony of voices calling to her from the old trunk in her room. As dusk approached she sat on her bed, clean from a shower, auburn hair wrapped in a towel atop her head, and gazed down at the trunk as she rubbed lotion onto her cream-colored legs. "Oh, shut up," she murmured, and reflected on the last few days. Two days. Two days since a kiss that should have meant nothing but continued to haunt her thoughts. Damn the man.

She dropped another dollop of lotion into her hands, and rubbed it gently into her neck and shoulders under the robe, spreading it across her lightly freckled chest, then popped the cap back down over the tube and set it on the table next to the bed. She rose and stretched, removing the towel from her hair, shaking the robe off of her body and pulling an oversized t-shirt over her head and bare breasts, and slipped her legs into her favorite boy shorts, before carrying the robe back to the bathroom and hanging it on the brass hook on the back of the door. Brushing her teeth, she looked at her reflection in the mirror, then went back to the room, sat on her knees on the floor, and opened the trunk.

This time, rather than opening the compartment with the letters from Matt, she pulled the entire compartment out and set it aside, peering into the cavern of the trunk. The inside of the trunk was lined with paper, now curled and old, smelling like an ancient library combined with the scent of smoke from the fire. Inside were stacks of notebooks, some looking very old, neatly bundled and tied with string, and on the top of all of them, an old dress, faded yellow, honed with tiny cornflowers, neatly folded with an envelope tucked inside the bodice. Claire carefully plucked the envelope from its nestling place, and felt her insides tighten as she read the face of the envelope that bore her own name in her grandmother's large, flowing stroke.

She felt her breath quicken as she slid her fingers under the lip of the envelope and unfastened it. Her heart skipped a beat. Inside was a letter, addressed to her, from Eva. She slid her knees out from under her bottom, leaned back against the old four-post bed with its cambric bed skirt, and began to read.

"Dearest Claire –

If you are reading this letter, something has, undoubtedly, happened to me in my old age; either I have decided to give you this old trunk, a gift to me from my mother, my trousseau, if you will, or I have passed from this earth. In either event, do not mourn, my dearest granddaughter. My life on this earth has been full and blessed, and I will soon join your beloved mother, who is awaiting my arrival. I do not go alone.

Inside this trunk, Claire, is the story of my life. Journals that I have written since I was a young girl, during the war, when life was so simple, and it seemed I had all the time in the world. It is the story of survival, and love, and forgiveness. You have heard stories; stories of the war, when gas was rationed, and young left, only to return broken, old men. But in these journals, you will find the breadth of my life, the dreams of a young girl, and memories that never fade.

When you came to me, that summer, so broken, I knew that someday, I would share this story with you. Please do not judge your old grandmother too harshly. Decisions made in youth, in volatile times, are not always good ones, most often driven by passion and not intellect. But true love, Claire, real, deep, hopelessly mad love, the kind that consumes every inch of you, never fades, no matter at what age it comes to you, whether you are seventeen and in love for the first time, or seven, and your prince carries you home.

Darling, you will read of forgiveness. I hope, Claire, that, as you read these journals, you will find it in your heart to forgive Matthew. I say this because, I know today, just as I knew then, that the two of you are intended. Without forgiveness, Claire, you will always be empty. Do not take these words lightly, my dear. The adage is true – life is too short to waste it holding onto that terrible pain you have inside of you. That boy loves you, Claire, and always will. Forgive him.

All my love, Princess – Gran"

Chapter Eight
The Diary

April 3, 1944

Last autumn, in English Composition class we were given an assignment by Mr. Stenberg to write a journal, every day, and include in it, our hopes, dreams, plans and things like that, until the last week of class. I have decided to continue to write, even if it is no longer an assignment. While I sit, on my windowsill, I realize I've always enjoyed the writing, but never considered writing about my life, which seems so boring. The glamorous life seems to be so far removed from this place of cows, and horses, smelling of fresh manure and black dirt.

It has been raining non-stop this spring. Betty and I have been driving together, in her brother, Tom's car, whenever we dare sneak into town so as not to get in trouble for not rationing gasoline. Betty says Tommy is sweet on me, but I don't really believe that; he's twenty-three, almost Joseph's age. Sometimes I see him glance my way when he doesn't think I know. He is surely handsome, but I think Susan Thommes has her eye on him. Mama says that Tommy spends an awful lot of time at the diner where Susan waits tables on Sundays, but Betty says that's because he helps Mr. Olson do his financial records. Tommy went to school in the Cities to be some sort of bookkeeper, and I think he is very kind to help old Mr. Olson with the books now that Mr. Olson's son, Bradley, is at war. I'm afraid

Tommy will be leaving soon, as well; when his draft number came up, he was in the hospital recuperating from a car accident.

We are at war. It is impossible to forget that day, when we heard the Japanese had attacked Hawaii, in Pearl Harbor. Two of my brothers are far away.

I heard that Wally Hendricks and Stanley Johnson have run off and joined the army. I am so sad and wish this would just end! Wally and Stanley are both in my class, and far too young to fight. I don't think Wally is eighteen yet. His family is very poor. Stanley is the star player on our football team; he is an exceptional athlete and has talked about going to play football for the Golden Gophers. Now, it seems, that dream is to be cast away.

I talked with mama about volunteering for the Red Cross, but she will not hear of it. She does not want me too involved; she says she needs me to help on the farm and the horses are my responsibility. I don't know why she is so stubborn about it; lots of the girls are volunteering. A group of them meet every Saturday afternoon at the church, sewing things and packaging food to be sent overseas. They even wrap bandages for the wounded; Patty Clark said she goes down to the fire hall and wraps bandages for a couple of hours every night. It seems harmless, but mama is very superstitious about it, and seems to think that me knitting socks, as bad a knitter as I am, will somehow bring damnation down upon us all.

Yesterday afternoon, I went to the first baseball game of the season, then over to Betty's house for supper. Betty's house is right on the edge of town, near the ball field. When I was younger, we used to walk to the ball field from her house and watch the games at night, when all the lights were on around the field. Now the Civilian Defense team of our town has followed orders for black outs, and we no longer have the lights around the field shining into the crisp night air.

We watched Betty's boyfriend, Jerry, play ball. She is afraid he will be called up to the war, and we've talked quite a lot about that. Jerry graduated from high school last year and has been working for his dad's electrician business. Jerry is a big boy, with a big heart, and has such a robust laugh, it would be hard to imagine life without hearing it. I cannot even think of it without feeling a sweeping sadness.

Tommy watched the game; his limp from the car accident is nearly gone, and, afterward, he asked if we wanted to join him for a coke at the diner. I like his smile; he is so kind and gentle, and has a voice that soothes, with a deep cadence that resonates. He is tall, and dark, a testament to what Betsy calls her mother's "gypsy" heritage; Betty's mother, Rebeka, left Hungary when she was young, to escape the Great War.

We sat at a booth overlooking main street, and ordered cokes, just as Jerry's teammates came in, to celebrate the win. Marty Stanford and another player I do not know, asked Jerry if he and Betty wanted to run over to Sanborn to the bar, and when Betty looked concerned, Tommy spoke up and said he would drive me home.

I felt shy, at first, but I don't know why; I've known Tommy all my life. I looked out the window, and in the dark, the star hanging in the window of the shop across the street is visible, its gold hue shining ever so slightly under the single street light that the city is allowing to keep over the street during the blackout periods. It reminds me of Chad Kirkpatrick, whose father owns the hardware store, and whose blue star was replaced by the gold when his parents got their telegram, telling them of his death somewhere in Europe. Chad is the first boy our little town lost to this war, but not the last; I have seen his father, now so thin and pale, sweeping the steps in front of the store; his hunched shoulders and distant eyes tell of his sadness. Chad was his only son.

I mentioned his name to Tommy, and he nods. "Yeah, his dad looks pretty rough. I know that they planned for Chad to work at the store after his stint with the army, and Chad and his family were going to live in the apartment upstairs. Now, it sounds like Chad's widow, Bernice, is going back to her parents after the baby is born." He said, referring to the girl that Chad brought home from Oklahoma.

"How sad for them," I said, "The baby will never know his daddy."

He nodded again. "I was there when the train came in carrying Chad's casket. It was hard to see Mr. Kirkpatrick standing there, so stout, holding his wife as she cried. Chad's wife just stood to the side, looking pained, didn't say anything; just watched them roll the casket out of the box.

"She didn't come to the church until just before the funeral and didn't stay long afterward." He was thoughtful. "Mrs. Kirkpatrick is devastated that she's taking the baby to Oklahoma. I heard her telling Mom how she'd been trying to talk Chad's wife into staying, but the girl won't even talk about it."

"Tommy when will you be leaving?" I ask, sipping from my cola. "Betty said you have another physical coming up?"

He looked grim. "Yes, I'll be leaving next month." He suddenly smiled. "Will you miss me? After all, nobody pulled your ponytails with such finesse as I..."

I shook my head. "I hated it when you pulled on my pigtails!"

He shook his head back. "No, you didn't. Besides, as you recall, I never let anyone else but me pick on you and Betty, even when you two deserved it!" Which was true, he had been our fiercest protector when the boys in town would pick on us at the park, especially if we were trying to play ball with them. Betty, who is 100 pounds soaking wet and is only about five feet tall, has a mean swing. But the boys from her neighborhood who hung out at the field all the time, never let us play. Unless Tommy was there, watching over us.

We finished our drinks, and while he paid for the colas, I pulled my sweater over my dress, smoothing it out, and stood near the door, just as Nancy Christian and Frankie Kadelbach walked in, with Billy Stewart.

He was alone, and when he spotted me, he quickly reached my side, leaning over me where I stood near the window. "Hey, baby, what are you up to?" He leaned so close to me I can smell the Barbasol he used to shave what little beard he has and see the glistening sheen of too much Wildroot cream oil he has slathered into his scalp.

"Oh, nothing, really, Billy," I replied. "I went to the baseball game tonight, with Betty."

He grinned, then, looking around. "I heard that Betty and Jerry are headed out of town. You want some company?" He leaned closer, still.

Suddenly, a hand comes over his shoulder and pulls him, none too gently, away from me, and I looked up into Tom's smoldering eyes. He takes me by the arm, pulling me around Billy's frame, to the door. "She's with me." He tossed over his shoulder as we walked out the door.

It was quiet in the car as we rolled out of town, headed toward the farm. "You want to take a drive, Eva?" Tom asked.

"Sure." I replied. "Where do you want to go?"

"We'll take a drive out by the river, if you want?" he glanced at me, and his face still held a dark look, like he was unhappy.

"Sure," I said again, feeling dumb, not sure what else to say. The car seemed small, and warm, and I could feel my cheeks flushing. He nodded, put the car in gear and we drove out of town.

We drove slowly along the river, with the windows down; the rain had slowed to a sprinkle, but in the distance we could still see the lightning that lit the skies to the west. I counted the seconds between lightning strikes and the thunderclaps, having learned from my dad that each second equals a mile between the storm and our location. I do not know if that is true, but I have always counted.

Although it was dark, there was activity out at the old labor camp on the river, which is being repaired and turned into a prison camp for prisoners of the war. It seems so unreal, that we will have Nazis right here, near our hometown, not far away from where I live. It makes me fearful, sometimes, knowing this. I have heard talk that the prisoners will be working at the cannery in Sleepy Eye and that some of them can be hired out to help in other industries, like our farm, perhaps.

I overheard mom and dad talking one day, last week, and saw, in a drawer of the pantry in our dining room, a paper titled "Certification of Need for Employment of Prisoners of War." I know that help is much needed; my brother, Daniel, is of no help; often, too drunk and mean to be of any use on the farm. I am very uncomfortable with the prospect of the enemy being on the farm. My imagination sometimes wanders to horrible thoughts, where German soldiers overrun the farm and kill us all. We can only hope that the war is over before harvest, and that we will not need to hire any of the PWs.

Tommy parked along the road and we got out of the car to take a closer look. He took my hand and we walked carefully along the woods, peaking at the camp, like two kids looking in a window. He put a finger to his lips, and we sneak further in, droplets of rain clinging to my dress and kid shoes as we made our way.

You can see the rows of cabins in the camp, now fenced, and carpenter workers are repairing one of the cabins in the line. The cabins were built several years ago and had been abandoned for some time. I wonder why they chose to have the prisoners come here? I am transfixed by the images that come into my head, of strangers slipping in and out of the buildings, and armed U.S. soldiers standing guard. It gives me an eerie feeling, and I stepped back, pulling my hand away from his and turning to go. He turns with a concerned glance at me, then puts his arm around me and pulled me along the freshly trampled path back to the car, just as the rain began to fall again.

Tom pulled his jacket off and held it over my head as we ran toward the car, and I clamored in, just as the rain began a heavy pelting on the roof of the car. He ran around the car to the driver's side and slid in, soaking wet, and we both gave a nervous laugh.

"Wow, that sure came in fast, huh?" he said as he slicked his wet hair back from his face.

"Yes, it sure did."

It is quiet in the car for a moment, and Tommy turned to me, thoughtfully watching my face. "Eva, how old are you?"

I return the look and feel my heart fluttering somewhere inside my chest. "Seventeen."

I heard him swear under his breath, so softly I could barely hear it, then he lifted his hands to my face, and gently pulls it to his. When he kissed me, I could taste rain on his lips. He stopped, looked at me again in the moonlight as another crack of lightning strikes nearby, and kissed me again, this time harder. I felt my lips parting under his, and his tongue briefly touch mine before he let me go, only to come back and kiss me again.

I felt his hands pull me closer to him, and his fingers slide across my breasts, and I stiffen slightly, frozen for a moment, not sure what to do next, and he stopped kissing me and held me close, caressing my hair and saying my name. "Eva. You are so beautiful." He was breathing heavily, and I could feel the pounding of his heart near where my cheek rested on his chest.

We didn't say anything as we made our way home, but when he stopped the car, he held my hand for a moment, looking at it in the pale light, and asked me if I would accompany him to the Spring dance next Saturday. I said yes, then quickly got out of the car and ran up to the house. When mama saw me come in the door, she asked who brought me home.

"Just Tommy," I replied as I jogged as quickly as I could up the stairs, knowing she would assume that Betty was in the car.

My brother Danny is shouting; he is angry because he found the papers in the pantry drawer. He doesn't want any Nazi soldier coming here and desecrating our soil, he says. He is a mean drunk, and more angry than ever since he was fired from his job at the brewing company.

My oldest brother, Daniel, was deemed not eligible for service when his number came up. He, along with Joseph, Jonathan Shank, and Eli Shutz, New Ulm natives, all boarded the bus for the ride to the army base in Sioux Falls, South Dakota, when they received word that they were required to go to war. Danny is a scrapper; a short, burly man with broad shoulders and a mean streak. When he was seven, he contracted scarlet fever, an infection that left him nearly deaf. Because of this, he did not do well in school, often being ridiculed by other students, and, sometimes, even some teachers.

Joseph always said this made him eternally angry, and, especially when Danny was mean to me, or Shane, he always reminded us that Daniel was not treated well as a youngster, and we should remember that. It did not lessen the pain he would inflict, especially on Shane, who was so sweet to everyone; he would never fight back or tattle. I, on the other hand, would tell on Danny, even when it was Shane, and not me, who got the brunt of his nastiness.

The worst of it came when my mom and dad, wanting to help, purchased a hearing device for Danny to carry so he could hear better in school. Daniel refused to wear it, especially in school, and, as he got increasingly behind, it became more and more difficult for him to control his temper. And he grew, big, bigger than most of the other kids, so that, by the time he was twelve, he was failing school miserably, but no one dared to ridicule him, anymore. Daniel quit school at an early age and began working at the brewing company as a laborer.

Daniel continued to work for the brewing company, even during the years of the Prohibition, when the company, which has been in New Ulm since the 1800s, began making soda pop. He began beer and soda pop deliveries when he was old enough to drive, delivering the large kegs to clubs all over Minnesota.

Unfortunately, when Danny wasn't making deliveries, he was drinking. A few weeks ago, Daniel came home in a foul mood, claiming that the company accused him of stealing some of their equipment, including a large keg barrel and some steel tubing.

I lie here, in my bed, and try to ignore my brother's voice, carrying up the stairs and through the heat grates that are in the floor above the dining room. He is pacing, and I hear my mother, Abigaile, trying to soothe him. "Sit down, Daniel. Eat your breakfast," she has a bit of an Irish lisp that comes out more when she is upset, and I hear it in her voice, now. "Nothing's set in stone, yet, Daniel. Your father is still deciding. It would do you well to stop the drink and do more around here, now that you are no longer at the brewery. Maybe you can come back to the farm, help out?"

"I do plenty around here." He replies, and I hear him sit down heavily at the dining room table. "Hire some kid from town or sell off some of those horses. Hell, we don't need them, and they're just more work for the old man."

"You know your father won't do that."

Daniel snorts, loudly. "'Head in the clouds, that one. And I ain't coming back to live on this place. I'll find work."

"I hear the cannery is looking for people; they're going to give jobs to the Germans when they come in June."

Danny snorts, again. "Cheap labor, that's what it is. They don't want to pay a decent wage to an American man who wants to earn a livin' but are going to hire a bunch of PWs to work for next to nothing."

"That's not what will happen, Daniel. We need workers around here, with so many boys off to war."

I can hear Mom setting the table. Dad's already out in the barn, milking cows, and will come in for breakfast soon. "Daniel, did you steal those barrels like Mr. Jansky said you did?"

Daniel's voice is agitated. "No, Ma!"

"Because I know I saw some things in your truck not long ago."

"Ma-," Daniel's voice is hard. "I found some junk, in the back—"

Daniel," Mom's voice is quiet. "God will strike you dead if you lie, or steal."

Mom is a deeply superstitious woman, and I know, as she points this out to Daniel, that she believes with all her soul that Daniel is going to go to hell for his drinking and carrying on. Adding lying and stealing to the list will only make his time in purgatory that much longer.

"I did not steal any god-damned equipment!" Daniel shouts and I can picture his face, red and angry. I hear Dad come in and tell Daniel not to talk to his mother like that.

Daniel grumbles something I cannot hear, and Mom's voice calls up the stairs. "Eva! Time for breakfast, girl!"

"Eva, go to the pantry and fill the salt shaker, will you?" Mom looks up from the stove as I round the corner to the kitchen. I comply, stepping over wooden boxes filled with crushed tin cans, what the Ration Board calls our contribution to the war effort, and reach for the salt. Behind it, there is a plain paper box, in which Mom has sugar hidden. She has been hiding it from Dad, who loves sugar in everything from his morning coffee to his pancakes, so that she can have extra to bake cakes for Easter. She doesn't know that I know, but, occasionally, to help her out, I dump a little bit of sugar in the box, too.

After breakfast, I fed chickens, picked eggs and tended the calves. Brushed Sasha, my beautiful Arab, and went for a ride. The rains of last night have washed away the winter dirt, and left mud in the fields and grass beginning to green in the pasture. It is a time of year that smells of earth and rain and reminds me of Shane.

Shane's letter requiring him to report for his pre-induction physical exam came just days after his eighteenth birthday. I remember riding the bus home from school and stopping at the mailbox like I did nearly every afternoon, wanting to hurry and change into my riding clothes, and take Sasha out before the evening meal. I opened the box, shooing a few lazy flies away from my face and pulled out the small stack of letters, pausing only long enough to slam the door and hurry up the long drive to my house. I lobbed the letters onto the table as I ran up the stairs, calling, "Hi, Mom." She didn't answer, so I assumed she was outside.

After I changed into riding slacks and hanging my school dress in the closet, I pulled my hair into a tail, pinned it, and headed down the stairs. The radio was playing in the dining room, and I was just about to skip through the front door when I saw my mother sitting at the table. She had been in town that day; her handbag was sitting at the table, and a basket of groceries were next to it. She still had her hat on, but she was leaning over the table, her hands over her face, and I could hear her breathing heavily. I stopped mid-step, uncertain, and she turned and looked at me.

"Mom, what is it?" I asked her, my voice sounding like tin in my ears. I could feel anxiety creep in. "Are you all right?"

"Child, go get your father; he's down in the barn." She replied, quietly. "Do you know where Shane is?"

"He went fishing with Jerry Hamilton."

Mom nodded, and looked down at the table. My eyes took in the envelope; addressed to Shane, in black print, all official and ominous, and I knew. My Shane was going to be the next to go to war.

Somewhere in the pre-dawn, I awoke in a cold sweat, calling out from a dream of Shane floating in a river, the water around him churning with blood. I am on my knees on the bank of this river, and reaching out to grip his hand, which is cold to my touch. He is floating face up, looking at me, reaching out, but I am not able to reach him, and I know that it is too late. He smiles up at me, and the water heaves and rushes him farther and farther away, until I can no longer see him. I am screaming.

I lay in my bed, breathing heavily, and the tears immediately spring to my eyes. I know. *I know.* I have always known this time would come, this moment of realization, that, no matter what the March 1st telegram says, he is not missing, he is not a prisoner in some village in Italy, he is dead. I sob, feeling grief pushing down on my chest.

The yellow telegram from Western Union, was delivered to my father on March 1st, in the late morning, as he scrubbed down the equipment after milking. He heard the automobile, assuming it was Mr. Zumbrovski, come to haul the milk into town, as he did every morning around that time. He walked from the milk house into the barn, intent on feeding the large, Holstein cows, and, just briefly, turned to look out the barn window, taking in the strange Studebaker sitting in front of the house.

Mom was at church study, a pastime that she has recently become obsessed with, and Dad walked out to greet the young man in the fedora hat, who was walking toward the house. He saw the yellow envelope, and stopped short, feeling his knees grow weak. Dad called out to the man, who carried the telegram to him, tipped his hat, and drove away while Dad stood in the drive, watching him go, clutching the envelope for several minutes before sitting down on the front steps, in the biting wind of a Minnesota March day, and opened the envelope.

"The Secretary of War has requested that I inform you that your son, Pvt. Shane W. Nielsen has been reported missing in action since January 30, 1944, in Italy..."

Dad is a very quiet and austere man. He does not share his thoughts easily, nor will he dwell on misfortunes that may befall him. That day, however, when I returned from school, he was sitting in the rocker, still in his barn clothes, holding the envelope. When I asked him what was wrong, he just looked up at me with tired eyes and seemed unable to speak. I saw the yellow paper, worn now from his rough hands, and felt instant fear.

"Dad, wh-who?"

He reached out and touched my arm, then said, "It's Shane, Eva. 'Missing in Italy.'"

I felt my legs buckle next to his chair, put my head on his knee, and sobbed. He brushed my hair with his rough hand; I could smell the sour smell of milking barns and calves and the pungent cow manure on his overalls. When I was finished sobbing and quieted, he reached into his pocket and took out a clean handkerchief for me to wipe my nose, and said, "It will be all right, Eva. Do not worry."

But, for the first time in my life, I could tell that he was very, very afraid.

I became obsessed with knowing, scraping up every magazine, newspapers, anything I could get my hands on, to find out more about the war in Italy. I read stories in the Life magazines that my friends gave me, leafing through the pages of advertisements for Victor records and the call to buy war bonds, and focused on the stories, not of the stars in the movies, but the boys in the war. The pictures of dead soldiers and villagers and the destruction made me ill, but I could not stop.

Shane entered Italy on September 25, 1943. He had left the Port of New Orleans, after traveling by motorcade from Camp Claiborne, Louisiana to the port city of Salerno, a city on the southwestern side of Italy, on the Mediterranean Sea, part of an Army division consisting mainly of Minnesota and Iowa boys, all young and fresh from the farm.

The fight against the Germans in Italy was intense; thousands of our boys are there, battling for Italy, and America. Shane is strong, an expert shot, who spent much of his life hunting rabbits and ducks in the marshes near our farm. He sent me letters from camp, with stories of the way the Louisiana sun beat down on his head under the heavy M1 steel helmet, intended to protect him from bombs and artillery, and the heaviness of the Army-issued clothing, stinking and damp from humidity and sweat. The helmet was too big; the boots too small, causing his feet to blister and ache. He wrote of the colorful young men in his company, most of them from Iowa, who were big, strapping boys ready to fight.

The last letter I received, v-mail, was from Benevento, Italy, in December. The division he was in was on a short break, and he let us know, in one hundred fifty words or less, that he was fine. The weather was horrible, but he was safe. The words were not of comfort to me; I had more questions than answers, and my heart has been sick with worry, because I know he is brave, and scared, and I don't want him there. I dream of him so often; he is running, the sound of bombs and gunfire around him, and I have been cursed with the *knowing* that he is near death at all times.

The German influence here is steadfast, and it is confusing to acknowledge that we are at war with people who have relatives who live among us. Germans in America have never been rounded up and sent to camps to live, unlike the Japanese after they attacked Pearl Harbor in Hawaii. I have never met anyone Oriental; I have only seen photographs of small, dark haired women in colorful dresses, and, recently, the Japanese flag, it's stark, off-center red dot splashed like a bloody sun, with rays of red and white emanating from it, a souvenir that Gregor Russell's brother sent back from the Pacific. We have received no such souvenirs of war from Joe, but, others in town, have, mostly Japanese items; swords, a helmet with a tiny yellow star affixed to its side, even buttons, or belt buckles taken from the dead or captured. It is all too macabre for me, to keep souvenirs of someone you have killed or who was trying to kill you. But that is war.

Joe is the oldest in my family; he is a quiet man, a philosopher of sorts, who, from the time he was old enough to ride bicycle, always wanted to fly. He is tall and willow thin, with short reddish hair that bleaches in the sun, and a crooked grin. He is reserved, and proud, and smart, smarter than most people I know. Joe also has a wicked sense of humor, and it creeps upon you, sometimes, when you least expect it.

When he was a youngster, he decided to build a flying machine. Resources were scarce then, it was just the start of the country's Depression, and there were not many extras around the farm to indulge a young boy's dreams. But, somehow, Joe came up with enough materials to build his dream machine, with wings made from branches of the old weeping willow tree that still stands down by the river, and an old canvas tent, worn with holes, that he found in the shed. He quietly and discreetly pulled the wooden artillery tires off an old Model T touring car that someone had abandoned by the old home site, taking other parts as needed. Joe attached the tires to his willow and canvas wings, attached the wings to a used Schwinn bicycle he got for his eighth birthday, and decided to test it one afternoon when no one was home to stop him.

Joe knew that Mom and Dad would not approve of his contraption, so he kept it hidden in the grove near the river, working on it whenever he could, between chores, until it was made to the specifications he had drawn on the back of a cardboard box he had in his bedroom. Then, he had to patiently await his move.

When Mom and Dad took Shane and me to deliver eggs in town one sunny afternoon, Joe employed Danny to help him pull his contraption from the woods and into the yard. The machine was heavy for the two of them, but they made it, and, using a rope from the haymow, lifted the bicycle up onto the barn and climbed to the roof, painstakingly settling the flying machine on the centerline of the barn's roof, next to the ventilation cupula. The intention, at this point, is not clear; Joe has never confessed whether he really thought he could fly, or if it was just for play, but, nevertheless, the boys took turns sitting in the "cockpit" of the machine and pretended to fly.

Sometime later, the boys got into a terrible row, the subject of which was never disclosed, and Daniel decided to push the machine off the roof, only he did so with Joe still sitting in the cockpit, strapped in with one of Dad's leather belts. With Joseph screaming at him, Daniel wedged himself between the cupula and the flying machine, and heaved the bicycle forward, pushing as hard as he could while Joseph tried to stop the machine from going off the roof with his bare feet. Joseph flew for the first time that day, landing heavily but miraculously into a stack of straw that was situated twenty feet from the barn.

Joe broke his arm in two places that afternoon, but his love of flying never wavered. When he joined up, after Pearl Harbor was attacked, Joe went with the intention of piloting bombers. Where others saw horror and fear, Joe saw opportunity. All his young life, he had dreamed of being able to fly. I remember the day, when I was nine, holding the soft downy chicks in the chicken coup, and listening quietly to the conversation he had with Dad in the barn. It seems all important conversations with Dad are held in the barn.

Though they did not know I was there, I could make out every word that was said from my spot with the chickens. Dad was walking along the alley in the barn, cleaning after the morning milking, and Joe was following with a bucket of water, scrubbing the stanchions after letting the cows out to pasture to feed. "Sir, can we talk?" I could tell Joe was nervous, and my little ears perked up at the subtle nuance I could hear in his voice. I leaned over and peeked at the two of them through a crack in the holding area wall, boarded over with a rough plank and rusty, 16 penny nails.

Dad straightened his sinewy frame hunched over the pitchfork, flexed his back muscles and casually leaned on the handle. "What is it, Joseph?"

"Dad, I've been reading, in the paper, about this new deal thing. The government is paying good wages in Minneapolis."

Dad didn't say anything for a moment, then slowly wiped his brow with a kerchief he had in his pocket. "Yes?"

"And also offering help in paying for college."

"There's no money for that, son."

"I know, Dad. I'm thinking I should move to Minneapolis and pick up a government job. They're hiring laborers to work crews for street construction. Maybe I would be able to send some money back home, to help here on the farm, and save some for college."

"Is this something you want to do?"

"I want to fly, Dad. I can't do that without education." Joe had always been the smartest boy in the class, but I knew that he could not attend school because we did not have the money for it.

"I can't get the education without money." Joe continued, "I know the farm is struggling; I hear you and mom talk it, sometimes." This was news to my young girl's ears, and I could feel a knot forming in my stomach as I tried to contemplate what that meant.

Joe continued, "Maybe, if I go to the Cities, I'll be able to help keep it going and get a job under this new WPA program. Daniel is here, to help with the chores and fieldwork, especially now that he's not in school, anymore. And I want to make sure that Shane and Eva can stay in school."

Dad's voice was heavy with doubt. "I think those projects are for family men, Joe; people who lost everything when the banks closed down. You leaving here might take a job away from someone who has mouths to feed."

"We have mouths to feed, Dad. With this drought, there won't be much of a crop this year." Joe's voice was confident, persuasive.

"Son, you don't have to worry about that; we'll get by."

"But every day it's getting harder. You can count on me, Dad." Even in the toughest times, my brother has always been an optimist. "Me going to the city to get a job can only help. I'll be all right."

Dad sighed. "Well, let's finish the chores and get inside for your mother for some supper before she sends out the calvary. I think she's roasting the chicken that we butchered this morning. I'll think on this and we'll talk later."

"Sure, Dad."

I thought about that conversation for a while, then put the chicks back down near the hen, who clucked as she fluffed her feathers and settled on the chicks in a feather light cocoon of warmth, somehow fitting all eight chicks under her like a down blanket, and stepped out into the evening sunlight. I ran to the house, washed up in the wash basin sitting on the porch, and went inside for supper, knowing that my curiosity would drive me to Joe and Daniel's room later that evening, where I could get Joe alone and ask him to explain the WPA and why he wanted to leave home.

After the supper dishes were cleared, and Mom and Dad were settled on the porch, Dad just leaning back with his eyes closed, listening to the news of the world on the radio through the open window, and Mom knitting in her rocker, I knocked on Joe's door.

"Come in," he called out. When I opened the door, he was sitting at an old writing desk, drawing. The room was divided into two sections; Joe's side, to the left of the doorframe, was tidy, with pictures of airplanes that Joe had drawn hanging on the whitewashed walls, while Danny's side was a mess, his bed rumpled. A tube of Barbasol shave cream squeezed down to the very base, its contents leaking on the little wood crate Daniel used as a bedside table, was strewn among combs and unmended socks. A crumpled pack of Lucky Strikes lay on the floor next to the crate, just under the metal bedframe.

"Hey, Pipsqueak," Joe turned from his drawing and looked up at me before resuming the drawing. Joe's talent for drawing has resulted in several near perfect replicas of the airplanes he loved so much.

The circular fan that sat on the top of the desk did nothing to relieve the oppressive heat, and he was sweating in the light cotton shirt, his hair silhouetted by the setting sun through the sheer curtains lightly blowing in the window. "To what do I owe the honor of your company?"

"Joe, what is the WPA?"

He stopped and set down the pen, and looked up at me, frowning slightly. "Why do you ask, Pipsqueak?"

"I heard you and Dad talking in the barn."

He looked down at me and crinkled his forehead into a mocking frown. "How much did you hear?"

I crossed the room and sat down on the bed. "All of it," I replied.

He set down the pencil, and leaned back, crossing his arms. "Now, Eva, you know you're not supposed to eavesdrop on adult conversations."

"Joe, *you're* not an adult! You're my brother!" I exclaimed. "Besides, I wasn't eavesdropping," which was a lie, because I had strained to hear every word. "I was just playing with the chicks when you and Dad were talking in the barn. I couldn't help but hear you!" I injected indignant drama into my voice so I wouldn't get into trouble. "Besides, I didn't say anything at supper, because I knew that you wanted to keep this strictly confidential."

Joe laughed. "Well, then, since you put it that way, and you're keeping it "confidential," I'll tell you what you want to know."

"So, what's the WPA?"

"It's a program that President Roosevelt has created to give jobs to Americans."

"Why?"

Joe was thoughtful, no doubt trying to find words a nine-year-old girl would understand. "Right now, there are many people who don't have jobs and money to pay for their families. So, the government came up with a way to help poor people get the jobs so they can feed and clothe their families, and make sure they stay in school."

"Are we poor, Joe?" I was wide-eyed. "I know that Joey Anderson and his mom and dad are poor, 'cuz Joey doesn't have shoes of his own and has to use his big brother's shoes, which have holes in them that are covered with cardboard. But I don't have to wear your shoes?"

"Eva, we're not poor; do not worry your head, so."

"Well, then, why are you going to move to Minneapolis?"

He sighed. "Because I'm old enough now, to help out, and get myself a job."

"But you can't leave! Who will protect Shane from Daniel?"

He smiled, stood and pulled me off the bed, my small hands, moist from sweat, enveloped in his hands, cool and dry. "Oh, Shane will be all right. Come here, take a look at what I'm drawing. Can you tell me which airplane this is?" Joe pointed to the pencil drawing on the desk.

I grinned, enjoying the game that Joe and I played each time he penciled a different one. "That's a Martin MB-2."

He smiled. "And, how do you know that?"

"Because you told me, Joe!"

With that he laughed. "Okay, how about this one?" pointing to a drawing, hung by a tack on his wall.

"That's the Spirit of St. Louis!"

"And this one?"

"That's the Wright Brothers flying machine!"

"How do you know that?"

"Because it looks really old." I replied proudly. "And, you told me."

Joe scratched his head. "Oh, come on, you know more than that!"

"Well, it's not made of metal, like the newer ones."

"Right!" Joe grabbed my hand. "Good job! Let's go see if there's a root beer we can share." He put on his best radio voice. "It's Heidt time for a Hires!" throwing me into a fit of giggles as we ran down the stairs.

By the time Joe stood on the platform, waiting for the bus that was to take him away from me, there were dozens of men standing there with him. It was January 25, 1942. The boys assembled first at the high school for a ceremony; the high school band, now want of several of its musicians, played patriotic music while a representative of the local draft board, our town clerk, stood and gave a great speech about the bravery of our men, the good of the citizens, victory and doing our part to support the men as they head into the unknown. None of us left there with dry eyes.

We traveled down to the depot, in small groups, to wait. It was bitterly cold, as it usually is in a Minnesota January, and we huddled together, our breath visible in the air, our cheeks and noses turning a rosy hue. The boys stood with their mothers, their wives, their children; some in borrowed overcoats that hung way below their knees, looking young and scared. Young fathers, their wives clinging to them, holding the hands of little girls in their best dresses.

One could hear the sniffles, the occasional sobs as each of us said our good-byes. Joe, Jonathan and Eli stood together, with their families, making jokes and smiling. Mama looked sick, trying her best to put on a brave face, but it only served to make her look grim.

I watched Dad watching Joe and saw such pride in his eyes. There is nothing like seeing the love and, perhaps newfound, respect that a father gives to his son at moments of great change. Danny was nowhere to be found.

A group of girls from town came together to see the boys off, and they were gathering among the crowd. I could tell they had planned for the occasion in their best dresses and gloves, lips painted brilliant red, hair rolled under sophisticated and colorful hats, right out of Hollywood.

Margaret Gunderson, a short, plump, flirty girl who worked at the grocery store, ran up and threw her arms around Joe, planting a big, lipsticked kiss right on his lips. The crowd around us grew boisterous then, laughing and cheering, as she reached into her own pocket, drew out a pink laced hanky and handed it to him. I liked Margaret and didn't mind; she always had a crush on Joe, but he had not seemed to notice. He flushed darkly and wiped the lipstick off with it.

When he tried to hand it back, she shook her head. "Keep it, Joe. It will remind you of me!" He grinned, hugged her, and slipped it into his overcoat.

Betty came to say good-bye, and I clung to her and cried as, all too soon, we saw the bus come 'round the corner. The crowd grew immediately quiet, but for a child or two, complaining of the cold and wanting to go home.

Joe hugged Mama, who was trying desperately not to cry, and turned to shake Dad's hand, solemnly. "You take care now, son," I heard Dad's voice break.

Joe nodded, turned to Shane and they embraced. When he turned to me, he swept me up into a bear hug and held me close. "I love you, Pipsqueak. Don't worry. I'll be all right."

And he was gone.

Joe spent two weeks in Sioux Falls, South Dakota before heading out for flight training, making his way southward into the deep heart of Texas, to a place called Randolph Field, eighteen miles northeast of San Antonio. The number of people training for war was unbelievable, and he said the base was very crowded; he was one of thousands of men who were there, and that, since Pearl Harbor, the army had grown their training program to try to keep up. Much of what he wrote was crossed out, and that was so strange; the censors must work, day and night to keep secrets.

He spoke about seeing the Alamo, and the smell of the cattle stockyards of San Antonio, where there were more cattle than he'd ever seen in his life. Having grown up around cattle, the smell of steer manure and decay did not bother him, but he shared, with amusement, stories of his new buddies, who had never been on a farm in their lives, gagging from the stench. He wrote of walking along the river, downtown San Antonio, where you could look into the sky and see the tallest building in the city, the Smith-Young Tower, thirty stories high, so high you barely see the flag on the top, and gargoyles perched high up on the corners of the building. He even sent me a postcard, and, although I could not see the gargoyles in the photograph, it did look huge and magnificent.

The airbase, he said, is beautiful. He described the clay stucco buildings, the heavy Spanish influence in the architecture and design, lush Bermuda grasses, and Spanish oak trees, not as large and old as ours back home, but beautiful. He said, from the air, flying into the base is like flying into a beautiful painting. There was beauty and art and green grass, and swimming pools, and even girls, but mostly, to Joe's eye, there were airplanes. Hundreds of planes along paved runways surrounded by green grass. To Joe, that was heaven.

Four months later Joe was transferred to Maxwell Field, Alabama for advanced training, near Montgomery. He was beside himself to be at the place where Orville and Wilbur Wright had begun their first flying school, on an old cotton plantation where the two brothers had finally found the perfect place to teach others to use their flying machines. Joe described flying a BT-13 Vibrator, so named because it shook so badly at times he said his arms would go numb from the constant shaking; it felt like he was in a giant jackhammer, and he swore he was going deaf form the pitch of the propellers.

As Joe wrote letters home, it became clear to me that he was exactly where he wanted to be. He he had gotten several letters from Maggie Gunderson, and he usually knew when the mail clerk was delivering a package from her because it was marked with a kiss and doused with Evening in Paris. It made me smile; although the perfume did not appear to impress Joe much, he said he appreciated hearing from the gals back home and noted that Maggie was not the only one sending him letters. I didn't have the heart to tell him she was sending the perfume laced letters to Jon and Eli also, and probably a few others; she might want to start rationing her supply; with the war going on, it might be a long time before she can buy another bottle.

He was more excited than afraid then. It was easy to see what he was doing as exotic and new and exciting, but, when his training was completed, he was headed to war. I am so proud of Joe; he graduated from cadet school at the top of his class, as a Second Lieutenant. We don't hear from him so much, now. He went to war in October of '42, flying missions over the Pacific Ocean, where the islands are so tiny you can barely see them on the Dymaxium map I ordered, now hanging on my bedroom wall above my bed, along with the pictures and models of airplanes Joe used to have in the room he shared with Danny. Days in the Pacific are hot, nights, cold, and the sea fog that shrouds the air in the early morning makes for impossible flying conditions. Joe says you lose track of all senses in that fog, but for the cold of the air and the salty smell of the ocean, your eyes straining to see what is before or behind you, your mind tricking you into seeing phantom objects, like land, or ships. Or the enemy, identified by the rising sun painted on each wing.

Joe was shot down in March, 1943, flying a mission in a battle near the Solomon Islands. The letter we received from the War Department gave us little information, only that he was injured and sent to an army hospital somewhere in Australia. The letter I received from Joe, later, gave more details, although some of the information had been censored out.

Dear Evie –

By now you have heard that my plane was shot down and that I am in Australia. I want you to know that I am fine and doing well enough to go back to the field. The Army has offered to send me on a leave, but I told my Captain that I would not leave until this war is over, and that I wanted to get back into the air. After some persuading, he finally agreed, so I will be back with my squadron soon.

I bruised some ribs and had a concussion from the bailout, but my airplane, the P-38 which I named "Maggie," suffered the most, and is now sitting at the bottom of the Pacific along with, by God, thousands of Japanese. We hit 'em hard, Pipsqueak. I was in the sky, on the attack, flying low over enemy destroyers, and the sea was pink with, what I could only assume, was the blood of the enemy, the sight of which was awesome and terrifying all at the same time, and was a distraction; I didn't see the fighter coming in on my left flank until it was too late. The bullets that hit my plane were loud like jackhammers pounding in the cockpit. Unfortunately, I lost an engine and, then I made the mistake that cost me my ship, pushing the old girl to full power, only ending up flipping end to end, crashing into the ocean with a jarring sound that I will never forget in my life.

It was quite the battle, Pipsqueak; the Japs are a determined foe, and, by the time it was done, as I tread the water, which, actually, felt nice and cool after being in the damn hot cockpit of my little Maggie, waiting for a raft to pick me up, I saw, all around me, fire and smoke, and men dropping off of the burning ships into the ocean below. I watched Maggie sink, and was struck with a sadness, that I would not feel her wheel in my hands again..."

I'm worried about Joe; his letters are strange and eerie, and about Shane, who is lost somewhere on the other end of the earth and feel helpless. I write letters, dozens of them, but, as days pass and the war continues I do not know if any of my writings are received, or read.

Everything around me is darkness. Mama and Dad do not speak. Dad throws himself into the farm, and does not come in at suppertime, like he used to. Mama just drifts, getting up each day, dressing, and heads to the church. My job is here, taking care of calves and horses, after school. Danny comes and goes, but he is of little use to any of us; he is so very dark and brooding, sometimes he frightens me, especially when he drinks. I do my best to avoid him, but sometimes I can't. He always smells of liquor and hair cream and sweat, and I cannot stand to be near him.

I pray, every day, and watch the skies when the sun is setting in the west, late in the day, and wonder what sun my brothers see. Does Shane, somewhere in Europe, feel the warmth of the sun, or is he swathed in wet, cold clothes, as depicted in the magazines, hungry, in pain? Does Joe see the paradise, the sandy beaches, the mountains and jungle I have read about, or does he see blood in the sea, and death on the beaches? I can only continue to pray, and hope, and wait.

Dearest Lord, please protect my brothers....

Chapter Nine

Wrong. Something is wrong.

Eva Nielsen stirs, feeling intense pain pounding in her head. Disoriented, she tries to reach to her head, but cannot seem to move. The smell of disinfectant is pungent in her heightened olfactory, and she begins to gag. Somewhere, in the distance, she can hear a shrill, repetitive bleating that pierces her skull like the blade of a knife.

A form comes out of the darkness; the light pushes through her thin eyelids, emphasizing the pain in her head. She groans around the tube in her throat, and a soothing hand reaches out to her.

"Hmmmgrghmm…" The voice, quiet and kind, is unfamiliar to her, and panic sets in as she thrashes, weakly, in the bed. "Shh…"

The doctors had begun the slow process of bringing Eva back from the medical coma they had put her in to reduce swelling and quiet her brain. The pentobarbital was slowly seeping from her body and Celia Woolard, on overnight duty, injected the IV protruding from Eva's thin veins with a calming sedative and checked her pulse, adjusting the monitor so the warning beeps would stop. Her cool hands touched Eva's warm forehead, and she frowned, worried about infection, a common side-effect that could take Eva's life quickly if it were not brought under control, stat.

She took Eva's temperature, adjusted her slight and fragile form under the blanket, then stepped out to contact the doctor.

Engrossed in the journal, Claire jumped when she heard the telephone's shrill ring. Reaching for it, she looked at the number and felt a quick sinking feeling as she noted the number for the medical center. Shaking, she answered. "Hello?"

"Claire, this is Celia."

"Hey, Celia. What's up?"

"I know it's a bit late, but I wanted to call you and let you know that Eva's starting to come out of the coma. She's doing okay, so please don't worry too much, but there may be a slight infection setting in. It's pretty common. Doc Johnson has upped the antibiotic dose."

Claire could feel relief overcome her. "Thanks, Celia. Is there any reason for me to come in tonight?"

"No, Claire," Celia's voice was kind. "I just wanted to let you know."

"Okay. I'll come by in the morning."

"That's fine. Get some rest, okay?"

"I will. Thanks for calling."

"Bye."

Claire sat back and stretched, then returned to reading the journal.

Chris Breuning couldn't sleep, thinking about the woman. He sat on the porch, feeling the cool air on his skin as he cracked open the beer he'd pulled from the refrigerator on his way out the door. He listened to the crickets sing, thousands of them, emerging from their winter slumber to chirp incessantly in the long grasses of the ditches, now swollen with rain. It reminded him of summers he'd spent on the farm as a child, catching fireflies and Northern Leopard frogs in the dark, hearing the frogs croaking to each other in the distance.

No frogs could be heard, tonight, the amphibious population had declined significantly. The air was cool, not stifling yet, but the continuous rains had left a moisture in the air that clung to his skin.

Two things he was certain of; Hank Beaudine had not been the one who trashed Lyneah Hamilton's house, or, at least, he was not alone. In his investigation of Beaudine, he found enough information to confirm that the guy was bad news, and his associates, most likely dealing in the world of meth, were worse. Beaudine was nothing more than a dealer who was also a user, an addict who wasn't smart enough to steer clear of the poison, and that made him unpredictable at best. At worst, his temptation to feel the dopamine rush made him susceptible to poor decisions, including snorting or smoking away all the profits. 'Might make Beaudine a wild card that his crystal suppliers want to control.

The other thing he was certain of was that Lyneah Hamilton could not be ruled out as a suspect in the crime against her elderly aunt. While she appeared to be more a victim than an accomplice, Chris had learned that women like her were attracted to the bad boy, the one who lived on the edge, and would often do things they were not brought up to do. While Chris's instincts were swaying toward victim, he decided to remain watchful. She was beautiful, and talented, but haunted, and Chris suspected this was not the first time she'd been in a relationship with a loser like Beaudine. He was going to find out more.

Miles away, Lyneah, too, was unable to sleep, tossing and turning in the single bed that still adorned her childhood bedroom, and knew it was time to go home. She had the next day off and had made plans with Claire to spend the day at the farm. They were going to make a day of it, and Celia Woolard, as well as Sadie, was going to join them. Maybe helping paint and clean out Eva's beautiful home would relieve some of the guilt she felt for the injuries that she was certain Hank had caused.

She sat up, aching for a cigarette, but opted for a glass of milk, instead. She tiptoed up the stairs to the kitchen and was startled to see her mom sitting at the table, in the dark.

"Jesus, Mom, you scared me!" she whispered, hoarsely. "Are you all right?"

"Yes, sweetie, I'm fine," Betty Lou replied. "Just couldn't sleep, tonight."

"Seems that's the way it is with everyone around here; is it a full moon, or something?" Lyneah asked as she pulled a glass from the cupboard. "Want some milk?"

"No, thanks, dear." Betty said, indicating to a cup on the table. "I've got some tea; thought it might relax me."

Lyneah sat at the table with her mother's tiny frame and was shaken at how frail her mom looked tonight. "You okay, really?"

Betty sighed. "Just thinking about Eva. You know, we've been friends for as long as I can remember, probably from the time we were just a couple of years old." She sipped her tea. "It's hard to see her in that hospital bed, all wired up."

"I know, mom. I feel that, too. She's always been good to me." Lyneah could feel emotion welling in her. "I just wish we knew what happened."

She felt her mother's cool hand on her arm. "Lynnie, you had nothing to do with that. Don't you feel bad about what happened. Eva would never, ever blame you. If there's one soul on this earth who understands human nature, it's your auntie."

Lyneah nodded. "She sure is understanding, isn't she? It's always been so easy to talk with her; she just draws you in and you feel like you can tell her anything. Why is that, I wonder?"

"Well, Eva's lived a long, full life. She lost a daughter, and a husband. She raised Claire and coped with taking care of a rebellious teenager at an age when many others would not have done so. You know, Ed's sister, Avis, offered to send Claire to a private school and pay for it. Eva wouldn't hear of it. She's just a strong woman with a soft heart and couldn't bear to have her granddaughter sent off to some school while Claire's heart was mourning her parents so."

Lyneah thought of Claire as a young girl, all goth and defiant. "Eva likes the misfits. I include myself in that category."

"Well, you were definitely a handful, but it kept life interesting," her mother laughed, quietly.

"I talked with the sheriff already, and he said he'd have his deputies keep a closer eye on your place for a while. I know I'd feel better if they did that." Betty's concern was in her voice. "I hope you don't mind; I don't want to step on your toes, but I want you and Travis safe."

Cottonwood Flowing

"Thanks, ma. We'll be fine." Would they? Lyneah could only keep her fingers crossed. "I think Jacquie is going to take Travis, again, this week for a sleepover and a ballgame, so I'll get everything ready and we'll be able to get back into the house in a few days."

"Sure, honey. Take your time." Betty rose and put her cup in the sink. "I think I'll go on up to bed and see if I can get some sleep; your father's snoring can sometimes wake the dead!" She reached down slightly and held her daughter's face, kissing her on the cheek. "Good night, sweetheart."

Lyneah patted her mom's arm. "'Night, ma." She watched her mother's robe-clad figure leave the kitchen, her satin ballerina slippers, in pink to match the robe, making a soft padding noise as she headed up the stairs.

Later, as she felt sleep creep over her, Lyneah was disconcerted to find her thoughts drifting to the detective, and she frowned drowsily. Just before sleep caught her in its inevitable grip, she caught herself wondering what he was like as a child. 'Bet he was a handful, too…"

The Watcher stood in the grove of trees beyond the fence, gazing through binoculars at the redhead as she moved systematically through the house, locking doors and shutting windows. He knew which bedroom was hers; he'd been watching the house since she arrived. Smokin' hot, she was, and he grew hard, desire exaggerated by the dopamine coursing through his veins. He'd love to go up and taste a piece of that ass, but he knew the boss wouldn't like it. He'd already been warned.

The Watcher considered himself to be smarter than the average meth head; he only used the stuff recreationally and didn't take enough out of the stash for anybody to notice. Not like old Hank, who couldn't get enough of the stuff once he was hooked. He absently picked at a scab on his face and wasn't cognizant enough to realize that the stuff was never, really, able to be used on a recreational basis only.

Old Hank had been put in his place, for sure. Not disclosing where the money or the stuff was until he'd been persuaded, so to speak. The Watcher snickered, quietly, as he recalled the moment when Hank finally 'fessed up on the using and the money, and now the question wasn't the location of the stuff, but where on the farm he'd hidden it, the one point that old Hank had not disclosed in a timely fashion. The Watcher knew that he had to be patient; no one wanted the cops snooping around, and it was only a matter of time before he could get in the house undetected. Maybe then he'd also get a taste of the redhead, lying in the ruffle bed with her fiery hair all spread over the pillow, the thought of which made him harder, still.

Maybe.

Next morning, Chris Breuning found Robert "Big Bob" Beaudine in his rundown milking barn, doing chores. He was an obese man, with an untrimmed beard, and missing several teeth, a wad of chew discoloring those that were left. Mean-tempered and slow, Big Bob could take a four hundred pound calf down with barely a blink of an eye, and most people in the area avoided him when he came to town in his bib overalls, covered in days old manure and smelling of strong body odor. Chris wasn't looking forward to the visit, but it had to be done.

"Mr. Beaudine," Chris began. "I have some questions for you."

Big Bob barely glanced his way. "I told you everything I know already."

"Well, sir, your cousin, Hank, hasn't been seen around here for a while. You heard anything from him?"

Big Bob continued down the lane, washing and wiping the teats of an old Holstein before pulling the milker from the line above him, and placing them on the cow. "I told you already, I don't know where the hell he is."

"You know anything about him breaking into Ms. Hamilton's house?"

"No."

"You know Ms. Hamilton?"

The man snorted as he bent with surprising deftness down on his haunches next to another cow, reaching between her hind legs to dip the teats and wipe them with a towel. "I seen her around town; she works at the bar where I go eat."

"You talk with her much? Know anything about your cousin's relationship with her?

"Ain't got nothin' against that girl, but I don't know nothin' about that, neither. Near as I know Hank was screwin' her. That's it."

"Where were you last Wednesday evening?"

"Right here, where I always am." He moved slowly to another, patting her on her bony rump and giving her a slight shove to move her so he could remove the milker from her udder.

"You have anyone that can vouch for that?"

Big Bob stood and faced Chris, and at full height, dwarfed the detective's 6'4" frame. "No. Ain't no one to "vouch" for me," his voice was almost a sneer. "I got nothin' to do with what Hank's done around here; bastard owes me money and left without payin' me back. I already did my time and I ain't goin' back to the clink. I been workin' my ass off and mindin' my own business these days, so you boys can go off and leave me the hell alone."

Chris backed off. "You hear from him, or find out where he's headed, you give me a call, you hear?" He boldly stuck a business card in the breast pocket of Big Bob's bibs and left the man smoldering.

He perused the old weathered farmhouse with barely any paint left to peel and stopped short when he saw a hand move a yellowed, ragged curtain in an upstairs window. He jogged up the steps and knocked on the door; no one answered, and he knocked loudly a second time. When, by the third try, he didn't get an answer, he jogged back to his car. Driving the sedan out of the yard, he saw that Big Bob was standing in the door of the barn, watching.

Claire was washing the walls in the living room when she heard Lyneah's voice from the dining room. "Hey, Geneva!" She stood for a moment, then wiped her hands on the old t-shirt she was wearing and stepped out to see Geneva. There she was in a colorful floral dress and a floppy straw hat, carrying a bottle of wine and a pair of strappy sandals in one hand, and a peach pie in the other. She bounced into the house, pushed the door shut with an ample hip, and Claire heard Lyneah say, "You're just in time for lunch!"

Claire watched Geneva envelope Lyneah in a quick hug while balancing the pie, noting that her elegance and dark-haired beauty had not changed a bit. She set the pie on the table and removed her sunglasses, her eyes adjusting to the house, and she spotted Claire across the room. "My, Sugar. Look at you!" she crossed the room and hugged Claire, too, and Claire returned the warm embrace, lingering for a moment, before she disentangled herself. "Honey, you are a lovely woman." Claire could hear the southern twang in her voice, still there after years of living among the Yankees in southern Minnesota. "Oh, it's so good to see you."

Claire cleared her throat, finding her voice. "You, too, Geneva."

"Now, I know I'm here without an invitation, but I just baked a pie this morning, and wanted to find someone to share it with. You know, Jack doesn't eat peach pie."

Claire smiled, recalling Matt's father, Jack, a handsome man who was always so kind to her. "I remember, he prefers apple, doesn't he?"

"Why, yes." Geneva rolled her eyes. "So many apples around here, and no peaches to speak of unless I have my sister ship them up from Georgia. Those peaches you buy in the supermarket around here ain't worth a damn. Only peaches worthy of my pie come up from Georgia." She still held the bottle of wine in her hand. "You got an opener for this bottle?"

Sadie and Celia came down the stairs, and there was another round of hugs before the five women took their lunch offerings, meats and cheese, crusty French bread and chicken rice soup, to the table on the front porch and feasted. While they ate, they opened another bottle of wine, and chattered aimlessly about life, catching up with one another.

Sadie had moved to the Cities and joined an airline as a flight attendant, and she shared stories that had them all in stitches, ranging from bowel movements to the "mile high" clubbers. She had spent a great deal of time overseas and enjoyed the travelling very much. Still, when Geneva asked her where her favorite place was, in all the world, Sadie just smiled. "Home." She said, simply.

Celia had four kids at home, all boys, and seemed to have boundless energy, even after working the night shift in the hospital ICU ward. "Those kids will drive me to drink, I swear!" she said, lifting her glass for a refill. "But you gotta' love them. When Frankie said he wanted to try for a girl, I told him I'd slit his sack with a butcher knife if he talked about it again." That brought a new round of giggles. "No way am I going to bring a little girl into that house! Thank God for my job, or I'd go crazy there, sometimes, all that testosterone…"

Later, Claire walked Geneva to her car, a black '65 GTO, which had been a gift from Jack on their 40th wedding anniversary. "Jack knew how much I loved those old cars. 'Reminds me of my youth.'" She leaned against the car, and breathed heavily, letting her air out slowly. "Mmmm, I love the smell of Spring."

"Me, too."

"Claire, you know, you don't have to feel bad, or avoid me forever."

Claire didn't know what to say. "I know."

"You know, I never blamed any of you kids for what happened with Jeremy."

Claire closed her eyes, wincing inwardly. "It was awful, Geneva."

"Yes, it was, Claire. I loved that boy. He was reckless; reminded me of myself. But if there's one thing Matthew is not, Claire, it's reckless. I know he's lived with pain all these years, blamin' himself for Jeremy's death. He'd have never let anything happen to his brother, if he could have stopped it."

"Jeremy's death was as inevitable as, well, his life." Geneva gazed out across the yard, watching a colt gallop awkwardly with its mother. "I know what happened between you, two, Claire. That boy was heartbroken, for a long time. Still is, I think."

"Geneva," Claire said gently, "Matt broke up with me. It wasn't the other way around."

"Oh, honey, I know all that. But he knew right from the beginning it was a mistake. He just started acting out a bit, after Jeremy died. Seemed to need to prove something to himself. What it was, I don't know. Jack was so full of grief, he hardly noticed. But I did." She turned her head and looked at Claire, but the sunglasses kept Claire from seeing her eyes. "Matt talked to me, the night before he married. I point blank asked him what the hell he was doing, knowing he'd never let you go from his heart, and he got so mad, madder than I've ever seen him." She chuckled, softly, shaking her head. "He never denied it."

Claire felt her cheeks redden; these were things that she didn't want to know. "Geneva, that's ancient history. We were just kids."

"Uh-uh, sweetie. I always knew you two should be together, even when you were just youngins playing in that old hayshed out back. Now you're back. And Matt's been waitin' on you for a long, long time."

Geneva, don't go getting your hopes up," Claire was beginning to get impatient. This could not go on. "We have nothing left of that old childhood fling. I'm in Illinois, Matt's here. I'm not going to be around long enough to pick up where we left off."

"Oh, you never know what the summer brings. You got someone you have to get back to?"

Claire rolled her eyes. "That's not the point, Geneva."

"Then, what is the point, Claire?" Claire could hear amusement in the older woman's voice. "You mark my word, Claire, that boy's gonna come courtin' and you'd better be ready to tell him what you just told me, because I know of no one who is more determined than my son, Matthew."

With that, she reached out and hugged Claire. "Don't be a stranger, now, ya' hear? I'll call you in a few days and you can come on over to the house for supper someday soon."

Claire smiled and returned the hug, warmly. "Okay, I will."

"And you take care of your Grandma, too. She's going to get better. You wait and see."

"I hope so, Geneva. Thank you. And thanks for the pie. I'll see you soon."

Geneva started the car, the delicate, throaty purr of the glass packed pipes sending rhythmic notes into the air. "Looks like you're gonna have to start explainin' sooner than later, darlin'," she said as she nodded down the driveway. "Have fun with that."

She laughed as she rolled down the lane, meeting Matt's truck in the drive. She stopped next to her son, and Claire watched as he rolled down the window and they chatted briefly, before he continued up the drive. Claire could see he was grinning, and she became incredibly annoyed, knowing she was the subject of conversation.

"Hey." Matt rolled to a stop next to where she stood but did not get out of the truck.

Claire was non-committal, acutely aware that she was covered in paint and had not a stitch of makeup on her face. She crossed her arms. "Hey."

"You have paint in your hair." He looked amused.

She did not like it. "What can I do for you today, Matt?" greeting him in a typically Midwestern way. "I'm busy."

"I stopped out to see the horses, and thought I'd ask you to dinner Saturday night."

She stared at him a moment, her senses at war. "Where?" she finally asked.

"At the new club in town. They have some pretty good food, and a band every other weekend."

Just as she was about to refuse, she heard Sadie behind her. "Hey, Matt. She'll go. Jason and I will join you after dinner," referring to her boyfriend, a pilot with the same airline she worked for. "He's going to come up for the weekend."

Claire turned around and her eyes shot daggers at her friend before turning back to Matt, again about to refuse but he'd already put the pickup in gear. As he rolled up the window, she heard him say, "Great. I'll pick you up at 7:00."

"Sadie, what the hell?" Claire was annoyed and let her have it. "Geez, of all people you should know how I feel about all this!"

"Come on, Claire," Sadie replied, bluntly. "You're an adult, now. Time to move on and let the past go."

"I *did* let the past go; you all seem to want me to keep holding onto it." With that, she stomped back to the house. Damn them, all.

After the women left, Claire took a long bath, then settled into her bed early, with a glass of wine and the journals, and continued reading. Eva had been a precocious girl, most likely because she'd been raised with three older brothers with whom she was driven to keep up or be left in the dust. It intrigued Claire to know about the time in her life when Eva was just becoming a woman, during a time of war, and the air of desperation that seemed to cling to every word she wrote.

April 25, 1944

It's Sunday, and rainy and cold outside. I'm in my room, and I can look out over the farm and see the rain falling on the rooftop of the barn, imagining two boys on that barn, playing with the flying machine.

The dance was last night. I went to Betty Lou's house to get ready and stayed overnight; we did each other's hair, and she let me wear one of her pretty chiffon dresses. I do not own anything so pretty, it is a lovely cream color, with a rose-colored sash tied around my waist, and a tiny lace bolero jacket across my shoulders. I'm glad it was floor length, because I do not have any stockings left to wear that are not full of holes, and we are not able to buy anymore because of the rationing. When I slipped my feet into Betty's slingback high heeled shoes, I felt grown up. I sat in front of the mirror while Betty pinned my hair up, and I was surprised at how sophisticated the reflection was; it was almost like seeing another person.

Betty's mom made a lovely dinner, but I was so nervous I could barely eat. It's strange to see Tommy through new eyes and be nervous around him as never before. He came through the door just as Betty and I walked down the stairs, and he couldn't take his eyes off me. I am unused to wearing high heels and was so embarrassed when I reached the bottom step and tumbled into his arms. We laughed while my face reddened, and he rested his warm hand across my back and lead me to the dining room table, seating himself next to me.

Tommy seemed preoccupied during dinner, and when I found out why, I nearly cried. Betty's mother, Rebeka, said that he would be leaving on Tuesday for Louisiana. I was not sure what to say. Tommy looked uncomfortable, and glanced my way, but didn't say anything, either. I wish I'd known he was leaving so soon; everything is happening so fast, and I do not yet understand how I feel about Tom, or how he feels about me. Two days is not enough time to find out, and I feel sick inside when I think that I may never see him again.

There were two other couples for dinner. Betty's mother so enjoys cooking, and there are often people around their home, which is boisterous and always filled with laughter. When conversation shifted, Tommy leaned nearer to me and whispered in my ear. "I'm sorry, Eva," he said quietly. I could feel his breath against my neck, and a warmth spread through my body. "I was going to tell you tonight."

I just nodded, too breathless to speak, and nervously played with the water glass in front of me.

Before we left, Rebeka took photographs of all of us, standing out in the front yard, by the lilac bush, which was not quite in bloom. She first took pictures of the girls, standing in a row, then of each one of us separately, and, finally, each couple.

The dance hall was decorated in the stars and stripes, as is everything now; the war influences all we do and all we say. There were a few GI's at the dance, in full uniform, looking handsome, all home on leave before shipping out. There were many more girls there than men, also due to the war, and the girls had their pick of suitors among the small crowd. As for me, Tom did not leave my side, and we danced to nearly every number. When the final dance number came, *Don't Cry Baby*, he held me close, and kissed my forehead. It was a glorious evening.

After we left the dance, we drove out by the river; the moon was full, and we walked along the path at the riverside park, occasionally running into other couples in the moonlight. When we sat on a bench near the river, Tommy pulled me close, gently caressing my bare back under jacket, and I shivered with anticipation. We kissed for a long time.

"Damn, Eva, how'd you grow up so fast?" he said, breathlessly, sitting back swiftly, and pulling my near him. "You take my breath away."

I did not reply but laid my head on his shoulder and closed my eyes, taking in the feeling of his jacket against my cheek, and the clean smell of the shirt underneath it. He stroked my arm, and took my chin in his hand, pulling my face to his and began kissing me all over again, soft, feather light kisses, deepening until I could barely breathe.

"Eva." He whispered my name. "Look at me."

I did so, looking up at him, feeling flushed. He pulled the pins from my hair, one by one, and ran his fingers through it. "How do you feel about me, Eva?"

"I don't know," I replied, honestly. "I know I don't want you to go away."

He sat quietly for a moment. "I have to go, Eva. I should have been gone long before now."

"I know. This war, Tom. It takes and takes. I just don't want it to take you, too. Like Shane. And Joe." I could feel tears starting to spill and blinked hard to hold them back.

"I'll be back, Eva. And so will Joe and Shane." He tried to comfort me. "You wait and see."

I did not have it in me to tell him that I *knew* that Shane would not be back. "Just promise me you'll be safe, Tommy. Please, promise me."

He stared into my eyes, in the moonlight, and slowly nodded. "I promise, Eva."

We talked for a long time. He asked me to write to him when he went away, and I said I would. He reached into his pocket and handed me an old pocket watch. "This was my grandfather's, Eva. Will you hold it for me, 'til I get back?"

I am young, but I understand the significance of this gesture, and I didn't know how to respond. So, I simply held out my hand, and he placed the old watch into it, and closed my fingers over it with his own.

April 27, 1944

I stood on the platform of the bus depot today, with a small gathering of friends and family, and watched Tom board the bus. He shook his father's hand, and hugged Rebekka goodbye as she wiped tears from her eyes. He hugged each person in the group, leaving me for last, held me for a long moment, almost awkward in its longevity. The crowd slowly faded away, even Susan Thommes, who had come to say goodbye, until we were alone on that depot, waiting for the bus to come in. When it finally did, he kissed me, hard on the mouth, and, without a word, boarded the bus and went to war.

For once, I am not cursed with the *knowing* if I will ever see him again.

June 1, 1944

I heard that Susan Thommes has volunteered for the Women's Army Corps. She left around the same time that Tom left, and is in training in Des Moines, Iowa. I do not know the nature of her relationship with Tom, but I do know they have been, at the very least, friends, for several years. She is a few years older than I and attended college at St. Cloud State Teachers College until this year.

Since the Women's Auxiliary Army Corps was converted to the WAC last year, there have been a number of recruiters showing up in town right in front of the movie theatre. According to her brother, Michael, the WACs are actually a part of the Army, and will be able to get the same benefits as men in the service overseas. Mike said that Susan really wants to serve and is hoping for some type of administrative job in Europe.

I drove the old pickup to town this morning, to deliver eggs. As I stood talking with Mr. Kirkpatrick in front of his store, a convoy came driving down the street. Trucks with open beds, led by a police car, and followed by army trucks with soldiers in them. People on the streets stopped and watched as the procession moved slowly through town. The trucks were loaded with soldiers, coming from Algona, Iowa to live in the old transient camp down by the river.

Mr. Kirkpatrick leaned heavily on the broom he'd been sweeping the sidewalk with and stared dispassionately as the convoy stopped in front of his store. The prisoners of war, who appeared German and, perhaps, Italian, all dressed in blue jersey shirts with the letters PW on the back, in glaring white, stared back. Some looked down, or into the distance. A few whistled at two girls who were walking down the street toward the post office.

Mr. Kirkpatrick sighed. "Ain't that a sight?" he said.

"Yes, it is." I replied, pushing my hair back behind my ears.

"I never imagined I'd see those Nazis drivin' down my street. No, sirree, never imagined it."

I felt a rush of sympathy for him and reached out to touch his arm. "I'm so sorry about Chad, Mr. Kirkpatrick."

He patted my hand. "I know you are, Eva. He was a fine young man," he trembled slightly, a tremor in his hand brought on by lack of nourishment and, perhaps, a bit too much Irish whiskey.

"Has Bernice left yet?"

"Yes, she did, a few weeks ago. Took the baby down to her folks in Oklahoma. She promised she'd write, and send photographs, but we haven't heard from her since. Mona's been writin' to her pretty regular."

I feel a surge of anger at the girl, and pity for this man, whose only boy was killed by the same soldiers who were riding past us, shifting nonchalantly in their seats. Some made eye contact with me, and I glared back defiantly. One man, a young soldier with silvery gold hair, held my glare in an uncomfortable stare, his eyes, even from a distance, were a startling shade of blue.

So many of our young men are gone, lost to this war, fighting for their lives in Europe and the Pacific, and we get to watch these men here, in our beautiful and peaceful home, where they will be warm and dry, and fed. It makes me so sad.

Betty came walking up to me on the sidewalk, just then, and I hugged Mr. Kirkpatrick. "You take care of yourself, Mr. Kirkpatrick." I could smell the pipe tobacco on his cotton shirt, and the pungent odor of old alcohol emanating from his rail-thin frame.

"You, too, Eva." He patted me on the back, continuing to watch the convoy edge past us.

Betty and I wandered, and she said she had walked downtown to see what all the fuss was about and to pick up some sulfa pills for her mother. "I feel so bad for Mr. Kirkpatrick," she said. "He just looks so old and frail now. You hear about Bernice?"

"Yes, Mr. Kirkpatrick told me she left town."

"She was a wild one, couldn't wait to leave," Betty reached into her purse and pulled out a small mirror, fussing with her hair. "I heard Mabel Clark talking at the drugstore just a few minutes ago, and she said that baby wasn't even Chad's."

"Oh, Betty, you know how Mabel is. She's always gossiping about something. If she can't find someone to talk bad about, she makes it up."

"Yes, but I know that Bernice was stepping out with Duke Elwood right about the time that she got herself with child. Nearly tore Chad's mother apart to see them go."

"Yes, Mr. Kirkpatrick, too." I couldn't help but think about his stooped shoulders and frail arms. "He's just wasting away."

"This war is just taking so damn long," Betty said, putting the compact back into her purse. She stopped and laid her hand on my arm when we approached my old truck. "Eva, I have something to tell you."

My stomach dropped; I could tell she was serious. "Jerry's been called up."

"Oh, no, Betty, not Jerry, too!"

She nodded, slowly. "We're getting married, Eva."

"What?" I was shocked. "When?"

"Next Saturday."

I stared down at her pixie face. "Wow, Betty, are you sure?"

"Of course, I'm sure, silly goose!" she said, breezily. "I love Jerry, and he loves me. We've talked about it for a long time; it just got pushed up because of the war. You understand, don't you, Eva?"

I felt suddenly very young and very foolish. Of course, she was going to marry Jerry; they had been going steady forever. "Of course, I do, Betty.

I was just startled by your news, that's all." I reached down and hugged her to me. "I'm so sorry Jerry's going away, but I'm happy for you, Betty."

"You will stand up for me, won't you, Eva?"

"Yes, of course, I will."

"You can wear that dress you wore to the spring dance. I'm going to wear my mother's wedding dress; it nearly fits."

"What are you going to do when Jerry leaves? Are you still going to go to school next fall?"

"No, I'm going to work down at the plant in Sleepy Eye. There are several girls from town who have already signed up to work there. I'll still be able to live with my mom and dad, at least, until Jerry comes home."

She chattered on, and my thoughts drifted to a time when we were children, playing dress up with Rebekka's high heels and old dresses. This was not going to be the affair of our dreams, but I could tell that, while she was worried about Jerry, she was excited about becoming his wife, and I was happy for her. Still, the lingering effects of the war was causing way too many of our friends to marry young, and way too many of our young men to leave their wives behind.

June 10, 1944

Betty looked simply stunning in the wedding dress her mother had worn on her own wedding day. The small ceremony was held at the Presbyterian Church on the edge of town, a tiny little church in a country setting, surrounded by an old cemetery and oak trees.

I stood as Betty's maid of honor, and Jerry's brother, George, who is my age, was his best man. It was a beautiful day, and Rebekka had managed to arrange a lovely meal to be served on the lawn of the church for a small gathering of friends and family, including a three tiered wedding cake that she had made herself.

Mr. and Mrs. Gerald Hamilton left the church in Jerry's Dad's sedan, to camp on Sleepy Eye Lake for a short honeymoon. They will return on Monday night, and Jerry will ship out by 8:00 a.m. Tuesday morning. Dad could not attend the ceremony because he was doing all the chores by himself, and Rebekka put together a plate of food for us to bring to him.

"Here you go, Evie," Betty's mother had always called me that, since we were little girls. "You take this to your papa, and make sure he gets a nice piece of that cake before you leave."

She handed me the plate, then hugged me. "Oh, Evie, honey, all you kids are growing up so fast."

"Yes, ma'am, we are." I replied, hugging her back.

"You don't be a stranger, now, you hear? Betty will be back soon, and you girls can get together at our house, just like you used to."

I promised I'd see her soon, and Mom and I headed home.

That day, we received a letter from Shane. I am overwhelmed with relief; these silly intuitions, the product of my mother, who believes she is the descendent of a magical Irish princess, even naming me after her, cannot be true, right? I am overcome with emotion and want to compose myself before I open the letter that I hold in my hand. Sometimes I am a silly child.

Chapter Ten

June 12, 1944

Shane Michael Kelly pushed forward, toward the west bank of the Rapido River with the US II Army 34th Division, facing mountainous terrain and a strong German resistance. The primary objective was to take Italy, village by village, back from the strongest foe the United States had ever encountered in its history. The terrain was rough, the weather miserable. The Red Bulls drove forward, advancing to the Valley of the Liri, and continuing toward that river, in a bloody battle. They were determined, having seen more hand to hand combat in the war in Europe than any other service units thus far. The cost of taking that river, one of many flowing through Italy's mountains like a swelling artery, was a significant and bitter one.

Italy was a mess; for months, the Allies had inundated Italy's small clusters of islands and its southern mainland with heavy bombing. The decision to move in from so far north was made with the assumption that the German stronghold was further south and that taking Naples, an important coup, would be quick and easy, an incorrect assumption. Italian armies began showing only weak resistance. With the continued fight between the Allies and the Axis armies, supplies were short, their homes in ruin, and Mussolini was losing his hold on his armies. Many did not fight the Allies, instead dressed in civilian clothes and disappeared into the mountainside.

There were rumors of Italy's surrender, boosting Allied confidence. But the 34th came into Salerno at night, and, with no preliminary bombing that was taking place south and in Sicily, they were trapped on the beachhead by a strong German front. By the time they were brought relief by the air forces battling in the south, they had lost thousands. And the invasion of Italy had only just begun.

The Division, along with Alexander's Brits, had driven forward from Salerno in September, ruthlessly pushing through minefields, barbed wire, and mud that sucked like a vice. Tucked into the mountainside were small cottages and abandoned homes. Those that were dead, shot to death by the German troops for what was perceived as betrayal, were left to rot on the ground, along with decomposing cattle, donkeys, dogs. Villages, at one time so beautiful and quaint, were left in rubble, surrounding olive groves, once lush, lay in a tangled mess. The Allies had dropped millions of pamphlets via air into Rome and Naples, warning of impending attacks and encouraging people to evacuate. Many that did not leave their homes did not survive.

For the young men of the 34th, the destruction was sickening. Most of them had seen death only in coffins at their local churches, tidy and ritualistic, where the people gathered to say final good-byes and have lunch afterward in cool, damp church basements. On the European front, the dead were sent down the mountainside on donkeys, strapped and hanging askew, or arranged in rows near where they fell, for there was no time and no dignity for the dead when you were fighting for your own life. Few of the infantrymen, if any, had seen such violence until their induction into the war. It was a time none who survived would ever forget.

The body readies for battle with the rapid beating of the heart and quickening of breath. They say that one of the hardest parts of war is the monotony in time, when you sit and re-read letters from home, in cold, dark trenches, wet and bone-tired, awaiting the next strategic move planned by officers in higher ranks who were safely nestled at Allied Command Centers stationed away from the front lines. The Officers who determine your destiny and whom you will never meet. You think about back home, and it causes a physical ache in your gut.

In this battle, however, there had been no monotony, only gripping fear, the constant smell of gunfire, blood and death. Such smells seep into your bones and never leave your brain, causing the mind to switch into primal mode. Whichever one you do, the rational mind decides, because for hour upon hour, all your senses tell you to run, back home to a life you will never know as the same again.

For six days, the Battery had met with strong, ugly resistance from a German army that had been instructed to hold the line at all costs. Clearing the mines planted along the mountainside had become all but impossible, the enemy was everywhere. Shane watched as brothers fell to the ravages, one after the other. To Shane's left Dom Patrick, a burly man, broad at the shoulders, slightly stooped, with a round face and an Irish brogue when he'd had too much to drink, was hit.

A tough bastard from the Bronx, he fell to the ground, his blood spattering several feet around him as his chest opened from the impact of the enemy fire. Shane, within just inches of him, felt the warmth of his friend's blood hit his face, tasted it on his lips, and reached out to grab Dom as he fell backwards without a sound, his helmet crashing to the rocks behind him before his body hit the ground, caught by Shane's compact but strong frame.

Shane heard screams, pushed his hands into Dom's chest, feeling the warm, fluid life leaving his friend's body, and realized the screams were his own. He closed his mouth but could not contain the sob that forced its way out of his throat in a guttural roar. No, no, no.

Lt. David Langford, on Shane's right, saw Dom's awesome frame go down, saw Shane fall under him, and was, for a moment, unsure of who was hit. David, the expert marksman of the battalion, spotted the helmet of the shooter, fired a single shot through the cold, foreign air, and hit the Nazi square in the face. Enemy gunfire erupted from what seemed like, every direction.

David returned the volley, until the clip was totaled, all the while Shane was holding Dom's body, trying to contain the blood flowing through his fingers. David heard no sounds but his own breathing, in, out, and each, precise click of the trigger on his left forefinger, *click, breath, click, breath.*

He'd gotten a lot of shit for being a lefty; it was unheard of for a lefty to be an expert shot, but David had grown up in the deep woods of the Black Hills, hunting coon with his dog, Henry, and pheasant in the fall.

Now twenty-five, he had been drafted in '41, and served his first leg of duty in Tunisia.

He liked the Kelly boy, all American, nice kid, oblivious to the horrific, bitter cold that settled into hands and feet until they were numb or tingling with pain. Only the adrenaline coursing through the blood kept the hands from fumbling while under fire in the rugged Italian tundra. The kid was smart, and quick, both attributes that had helped keep him alive in this hell. He liked that bulldog Dom, too, but it was probably too late to tell him that. *Click, breathe, click breathe.*

Shane saw the enemy advance from the South, to the right of where David and the other GIs were tumbling into the shelter of the rugged crevices, firing to the west, and shouted, "Get down!" as he pulled a hand grenade from Dom's belt and threw it, hard, over David's head, and ducked down near Dom, who was now dead. He rolled over a jagged outcrop and grabbed both his and Dom's army-issued weapon and began firing at the line advancing rapidly toward the dozen or so soldiers who had gotten trapped between advancing Germans on all sides. Not aiming, just shooting, screaming at his comrades to retreat easterly, where the rest of the platoon could cover them.

David turned and began firing to the south, covering the others who were retreating down the rough slopes, pulling themselves out of the gulley, trying to escape. The bullets would whistle as they whizzed by, and the sound of them hitting rocks was very different than the distinct *whap* of a bullet entering the body. David heard these sounds as he re-clipped and began to fire again, just as mortar shells and "screaming meemies," named so for the sound they made, rained down on the small group.

David felt a searing tear in his left arm and looked down to see it hanging limp at his side, the shocking white of bone sticking out through a gaping hole where his elbow had once been. He watched the Germans advance down the slopes, saw Shane's right arm wave him to go, the rifle flinging crazily around him as he shouted, "I'll cover you! Go!" All the while he continued a steady fire from the rifle he'd taken from Dom.

The mortar shelling was heavy, plastering shrapnel around them, pinging off the terrain and ricocheting into the skin. David felt the sharp metal stinging into his arms, legs, face, and pulled his service revolver from its holster, using his right hand to fire shot after shot, picking off the enemy one by one, as he climbed backward on his back and legs over the crevice toward the rest of the division.

"You come, too!" he shouted over at Shane.

"'Right behind you! Now, get the fuck out of here!" he heard Shane shout out, when he felt the hands of Private Johnson and Doc Benjamin pull him backward over the slope just as the Nazi line came over the crest, less than twenty yards to the south.

Shane's voice spoke, loud and clear, shouting above the sounds of artillery surrounding them. "Our Father, Who art in heaven, come on, you Nazi Bastards! Hallowed be Thy name-"

David watched as the Germans surrounded the Kelly kid in the gulley and watched as one fired a shot into the kid's leg before the kid shot him in the gut. David suddenly closed his eyes and leaned his head back, blacking out. That was the last time he saw Shane Kelly.

I know this because, the day after Shane's letter arrived, a letter came from a Lt. David Langford from a veteran's hospital in London, smuggled out by an attending nurse, a classmate of his from his hometown, so that it would not go through the censors and all detail blacked out.

It was a long letter, written by someone who obviously cared a great deal for Shane, and was addressed to me, because, he said, Shane had spoken of his little sister so often. David lost his arm after that battle, and part of his intestines from shrapnel, but was expecting to come back home in a few months, to the family farm. Shane, he said, had saved the lives of all the other men who had been trapped in that jagged gulley in the Italian mountainside. He intended to make sure that it was never forgotten. The date was January 30, 1944.

I am certain my Shane did not survive; it does not matter what the government notice says in letters coming several weeks too late. They cannot keep up with the body count in this war. By now, Allied forces have taken most of Italy. Shane has yet to be found, dead or alive.

He is never coming home.

July 4, 1944

The grief weighs heavily on my chest as I toss and turn into the darkness of night. I cannot get the images of Shane falling at the hands of the enemy and can almost feel the wrenching fear he must have felt facing death. How can someone so full if life, so vibrant, be no more? I cannot sleep for facing nightmares filled with blood and death; I cannot eat, for the pit in my stomach grows and consumes me. My Shane is gone. I sob into my pillow, seeing Shane's face so clearly in my head, that his image overwhelms me.

Papa has all but given up; he seems to have aged overnight. His hair, usually peppered with grey, is now pure white. He is stooped and having coughing fits while he stands in the morning sun, leaning his forehead heavily against one of the horses he is so fond of, spitting phlegm and doubling over. I worry about him, but he refuses to see Doc Johnson, saying he's fine, he's just got a cold. What will we do if something happens to Dad? Daniel has disappeared, no doubt lying somewhere in a drunken stupor. No one knows where he's gone since the telegram came.

Mom has fallen into a religious fervor, praying and moaning. Shane was the life of this family. It is frightening to see what the grief has done to her, and to Dad. Each day, Dad has gone out to the barn later and later. No longer interested in milking the cows or tending the horses, he just wanders around, or sits in his chair, staring out the window. Finally, a few days ago, he just didn't get out of bed. I did the chores alone that day, and have since, rising early to try to keep up. I am now glad that we have sent the application for assistance, even if it is from the enemy, because we cannot continue this way.

Chapter Eleven

Claire stared nervously at her reflection in the bedroom mirror, and glanced, once more, at the black forest chalet style cuckoo clock that had always hung in her bedroom. The clock was beautiful and ornate, its birdsong long since silenced. But the clock continued to keep perfect time, and she realized she had just minutes to put the finishing touches on her makeup before Matt came for her.

She grimaced, refusing to call it a date. It was warm in the old house, and Claire pulled her damp curls into a chignon and clipped it with an old tortoise shell clip she had found in Eva's bedroom before stepping into the little black dress she had plucked from her suitcase. She slipped on a pair of delicately heeled sandals and headed down the stairs just as she heard Matt open the screen door on the porch.

"Hey," she said, breezily as she swept past him, not inviting him in. The intoxicating scent of woman and expensive perfume floating into his nostrils as she headed toward the door. "I'm ready. Let's go."

He followed, watching the swing of her hips as she stepped into the evening sun. "Beautiful night, huh?" he heard her say over her shoulder as she walked quickly to the vehicle.

"Beautiful. Right." Matt managed to reply and took a few easy strides to catch up with her, faintly amused and wondering what she was afraid of. "Here, let me get the door."

He held out his hand to her as she paused briefly, assessing her best options for getting into the pickup without losing grace. Or a heel. She took his hand and he guided her up the step, slamming the door after she was settled. Claire was breathless, a condition she chalked up to humidity, and was grateful she felt the soft whir of air conditioning brush against her flushed skin.

She was overcome with nervous tension, and conversation between the two of them was awkward on the drive to the dance. When they pulled into the drive of the eatery, she felt vast relief to see Sadie standing in the arms of Jason Boedke, a pilot that Sadie had been dating for several months. She looked happy and waved at Claire as Matt parked the truck.

"Hi!" Sadie's voice floated across the parking lot as Claire and Matt walked toward them. Claire was deeply conscious of the touch of Matt's fingers resting lightly on her elbow and could barely speak a greeting.

"Matt Hendricks and Claire Beaumont, I'd like you to meet Jason Boedke." Sadie's voice had always had a silvery ring to it, especially when she was excited, and Claire could tell that the introduction was important to her.

Claire moved forward, breaking contact, and greeted the tall and handsome pilot warmly, taking his hand in both of hers and smiling up at him. "It's so nice to finally meet you," she said. "Sadie has told me so much about you."

Jason's grin was broad and strikingly white. "You, too."

The four of them stepped into the cool darkness of the newly remodeled ballroom. It had been made into a winery, and the décor was modern and simplistic. The hostess, a fiftyish woman with red hair that was streaked with platinum took them to a reserved booth toward the back of the dining room. "Here you go," she said in a smokie voice. "Your server will be right with you."

Claire could see the band setting up in the adjoining room, the sound of a steel guitar tuning and acoustics blaring from the oversized speakers near the stage. She glanced around, wondering if she would see anyone she knew. It had been a long time since she had been in town, and she wasn't sure if she wanted to see anyone she knew or not; the thought was rather unsettling to her, especially with Matt by her side.

She ordered a vodka tonic and glanced through the menu while Jason and Matt made conversation. All the while, she could feel Matt's body near hers, and the warmth of his thighs nestled in the booth next to hers made her insides all fluttery, so much so that she tried to slide just a little further into the wall on the other side of her. Sadie sat across from her and grinned, fully aware of Claire's discomfort, and Claire glared at her across the table as their drinks arrived.

They talked about the winery. "My mom says that, when she was a kid, this used to be a roller skating rink, and they would come here and skate every Friday night, unless there was a dance." Sadie took a sip of the local wine while she talked and brushed her hair behind an ear. "About eight years ago, something like that, one of the Kirkpatrick boys, Gil, I think, bought it and the acres behind the fence you saw when you drove in, and decided to open a winery. Anyway, this is the first year that they have been able to bottle and sell the wine. It's good."

Matt poured Claire a glass of wine from one of the two bottles in front of them, a shimmering, crisp chardonnay, and handed it to her. "This is one of the wines I brought over to your place for our Sunday date." He grinned, and she found herself blushing. "I believe you enjoyed the, um, bouquet..."

Claire murmured, "Thank you," and took a sip of the delicate liquid. She smiled at Sadie, commenting that the wine was nice, and then hid behind the menu before her, noting Sadie's questioning look, but refusing to say anything further.

"The menu changes on a regular basis, here, but everything I've ever tried seems to be really good." Sadie said. "They have a lovely Brie that is baked in honey and pecans and served with this wonderful bread that reminds me of a brioche I tried when I was in Paris for a layover."

"Sounds good," Claire said. "How about if we start with that?"

"Sounds good to me," Jason replied. Claire watched as he brushed a tendril of Sadie's blond hair, now set in a pageboy cut with short, cropped bangs, behind her ear, his hand caressing as he slid an arm across her shoulder and snuggled her close for a kiss. "How's my girl been this week?"

Sadie smiled back. "Good. How's the plane coming along? Matt, Jason is rebuilding a plane his uncle flew back in the '40s. What kind of plane is it again, honey?"

"It's a Cessna 140," Jason explained. "My dad's family is from Kansas, and all the brothers flew in World War II before coming back home. My uncle, Wayne, worked for Cessna for several years, and also did some civilian flying on the side. Anyway, when he died last year, my dad bought the plane from my aunt Sissy, Wayne's wife."

When Matt asked what kind of condition the plane had been in, Jason explained it had been stuck in the back of an old barn on the original home place for many years. "Wayne developed diabetes and his eyesight went bad, so it sat for many years. It's been a great project for me and Dad, but I'm gone quite a bit; don't get to Kansas that much, anymore." He smiled wryly, and snuggled Sadie. She grinned back, and Claire was briefly envious at the ease between the two of them, and glanced at Matt, who was nonchalantly buried in the menu before him.

As the evening progressed, Claire found herself relaxing. The food was excellent, the company as well, and by the time the music started, she was thoroughly enjoying herself. When the band played an old slow song from her youth, she felt Matt's hand touch her knee, and she looked up. "Shall we?" he beckoned, and she nodded, feeling his hand guiding her to the dance floor. The lights were dimmed, and strings of twinkling lights, like raindrops cascading from the domed ceiling, cast a soft glow on the two of them as they swayed to the rhythm of the music.

When it ended, Matt held her close for a moment, and she felt his breath on her skin. "Honey," he said, softly. "You smell like honey."

She tried to detangle herself, but was lost. When the lights brightened, the two of them were still entwined. When *Fishin' in the Dark* began to play, Matt grinned, encircled her waist with one hand and grabbed a hand in the other, and the two of them two-stepped around the floor, swinging and twirling, song after song, until she was breathless.

When her tresses escaped the hair clip, Matt reached up and released it, and watched as the heavy mass of hair tumbled wildly around her face.

"Wait!" she protested, trying to tame the curls with her fingers. "I'm sure it's a mess!"

Matt grabbed her hands. "Don't." he said softly, bending slightly to bury his head in her soft tresses. "It's beautiful."

She caught her breath, then, quickly moved away. "Let's sit this one out; I'm thirsty." She said as she headed for the table.

Matt followed, and they sat, sipping drinks and talking more, until Jason and Sadie, too, left the dance floor and joined them when the band took a break. "Hey, how's Eva doing?" Sadie asked. "I haven't heard for a few days."

"Not much has changed," Claire sighed. "But the doctors said she has stabilized, and we'll probably have to move her to a long-term care facility and see what happens from there."

"Any new leads on who did this?"

"No, nothing yet. But I know that the sheriff's department has been working on it. There's a new detective who seems to be pretty sharp."

"Claire, I wish you would consider not staying out there by yourself, at least for now. I worry about you," Sadie was concerned. "It seems so remote, sometimes, especially knowing you're out there alone."

"Oh, I'm all right. By the way, where's Max?" she asked Matt. "With him around, Gran always felt pretty safe."

"Hmm," Matt frowned. "I can't say I've seen him for a while. I'm sure that Eva would have said something if he were sick. You might want to check down at the barns; I'll look around next time I'm out for the horses. I'll talk with Dave."

"Okay. I'd like to talk with him, too, and haven't gotten down to see him yet." Claire was puzzled by Max's disappearance. "I haven't met the kid that Grandma hired, but I saw him the other day. He does seem to be a bit rough around the edges, like you said. Do you know anything about him?"

Matt took a swig of the beer he'd switched to after dinner. "Not much. His name is Ben, one of the Weaver kids who lives in those Shady Oak apartments."

"Oh, wow," Sadie said. "Those are not the nicest apartments in town. My mom volunteers sometimes to deliver meals and do welfare checks, there. She told me there are lots of drugs and young kids, sometimes as young as four or five, running around with no one taking care of them. She always feels bad for those kids. Weaver, you said?"

"Yeah. I think he may be the oldest of three or four. His old man's been gone for several years, now, and his mom doesn't leave the apartment much, except to get drunk." Matt said. "Too bad, the kid seems to have some talent with the animals, and isn't afraid to work, but he's got a record. I think that Eva worked a deal with the judge down at juvie to have him work for her rather than on a community service deal."

"How do you know that, Matt?" Claire asked, curiously.

"Eva told me," he replied. "'Said Dave agreed to keep an eye on him and give him rides to and from the farm a few days a week."

"Any idea what he did to end up in juvie?"

"She didn't say, only that he needed guidance more than punishment, and sometimes it takes a community to raise a child."

Claire nodded. "That sounds like something she'd say. I think I'll mention him to the detective, although I'm pretty sure he's already spoken with Dave, and probably knows that the kid has been working at the farm."

"Well, just be careful out there, Claire," Sadie warned. "You know, Matt's just a phone call away."

Claire rolled her eyes and sipped her drink while the band stepped back onstage. She shook her head and laughed with her friend, and the music began to play.

Across town, Lyneah was ending her shift at the bar early; with a popular band out at the winery, business was slower than usual. She went into the employee restroom and washed her face, glancing at the clock. Eleven o'clock. Early, but she was beat, and was glad that her sister had invited Travis for a sleepover once again; Lyneah planned to pick him up in the morning.

She thought of the detective, Breuning, whom she had seen regularly since the break-in at her house. He'd taken to stopping in the bar on her shift, sometimes having a meal at the bar, other times, having a few beers with another, younger cop who had been in the bar before. Chris often came in late in her shift, and walked her out to her car, following her home to see to it that she made it safely, before he continued to the home he shared with his grandfather.

At first, Lyneah had been intimidated by the gesture, and had felt rather paranoid that she was somehow suspect. But, as she got to know him, she realized that the detective was just doing what he thought was right and wanted to make her feel safe. She'd become almost reliant on his presence.

On this night, however, she had agreed to leave her shift early, and would have felt silly trying to call him to see where he was. After all, she was a big girl, and it wasn't his job to look after her all the time.

She pulled into the driveway, slowly coming to a stop in front of the house. The motion light that her dad installed when he replaced the door, shown brightly across the deck, and she was comforted by it as she reached into the car to grab her purse and jacket before heading up the steps.

Suddenly, out of nowhere, an arm grabbed her from behind and pulled her from the car, roughly, wrenching her around her waist. She let out a yelp and a hand came across her mouth. She heard his voice, Hank's, and her heart sank. "Shhh, little girl," he breathed into her hair from behind. "I been meanin' to pay you a little visit for a while now."

She tried to cry out, but his hand stayed over her mouth as he dragged her to the house. "Give me those keys." She acquiesced, trembling.

"Keep your mouth shut." He said as he released the hand clamped over her mouth and grabbed the keys, reaching over to unlock the new door and push it open with his foot. He dragged her in the house and slammed the door behind him, locking it.

Lyneah stumbled, then backed away, shimmying backward on her bottom and her hands, fear gripping her. She was shocked at his appearance; his hair unkempt, his clothing ragged and torn. He had a black eye and an obviously swollen lip.

As he sneered down at her, she absently noted a front tooth missing. "You didn't think I'd let you all get away that easy, did you?" he snarled as he stepped toward her.

She quickly turned on all fours and tried to stand, but he grabbed her by the hair and yanked her back. She bit her lip and winced, tried to be brave. "Hank, please, get out of here."

He didn't say anything, just pulled her back to him and picked her up, heading down the hall toward her bedroom. She fought, grabbing the walls with both hands and her legs, trying to kick away, but he was strong. She wondered, briefly, what he was on that would make him so crazy, then felt blinding pain as her head hit the bedside table when he flung her onto the bed.

She moaned and pleaded. "Please stop this, Hank."

"I saw that cop following you around like a puppy dog, you little bitch," he said softly, leaning over her, and yanking at the buttons of her shirt with one hand while holding her hands with the other. "You been fuckin' him, Lyneah?"

She stared up at him. "God, no, Hank. Please, don't do this."

"You been, haven't you? What did you tell him, Lyneah?" He demanded, roughly. "You tell him I had something to do with your old Auntie? He's been checking up on me, and I don't like it."

"No!" she replied. "No, I didn't!" She tried to pry her hands away from his. "Geez, Hank, did you have something to do with hurting Eva?"

'He didn't answer her, just pulled harder on her blouse, until she felt the buttons give and the fabric rip. He was crazed. "Stop, Hank!"

"Where'd you put the stuff?"

"What stuff?"

"The stuff I hid in the barn?"

"What barn?"

He backhanded her, hard. "Don't fuck with me, Lyneah."

"I don't know what you're talking about!"

Hank grabbed her around her neck, squeezing. She felt panic, clawed at his hands. It seemed to excite him, even more, and he laughed as she reached around, trying to grab the lamp on the bedside. "You think that will protect you?" He released her neck and pulled at her bra, roughly grasping her breasts through the thin fabric. "You don't know where it is, huh? No matter, I come here to take what's mine, and give you what's been comin' to you."

He reached down to his pants and unbuckled his belt. Lyneah fought nausea as she tried to buck him off her, but he held fast. He pulled the belt form his waist, wound it around her wrists and yanked her arms up above her head.

"No, please! No!"

He ignored her and began unzipping her jeans. She bucked and writhed, pulling her legs up and kicking as hard as she could. He pulled back and punched her across her jaw, and she fell back, stunned from the blow. He worked her jeans down, and then his own, and she felt his erection against her leg.

Lyneah moaned, "Nooooo-…." as Hank straddled her, pulled her legs apart roughly and rammed into her. Lyneah fought nausea, gritting her teeth against the sickness that had risen from her panicked insides. She prayed. Prayed that he would be done, soon. Prayed that someone would save her, that she could undo this moment.

All the while he pumped into her, his gruff voice was breathing heavily into her ear. "Come on, baby. Lighten up. You need to relax."

Her insides were raw from his brutal attack. She felt his hands, rough on her body, and found herself drifting, drifting, away from this moment in time, back to another time, when she had been young, and carefree, running through the woods with her sisters. She kept her eyes clamped shut, and thought of Travis, thanking God he was nowhere near the house. She thought of dying. She heard Hank grunting, and a snarl, something about how frigid she was, but she was too far away to hear it. When he finally climbed off her, she lay, unmoving, in the exact position he had put her in when he began his attack, eyes closed.

She heard him ranting about her inadequacies, heard him shuffling around the room, pulling his clothes on, heard him zip the jeans. She felt him yank the belt form her wrists, and a foot nudge her roughly on her side. Still, Lyneah kept her eyes closed, an empty calm engulfing her body, detaching her.

When he finally left, she lay still for a long, long time afterward, unmoving, until dawn. She did not bother to get up and lock her door; he could get to her no matter what she tried. She just lay there, naked, bruises covering her thighs and blood caking the corner of her mouth. At some point, she curled on her side, pulling the quilt over her cold body and shivered, but no sound came. And no tears. She shivered uncontrollably for a long time, then, exhausted, she dozed.

The sound of her doorbell startled her awake, and she gripped the covers around her, her heart pounding at the sudden sound. She curled even further into herself. *No. Go away. I don't want to see you.*

Lyneah heard her name in the distance but did not move. It was that detective, she could hear him calling through the thin walls of the mobile home. Still, she did not move, did not make a sound. She pushed her fist against her mouth and fought back a panicked sob. *Please. Go away.*

She sensed rather than heard him enter her bedroom, and lay still, wary. Felt him slowly approach her bed, softly saying her name. "Lyneah?"

She felt him touch her bare shoulder just above the quilt, and she winced. "No. Go away!"

Chris pulled his hand away, but continued to stand by her bed, looking down at her still form under the quilt, her tangled blonde hair covering the bruises on her face. He looked around the room, saw her torn blouse, the lamp on the other side of the bed, its glass globe broken into pieces, and felt a jolt of shock. The cop in him kicked in, but the man inside of him, boiling with rage, wanted to find that bastard and rip him apart with his bare hands.

He pulled his cell phone out of his pocket, and quietly said he was going to call for some assistance.

Lyneah heard him, finally turned and grabbed at the phone. "No!" she shouted. "No cops!"

He saw her face, the bruises, the vacant look in her eyes, and winced. "Lyneah, I *am* a cop."

She looked up at him, frightened, and a keening rose from her throat. The quilt had fallen away from her body, and Chris saw bruises on her neck and breasts. Dear God, he thought. She began to rock and sob, and he gently pulled the quilt back up over her body and sat on the bed, carefully enfolding her and holding her until she stopped sobbing.

When she had quieted, he moved her damp hair from her face, all the while talking to her about how important it was for her to see a doctor, to let him find whoever had done this to her, to let her know he was going to make sure she was safe. She said nothing, just sat against his warm body, and wondered that she could feel such security after what had happened.

She never wanted to move, so mesmerizing was it to just lean on something so strong and warm and comforting. She felt the softness of the sweatshirt he had thrown on, large embroidered letters etching print on her cheek, and did not care. She felt the beating of his heart.

When he sensed that Lyneah was calm enough, he disentangled himself, and said, softly. "Lyneah, I need to ask you some questions. Do you know who did this to you?"

She looked up at him, and felt cold, harsh reality again. She didn't say anything, only nodded, slowly, before looking away in shame. "Was it Beaudine, Lyneah?"

She continued looking down, and withdrew from Chris's side, leaning back against the headboard, pulling the quilt up around her. She started shivering again.

"Was it Hank Beaudine, Lyneah?"

She nodded slowly.

"Did he-?"

She could not look up, just nodded, slowly, again, and a single tear fell down her cheek. Chris worked hard to squelch the rage boiling inside of him. If only he'd caught the bastard. If only he'd been able to accompany her home. But he'd been on duty last night, late, and when he got to the bar, he'd been told she left early.

He'd gone home, then, exhausted after a double shift. He'd gotten up early for a run, chatted with his grandfather, who was on his way to coffee with the boys, and decided to drive back to Lyneah's with coffee and Danish for breakfast, since it was his day off.

He took her hand and held it. "Lyneah, tell me what happened, if you can. It's important for you to give me as much detail as possible, even if this is uncomfortable for you. Do you understand?" he asked.

She closed her eyes, still unable to make eye contact with him. "I- I don't want to do this." She said weakly.

"I know." He reached, tentatively, to her and brought her chin up so she could meet his eyes. "Trust me."

She shook her head, vehemently, blonde hair catching in her lashes and falling into her face. He slowly, carefully, pushed it away from her face, and she winced away. "Lyneah, you can trust me. I will never harm you. I will do nothing until you agree, okay?"

Chris clasped her cold hand in his warm grasp, and waited, slowly caressing her hand with his large fingers, all the while encouraging her. "Lyneah, I will never harm you, you understand that, don't you?"

She nodded.

"You can trust me. I will not judge you. I will not do anything you do not want me to do." His soothing voice seemed to calm her a bit. "I'll be right here, until you're ready to talk."

"Okay." She said. And she told him her story.

"You did not shower after the incident?"

She felt ashamed. "No."

"It's okay. But it's important to get you up to the hospital to do a rape kit."

Lyneah vigorously shook her head. "No! I don't want to do that!"

Chris tried to soothe her fears. "Don't worry; they will take care of you and I'll be right there with you."

"No," she pleaded again. "I just don't want anyone to know. No one will believe me."

"I believe you."

She set her chin and shook her head, firmly. "I don't want to go to the hospital. I don't want this to get around. I just want to forget it."

Chris knew that, in a town this size, no matter how discreet, people still found things out. There was no way to guarantee her that people would not know, but he let her know that he would respect her privacy and so would the team of people who would work together to find Hank Beaudine.

Still, she wouldn't budge. "I do not want my parents to know. Or anyone else." She glanced at the clock. "I'm supposed to go and get Travis this morning."

"Where is he?"

Her lip trembled. "My sister's."

"How about if I give her a call?"

"And tell her what?"

"That she should make arrangements for Travis and meet us at the medical center this morning. You need the support of someone you trust."

She shook her head. "You are not understanding me. This town already thinks I'm a sleaze. I just don't want to go up to the hospital where everyone knows everyone and walk in like- like this." She looked at the floor helplessly. "Hank and I were dating; there are some people around her who would just say we got too drunk or something. That I deserved it. I just don't want anyone to know."

He stared at her, perplexed. "Why are you trying to protect him?"

Lyneah shook her head vigorously. "I'm not trying to protect him! He should rot in hell for what he's done to me and probably to others. But I am trying to protect my family, and my son. I don't want them to be hurt by this, or any talk, or anything else. So, do not tell Jacquie that she needs to come hold my hand for a rape kit!"

He was quiet. "What do you want me to tell her?"

She stared back at him. "I don't know." She paused. "A rape kit won't matter, anyway. He couldn't, um, finish." She quickly looked away.

"That doesn't matter; an examination by a doctor can reveal all sorts of things, and we want to make sure you're healthy, and there aren't any injuries that could be serious, or life threatening. Look, if something happened to you, what would happen to Travis? This isn't something you can hide from, Lyneah."

She leaned her head back. Silence filled the room, as the sunlight flickered in the east window, sending rays of sunshine into the room. It was going to be a warm spring day, the kind she loved to be out in, the kind that she would spend with her mom and Jacquie, getting the gardens ready, planting flowers, biking with Travis. Would things ever be like that, again? Just normal? If she came forward, there would be no normal days. There would be a trial. Facing her family. Facing people, with her shame. Facing Hank. Hank, who could hurt her again, or worse, hurt her little boy.

"Okay." She finally said. "Let's go."

Chapter Twelve

Claire awoke to brilliant sunlight and kicked the covers from her legs as she stretched slender arms above her head and snuggled, happily, into the pillow for just another minute. She lay there on her back, wearing an old sweatshirt and shorts, staring up at the ceiling, and found herself thinking about the evening before.

Matt still affected her like no man had, before or since. His touch on her back as they danced, his breath in her hair, like a dream had drawn her in, and, when he'd driven her home, led to some heavy petting in the front yard of her grandmother's home.

She knew, without question, that before long, they would end up in bed together, and the thought sent a flush through her body and across her cheek. She frowned, and turned on her side, burying her head under the pillow. 'How am I going to get myself out of this one?' she asked herself. All signs warned her, but, when it came to Matt, even now, she was lost.

She tossed off the blankets, padded across the hardwood floor to the bathroom in bare feet, brushed her teeth and put her mass of hair up in a pony, before heading downstairs to brew a cup of coffee. Before long, she was curled up on the porch swing, its brightly flowered pillows enveloping her, and she was reading her grandmother's journal once again.

She did not hear the insistent vibration of her cell phone, which was tucked away in her purse upstairs.

September, 1944

It seems so odd to know this fellow, who is my enemy. He intrigues me; I want to hate him, but I can't. He does not say very much, but when he does, he is very polite. He speaks English very well. Mama says it is because he has been in America for over a year; she checked up on him before we would agree to take him on as a worker. He is tall and has blonde hair that turns silver in the light of the sun. His blue eyes sometimes follow me when I am in the barns. They are a brilliant blue, almost green, and when I catch him looking at me, he turns quickly.

When he came to us, I tried so hard to hate him. I would not look at his face, and, when I had to work beside him in the barns, I would stomp around in stony silence. He, always polite, always kind, would accept this behavior without question, I suppose because he has no choice; he is a prisoner.

One afternoon, in August, a thunderstorm hit with such severity that it toppled trees and blew the cedar shakes off the chicken barn. The horses, led by a spirited colt named Chance, became wild, running around their pasture, their whinnies becoming screams as bolt after bolt of lightning split the sky. Chance, panicked at one particularly bad jolt, raced across the grass toward the woods, oblivious to the barbed wire fence standing between him and the shelter of the trees.

I heard his screams from where I had sought shelter from the storm, in the hay barn, and without much thought, ran out toward him. Erich, too, heard his cries and appeared from nowhere, running alongside me, carrying a tin snip in his ungloved hands. By the time we got to the colt, he was tangled up in a mass of barbed wire, bloody cuts gashed into his painted coat, and his eyes, one blue and one gray, were wild with terror. He thrashed around so much I could not reach him without getting kicked.

I started pulling at the wire with my bare hands, and Erich said, "No, Eva, let me do that."

I had never heard him say my name before that moment. He spoke in soft German to the horse, whispering quietly, close to Chance's ear, words I did not understand, but they were calming to both the horse, and to myself. He gestured for me to come closer, patting the horse's flank, and I stood near him, stroking Chance, calming him as Erich snipped the wire from his body.

The work took a long time. Rain poured down upon us, and I could feel the animal quiver every time a bolt of lightning crackled with thunder across the western sky, but he did not again move, until, at last, he was free. He struggled to his feet and took off across the yard at a full gallop all the way to the other end of the pasture, stopped, turned, and came charging back at a dead run.

At first I was afraid he would try to jump through us, still seeking the shelter of the tree line, and Erich must have felt the same, because he covered me with his body, holding me protectively to the ground while he cradled my head against his shoulder. I was aware of the scent of him; sweat, hay, and something more, and my heart skipped a beat at the moment that Chance stopped short, just a few feet from where we huddled by the broken wire. I breathed out slowly and told myself this moment of madness was nothing more than fear of the horse.

We slowly disentangled from one another and stood in the pouring rain, staring at each other before he began to repair the fence. I turned to lead Chance to the stable to attend his wounds, but stopped, turned back to Erich, and said, "Thank you."

He smiled down at me, and I saw his even, white teeth, noting I had not seen him smile before that moment. "You are welcome." He said in his throaty accent-tinted voice, before he turned back to the fence.

I have thought about him, nonstop, ever since. Sometimes, these thoughts keep me awake at night, and I awake tired and cranky, and when he greets me, I grumble at him because I am angry at him for making me think this way. He does not show his curiosity at those moments, just seems to accept them, and I need to remind myself of why he is here, and where my Shane is. It eats at me that Shane will be forever gone, somewhere a million miles away, and I could feel such disturbing things for one of the men who put him there.

It is getting colder now, especially at night. When I was little, I loved the snow, but now I dread it. Snow means more work with the cows, more bedding, no more pasture grazing, so more feeding.

Erich is very good with the cows. Sometimes I hear him speak to them in German, quietly whispering to them as he works. His English is excellent and I asked him what he did before the war. He said his father was a lumberman and a wood carver, and he lived in beautiful mountains, very different from our plains in Minnesota. They also had cattle. He seemed so sad when he spoke of his home.

I heard Dad and Danny quarreling behind the granary yesterday. Danny was yelling that Dad, who has such trouble with his arthritis that he can't walk some days, should never have agreed to take on that "god damned Nazi." Dad's booming voice carried over to where I was, in the east shed feeding calves with Erich, and Dad replied that he would not have had to if Danny were not a drunkard and a fool.

I looked at Erich's face; he returned my gaze, but his face was blank. I know it was hard for him, though. He left the shed quickly, headed back toward the milking barn so they would not know he heard anything. I am embarrassed. I peeked out the paned window to see Danny stalking off to his old truck, and Dad, standing in the door of the granary, watching him leave, his shoulders stooped as he leaned weakly against the doorframe. Since Shane died, Dad is so preoccupied that I hardly see him, and when I do, he is so distant, I cannot seem to reach him.

I went to find Erich, and apologized for my brother, feeling such mixed emotion. When I spoke to him, he shook his head, and said it was not for me to feel bad about it. But I did. I started asking questions about himself, and how he got here.

He said he was not a part of the SS, but was actually in the German navy, the Kreigsmarine, and was some type of sub-lieutenant. He said he was conscripted, which means drafted, into the navy. I am bold; I asked him his thoughts about his country's leader, and he studied me for a long time. He shook his head, and said that many of his countrymen love Germany, and feel that Heir Hitler is not good for his country.

Erich heard rumors, he said, about the resettlement of the Jews, and that really meant that they were going to die. He talked about refusing to wear the issued stockings, because there were rumors that the hair used to knit the stockings was from the dead Jews. It was horrible; the more he talked, the more, clear it became how evil Adolph Hitler really is.

My parents went to Minneapolis today to visit my Aunt Gert, who is my Dad's sister. She is at Glen Lake Sanitorium in Minneapolis because she the TB. She is a spinster, and Dad's only sister. Mom told me that, many years ago, Gert was in love. Dad and Gert moved to Minnesota, in 1906, when Dad was just eighteen, and Aunt Gertie only sixteen. They moved here from out East, after their parents died in a fire. Dad's life was the horses. They did not have much money, but Dad put everything into buying the land here and raising horses; drafts and a line of thoroughbreds.

Times were difficult; the government had shut down gambling and betting on race horses. Dad farmed the land, and raised cattle, too, but his life has always been the horses. I have watched him, sometimes, with them; it is almost mystical how they respond to his voice, and touch.

Gertie, who had been schooled out East, began teaching in the country school just miles from the farm. It was difficult for her; she was a city girl, and unaccustomed to farm and country life. Most of the children were German farm kids who didn't know much English. There, she met my mother, Abigaile, who was her oldest student, and they became good friends.

Mama says that she fell in love with Dad the first time she met him, at a Christmas program at church. He was quiet, distinguished, and handsome. She felt, she said, weak and childish in her fascination with this regal figure, and never thought he would love her. But he did.

They settled on the farm. One day, during the Great War, a man and his son came up, a horse broker from out east, looking to buy horses that were going to be shipped overseas, and used in battle. He said that the English were running out of horses, and there was good money to be made in selling draft horses for the war. His name was Thorsen, I think, and his son, Jacoby, was a handsome and charming lad.

They stayed in town, and wagered for horses, returning every few weeks. He and Gert fell in love. Unfortunately, it was all a ruse, and the deal went sour. My dad lost a lot of money when Thorsen disappeared with two horses without paying for them, and Gert lost her first and only love.

Dad recovered and did send some of the Belgians overseas, but Gert did not. She never married, never loved again. 'Sounds so dramatic, and forlorn. But the truth is, she is often a bitter and unhappy woman, pale and thin, and severe, and I think she is a spinster by choice, not necessarily because of that incident.

Mama would not agree, but Aunt Gert would not have been a very nice wife! She taught school for several years, and then, when she got sick, retired a lonely woman, leaning on Dad quite a lot, until she finally entered the sanitorium, long after the disease had taken such a grip on her that it could not be undone.

They try to visit Gert often, saving gas rations as much as they can to be able to see her. Today is beautiful. The skies are bright, and the sun is shining. I'm going to do chores this morning, and then spend some time riding; it is lovely, and I know that Sasha needs a run. I will return to write later.

I am back, sitting here, with flutters in my stomach. I do not know how this is possible, but something happened today that takes my breath away. Erich came to the farm, as he does each day, to work. I was in the potato garden, digging, and he walked up the drive, past the horse barns and paused by the calf shed. He saw me in the garden, waved his hand, then went into the shed to feed calves and clean stalls.

I continued digging the potatoes, but could not seem to concentrate, and kept glancing toward the barns. When I had a basketful, I stopped, and carried them to the barn to rinse them from the well, trying to be calm and nonchalant. Erich paused from his chores when he saw me come in and turned to watch me. I was nervous and did not know why. I could not stop chattering, telling him that my parents were not home, and it is such a lovely day, babbling and feeling like an idiot with a loose tongue. He was quiet, and smiled at me, asking me if I needed any help in the garden. "Yes," I replied. "I have to pick tomatoes and carrots, and some other things…"

After we picked vegetables, I invited him to ride horse. He seemed hesitant and asked about my parents and brother; he did not want to do anything improper. You can tell he loves horses as I do, and when I asked him, he said that he had a favorite back home, but that she was taken for the war effort.

I packed a lunch, and Erich saddled the horses. We set off for the old farm, an old cabin that is in disrepair, but a wonderful spot to explore and to picnic. We spread an old wool blanket on the grass, under an oak tree, and had lunch.

"I had good life in Germany. My papa is a woodcarver. We live in the Schwarzwald, eh," he hesitated trying to find the English words. "Eh, black forest. It is a mountain area. I live near Bodensee, a large lake near the mountains."

I took a bite of the ham, nestled between thick slices of mama's bread. "How did your English become so good?"

He smiled. "We have many English tourists come to where I live. My papa makes beautiful wood carvings, and clocks in his shop. We sell nice gifts to tourists, until the war."

I took a bite out of an apple, fresh off the tree, tart but sweet and crisp, catching the juices with my tongue while he told me of his family.

As the sun moved across the sky, I could feel its heat on my back despite the season. It is Indian Summer, a time when we have a renewed dry warmth in the air. Erich talked of his brothers, twins Jens and Jonas, who were young and rebellious and impressionable, and his worry about them. He held up his hands, they are fourteen, he said. The war will take them from my mama. They are *gewagt* he said; reckless and daring.

He told me of his mama, Sophie, the talented musician who grew up in Austria, who, from a young age, made beautiful music in Vienna. She played the pedal harp with tiny, deft hands for Austrian nobility. The world war, he said, changed all that.

"What happened?" I asked.

"Mama's brother, Franz, was much like the brothers," he replied, referring to the twins. "He was spoiled, and unkind. Mama is sweet, and kind and talented," He paused, thoughtful. "Mama 's family was good family, some money."

Erich's accent is rich with the dialect of his heritage, but he rarely stumbles when he speaks nearly perfect English. He is serious, carefully putting thought into every word, and I felt myself relaxing as he spoke of home.

Sophie's father was rising in the ranks in the political arena of Austria before the Great War, and was a well-known business man in Vienna. Erich did not know his grandfather; by the time Erich was born, Julian, a tall, dark haired man with a long mustache and wire glasses, was already dead; gone, he said, due to the influenza that had ripped through the world before the '20s. As he spoke, I closed my eyes, basking in the warmth of the sun, feeling lazy and relaxed, and pictured the world he described; the music halls, alive with flowing gowns and noble gentlemen in top hats and waistcoats, while his tiny mother sat upon a stage, gliding her fingers across the strings to create haunting music for the wealthy.

Franz, three years Sophie's junior, had been a naughty, spoiled boy, who rebelled against every ideal that his Catholic Socialist upbringing had enforced. Julian kept a firm hand on his son's education, sending him to the best schools, affording him luxuries of nobility that were beyond his means. Sophie's natural gift for music was fostered with her enrollment, at a young age, in private music tutoring with some of the most well-known musicians in all of Austria.

But Julian was not so attentive to the needs of a head-strong boy; the social life and business dealings and political meetings kept him busy, and by the time Franz was a teenager, the boy had begun sneaking out of the lovely house on the expensive edge of the Third District, running with the young artists and beggars and students near the beer halls, where political movements were beginning to draw the working class. There he became enamored with a pale, thin-faced man with vacant eyes and a dramatic penchant for furious and passionate oratory.

"Mama knew that Franz was being bad," Erich said, "but, she could not convince him to stop going out into the streets. She was afraid he would be hurt or killed in the streets, but he just laughed at her. She told me that, sometimes, when he came in, he smelled of schnaps and smoke, and her *Mutter* would hurry him past the salon, where men of the Christian Social Party would be gathered, smoking cigars and drinking schnaps in small, beveled snifters."

"You mean, your uncle Franz knew Adolph Hitler?"

Erich smiled softly, shaking his head slightly. "Yes, but only from a distance. Franz attended meetings where Der Fuhrer would speak." It had grown warm in the sun, and Erich unbuttoned the blue, standard issue shirt with the large "PW" letters emblazoned on its back as he continued. His eyes met mine, crystal blue, and warm. "Der Fuhrer was once a young man, also. He was a street artist then, in Vienna, before the war. He lived in a, eh, how do you say it, Asyl Fur Obdachlose, uh, mans home. Eh, for the poor…"

I sat forward, idly braiding strands of long, golden grass. "You mean, the German dictator was poor?"

Erich nodded. "Yes."

"Wow." I mused.

"Ja," Erich said. "Wow." He smiled broadly, looking directly into my eyes, and my heart skipped a beat as I grinned back. He cleared his throat and continued. "My Opa would talk with his comrades about the movement, and laugh about Hitler; Opa knew many people, and one of his employees lived in the same house as Hitler. Franz's idol left Vienna, moved to Germany. Franz was but a boy; he lost interest in one cause for another."

Erich had such knowledge and lulled me with his story. Austria, he said was a powerful and awakening empire, a sovereign nation in the early 1900s. There was much strife in Europe then, Erich said, and much political maneuvering was taking place.

Prussia, the power kingdom of Germany, was unscrupulous in its ambitions, intending to acquire territories across the continent, and even into Argentina, with an ultimate goal of encompassing the entire civilized world under its own power. Before that, however, there was the small matter of Austro-Hungary, the great sovereignty whose lands stood between Prussia and its desired holdings in the Balkans to the south. Germany and Austria built a great railway to Turkey, giving Germany greater access to the Balkans, only to lose it to Serbia after Turkey's defeat to the Serbs during the Balkan war.

There had been many wars between the various European states, for centuries, strife among territories, and Bosnia had been annexed to Austria-Hungary, a move of bitter resentment among Bosnians. But this was a time of diplomacy, and Austria's heir to the throne, Archduke Franz-Ferdinand set out to make change. He had married a Commonor, the beautiful Sophie von Chotkowa und Wognin, breaking with Austria's requirement that royals marry only other royals. Sophie was not allowed to ride in the same automobile as her husband, was not able to appear with her husband during public or social engagements. The lovely Sophie was often snubbed by the wives of the aristocratic upper class.

As Field Marshall of the army, Franz could travel and make public appearances with his wife. During these times, Franz often traveled with his wife, overseeing his troops in various parts of the regime, and in June of 1914, he and his wife visited the occupied city of Sarajevo. The city was alive with secret political animosity, particularly toward Austria.

Peculiarly, there were no efforts to protect the Archduke and his wife; by the end of that Sunday, June 28, 1914, the Archduke and Duchess's fourteen year anniversary, both would be dead of gunshot wounds, and Europe would be embroiled in even further turmoil.

Julian, too old to go to war, and Franz, too young, would watch as their world became enmeshed in the Great War. In the beginning the entrepreneur in Julian thrived on the war efforts, capitalizing on the need for resources to feed the frontlines. But as early as 1916, resources were increasingly limited, and provisions were scarce.

The government put a moratorium on spending, and rations, and even those of the upper middle class were left with little to survive on in the once thriving city of Vienna. Julian was forced to sell assets at pauper's prices, and Franz ran away to join the effort when he was barely sixteen, much to the apprehension of his sister, Sophie.

Sophie, by then a grown woman, left her privileged world and joined the work force, eventually making her way through Germany, into Munich, where she worked as a hospital clerk. It was there that she met a young and handsome German soldier by the name of Willhelm Anton Gebhardt.

Erich paused and smiled at me, then, when he spoke of his Papa and Mama. "Mein papa was in the hospital with battle wound. He was in the same *truppe* as *Onkel* Franz. They were comrades, yes?"

I nodded, smiling back, and realized with a start that the sky was beginning to darken. "Oh, dear, I think we need to get back to the farm."

"Ja," he answered, his brilliant blue eyes never leaving my face. Neither of us moved, and I held my breath. Time stood still, just then. He reached for my face, cupping my chin with one hand as he gently pulled the scarf away from my hair with the other, and he kissed me softly.

He drew back, slowly, then reached down and kissed me again, and again, until I was breathless, his warm hands running through my hair, cupping my face. I did not stop him, but kissed him back, with more urgency, until he finally stopped and pulled me close to him, resting my cheek on the cotton undershirt he wore, and held me there.

Wordlessly, we stood and pulled everything into the blanket, and he helped me mount my horse, touching my knee. I looked down at him and felt suddenly shy. We road back in silence, running the horses, in order to rush through chores before he had to leave with the truck that stops at the end of the driveway to pick him up each day, to take him away from me, to the prison camp he now calls home.

I watched him walk hurriedly down the drive in the dusk, the stark, white letters on his back reflecting eerily in the moonlight, distorting as he moved further down the lane. I stood in the shadows of the barn doorway, where he'd pulled me to him just a moment before, and kissed me with such passion I could barely stand on my feet, and I felt such an ache to see him again as he disappeared into the darkness just as the lights of the bus came rolling past the grove of trees.

October, 1944

Dearest Journal –

I have begun an affair.

My life is spinning, spinning out of control. I feel wicked, and deceitful, but I do not stop wanting him. Letters come to me, from across the sea, which I leave unopened, too tired at the end of the day, too weak with shame, as I plan how Erich and I can be alone, again.

Nights are getting longer, colder. It is easy to sneak away from camp, Erich says. There are few guards, and he can move quietly. We meet, sometimes, in cover of darkness, and lie in the grass, shivering with cold, and excitement. We are mad, it can only be doomed, but I cannot stop wanting him, and find every chance to steal away.

It is a dangerous game we play, but we continue to play it. Tonight, we did chores; Mom and Dad went to a church social, the first function my dad has attended in months. Erich and I rushed through chores and came to the house to clean up. We kissed by candlelight, touching and caressing. He was hesitant, at first, not wanting to hurt me, or my reputation, but I shushed him with my lips and held his hand to my breasts.

He touched me, tenderly, entering me with his fingers, and I felt a flush across my body, unlike anything I've ever known. He continued to caress, and touch, and lick, until I cried out his name, over and over, and then, very carefully, he pushed his way in. I felt a prick of pain, and cried out, and he stopped for a moment, holding me close and whispering in my ear, in a language I did not understand, and then I was lost in it.

After, while we were dressing, there was blood, in the worn percale sheets, and in my clothes. I found an old cotton shirt in the drawer and wiped myself clean, then, we rinsed the clothes outside, watching the water turn pink as it seeped into the ground under the cistern. I saw the blood, thought of war, and Thomas, and Shane, and felt hollow inside, shame creeping in.

Erich seemed to sense something, for he gently took the few bits of clothing from my hands and wrung them out, reached for my hand and gently led me into the house, where we hung the clothes in the back of my closet to dry.

He has gone, and I lay here, in the bed that feels cool and damp from the scrubbing of blood, and I write this. Dear God, what have I done? I am so ashamed, and feel wicked and lustful, words my mother would use to describe my wanton behavior.

And yet, I know, I will do it again.

Chapter Thirteen

Claire's heart was racing as she rushed through the corridors of the hospital, intent on getting to Lyneah's room. She'd been shocked by the revelations in her grandmother's diaries and had been intent on reading further until she heard her cellphone chirp. The call from Jacquie had been rushed; Claire, Lyneah is in the hospital. Will you come?

Of course. She'd stopped at Jacquie's first, to pick up a bag of clothing, and Jacquie's face was lined with worry as she came to the door and handed the bag to Claire.

"How is she, Jacquie?"

"I don't know, but it can't be good." Jacquie tried to fight back tears as she spoke in hushed tones. "She doesn't want anyone to know, and I've got Travis here because she worked last night. I called Mom and Dad and had to practically order them not to run down to the hospital. She only wanted to see you, and Diana…"

Travis peaked around his aunt's leg. "Hi, Claire!" he grinned up at her.

"Hi, sweet cheeks!" Claire replied, putting her best effort into a grin. "Come here and give me some lovin'!"

He came around and barreled into her, his small frame hugging her tight. She hugged him back and told him she had to run but she loved him and would see him soon.

He looked up, solemn, and said, "Hank hurt my mom. He's a bad man." Jacquie and Claire exchanged glances, puzzled. Her cousin looked baffled and lifted her shoulders, gesturing uncertainty. Claire knelt to look into Travis' eyes. "How do you know that, sweetie?"

"I just do." And with that, he turned and ran back into the house, calling a goodbye over his shoulder.

Jacquie shook her head. "That boy is truly a mystery, sometimes."

Claire reflected on that as she approached Lyneah's room. Outside, in the corridor, she saw Chris Breuning, and a female cop with olive skin and deep brown eyes, talking quietly. As he turned to greet her, she could see concern in his face, and he took her by the shoulder and drew her near them.

Chris introduced Claire to the officer, and identified her as Steph Vasquez, an officer who was assigned to the victim task force for their county. She was short, stocky, and muscular, and spoke in hushed tones. "It's hard to prove, even with the injuries she has. She's going to have to be strong."

Chris looked grim as he nodded, and Steph continued. "She has some slight vaginal tearing; the swabs are being sent for analysis, so we won't know much until later. She's got a nasty shiner, you know, and some bruising on her wrists from the belt. Lots of marks on her thighs, legs…"

Claire winced, and closed her eyes, feeling sick. When she opened them, Chris was looking at her with concern. "Lyneah's in the shower now. Do you want to wait in the room?"

Claire shook her head firmly, and he turned back to the officer. "Even without a sex assault, we should have a domestic and aggravated assault, enough to bring him in. We've got time to file formally on Monday. I can give Judge Aldren a call, see if he'll approve the warrant and sign an OFP. Any trace on the clothes?"

Steph shook her head, "not really. I mean, there's a lot of fiber, hair, and stuff, but as I understand it, he'd been living there, at her place, so it won't be very useful, especially if the clothes were scattered on the floor and under the bed. We did pull and bag everything we found and sent her undergarments in for testing."

"The team finished at her house?"

"I think so."

"Thanks, Steph."

"Sure. I'll file the report and follow up with her and ask Gina to set up some time for her to meet with the victim advocate right away."

"Okay."

After the young officer left, Claire turned to Chris. "How is she?" she asked him, quietly.

"Not good. She's going to need help staying strong." He paused, as if to search for the right words, before continuing. "She doesn't have the confidence in herself to face this on her own. It's what happens to battered women."

Claire felt sadness. "Yes, I know she's had some rough spots."

"She fears that the town, and your family is going to judge her harshly because of this. She's worried about Travis, and her parents. It's tough in a small town."

"Yes, it is. But I know people love her, Detective. She's well-liked; people don't really harbor anything like that. I think she just needs to forgive herself; she'll be surprised at how much support she gets."

The door to Lyneah's room opened, and the bath aide, a young, heavy-set woman dressed in a floral shirt, scrubs and slippers, stepped out. "She's lying down." She smiled at them as she pushed a cart through the door.

"Thank you." Claire pushed her way into the room and saw her cousin in the hospital bed. The bed was raised up, and Lyneah was lying back, motionless, with a towel around her hair, wearing a pink hospital gown. Her face, scrubbed of makeup, looked pale in the light streaming through the window. She slowly turned to see Claire walk toward the bed, and her composure crumpled. She started to sob, reaching her arms out to her younger cousin. Claire kept a strong face as she looked at her cousin's bruises and felt a flash of anger at the monster who caused such pain.

She dropped the bag of clothing, kicked off her shoes and crawled into the bed with Lyneah, holding her, stroking her hair and rocking gently back and forth. "Shhhh, it's okay." She murmured.

She held Lyneah for a long time. Chris pushed a box of tissue nearer to them, and she pulled a few out, first wiping tears from her cousin's eyes, and then, her own. When the sobbing subsided to an occasional sniffle, she carefully removed herself, and sat on the edge of the bed, holding Lyneah's hand.

"Sweetie," Claire said softly. "I'm so sorry."

Lyneah leaned back, exhausted, and whispered, "I know."

They talked quietly for a time. Lyneah carefully avoided the topic of Hank, and the rape, instead making small talk. How is Travis? Do Mom and Dad know? What did Jacquie say? Claire spoke in soothing tones, reassuring her that her everyone was worried about her, but all right.

"Thank God Travis was not there. I can't protect him," Lyneah said, tears starting again. "I don't know what to do, anymore. What if *he* comes back when Travis and I are alone? I just have to take him and move away--" her voice was bordering on hysteria.

"He's okay, Lynnie," Claire reassured. "Jacquie and Dave won't let him out of their sight, not even for a minute. And you won't be going back there until this guy is caught. Detective Breuning and I will go and pack some things, and you can come and stay at the farm with me. It's safe there, and I've had a new security system put in." She glanced at the Detective, and then back at Lyneah. "We'll figure this out."

"Did someone call Diana?"

"Yes, Jacquie did; she's in Chicago at some convention; I think she'll be flying in later today."

Lyneah nodded, then turned to stare out the window again. Chris spoke up. "I'm going to step out and make a few calls. I'll drive you whenever you're ready."

After he left the room, Claire spoke. "He's a nice guy."

"Yes, he is." Lyneah replied.

"Good at his job, too. He'll find this asshole and bring him in. I'm sure of it. One way or the other, that guy will pay for what he did to you, and to Gran."

Chris returned to the room, and pulled the solitary chair closer to Lyneah's bed, placing it protectively between her and the door. Claire wandered down to Eva's room, and spoke with her a few minutes, marveling at the things she had learned about her grandmother from the diaries.

"Thank you, Gran," Claire whispered close to Eva's ear. "Thank you for the words you wrote for me."

The ventilator had been removed, and the bruising on Eva's face was fading to a greenish-yellow. She still looked so frail, and Claire marveled at Eva's body's fight to stay alive. She seemed to be restful, and, when Claire touched her hand, her grandmother's fragile, shaking fingers grasped hers weakly."

You're getting better, Grandma." Claire said to her. "Time, soon, to come home."

But Eva did not move, or utter a sound and mere seconds later, her light grasp loosened, leaving Claire to wonder if she had imagined it. She kissed Eva good-bye, and went in search of the doctor, to talk about a care plan for Eva during the next phase of her recovery.

Eva is standing in the sun, holding Isabelle's hand in the meadow. It is warm, and light, and she feels as though she is floating through the long, softly swaying fronds of grass. She sees, across the meadow, the sun, shining so brightly, and there, in its silhouette, a young, handsome soldier walking toward her, with his hand in the air, waving enthusiastically at her.

"Evaaaa..." she can hear him calling her.

"Mama, who is that?" she looks down at her daughter's face, the high cheekbones and almond eyes already showing signs of great beauty, and smiles. "That's your Uncle Shane, child." She again looks up, and he is jogging now, closer and closer. "He has come home..."

Chapter Fourteen

Days passed. Chris worked doggedly to bring Beaudine in. Lyneah, haunted and withdrawn, moved in with her cousin, Claire, staying at Eva's with its old doors and new security system. Travis took the guest room at the top of the stairs, a long, narrow room, just wide enough for a single bed and a small nightstand next to it.

Claire went shopping and loaded up with things she thought every young boy should have; new curtains, a sporty bed set, tiny glowing stars for the ceiling and walls, and a fish tank. She and Matt picked up some of his things from the house he shared with his mom. He seemed content, comfortable with the idea, but stuck close to his mother.

Matt stopped by often, sometimes late at night, after work, the smell of milk cows still clung to his clothing after he'd been on a call. Spring was upon the farm; daffodils and tulips were popping up in the gardens around the yard where they had full sun, and Claire and Lyneah spent evenings cleaning up the gardens, burning the leaves that had been left from last fall, watching Travis pick up twigs and toss them into the fire. Claire's classes for the spring session officially ended, and she had yet to make plans to return to her apartment in Illinois.

Eva had reached a plateau in her recovery, and the decision was made to move her into the long-term care facility. There was little discussion about her returning to the farm; all they hoped for was that she would continue to gain strength and be comfortable.

There were so many things that Claire wanted to talk with her about, but she could only hope that there would be a time when those conversations could take place and her questions could be answered.

On an evening when the age-old lilacs that formed a hedge at the edge of the yard were just beginning to bud, Matt showed up, driving slowly up the drive. Travis ran to greet him; they had become fast buddies, the two of them, and Claire, who was preparing charcoal for steaks, saw from a distance that he had a passenger in the truck.

As he drew nearer, she could see that the passenger was rather large, furry, and had a black nose that was, at the moment, planted at the top of the partially rolled down window.

"Travis," she called. "Wait until Matt parks the truck." She lit the charcoals, then walked toward the truck, wiping her hands on the jean shorts she was wearing.

Matt stepped out of the truck, and watched her approach, saw the way her t-shirt, with the word "Illinois" printed across it, stretched across her body, the way her legs, creamy and smooth, tapered beneath the tattered hem of the shorts. He had a flash of a life, a glimpse of him, coming home at the end of a day, and watching her run across the yard to kiss him. Only a glimpse, but it was enough.

"Who's your furry friend?" she asked him with a wry smile.

He let the pup jump out the driver's side and grinned back. "'Thought you could use a guard dog."

The pup ran around and round, chasing its tail and barking, nearly knocking Travis over when it barreled up to him and jumped, licking the boy's face. Claire chuckled,

"Some guard dog!"

Matt impulsively pulled her close, hugging her against him tightly, and she stood rigid for a moment before she relaxed into his arms. She, too, had seen a moment, a tiny sliver of life beckoning, it was *home*. That's what it was, home, and it felt *good*. She had not felt that contentment in a very long time, if ever. One thing she knew for sure; she had never had it with anyone but Matt.

Lyneah, coming down the stairs from a brief nap, saw the two of them, and felt envy. She knew their history, but also knew that they were still in love with one another, even if they would not admit it. She called a greeting to Matt when she walked outside.

"Mom! Look what Matt brought us!" she heard Travis squeal.

"Oh, honey, that's so sweet," she replied. "Matt, where on earth did you get that thing?" she laughed. "It *is* a puppy, right?" She was referring to the fur, a mass of many colors, the looked to be lab, sheep dog, and some other mix that she couldn't quite figure out.

Matt laughed as he reached down and rubbed the dog's ears, to which the dog lopped down and rolled onto its back, beseeching a tummy rub. "Yeah, he's a pup. Seems Harry Johnson's boy got a female shepherd, and she got out of her kennel one morning, oh, about eight months ago, and wandered around the neighborhood for a while."

"How old is the dog, Matt?" Claire asked.

"'About five, six months…"

The pup stood, suddenly, and set off on some chase, and Travis ran after him, around the yard, picking up a stick and throwing it. The pup, however, had no interest in the stick, instead launched himself at the boy, who fell back, laughing, as the pup lapped at his face and neck.

Lyneah put her hand on Matt's arm and thanked him. "You know that boy isn't gonna' want to let the dog go, like, ever…"

"He may not have to," Claire said, lightly. "When I go back to Illinois, someone will have to take care of him…" She trailed off, and an awkward silence followed. Matt let his arm, which had been casually draped over Claire's shoulders, drop to his side.

Claire broke the silence, asking Matt if he'd like to stay for supper. "We're going to grill some steaks and brats; you're welcome to join us, if you'd like."

"Ah, I'm pretty dirty; I was just going to go down to the barns and take a look at the horses."

"It's okay, Matt, you're fine. We'll just eat out in the porch. You want a beer or an iced tea when you come back up?" Lyneah asked.

"Sure. Hey, Travis, you wanna' walk down to the barn with me? I think mama cat has some kittens in the back of the feed room. Bring the pup with you."

Chris Breuning met Ben Lahr at Lyneah's house that evening; there were parts of the puzzle that didn't quite fit, and he wanted to dig around a bit more. Diana had given Chris a key, without letting Lyneah know, saying that he'd "be better off not saying anything to her" about going through the house, and "what she doesn't know, won't hurt her."

She'd also added that she'd be "damned happy to run into that Beaudine sonofabitch out on some country road somewhere, anytime, and kick his sorry ass." Chris had little doubt that she would kick the guy's ass if given the chance.

When he explained to Ben what they would be doing, he was not surprised when Ben jumped right on board. "Hell, yeah; I'll help you out with that." They had become friends since the Nielsen case, and Ben didn't particularly like Beaudine, having run into him once or twice around town. He wasn't all that worried about the legality of the search and seizure, either.

They began searching on one end of the house, moving slowly through drawers, looking under cabinets, furniture, careful to keep things neat and tidy. Lyneah didn't have much, but what she did have was tasteful, and cozy.

In the kitchen window sat an old blue porcelain coffee pot filled with yellow and pink-tipped tulips, the flowers dropping seeds and petals on the doily positioned beneath the pot. Two chairs at the table, painted sage green, with bouquets painted on the backrests, no doubt Lyneah's work. An old floral sofa and loveseat, clean but well worn, with a throw blanket crumpled on one end, as if she'd just been there, curled up underneath it, reading or watching an old movie.

Chris removed the cushions of the sofa, checking for any new stitches or holes, finding none. Methodically they moved through each room, Ben moving through the bath and Travis's nearly vacant bedroom, and Chris searching Lyneah's room. The cops who processed the scene of the rape had left quite a mess behind, fingerprint dust, items strewn around the room. The sheets had been stripped from the bed and taken to the lab for analysis, including pillows, clothing on the floor.

Chris did a perimeter check first, moving along each wall, through the master bath and closets, then moving furniture to look for hiding places. Chris was pretty sure the first time the house had been ransacked was because someone, namely Beaudine, had not made payment to his supplier, and they had come to collect.

Ben stepped outside and started walking casually around, swatting the occasional mosquito that would soon overtake the Minnesota summer. By now, the sun was beginning to set, and he felt the chill of a spring evening settle on his skin. He pulled a flashlight from his squad car, and started searching around, under the fuel barrel to the north, through the garden shed. He looked under the steps leading up to the door, and slowly began a walk of the outside perimeter of the mobile home.

The skirting around the foundation on which the mobile home sat was insulated with a layer of plastic, nailed in place with laths, probably placed there to keep the frigid winter air from freezing the pipes. He stepped close, scanning each section, fingering laths and the sheeting to see if he could spot anything worked loose.

Bingo. He called to Chris, who was still in the master bedroom, and rapped on the back window. When Chris approached, Ben beckoned for him to come out. The two men carefully removed the loose laths from the corner, where it had been removed and reattached previously. Ben held the light for Chris as he pried the sheeting away from the house, peering into the cavernous area that was sheathed in skirting. He crawled in, and Ben followed with the light.

The two surveyed the area in the growing darkness. There was fiber insulation covering the underside of the structure, otherwise, it was clean. Chris pulled a penlight from his pocket and shown it on the ground in front of them.

"See that?" he asked Ben. There were marks in the gravel, where someone had crawled in from the corner they were at, across the trailer, diagonal to the other end.

Ben nodded, and they made their way to the other side, skirting along the edge of the house rather than to disturb the trail, and stopped where it ended. With both flashlights shining, Chris was able to see a small hole that had been taped in the insulation, under the kitchen. "Let's see what kind of surprise the asshole left us."

He pulled a glove and pocketknife from his suit jacket and sliced evenly along the side of the hole. When the insulation gave way to the weight of what was tucked inside, a clear, gallon sized plastic bag fell to the ground in front of Chris, kicking up dust and insulation.

Crystal meth. And a lot of it. "Shit," Chris heard Ben say under his breath.

Chris didn't touch it, just indicated to back out. "We'd better process it. You call the chief; I'll call Diana Hamilton."

Lyneah picked up her cell phone when a call came. "It's Diana, I'd better take it." She grabbed her glass for a refill, got up and stepped into the house from the porch. "You need anything else?"

"No, thanks."

Claire heard Lyneah answer the phone through the open screen door. "Hey, Diana."

Silence, then an audible gasp. "What? Oh, my God." Claire stood and entered the house, looking concerned. Her cousin's face was pale, and her eyes wide. She glanced at Claire as she entered the house and held her gaze while she listened. "Okay. That's fine. I'll run over there."

She disconnected and said, "I have to run to the house. Would it be okay if I left Travis here for a while? He's asleep already. Something's come up."

"Sure, Lyneah, go ahead."

Matt noticed Lyneah had lost weight, picked at her food over dinner, and now looked scared to death. "Anything I can do? You want me to drive?"

Lyneah shook her head as she hurried up the stairs to grab a sweater and her purse. "No. I'll explain; just a minute." She called as she took the steps two at a time. When she returned, she talked quickly. "Apparently, they've found drugs, or something at my house. I'm going to run over there." She hurried to the door, throwing over her shoulder, "They're not mine, by the way. I don't do that stuff."

Matt and Claire went back to the porch and cleared the plates from the table. "Thanks," she said. "She's been through so much. She's not eating, and sometimes, I hear her crying at night. I worry about her. I can't believe they haven't been able to track that guy down."

They carried the plates to the kitchen, and together, loaded the dishwasher and put the food away. When Claire's cell phone rang from where she'd left it on the sofa table, she went to answer it, concerned that it may be Lyneah.

"Hello?"

"Hi, Claire," she heard Marcus's voice on the other end, and her stomach did a little lurch.

Claire glanced over her shoulder to see if Matt had followed and heard the clanging of glass and flatware being loaded into the dishwasher. "Hey, Marcus."

"I haven't heard from you for a while and thought I'd give you a call and see when you're going to be coming home." His voice was warm, kind, but hesitant, and she felt a niggling of guilt, as she glanced behind her again.

"I'm not sure, Marcus," she replied, keeping her voice low.

"What? You must be in a bad area or the connection's bad."

"Yes, sometimes the connection is bad."

"I'd like to see you, Claire. Summer semester doesn't start for a few weeks; how about if I come up to Minnesota and spend a few days with you?"

"Oh, you don't have to do that; I'm in the middle of a mess with the kitchen remodel and working on getting my grandmother into a different living arrangement." She groped for excuses. "Plus, I have a cousin staying with me for a while, and there's no room here. I think I've got another week or two before I know more, and we can get together when I come back."

Marcus sounded disappointed. "I'd love to see you." He said. "It would be easy for me to fly up for a weekend."

"I know, but I'll be home soon." She reassured.

"How's your grandmother, Claire?"

"Oh, as well as can be expected. She probably won't come home, again."

"What are you going to do with the house? The market is rough right now, but I imagine you can sell it off for development, or ag, or something."

"I don't know, Marcus; I have not thought that far ahead."

"Well, the old town hasn't been the same without you."

She smiled. "How's everyone doing?"

"They all miss you."

"How's Shea?"

Marcus talked about Shea's summer job, and how excited she was that Claire had gotten her hooked up on an internship, assisting Tamara McCoy in New York. "Shea says she has you to thank for that."

"Oh, I think she did that on her own; her paper was really, really good." Claire sensed, rather than heard, Matt come up behind her. She felt his hands brush her hair across her shoulder and run down the middle of her back. She didn't dare turn around; instead, stepped away. "Well, I'd better get going."

"I didn't know you were busy, Claire. I'll give you a call tomorrow. Just in case I can change your mind, I'll take a look at some flight options and try to get up there to see you."

"Marcus-"she tried to protest, but he cut her off.

"I miss you, Claire."

Matt followed her, close enough that she could feel his breath in her hair. She knew he could hear every word. She became defiant for a moment, and turned quickly, glaring at Matt. "I miss you, too, Marcus."

She saw Matt's jaw clench and heard only part of Marcus's response. "'Glad to hear that. I was beginning to wonder..."

"Well, I'll talk with you later, Marcus. Bye-"

"Bye, Claire."

She flipped the phone shut, heard Matt swear under his breath, and he was upon her, crushing her to him and kissing her deeply. She tried to push him away, but he backed her into the wall, grabbed the hand that she was using to push him and held it above her head as he kissed her lips, her face, her throat. She protested, hotly, but he ignored it. Instead, he used his free hand to pull her body to his, meshing it into his own and glared down at her. She heard the phone drop to the floor as her hand, as if having a will of its own, reached up and roughly grasped the hair at the back of his head and pulled his face to hers, claiming him.

He kissed her, hungrily, and slid his hand down her arm, to her breast, then her buttock, lifting it and her bare leg to wrap around him as he lifted her and swung her around to fall upon her on the sofa, barely missing the coffee table with his knees.

They wove tightly to each other, and his hand reached under her shirt to touch her skin. He sat up on his knees and slowed, all the while watching her face, and pulled the shirt up before laying his lips on her tummy. She gasped as his hand cupped between her legs, rubbing her through the jeans and sliding a thumb under the cuff of her shorts. Her breath came in short gasps and he reached up to kiss her again, his tongue dancing with hers, and she felt his hand cup her breast.

Claire tried one last effort to stop the madness. "My God, Matt…" she breathed hollowly. He continued showering kisses on her neck, shoulder, and she felt her shirt pull up and his fingers across her nipple under the thin sports bra she had on. "This is crazy-"

He shushed her; she let him loosen the zipper on her shorts and she lifted her hips to allow him to slide them off her. He stopped, looked into her eyes, and she felt his fingers glide smoothly into her body and caress as she cried out, and closed her eyes, felt the heat of the orgasm deep within her, could feel it radiate across her limbs, down her thighs, into her center, and she heard a keening sound that some primal part of her knew was her own.

As the spasms continued, she moaned, deeply. Through her lashes she saw him remove his shirt, saw the beautiful body that she had once owned, older, now, but still the same, saw him unbutton and pull the hips over his jeans, and the moan turned into a low, guttural howl as he sank into her, as far as he could go.

They rocked, and moaned, called out to God, and to one another. All sense of time was lost; the rhythm of each other, the dance, overtook them both, and, when the music subsided and faded away, Matt pulled her body, glistening with sweat and lovemaking, into his and wrapped himself around her on the narrow sofa.

It was Claire who moved first, without a word, slowly disentangling from his arms and searching for her panties and shorts on the floor. He reached out with his hand to touch her softly, and she slid away and crept up the stairs carrying her shorts. He watched her bare bottom sway as she went up the stairs and wanted her again.

When he heard Lyneah's car in the drive, he yanked his jeans on, this time banging his knee into the table as he balanced on one leg while he pulled his other leg

Lyneah walked in the door and popped her head around the corner of the living room. She took in his nonchalant look, the flush in his cheeks and his unruly hair, and grinned. "You all look like you just got caught with your fingers in the cookie jar, Matt." She drawled.

Claire came down the stairs, with her hair tied back and her clothes intact, looking cool but for the flush in her cheeks and the swelling of her lips. That, and she looked guilty as hell.

"Hmmph," Lyneah smiled, enjoying the obvious discomfort of the other two.

Matt smiled broadly, and Claire looked pained. "How did things go at your house?"

"Well," Lyneah sighed, "apparently, Diana and Chris Breuning cooked up this idea that they needed to search my house. Which, as it turns out, was not a bad idea. They found some smack under the trailer."

"Wow, really?" Claire.

"Yep. So, I went there, and they wouldn't let me in the house, and now it's really a mess, all torn up." Her eyes misted a bit. "Oh, well, Travis is here, and safe. Chris is going to stop here when they're done at my house and ask for my statement."

They talked for a while, until Matt said he'd have to get home. "You take care of yourself, Lyneah." He said to her as he hugged her good-bye. He turned his eyes to Claire, who wouldn't meet his gaze, and her cheeks turning a rosy hue when he reached down and pulled her to him, planting a hard kiss on her lips before he said, "Talk with you tomorrow," and headed out the door.

The two women looked at each other, and Lyneah burst out laughing. "Honey, you can't deny what happened here tonight. I can see it all over your face!"

Claire scowled. "Look, it's not going to go anywhere. We just got caught up in the moment." She shrugged her shoulders and padded in bare feet to the kitchen for a glass of water.

Lyn followed her there and leaned against the doorway. "Why not, Claire? That boy's crazy about you, has been since you were ten years old."

"Come on, Lyneah, not you, too."

"Me, too, what?" Lyneah's voice, normally fragile, was surprisingly strong. "Me, too, care about you, and want you happy? Claire, it might be worthwhile to just step back, close your eyes, and picture what it could be like instead of what it's been. Hell, I do it every day."

Claire felt apologetic. "I'm sorry, Lyneah. After what's happened-"

"No," Lyneah held up her hand. "Don't be sorry. There's nothing you did to feel sorry for. We can't rewind this tape, Claire. No one but Hank is responsible for Hank, or what he did. Not even me-" She closed her eyes, momentarily hesitating, as if to convince herself. "I wasn't around here when you and Matt had your thing, but I was here before, and I've been here since. I was here when he was married."

Claire bit her lip, not sure she wanted to hear any of this, but Lyneah continued. "People talk in a small town. They thought she was all uppity, and full of herself. 'Wouldn't go down to the clinic, like Doc Zen's wife used to do before he retired.' 'Looked like she was afraid to get her hands dirty.'

"She was a looker, but not in a stunning way. She was pretty, and petite, and had nice nails and nice teeth and nice clothes, but she never really quite fit in. People would snicker behind their menus, just the mean, small town ones, of course, the same ones that liked to talk about me. 'Couldn't really believe that a country vet married such a woman.'"

"Trust me, a waitress at the local bar gets to hear and see things most people probably don't want to," she smiled, wryly and reached for a glass. "Matt came in, acting like the devoted husband, and all that. Put on a happy face, always the gentleman, seemed like he was compensating somehow. Never once, though, did he ever look at her the way he looks at you. I've seen it. It's the same look he had on his face that day he carried you home after you fell when you were a little kid."

For a moment, Claire was speechless. "I don't know what to say," she finally replied. "I've been away too long, and we're all grown up now. Matt and I made too many mistakes with each other, knew each other too long, and got too comfortable. I just don't see me picking up my life and moving back here to try to rekindle something that died a long time ago."

"What do you think you've been doing, girl? 'Cuz when I walked in that door, it seemed to me that old flame was burning hot enough to singe my carefully tweezed eyebrows!" Lyneah raised her eyebrows a few times, licked a forefinger and touched an eyebrow, making a hissing noise. She and Claire laughed together as she filled the glass from the faucet.

Serious again, Lyneah sighed. "I think, just once, if you let yourself heal that scarred up heart, you will find that I'm right."

"I don't know, Lyneah. I've got a good life back in Illinois now. It's not something I can easily move away from." She paused. "Fact is, there's a man I've been seeing there, someone I care about very much, and I don't want to hurt him, or mislead him. He's been calling, wanting to come here."

"Oh, girl, that will not be a good idea."

"Oh, I know," Claire said quickly, "but the idea reminds me of the life I have that is not here, anymore. My job. The University. My friends. My students. And Marcus. If I really think about this, I realize that this dalliance, or whatever it is, cannot lead to anything. Matt, well, I'll always, always love Matt, but that's, like, a little girl's fairytale. I'm not that little girl, anymore."

"I really don't think Matt would like to be considered a dalliance."

Claire sighed. "You know what I mean. I knew when I left here all that time ago that I'd have to deal with Matt sooner or later, but I really didn't expect any of this to happen. I was going to keep him at a distance until Grandma got better, then I was going to go back home."

"But you *are* home here, Claire. Don't you feel it?"

It hit Claire that it was exactly what she felt, as recently as this evening when Matt had arrived with the puppy. And she wasn't ready to face it. Not yet, anyway.

"Well, like you said, Lyneah, we don't have a rewind button; none of us can go backward and make things different."

"Tell me about Marcus."

"Well, he's a Professor at the University. We've known each other since I started teaching there. He's smart, and funny, and nice..." Claire's voice trailed off.

"Sounds like he really rocks your boat."

"Well, what do you want to know?" Claire asked. "He's been my friend for a long time. We started dating, maybe a year ago, off and on. We're both pretty busy, and he's working on tenure, while I've been doing research for publication, so neither of us has much time. He's funny, he's charming, he's handsome. He cooks…"

"Okay. But does he rock your boat?"

"'What do you mean, rock my boat?" Claire demanded.

"Has he ever, ever made you feel like Matt made you feel tonight?"

"Oh, for God's sake, Lyneah, it's different. It's always been different with Matt, but that does not make it real. Marcus is a good man. Matt's more like, a drug, like something that makes you feel good now, but when it's gone, and the euphoria wears off, you think maybe you shouldn't have taken it, because it's not good for you. I care about Marcus. But you can't compare my feelings for each of them, because they are not the same, nor will they ever be." She was feeling troubled. "It doesn't mean that our relationship can't grow into something more. He fits my life."

Lyneah's voice was gentle. "I just wish you would let yourself realize that, if you cared about this guy as much as you care for Matt, you would never be able to let another man even glance your way."

"I know." She looked downcast, troubled. "Quite frankly, I'm mortified at my own behavior. I know that Marcus cares for me, perhaps in a way I can't care for him, but he does not deserve a relationship with someone who is not with him fully. I can't go back and undo anything, but I do have to step back and think about this. 'Which is never possible when I'm around Matt."

Lyneah nodded, then put her arms around her shorter cousin. "Somehow, this will all work out. No, you're right, you can't undo the past, none of us can, but it's what you do now that matters most."

She reached for the phone on her hip and answered its ring. It was Chris Breuning, saying he'd gotten delayed and would not be stopping by, since it was late. Could he come by, tomorrow?

She said yes, and the two women locked down the house, checked on Travis and the pup, who was curled up beside him, and headed to their rooms. Neither woman slept.

Chapter Fifteen

Chris secured a search warrant for Hank Beaudine's last known address, and Big Bob was not happy about the process.

"Fuck you think you're doin'?" He demanded as detectives swept into the house mid-morning. Big Bob was sitting at the table, in a kitchen that was surprisingly clean, still wearing his chores clothes.

His Key bibs were damp from the hose he'd used to clean the barn after milking; cow manure had spattered the cuffs and leggings. He'd been in the middle of making breakfast on an old gas cook stove, the aged cast iron pan smoldering with thick slabs of side pork. He'd gone to the chicken coop, picked some nice big brown eggs, some with the down feathers from their nests still floating around the basket that was sitting on the Formica countertop.

The house had not been updated since the '50s. It was surprisingly neat, considering Big Bob was a bachelor, and lived alone in the house where he was raised. Both of his parents had passed on, and he, and his brother, Kenneth, who lived on his own place to the south, were the only siblings left who had interest in the farming. Too much work, they'd all said, as, one by one, they'd drifted away from the home place, leaving only Bob and his frail parents before they died.

Bob's dad, Walt, had been a heavy drinker in the day, getting up each morning to strong egg coffee, and a bottle of whiskey in the milk house to top it off. By mid-day, when the coffee was gone but the whiskey still there, Walt was usually three sheets to the wind, but surprisingly efficient. Bob, the youngest of the clan, big, quiet, and a little slow, would help his Dad to the house, piling him onto the vinyl easy chair, and go back out into the barn to finish the chores.

Bob's mother, Agnes, with an air of resignation around her thin lips, would take Walt's boots off, without a word, then go back into the kitchen and continue kneading the bread she made each morning. She was a fine cook, and kept the house neat and tidy, but, after Walt died in the '80s, when arthritis set in, she had been largely confined to her bed.

Big Bob moved one of the twin sized beds down the stairs to the small sewing room in the back of the house, next to the tiny bathroom on the main floor. The arthritis had gotten so bad in her knees that she couldn't navigate the stairs. Big Bob, surprisingly gentle with his mama, had taken care of her, helping her get dressed each morning, feeding her when her hands, gnarled with arthritis, could not lift the spoon to her lips.

When she passed a few years after Walt, Bob had a time of rebellion, drinking and carrying on. Had gotten into some trouble, and landed himself in jail for a few years, the last time for beating some rich kid to a pulp for talking smack at him in the bar. Luckily for him his brother had kept the farm going, and, when Bob got out the last time, Kenneth, who was even bigger than Bob, had taken him down and they'd had a "come to Jesus" meeting.

Now, Bob was angry, swearing up a storm, but he knew better than to cross the line, even if he wanted to take a swing at Chris, who was rather enjoying seeing the big guy squirm.

"You stay out of my ma's room!" Bob shouted to the ceiling, as detectives climbed the narrow stairs to the second floor. "Ain't nothin' in there you want." He glared at Chris, who grinned back and asked the two uniformed cops to stay with Bob while he conducted a search.

Chris climbed the steep stairs that creaked with each step, and walked through each room, as another agent who was searching through the second floor, glanced his way. The upstairs had not been dusted in years; a thick layer of dust covered all surfaces, but for the one room that was obviously Bob's. The room was his boyhood room, an old chest of drawers, worn from years of use, stood in the corner, some of its drawers open askew, and full of clothing that had been tossed in rather than folded. Dirty sheets covered the bed, clothes and old porn magazines were strewn around the floor. The room smelled of sweat and barn, and was, apparently, the one room in the house that Big Bob did not keep clean.

Chris opened each of the other two doors, one to the master bedroom, which had apparently remained untouched since Bob's mother died. Dust and cobwebs covered every surface.

He climbed back down the stairs. "Which room was Hank's?" He asked Bob.

Bob defiantly nodded to the back of the house. "Back there," he said. "Can I finish making my breakfast?"

"No. You won't starve." Chris walked through the house to the tiny room where Hank had spent his time. An old singer sewing machine stood in the corner; twin bed under the window. Antique dresser. No closet in this room, just a narrow, tin wardrobe that was hanging open, with some wool blankets and a few sets of sheets, faded and worn, on the shelf.

The bed was stripped bare of sheets and pillowcases, and a single down pillow, worn and stained, had been carelessly tossed on the bed. The smell of cheap men's cologne still lingered in the room. Chris searched every drawer. The waste basket in the corner was clean. There was nothing but a thin layer of dust and the stench of cologne that indicated anyone had stayed in the room recently.

Back in the foyer sat an old writing desk, and Chris sat down on the wood chair in front of it and opened the desktop, pulling out envelopes, one by one, from the stacks in the slots. Tax statements, milk checks, bills. He pulled out several envelopes addressed to Henry J. Beaudine, Hank within his circle of friends, from the Indiana Child Support Bureau, and placed them in a plastic bag.

He could hear the cops in the kitchen, talking as they worked, pulling out drawers from the cupboards around the sink, dumping kitchen gadgets, stainless flatware and hand-hewn knives on the countertop, far beyond Big Bob's reach. "Why don't we move to the living room," he heard one say to Bob, and heard the chair being pushed back from the table. 'Probably a good plan; wouldn't want Big Bob to get any idea about using the knives.

The watcher stayed in the shadows of an old hay barn on the far end of the grove, where he sat near the rafters, having climbed, like a kid, onto the top of the dusty bales. He was thin, wiry, and full of meth. He could barely see them from the distance, but he watched, catching glimpses of the cops as they walked around the farm. He saw a young officer pull into the yard, and reach in the back with a long leash, leading a large, black German Shepherd out of the car. He shook with paranoia, scratching at the scabs on his face, but did not leave his perch, convinced that he was invisible in his hiding spot.

He knew the Boss Man would be very unhappy about this turn of events and would come to clean up Hank's mess. The thought, along with the paranoia enveloping him in the aftermath of the smack he'd injected, made him shiver uncontrollably. It was time to find that fuckin' Beaudine and kick his ass before the Boss got back, or he and his goons would take care of them both.

He watched the cops filter out into the outbuildings, searching with flashlights in an old granary, the milking barn, various ramshackle sheds. He watched the dog, searching, trying to sniff out drugs around a place full of the smells of stillborn calves, cow dung and chickens. The watcher stayed put until he saw the cops leave the farm, waited until he saw Big Bob, the idiot, walk, in shit covered boots, out to the barn for his evening milking. Then, in the half light, the watcher slithered down the side of the shed and around the back, slipping into the grove surrounding the farmstead, running with constant, artificial energy, stopping every few yards to duck behind a tree, or slither through the shrubs.

He was paranoid, constantly looking into the sky. Fuckers are watching me. They got satellite tracking. It took him an hour to reach the car parked a mile away, so full of fear and drugs that he circled and zigzagged across fields, marsh and swamp, until he reached the car he'd parked along a dirt field road. There he stood leaning on the hood, coughing and hacking and twitching, hating the clean, cold air he'd endured because he'd been sent to take care of some business. When he could breathe again, he got in and started the car. He held his cold hands over the dashboard heater and cursed his hard luck.

Once again, Claire went into avoidance mode. Images of Matt filled her days, and sleepless nights. When she closed her eyes, she could taste his body, and feel his warmth against her skin. When he called her, she let the messages go unanswered. When his pickup turned into her drive, she quickly left through the back door of the house, skirted around the house and wandered down the beaten path that led to the old place, now overgrown from lack of use. She became restless. At night, she lay in bed, and read Eva's diaries, intrigued by the story of her grandmother, and the boy with whom she had fallen in love.

Claire and Lyneah took Travis to Flandrau State Park, the current site of what had been the POW Camp, Camp New Ulm, during World War II. The cabins were still maintained at the site of the old camp and were part of a park that included walking trails, a beach house lodge, and a swimming pool. The park was not yet open for camping and swimming, so Travis and his mother played on the playground while Claire walked through the camp, now modern and fresh, and marveled at the piece of history she had found in Eva's trunk.

She wandered between the cabins, peaking in the windows. Where had Erich slept? What had become of him? Claire knew that, when the war was over, in 1945, prisoners of war had been repatriated, and sent back home. Perhaps he still lived, at his home in the Black Forest, with a family, enjoying grandchildren, beautiful days. Now he would be old, perhaps stooped, and Claire's imagination pictured him sitting in a sunny window in a wheelchair, his gnarled hands, once rough with hard work, now idle, folded in his lap, and hair as white as snow atop his head, the brilliant blue eyes that Eva had described now faded.

It must have been difficult for Eva to watch her lover leave, first to spend the winter at Algona, then to leave the United States for good, never to return. What had it been like for the seventeen-year-old girl to watch him go? Did she await his return? Or was the young heart, easily mended at that age, no longer longing, as time, distance and life moved them farther apart?

Of course, Claire knew that her grandfather, Tom, Betty's brother, had been Eva's life partner. She wondered what he had known. To her knowledge, Tom had served in Europe during the war, had come home to marry his sweetheart, although there had been some time spent apart, since they had married in New Ulm in 1948, and Claire's mother, Isabelle, had been born just over a year later. They had immediately moved onto the farm, to care for Eva's ailing mother.

Claire had seen images of William and Abigaile, her great grandparents, in the old family photo albums that were perched in the bookshelves of the farmhouse. They had been a handsome couple, although William had a rather long face with a severe expression. Abigaile had been quite lovely, her hair swept up in the fashion of the time in a full chignon at the back of her head, soft tendrils of hair curled tightly around her face, her full lips somber, but her eyes seemed to dance with amusement in the sepia toned cards, as though she could see right into you.

Claire, during the annual trips to Minnesota, would sit in the living room on rainy days and pour over the old albums, searching for pictures of her great grandmother, and, when she found them, she would carefully lift the pictures from their paper corners so as not to pull the fragile glue from the black paper, and hold the pictures up, moving them slowly back and forth, so as to watch Abigaile's eyes follow hers.

When she told her mother, Isabelle had chuckled, the sound that even now Claire could hear, its soft tinkle, crystal clear and sweet. She confessed that she, too, felt that their grandmother watched from the faded pages of the photo album.

"There, you see this one," Isabelle's long finger had pointed to one of the entire Kelly clan. "This is Uncle Joe; he was a pilot, and Uncle Shane, who died in the war."

Her finger drifted lightly across the page. "And there is Grandma Eva, sitting in front of her Mom and Dad." The photograph was taken on the front porch of the farmhouse, the boys in jackets and slacks, standing behind where William and Abigaile were seated in wicker seats, and Eva was situated on a small stool in front.

In this picture, Abigaile looked severe, and her expression seemed more distant, unlike the photos of her when she had been a new bride. Eva's long hair was pulled into a bow at the back of her head, and she wore a sweater over a pretty dress dotted with tiny flowers. Joe was dressed in uniform, his visor hat sat jauntily tilted over his eye, and he grinned at the camera. Shane stood next to him, in the middle, a boyish grin on his handsome face, showing white, even teeth, and a dimple in his cheek.

"Who is that, mama?" Claire had asked, pointing at the man on the far right, standing nearest the window, and whose face was shadowed from the light in such a way that you could not see it but for the eyes, which sent a shiver down Claire's spine as she stared into them.

He had a look of cold defiance, and Claire snatched her hand from the image, feeling an alarming sensation of fear grip her. "He's really creepy, mommy."

Isabelle looked at the picture absently. "That is your grandmother's brother, Daniel."

"What is he like?"

Isabelle sighed. "Grandma never talks about him, but I think he was not a nice person. Not like Joe or Shane. Grandma says Daniel used to be rather mean, and then he went away. No one knows for sure where he is now." Young Claire continued to stare at the image, the glaring eyes, the defiant lift of the shoulders, the clenched jaw.

Later that evening, Tom and Edward had decided to go fishing. The evening was cooling off after a hot and humid day, and one could feel the breeze coming through the screens softly touch your damp skin.

June bugs, their fat brown bodies dancing awkwardly in the air, would periodically hit the screen with a soft tap, and in the distance, in the slough that furrowed through the ditch across the road, fireflies danced in the near darkness. Claire remembered sitting at her mother's feet after having taken a cooling bath, and her mother was brushing her hair while Eva rocked in a chair next to them on the porch.

The two women chatted for a while, then, Claire spoke up. "Grandma, I saw a picture today; you were really pretty. Your dress had flowers on it, and you were sitting with your Mom and Dad…"

Eva responded, looking over at her daughter's face in the shadows. "Which one was that?"

Isabelle replied, "The one of all of you, just before Joe went overseas."

"Ah, yes. Joseph was so handsome in his uniform that day. It was a Sunday, and he was home just for a short leave. We'd invited a bunch of friends and family to see him off." She sipped the lemonade she had squeezed earlier. "We were sitting right here, in fact. It was so cold that day, but Mama insisted we take the picture on the porch." She laughed, softly. "I remember sitting there, shivering, waiting for Betty's Dad to finally take the picture, and ran into the house as soon as it was done, trying to get warm."

"Was Grandpa here that day?"

"No, but his family and Auntie Betty were there. Your Grandpa Tom had been in an accident and he was recovering."

"What happened, Grandma?"

"Well, he was riding with a friend from school, Bud Fischer, I think, and they went off the road and ran into a tree. Bud wasn't hurt as much, but Tom ended up with some broken ribs and a broken leg, I think. I don't remember very much, but I do remember that he was pretty banged up. I went with Betty to the hospital to see him, and he had a big, black eye like he'd been in a fight!"

"Didn't he go to the war, too?"

"Yes, he did, but not until later."

"Grandma, who is Daniel?"

Eva's voice was quiet, and she took a while before she spoke. "Daniel was my brother, Claire."

"What happened to him?"

"He went away. He had a terrible temper. You never knew when he was going to get angry, fly off the handle; he threatened to leave so often most of us just didn't listen, anymore. One day he just left, and no one has seen him since then." She stopped, staring into the distance.

"You mean, he moved away and never called or wrote or anything?" Claire could not imagine ever leaving her mother and father. "Even his mom?"

"Yes." Eva said, distantly. Even at her young age, Claire could sense that it was painful for Eva to talk about Daniel. "It was hard for my mother; she had been through so much. When she died, we tried to locate him, but, back then, there was no internet to help track people down, like there is now, so we had no idea where he was at. He'd always talked about leaving, though, maybe going west."

"Did you ever try to find him after that?"

"I never really wanted to…"

Headlights from the road turned into the driveway, and Claire's mom spoke up. "Oh, look, Grandpa and Daddy are home! Do you think they caught any fish?"

And the conversation about Daniel had ended.

Chapter Sixteen

The body is a superiorly crafted machine; it is designed to withstand the pressures of gravity, and millions of cells work together to regenerate themselves, repairing the body from trauma. The mind, however, is delicate and mysterious. Damaged cells are not replaced; the brain cannot repair itself. All it can do is relearn and compensate for the loss. For some, the damage can be so crippling as to render the person to be a fraction, or a shadow, of the former self.

Claire stepped through the automatic doors of the Shady Oaks Elderly Care home, a modern, three-story nursing home, nestled in a quiet, upscale neighborhood in town, and felt the cool air caress her skin. The building was strategically placed in a grove of mature trees with a walkway lined in hostas and a spirea, now in full bloom.

The name of the nursing home made her cringe, connoting something out of a movie, the scary place that people threaten to send their elderly parent, played by Cloris Leachman or Olympia Dukakis, if they continued to misbehave. In truth, however, it was a wonderful place for her Grandmother, the care superb, and Claire smiled as she stepped into Eva's room.

Eva's physical therapist was Tammy, a tall, willowy figure, who had a bubbly personality and short cropped hair, streaked in an array of colors, some natural, some not, and a nose ring. She smiled back at Claire as she maneuvered Eva's limp arms. "Hi, there." She said. "Eva, your granddaughter's here!"

Eva, whose eyes were closed, did not respond, and Claire felt a tightening in her chest. "Hi, Grandma," she said breezily and bent down to kiss her grandmother's cool forehead. "How's it going today?"

Tammy placed Eva's arm across her lap, moved further down the bed, and began to massage and maneuver her left leg. Tammy's voice was robust, used to talking to people who could not hear well. "She's doing well, today, aren't you, Eva?" she said. "She slept well last night but wanted to take a little nap while we do her therapy today!"

During Eva's care conference, Tammy had impressed Claire with her philosophy on treatments. "We're not only treating Eva's body, we're treating her brain, teaching it to re-route signals from the area damaged by the impact and subsequent stroke."

While she was a certified physical therapist, Tammy also believed in the healing of body and mind through reflexology, and her words to Claire had been poignant and direct. "If there is anyone who understands the place where your grandmother is right now, it's someone who's been through the experience. I know I can help her; there are no guarantees of how much, but I know I can improve her quality of life."

At the age of fifteen, Tammy had been an avid athlete. She'd participated in a variety of sports, but hockey had been her passion. She was, she said, raised with two brothers and she had been fortunate to have learned how to be tough. They had lived on a lake near Ely, Minnesota, and her Dad had flooded the shore, year after year, creating an ice rink as smooth as glass right in their own back yard. She and her brothers had spent many days and nights on that rink, ripping pucks into the net, in the half light of the flood lamp that was attached to the back deck of their house.

'It didn't matter how cold it was, we were out there.' On one particular night, her brother challenged her to a race, from one end of the rink to the other. It had been a warm February, and the ice had begun to change, thawing and freezing, leaving rough spots. That night, Tammy was not wearing her helmet, just the old North Stars stocking cap her dad had given her, and she remembers feeling the crisp air on her breath and seeing the stars in the clear sky and knew she would beat him this time.

She took off, flying across the ice, hearing the swish, swish, swish of her skates slicing into the ice, and hearing her brother, Rob, right behind her. As she gained momentum, she turned to watch him gaining on her, and failed to see the chunks of ice that had formed from the early thaw. She tripped, lost her balance, and flew headfirst into the pipes, knocking her out.

When she came to, she was in the hospital. Her dad and Rob were there, and doctors all around her. She couldn't move the right part of her body, and she could not understand any of the words they said to her; it was like they were speaking in a foreign language. Tammy had been out for several days. She was frightened, not only hearing gibberish, but, when she tried to speak, was incoherent.

She would later find that, when she struck the pipe with her head, she had suffered a massive hemorrhage that had caused damage in her temporal lobe and her cerebral cortex, leaving her with almost complete aphasia. It had taken months of therapy to relearn how to understand language, and just as long to be able to walk. "I had a great team of therapists." She told Claire. "That's why I'm here today."

Claire crossed around the bed as Tammy was finishing up, and pulled a book from the drawer, sat down and prepared to read to Eva's quiet frame. She'd begun doing that on a regular basis, reading to her grandmother from old favorite books; it gave her a feeling of connection that was difficult to grasp when one tries to carry on a conversation with someone who was unable to engage.

"Okay, Grandma, we're on Chapter 3 of 'The Awakening," Claire continued reading the Kate Chopin novel, *"A feeling of oppression and drowsiness overcame Edna..."*

When she'd finished, she reached out her hand. "I'm going to be going back to Illinois this week, Grandma." She said gently. "But don't worry, Betty and Jer will be in to see you often, and Lyneah and her little boy, Travis, are staying at the house. I'll be back soon." She kissed her grandmother, goodbye, squeezed her hand gently, and left the room, all the while praying that nothing would happen while she was gone.

That evening, the old farmhouse was unusually quiet, and the heat of her upstairs bedroom was oppressive. She packed a few bags for the trip and pulled together some of the journals that were her grandmothers, crawled into bed, and continued reading.

October, 1944

It is an unusually warm October; almost like August. We are fortunate to have Erich helping on the farm, because it is near time for the crops to come in, and, from what Dad says, it will be a bumper crop, if it would just dry up, we've had so much rain. The normal workday for a PW is only eight hours per day, not something that is possible on a working dairy farm, particularly during harvest. The War Manpower Commission was smart enough to allow farmers to keep their hired hand for longer hours in the day, and that means that someone will drop Erich off at the camp later in the evenings, when the day's work is done.

Sometimes, I am the one who gets to drive Erich back, for my parents trust me, and Erich; he works hard, is polite and kind. Dad has been increasingly sick this year, sometimes doubling over with pain in his back and I notice he seems to have a tremor of sorts, ever so slight, but it is there. I am concerned; he will not, however, go to the doctor, and, instead, leaves more and more of the responsibility of the barn to me. Erich and I work well together, and we visit while we milk.

"Tell me about the camp, Erich," We are feeding the heifers from the freshly cut haystack, wheeling in load after load and dropping it into the feeder. It is warm, and I can feel the damp sweat as it catches in the scarf I have tied around my hair. "What are the others like?"

The sun has made him flushed, and he has removed the tunic he is required to wear; it is hanging on a hook in the milk house. He shrugged, "It is nice. Food is good."

"How about the others that live with you, other soldiers…"

"We haf' many there, some who are old-timers, great Nazis, and others who are young, who do not believe so much in the, eh, purpose of the war. You must be careful, keep your mouth shut, sometimes. The officers are arrogant, still believe that they must command their soldiers as they did back in Germany."

"How do they treat you," I asked.

He glanced my way, then grabbed the wheelbarrow and hauled it back to the hay pile. "I am careful. Sometimes, the walls have ears. I am fortunate that I am not there very much. One of the higher officers does not like me much. He thinks my English is too good."

I stopped next to the hay pile and picked up the quart jar that we had filled with water from the sistern moments ago, taking a drink of the tepid water. "What can you do about it?"

Erich shook his head. "Nothing, Eva. Here, I am a farm worker; there, I am a Leutnant zur See, a soldier. The officers who serve my country under General -Feldmarschall Rommel take this very seriously, and believe that, one day, they will be here to greet their comrades when Germany invades the United States."

I was a bit taken aback by that. "That's not going to happen, Erich. I mean, the newspapers say we'll be done with this war by the New Year." I handed him the jar.

He took a swig and wiped his mouth with the back of his hand, pulling a kerchief from his trouser pocket and wiped his brow. "The young ones, the ones who came to the army later, they are rebellious, and disinterested. They like it here. They have more food and are safe. They even sometimes, sneak out of camp at night, and cross through the river, sometimes to meet girls from town."

He smiled and shook his head. "But, you see, if they are not careful, and do not keep quiet, the SS officers will accuse them of being traitors. They may be beaten. That is why I stay silent." He smiled down at me.

I shook my head, not believing what I was hearing. "What about the guards?"

He again shook his head. "The guards are blind. They are not real soldiers. They do not want to be involved and, I think, are happy to leave the disziplin to our Kommandeure."

"What kind of discipline is there, Erich?"

He shrugged. "I do not know, but I have heard of some having their food rations cut and being confined. 'Extra work around the camp. There is a new woodstove in the main building, and one solder, Ludwig, was caught sneaking back *into* the camp, so he spent a week chopping wood!" He laughed at that. "I hope it was a worthy trip!" his eyes twinkled, and I felt myself blushing as I laughed with him.

After feeding the heifers, we cross over to the barn and begin setting up for the milking. I pull my barn shirt from the hook next to Erich's, and hand his to him. In the pocket, is a book, and I ask him about it.

"Ah, yes," he pulled it from the pocket, handed it to me to look at. The cover has a bird on the front and is titled Soldbuch. I page through it, and, of course, it is in German, a language I cannot read. I glance at the cover again, and see that there is an eagle, with the Nazi symbol on the cover, and I feel uneasy.

"What is it?"

"It is my papers. Eh, *my* documents. My number, and rank," He pointed to words in the book, but I only shake my head and paged through, spotting a photograph of him in the cover.

"Oh, Erich, you are so handsome!"

He grinned. "Here," he said, and carefully pulled the photo from the book. "You keep."

I thanked him and fingered the photo. "It is so worn, I can barely see your eyes."

"Yes. When I escape the u-boat, all was wet. I wrapped it in cloth, to dry out, but much of the book is destroyed."

"You carry it always?"

He nodded. "Yes. It is the book of my life. I am fortunate to still have it; many others whose soldier book was not so worn, had theirs taken by the American guards when we were moved from camp to camp."

As I handed him the book, some coupons fell to the ground. He picked them up and placed them back in the book. "Canteen coupons," he said, absently. "They are to buy things at the store at camp."

As we set about doing the chores, I have a moment of melancholy. He is not of this world, and, soon, he will be taken from me. It is unsettling, and I grew quiet. Erich, too, seems deep in thought, perhaps thinking the same. We both know that, at any moment, he could be sent away. When the canning season is over in Sleepy Eye, many of the soldiers will be sent back to Iowa for the winter. We may never see one another again, and that thought leaves a heavy knot in my stomach.

Sunday mornings, Erich does not come to the farm, even for harvest. I dressed for church, and mom and I drove into town. I am so happy to see Betty there, and my eyes mist up as I hug her at the door of the church. She looks well, but thin, although she has the same beautiful smile as she hugs me back. "Let's go downtown for breakfast, shall we?" she said.

'We linked arms and walk the few blocks to the cafe, crowded with people stopping in after church. We finally found a tiny table in the back and clamor into them before they are taken. Betty talks as she removes her gloves; her nails were painted a brilliant crimson, but rough from the work she was doing at the cannery.

"I have so missed you, Evie!" she breathes and turns the ceramic coffee cup right side up from its cradle on the matching plate as the waitress stops to fill the cup. I, too, overturn my cup; it's been so long since I had real coffee, the smell is luxurious, and I close my eyes and soak it in for a moment. Barley coffee is not a good substitute for the real thing.

"Tell me, Eva, how are things going?" she poured cream into her cup and stirred, leaving out her customary sugar because, due to rationing, sugar was no longer available on the tables of the coffee shop.

We talked. About Shane, and Joe, and Jerry, who was completing his training in Texas. I could tell that Betty was worried, but she tried not to show it, and kept a positive outlook. "I hate this damned war," she said. "But we all have to keep going." She sipped her coffee. "Tommy is also completing his training." She said casually, setting her cup down. "He sent me a letter the other day."

"Oh?" I replied. "That's nice." I took a quick sip of my coffee, burned my tongue, and winced. "How is he?"

"He's doing well. He's also in Texas, but I'm sure you know that, because he said he'd sent you a bunch of letters, and has not heard from you, yet."

I looked away and shook my head. "I've been, well, busy. Dad's not been well, and I've been working more." I felt guilty. "I should write to him, soon."

Betty leaned over and put her hand on mine. "You know, I would not ask, but he's my brother, and it may ease his mind a little, make him focus more on winning the war."

"I know, Betty. I'm just busy."

"Clark tells me that you have a hired hand from the PW camp." She said. "'Sounds like he's at the farm, quite a lot. What's he like?"

I shrug, trying to be nonchalant. "He's very German. He's quiet. He works hard." I laughed, a sound which to my ears sounded like a nervous chortle. "I don't know what to say, Betty. What do you want to know?"

"Oh, I don't know. Is he handsome?"

"Well, yes."

"What does he look like?" she asked. I was acutely aware of the buzz of the busy little coffee shop, the people around us, and the gossip that would often have its roots right in this little establishment.

I lowered my voice. "Really, Betty, let's talk about something else."

"Oh," she replied, looking around. "All right."

"Tell me what it's like to be married."

"Well, I really don't know, since Jerry left right after the wedding night!" we both laughed at that and spoke more about her family. Then she said, "Say, I hear that Danny got a job as a driver for the prison camp. Is that true?" Betty was very aware of how much I disliked my older brother; she'd grown up along with me and had done her best to steer clear of him as a child.

"I don't know. If so, Mom and Dad have not said anything to me about it." The thought of it made me slightly ill, for it was the last thing we needed, with his hatred of all things German, and his arrogance.

As we walked back to the church where Betty's car was parked, we stopped in front of the hardware store, and took in the sight of the display in the window. Along with the usual Halloween jack-o-lanterns and black cats, there were, leaning into the far corner of the bay window, two guns and a dome helmet which had the same insignia on the side that was on the cover of Erich's soldier book. There was a handwritten note pinned to the wall that said they were "tommy" guns, souvenirs, sent back to the United States by the son of a local merchant, as a Christmas present.

After Betty drove me home, I hugged her, and she gently touched my face. "Eva, please, even if you are not sure of your feelings for Tom, please, send him a postcard, just to lift his spirits a bit. He needs to put all of his energy into staying alive."

"I will, Betty. I promise."

Chapter Seventeen

Claire drifted to sleep, only to be awakened by a loud banging noise. Startled, she sat up in the bed, feeling her heart pounding in her chest. The banging continued, and she realized it was coming from the front porch door. She quickly climbed out of the bed and threw a light cotton robe on before heading down the stairs, cautiously, to see what all the commotion was. Lyneah and Travis had gone to the cabin with Diana, and had taken the pup with them, so Claire was alone. She approached the door and heard shouting on the other side.

"Claire, open the damned door." Matt. And sounding none too happy.

Not sure if she was relieved or even more anxious, she entered the security code into the pad next to the door, slid the lock, and opened it. Matt stepped past her without so much as a sidelong glance, stepping heavily into the house.

They faced each other across the table, neither one willing to start the conversation. Finally, Claire took a deep breath and began, quietly, "I have to go back, Matt."

"What the hell are you doing, Claire?" He demanded.

She didn't respond, and he continued, "What was this? Huh? What was the other night? You think you can go to him and just forget all about what's happened here?"

"It's what *you* did."

He stared down at her, then brushed a hand through his hair, and started to pace. "Claire, Jesus, we were kids then. Impulsive. Stupid—I don't know, but this, this is real."

Claire shook her head. "No, it's not real. It wasn't then, and it isn't now. I came back here because of my grandmother, not to take up with someone I haven't known in almost twenty years. I mean, did you think that we would just pick up where we left off that long ago? I have a life, separate from here, and, I suppose, I have you to thank for some of that."

"What?" Matt's voice was explosive. "*Thank* me? Are you kidding?"

Claire fought to remain calm. "Maybe that didn't come out the way it should. I just meant that, if we'd stayed together all those years ago, who knows where we'd be? I could be stuck here, in this town.." she faltered, uncertain.

"Oh, I get it. You wouldn't want to be stuck with some small-town animal doctor living in the sticks, surrounded by people who love you."

Claire knew that hit home with Matt, considering what had happened in his marriage, but she held her ground. "No. If you're talking about yourself, then don't bring that word into this, Matt. We don't even know each other. One moment of indiscretion does not make this love."

"*Indiscretion*! Is that what you call it?" Matt was incredulous. "Well, I guess what we call it in these parts is a roll in the hay…"

"There's no need for sarcasm. Can't we discuss this like rational adults instead of ending up fighting?"

"Sure. Like you did when you decided to hide from me every time I drove in the yard. Nice, Claire."

She shook her head, derisively. "I just didn't know what to say. It seemed better not to say anything at all."

Matt just looked down at her, shaking his head. "So, now what? You gonna go back to the boyfriend? Is that what you want, Claire?"

She looked down. "I don't know what I want, Matt. But I have to go home and take care of some things."

"That includes him." It was a statement, not a question.

"Yes. I guess it does."

He walked out. She cried herself to sleep.

November, 1944

We are a few weeks from Thanksgiving; the autumn leaves are gone, and the nights are so long, it is dark by 4:30. It has become bitterly cold. There is gossip that the PWs are going to be sent south, for the winter, to Iowa, or maybe even further. I can't think about losing Erich, but, at the same time, I cannot picture a future. When I look into the future, it is empty of Erich, and this sense makes me fearful for him.

We do not get as much time together as before. With the change in season, the rules have tightened. Daniel is driving the PW bus now, which makes it very difficult; he is always angry, always mean. Dad rarely leaves the farm. He is growing thin, his face is gaunt, haunted, shoulders stooped.

Mama nearly caught Erich kissing me in the milk house the other day; we stepped apart and Erich slipped into the barn just as she swung the door open. She stood there in the door, sunlight like a hallo around her head blinding me for a moment for its brilliance, shining into the dark room with its single swinging bulb and small window. She watched the half-door swing then crossed over to push her way into the barn and looked about. Erich had managed to slip out the back, into the calving pen, and when she came across him, he was pitching straw around the calving cow.

Mama came back into the milk house and stood next to me, eyeing me suspiciously, before speaking.

"Eva, you spend too much time with that boy."

"Mama," I protested, cheeks flushing. "We work together."

"You're too close to him. I want you to stop spending so much time together."

"Who have you been talking to, Mom? Danny?"

"That's not what this is about. I don't want you alone with him, anymore."

"How, Mom?" I asked, callously. "Who else is going to come out and work here? Danny's a drunk, and Dad can't even get out of bed."

"Do not disrespect your papa, you hear me, Missy?" Mama's Irish heritage comes out when she's angry, and you can hear the lilt in her voice. "Your father is a good man, child, and you will not speak ill of him on this farm."

"I'm not. But Erich and I are the only two here. You're being silly…"

Her eyes narrowed. "Heed my words, girl and watch your step. I can have them send someone else, you know."

I stared, helplessly. "Mom don't worry. I'm –I'm a good girl."

She gripped my arm. "You'd best stay that way." And she turned and walked firmly back to the house.

Joe has been reactivated to the 20th Division and battles the Japanese somewhere in the Pacific. Letters from him are sporadic, but I believe he's somewhere in the Philippines, where a battle rages for a tiny place called Leyte. The things I see in pictures from Europe are horrific, dead soldiers, callously photographed and printed next to advertisements for Old Crow bourbon and models in the newest fashions for the "under 20" girls. I am both fascinated and repulsed by these images, sometimes imagining Erich or Shane there, lying crushed and bleeding in the rocks next to tanks and dead horses.

We will have Thanksgiving dinner at home. We've been fattening up a couple of turkeys that we bought as chicks last spring, from the turkey barns, and have raised throughout the summer. Mom will butcher the largest of the birds for our dinner, stuff it with herbs and bread, and bake it for most of the morning. The house will smell of heaven, and, when I come in from the barns, I will feel the heat of the kitchen on my cheeks, making them tingle, and the scents of sage and onion, mingled with apple pies and molasses cookies fresh from the oven. She will use the syrup that we tapped from the maple trees in the grove and cooked down for days over the woodstove in the shed, to make pumpkin pies, because sugar is in such short supply, and the pies will taste of pumpkin and nutmeg, with a distant flavor of smoky maple.

We will invite Betty and her parents and have homemade dandelion wine and apple cider and fresh, frothy milk from the barn; the only thing missing will be my brothers and Jerry. And that breaks my heart.

December, 1944

The days are cold, and short. We continue to hear word that the war will be over soon. Thanksgiving came and went. I continue to be careful, so as not to fuel Mama's suspicions. Erich is working shorter days, now, and we do not see each other as we did, just weeks ago. We are preparing for Christmas, this year a dire affair, and waiting for some sign that our friends and brothers and husbands will return to us, soon.

I am torn, ravaged with guilt and fear, and sadness. Each day I realize that Shane will never come home again. I will never hear his lilting voice as he calls my name, often teasing Mom by fashioning a fancy Irish brogue, and wearing her apron, like a kilt. Oh, how she would blush, and laugh at him as he swung her around the kitchen, his eyes twinkling, singing "Danny Boy" as loudly as he could. He'd put a sad look on his face and dramatically touch his heart, and she would giggle and tell him to shush. I am certain I will never hear my mother giggle again, as long as I live.

The hardware store and downtown shops are busy, strung with lights, and wreathes adorn every door. At least, pine trees are still in abundance, even if everything else is rationed. Artificial mistletoe adorns the door between our kitchen and dining room, and I wonder who will kiss whom under that door this year.

I receive fewer letters from Joe and even fewer, now, from Tom. I haven't even opened any from him, yet; they are hidden in an old hat box underneath my bed, and I sometimes lie awake at night and want to open them but am too ashamed to do so. I cannot bear to see the words, at first optimistic and caring, then increasingly impatient. I am not doing right by Tommy, and I cannot deny that I do not open the letters because I do not want to know. It is heartless of me, cruel, not to respond, and, although Betty does not say anything, anymore, she looked upon me with curiosity, a guarded expression on her face, when, at Thanksgiving, conversation turned, more often than not, to the war.

Betty has grown thin. There is worry etched into her lovely face, the same look I see in so many faces. Jerry is completing his training now and is now learning aircraft maintenance in Indianapolis. Betty had hoped that he would be stationed for that training in Sioux Falls, so that she would be able to see him, but that was not to be. He will ship out soon; she does not know where, but we all tried to encourage her; maybe he'll be the mechanic for Joe. At least he will not be in the infantry. He and Joe together can bring the Japs down so they can all come home.

Tom is in Europe, a Lieutenant. It appears that he is some sort of radio operator, and is close to the frontline, which is frightening for all of us. From the news that the Nielsen's have gleaned, he is somewhere in a mountain area called the Ardennes, a mountain region stretching somewhere between Germany and France. He reads maps and coordinates the men in battle. Tommy is smart, and confident, and always reassuring that he is safe in this dangerous mountain region, but I know it wears on all of them, particularly Rebeka.

Yesterday, I drove into town and met Betty to look at the Christmas decorations around town, and to do some shopping. It is bitterly cold, and we both bundled up in our coats and walked along the sidewalk, peering into the windows of the shops and browsing the aisles. There is a war bond going on, the sixth for our state, and there is a table of volunteers set up at the hardware store. Betty stopped and chatted with them, and purchased a few, but I wandered the aisles, picking up a colorful scarf and a tiny bottle of perfume for my mom to wrap in brown paper and stick under the tree when she is not looking.

The cafe was warm and inviting when we stopped for lunch. We sat in our favorite corner, as close to the old fuel burner as we could get, and warmed our hands around the porcelain cups, Betty with tea, me with coffee, which was a wonderful treat.

We joked that the owner of the shop, old Mr. Shumacker, had an inside person on the black market, because he always had coffee, the best around, and never seemed to ration. Betty sipped slowly but did not touch the warm slice of pie that Beatrice placed in front of her. We stared out the window for a while, enveloped in silence as the bustle of holiday shoppers walked by, sometimes stopping to greet each other, or stopping to chat but not for long, the cold was so deep it would seep into your bones and leave your feet numb if you stood too long.

Finally, Betty spoke. "I'm pregnant."

I reached out to touch her hand. "Oh, Betty, that's wonderful…"

She smiled, her cold fingers clasped mine, briefly. "Yes, it is."

"Have you told anyone? Does Jerry know?"

She looked down. "I have told no one but you."

"When will you have the baby?"

"Next Spring."

I was happy for her, for this gift, but it seemed so unreal. "How are you feeling?"

"I feel scared, Eva." Her eyes filled with tears. "I am so frightened that Jerry won't come home and meet our baby." She pulled a neat, monogrammed kerchief from her handbag, and dabbed her eyes quickly.

"Oh, Betty, he'll come home. They all will..." my voice trailed off, thinking of my sweet Shane, who will never come home, forever buried somewhere a million miles away.

She shook her head. "We know that's not true, Eva. This war never ends, and so many of the people we care about are gone."

"Shh, it's ok, Betty." I tried to give her comfort, even though, inside, I felt the same. "Jerry and Tom are strong and smart. They'll be back. I'm sure of it."

Betty worried over the kerchief and dabbed her eyes again, and sipped her tea, stared out the window before speaking. "Tom's in Europe." She turned her clear, deep eyes back to me, and I looked down, busying myself with pouring fresh cream into my coffee.

"Eva, look at me." She beseeched me, and when I did, she reached her hand to mine. "I'd understand that you do not feel the same way that he does. It's all right, but please, know you can talk to me, too, any time you need to." She squeezed and released my hand. "I worry about you, too..." Betty's voice trailed off.

I let out a little laugh and put on my best Vivian Leigh look. "Why, whatever for?"

"Because you are not the same, and I know that something's going on with you."

My heart skipped a beat. "What do you mean, Betty?"

"It's all over town that you've been carrying on with one of the PWs that work on your farm."

I sat back and stared, suddenly feeling ill. "That's ridiculous." I scoffed. "Who on earth is saying that?"

"Susan Thommes' sister, Sharon, was talking with someone at the canning factory, and I overheard her saying something about a handsome blonde German that she saw you with, out in the fields."

"Oh, for heaven's sake, Betty, you know how people talk. It's nothing." I sat back in the chair and daintily dabbed my lips with a tissue. "Really, Betty; Sharon has been running with that crowd Danny's in. He's just a troublemaker, does nothing around the farm, but goes off and drinks his moonshine and talks like he knows, but he's just a gossip."

She shook her head and leaned forward. "Eva, you can tell me. I will always be by your side." Her beautiful Bohemian eyes grew even darker.

"But be careful," she warned. "This could get back to your mother. Who knows what could happen really? We're talking about *treason* here, Eva, not some summer romance! *Treason.*"

I didn't know what to say at first, but then I shook my head, knowing inside that I could tell *no one*, not even my best friend for a lifetime. It was a secret too deep and too dark to share of my shameful behavior, and how could Betty understand what I cannot understand myself?

I changed the subject. "Tell me about Tommy, Betty. Where is he? I have heard horrible things about the Nazis."

She looked at me skeptically, and replied, "You'd know if you read the letters, Eva."

My face flushed with shame. "I know."

She sighed, sniffled again, and began to tell me of Tom. The more she talked, the more shame I felt. Tommy had completed his training and moved up the ranks as a Lieutenant, and was now, somewhere in Belgium or Germany. The news is ominous; there are report coming in that heavy blizzards of snow and blistering cold have hindered our progress in Europe.

Our local draft board has been busy, sending young boys for training. There are rumors of untrained boys being sent to battle Nazi monsters, only to be slaughtered or taken into captivity. Some say that there are even Generals who are cracking up, leaving the men in their command and being sent to military hospitals in Great Britain.

Susan Thommes is also in Europe and Betty said she had a call from Susan's brother, Al, who said that he heard Tommy was somewhere in Belgium as a radio specialist. I do not know what that means, but Betty said he would relay information between divisions out in the fields. He was not in artillery but was close to the front lines.

Al also told her that Susan was in a makeshift hospital somewhere near the lines, and I wondered if she and Tommy were together, somewhere, there, and felt a sinking feeling inside of me. Does Betty know how much I feel so separated from the girl that he kissed goodbye that day to the woman who is unable to stop loving an enemy? I am loathe to hear more, and turn the topic to other things.

"We should walk down to the hardware store, Betty; I hear that Santa is going to be there today. Would you like to go see the children?"

"Sure," she replied, and we finished up in the coffee shop, slipped our coats and hats on, and strolled down the lane to watch children stand in line to talk with Santa, who had ridden into town on a horse-drawn buggy, bedecked with bags of candy, peanuts and apples to give to the children.

They wait, patiently, holding the hands of their parents, bundled up against the cold. If only there were snow, the picture would be perfect. But this year, it is cold and the landscape still dreary and cavernous, the beauty of autumn has faded into patches of black and brown. Still, it is a joy to see them so excited.

I finished chores alone tonight, a few evenings before Christmas. Mom and Dad are gone, visiting Auntie, and I hurried to get through the last feedings, my fingers numb and the cold is biting through my overshoes, leaving my feet painful and I feel as though I'm hobbling to the house. It is dark here, already, at 4:30 and I clean up, feeling the steam of the bath envelope me as I pour in a tiny bit of the scented soap mom keeps in the linen closet.

Dad had called earlier this evening, to tell me that they had blown a tire somewhere near Waterville, and they were not able to get it repaired until morning. They were staying the night with a friend there. Please don't worry, I had told them. I'll be fine; I'll do the milking and be in by dark. When Mom got on the phone, she insisted that she call someone to stay with me, and I insisted that I was not a child anymore, and please, don't worry. I'll bake bread out of the yeast mix you have going for Christmas and eat the chicken in the icebox with it.

She finally agreed, but reluctantly, I could tell. I stepped out of the bath and was drying off when I heard a knock down at the door, which startled me. I threw on the first thing I grabbed, which was a tea dress hanging on the door to my room, and quickly buttoned it, calling "Coming," as I ran down the hall when the knocking became more insistent.

I approached the door and peaked through the draperies. Erich was standing in the cold, rubbing his hands together. He had a wool coat over him, and a hat on his head. I threw open the door and pulled him in.

"What are you doing here?" I asked, breathlessly.

He said, "I was working at the place down the road. And, when the bus came, I hid." His German accent seemed heavy tonight as his teeth chattered from the cold. "I wanted to see you, Eva."

"Erich, you must be careful." I stood quaking. "What will happen if they find you?"

"They will not, not yet; I'll run back later. There are festivities tonight, and my friend will cover for me for a while."

"What friend?" I was demanding, feeling fear in my heart, and also, joy that he had risked so much to see me. "How could you know my parents were gone?"

"I did not; I thought I would find you in the barn or wait until later. Then I saw that the car was gone. And I knew you were here…" His voice trailed away.

"Oh, Erich," I breathed and he came to me, wrapped his arms around me and kissed me deeply. I took his hat off and touched the silvery strands with my fingers, feeling stubble where it had been cut short. "You've gotten a haircut."

"Jah," he smiled down at me, caressing my wet tresses. "You have not."

We went to sit on the sofa, and I snuggled next to him. "I do not have much time, Eva." He said. "We will be leaving the camp soon, I think. There is much talk; much of it not shared with me because they are suspicious of me, I am too "English"."

He smiled at me. "Ve are very careful there, to not anger the officers, who believe that the war will be won by Germany soon. But, Eva, I know that is not true." He held my hand as he spoke. "They think the newspapers are just propaganda, but I know that we will not win, and I know that I will be set free, to leave here."

His blue eyes were insistent. "Eva, I love you. When I can, I will come for you. I want you to be my wife."

"Oh, my God, Erich," I was astonished. I had never considered the possibility that this could happen.

"Yes, Eva! This war will end, and, because I am here, in America, I am safe. It is only time, now, until we are liberated and can be free of the war, and this, this secret." He drew me close and we held tightly to each other.

He reached into his pocket and drew out a small object, wrapped delicately in a U.S. issued PW handkerchief. "This is for you, Eva. Merry Christmas."

He handed it to me, and I opened it slowly, to reveal a tiny carved horse, intricately carved into walnut, every curve and flank perfectly honed and polished to an impossible shine. It was tied to a long piece of leather bootlace, and glimmered in the dim sitting room, lit only by the kitchen light in the next room.

"It is so beautiful, Erich." I breathed. "You made it, didn't you?"

"Yes. My father is a carver. He taught me. We, at the camp, have many carving tools that someone brought for our use. We had a contest, and carved the, the, eh, krippe." He searched for the words. "Baby Jesus. Mutter. Father."

He smiled, and I felt such a flush of pleasure to see his beautiful face. "I carved this, at night, when everyone was asleep. For you, my Eva." He gently placed it around my neck, and I felt it against my skin.

I stood and took his hand, then, walked through the kitchen to the stairs to my room. We made love then, sweet and, for once, unhurried. I was so in love with this man, who was to be my husband. Every touch, every sense awakened, until we lay back, together, spent, stroking each other softly in the sparkling light of the bright winter moon.

Soon, though, he had to go back, and he dressed quickly as I put on my robe. Downstairs, by the door, we stole kisses, and he put on his coat and cap, lingering for just a moment to touch my hair and kiss me a last time before heading into the cold night. We smiled to each other, professing words of love. "Soon, my Eva," he said and opened the door.

"Oh, my God," I could hear the whisper of my voice inside my head; did I say the words? "Daniel."

Chapter Eighteen

Claire's drive from the airport to the farm seemed endless. The constant, unseasonable rain was pounding down on the windshield, and she drove slowly. The windshield wipers could not keep up with the torrent of rain and the highway was flooding out in several areas. She kept her distance from other cars, but sometimes they came too close for comfort, and her hands clenched the wheel as she tried to stay the course.

The last ten days had been filled with such a mix of emotion that she could not even contemplate. Marcus had been so kind, genuine, she had so enjoyed the company. She had spent time in her office again, where she caught up on paperwork, spent time with other faculty and caught up on the campus events. It had been relaxing, a place where she felt safe, in her little cubby, with its tall, narrow window overlooking the lawns. Everyone had welcomed her back, and it had felt good, and real.

She had spent moments alone, in her home, reading Eva's journal, and had been completely shocked by the revelations she had found there, which she had been unprepared for. The secrets Eva had harbored all these years were so well kept; Eva had never, ever let on the love that she had encountered as a young girl. And Grandpa Tom had always been so happy, so full of love for her, it had never occurred to her that the love story they had always shared had not been as they had implied. What had he known? What had Betty known, and kept all those years? Claire had only taken a few of the journals with her, and she was anxious to go home, and continue Eva's journey.

She also knew that she had to see Matt, and she was filled with anxiety about how it would go. One thing she knew for sure; she had waited her entire adult life to come to resolution regarding Matt, and now was the time.

She turned down Main Street and slowed, looked into the old cafe, now an insurance office, and felt sadness for the times gone. How do we really know what we will become? In all her life, she had continued to seek and search the answers to that question. There had been so many lives touched by war, by changing times. Perhaps, after all, she would finally find her destiny. She smiled to herself wryly as she drove, turning to the road that would lead to the farm, and, with hope, resolution.

She climbed out of the car in the pouring rain, pulled her carry-on bag from the car. Leaving the rest of her luggage, she ran up the steps, pet the pup, who was dry on the porch, chewing on a rawhide bone, and the leg of a chair.

Lyneah came to the door and opened it. "Hey, cousin! Welcome home!" she opened her arms and gave Claire a quick hug. "You're soaking wet! Come in and we'll get you dried off."

The two women entered the house, and Claire could see that the reconstruction of the damaged kitchen had been completed. There was still a lingering odor of old ashes, so faint you could barely sense it. The most powerful smell, however, was of Lyneah's cooking.

"I made a pan of lasagna; it was crappy and cold outside, so Travis and I have been in all day." She shrugged as she stepped into the kitchen and pulled a fresh Italian loaf from its wrap. "I cook when I can't do anything else."

"'Smells wonderful, Lyneah." Claire pulled her damp, messy hair away from her face. "I had no idea you cooked!"

"Ah, lasagna is easy. Go and dry off, and we'll have a glass of wine."

When Claire, dry and changed into comfortable slacks and a red blouse, returned, the two women sat in the living room and sipped merlot. It was good to be here, in the house, and Claire relaxed, doing her best not to think about the upcoming discussion with Matt. She knew she had to, but she was afraid, of what she was not certain. But it had to be done, for both of them. Resolution.

"I hope you don't mind, but I invited Chris for dinner," Lyneah said, interrupting Claire's thoughts.

"Chris? You mean Detective Chris?" She grinned. "Of course, I don't mind."

"Oh, don't get any ideas. It's not like that. He's been so kind to Travis and me. I just want to thank him."

"Mhmm..." Claire mumbled through an even larger grin and a sip of the wine. "So, what have you been up to since I've been gone?"

Lyneah rolled her eyes, then shook her head and smiled; a smile that lit up her face and made her look like a girl again. "Oh, seriously, it's nothing! He just took Travis and me out to his grandfather's place. Well, actually, his place, but it was his grandpa's when Chris was growing up, and he bought it..."

"And?"

"His Grandpa's name is Bill Breuning. He's a sweet man, and both he and Chris live on the farm. He's got a big beautiful garden, and he plants annuals all over the place, in homage, I think, to his wife. She died some time ago, I think." She sipped of the wine and continued. "Anyway, Chris took us on a tour of the farm..." Lyneah's voice trailed off.

Claire set her stemmed glass on the table and reached out to hug Lyneah. "Hey, you don't have to tell me, but I do believe, Lyneah Hamilton, that you're smitten."

Lyneah blushed, and smiled, but shook her head. "I don't know what I am. He's a kind, generous man and I'm not, well, I've not met anyone like him before. He's like Dad, in ways. He even bought a couple of horses, two quarter horses; a mare and her colt." She looked away. "A lovely mare, about sixteen, who had been in competition for many years but was growing too old for the ring. He told me that he'd bought them, knowing she would be an easy rider, so that Travis would be able to learn to ride."

"Wow," Claire breathed. "That is so sweet. I don't know what to say; that is one of the kindest things he could have done for Travis; he loves those horses, Lyneah. I'm sure he's so excited."

Lyneah, glanced toward the stairs, and heard Travis playing in his room. "I didn't tell him."

Claire cast a puzzled look at her cousin's face. "Why not?"

"Because I don't want Travis hurt again. He's seen Hank come, and go, and somehow *knows* how much pain Hank has caused, even if I try my best to keep him safe from those things."

"But, Lyneah, Chris is not like that."

Lyneah took a deep breath. "Yeah, I should know that. But, in my life, love has always come at a price."

Claire took note of that four letter word and did not comment on it. Instead, she rubbed her cousin's shoulder and spoke carefully. "It doesn't have to be that way. Not for you, and not for Travis. Trust yourself, trust your heart this time, and, take it slowly. This could be what you have been waiting for all your life."

Lyneah patted Claire's hand. "And, you, Claire? Have you found what you've been waiting for?"

Claire smiled softly and picked up her glass. "I don't know, but it's time to stop searching."

The two women sat in comfortable silence, sipping wine and listening to the slow strum of the songs playing on the CD player; Van Morrison's voice filled the room with dreams of the mystic. When the knock came to the door, both women jumped, sloshing the wine in their glasses. Lyneah got up straightened her hair absently, and went to the door, greeting the man that had no idea how much he had changed her spirits.

After dinner, Claire cleared her head and took a deep breath. "I have to go out for a while."

Lyneah smiled and hugged her cousin. "Yes, I know. I love you and hope that you finally find peace."

Claire was shaking but thankful for Lyneah's understanding. "You have a great evening; I'll see you later."

The drive to Matt's home was short, and Claire felt nervous as she approached the doorstep. Matt opened the door before she was halfway there, and she stood in the pouring rain, uncertain of what to do, or say.

Matt's form stood, backlit from the lights glowing in the house, and her heart skipped a beat or two as he stood, not saying a thing. Not inviting her in. 'Only watching her.

She finally began. "Hello, Matthew."

He just stood there, waiting.

"I-I wanted to come and talk…"

"Say goodbye, Claire?" he finally spoke, his voice tight. "'How was your trip?"

"Can I come inside?"

He shrugged and held the door for her. She climbed the steps and felt the heat of him reaching out to her and her damp skin shivered from its warmth.

She stepped in and stood there. "I'd like to talk to you about things, Matt. I think it's time."

He walked past her, into his living room, a warm, inviting room with vaulted ceilings of cedar plank, honed and polished to a beautiful, deep red. He did not invite her, and she knew that these were not good signs. She followed anyway. He plumped down into a soft leather chair and beckoned her to sit across from him on the matching sofa. She did and began.

"When we broke up, those years ago, I cried for days. I bled for months, and it took a long time for me to get over you."

He cocked his head, his face revealing nothing.

"I had always believed we would be together forever," her voice quaked, and she turned her head away, looked instead at the stone fireplace set into the north wall, its stone chimney reaching up through the vaulted ceiling. "But I had to reach a place in my heart, and in my life, where I could be free of that belief. And I did. It took a long time, but I did. I moved on with my life, and you did. I have a home and a wonderful job, and a good life."

Still, Matt said nothing; she could see his jaw clench. She waivered for a moment but kept going. "It felt good to go back. To see friends, to work in my office. To see Marcus-"

Matt's angry voice cut her off. "Why are you here, Claire?"

"Please, let me finish. I've been trying to find the right way to do this and it's really hard, Matt. Please…"

He looked away, his jaw clenching.

"Marcus is a good man. He's been in my life for a long enough time for me to see that. He's stable, and intelligent. He has the same interests as I do. He would do anything to make me happy…" her voice trailed off.

Several minutes went by as they each stared at anything but each other. He sat poised, waiting for the words he'd dreaded since she'd gotten on the plane.

"But I don't love him, Matt."

She watched him close his eyes and breathe deeply. Relief swept over him like a tidal wave, making him lightheaded. Still, he did not speak, or move.

Uncertain, Claire continued. "Not the way I should. I love my life in Illinois, but I know that I can't continue to hold Marcus on a tether because it's not fair to him. He deserves someone who will give him the kind of love that I can't."

Matt's thoughts drifted to his ex-wife, to the pain she must have felt when she realized things would never work between them. "Does he know that?"

"Yes."

Matt finally looked at her, his eyes softening, just a bit. Finally, he stood and walked slowly to where she sat, held out his hand. When she took it, he pulled her to him and crushed her in his arms, holding her close, not kissing, just touching her hair. She clung to him, also, feeling his warmth, and his strength, and felt the energy drain from her body as the stress washed away. Resolution had begun.

Chapter Nineteen

He was drunk, standing on the stoop. His ruddy face took in first Erich, then me, standing in the cold air in my robe, and I watched the rage build.

"What the fuck is going on here?" He demanded as he reached forward and grabbed Erich by the collar of his coat and pulled him down the steps.

I screamed, "Nothing, Daniel. Stop!" and followed them out to the cold, dark ground in bare feet. I reached them just as Erich regained his footing and was trying to pull away from Daniel's drunken grasp, strong, stronger still, in his state of intoxication. "Leave him alone!"

I grabbed Daniel by the arm, and he let go of Erich, only to reach out with his other arm, and punch me in the side of the head. I fell back onto the cold, solid ground, splayed out for a second, my eyes watering from the blow, but flew back up from the ground and came at Daniel with all my strength. He and I tumbled and rolled on the ground, until I felt Erich lift me.

"Eva! No," I heard his voice, demanding and forceful. "Come."

He helped me up and pushed me behind him. "Daniel. Stop."

But Danny would hear nothing, his body was clenched in rage, and I knew that no good could come. "Erich, go. Please…"

But, Erich, my protector, would not budge. He stood there, before Daniel, a shorter but stronger man, and would not leave my side. "No. I will not leave you alone with him." He spat out the words. "You go inside."

I shook my head, unaware of the cold on my bare feet. Daniel lurched as he stood up, unsteady from the drink, and tossed us a glare, first Erich, then me, standing behind him, watching. "'You whoring around, with, with this Nazi, Eva?"

"No! No – it's not like that, Daniel," I replied. "Go away. You're drunk."

His malicious grin unleashed fear inside of me; he had always been a cruel boy, who had grown into a cruel man, and I knew that look well. "Daniel, please, just listen. Please!" I begged him.

"I come here to check up on you, you little bitch, to help you with chores, and I find you damned near naked with this piece of garbage! You tramp!"

Erich lunged at Daniel, delivering a punch to his chin that knocked Daniel backward, to the ground. Daniel sat up, and wiped the blood dripping from his lip, looking up at Erich, then, slowly, got himself up from the ground.

I was terrified, and moved forward, just as he swung back at us. Erich stepped in front of me again, but it was too late; the blow struck me across my jaw and sent me flying. I lay, on the ground, feeling the bitter cold of the winter grass on my cheek, unable to move but for the quaking of my body, partly from cold, partly from fear. I could hear the two of them brawling, shouts of anger from Daniel. Erich maintained himself and spoke calmly when he could.

"Calm down, Daniel." "Let's settle this like gentlemen."

Daniel backed away, the first to exhaust. He was a fighter, but not in the physical shape that Erich was, his body overcome with liquor and laziness. They stood, facing off, the warm vapor of breathing visible in the winter moon, and I slowly began to try to get up, feeling cold and sharp pain and tasting blood.

Erich spoke first. "Eva, go inside."

"Yeah, go inside. I'll drive *him*," Daniel spat out, unable to say Erich's name. "I'll drive him back to the prison camp. Where he belongs…"

I tried to shake my head, no, that is not a good idea. Erich reached down and gently helped me up, holding me steady, nudging me toward the door.

"Daniel, you will get a doctor, yes?" he said as his worried eyes took in the bruise already forming on my face. "Yes?" He said again.

"Sure. After I take you back."

Erich's hand touched my face. "Are you all right?" he asked.

"Yes." I replied, tearfully, "Please don't go."

His eyes warned me. "Shh... let me open the door for you." He helped me into the kitchen where I sat on a chair. "Daniel and I will talk." Erich's confident voice spoke to my ear. "Ve vill settle this. Like men."

He stood there, looking down at me, for the briefest time, and then walked out the door.

Daniel did not return until early morning. I'd had a sleepless night, tossing and turning, and had gotten up once or twice to heave, sick from the headache that would not let up. I saw my mottled face in the mirror, wondering how I would explain the swollen lip and bruised face to my parents. They would be anxious to get home, to check on the cows, to check on me, to prepare for Christmas Eve.

I heard him pull into the driveway and rose from my bed, stepped into the kitchen as he came in. His coat was dirty, and he was disheveled, not only from the fight, but from dirt and oil.

"Where have you been?"

"None of your damned business," he replied gravely as he pulled off his coat and undershirt. He still had blood on him from the brawl, and I wondered if Erich had been able to get past the guards without having someone notice his appearance.

"Did you bring him back to the camp?"

"Yes."

He walked past me to the sink, splashing cold water into the basin then onto his face.

"How was he? Did he get back in?"

"Eva," Danny said, impatiently, "what did you want me to do, babysit him? I dropped him at the gate, and I left."

"Danny, where have you been?"

"I had a breakdown and had to fix it coming back. Took me half the 'fuckin' night."

"What did you talk about?" I approached him, grabbing his sleeve, and he flung my hand off.

"Don't touch me, you filth." He said. I flinched and felt the pounding in my head. He noticed my pale face and bruise. "As far as I'm concerned, you got what you deserved. But you won't breathe a word of this to anyone, you hear?" He roughly grabbed my arm and tightened until I felt pain. "You hear? *No one!*"

I nodded dumbly as he stepped past me. "Make some coffee, and none of that damned Postum stuff that tastes like shit; time to do the chores."

After Chris left, Lyneah put Travis to bed, then sat watching tv for a while, unable to sleep. Her hours at the bar had made her a night owl, and she usually stayed up later than most. He'd given her a hug when he left, a warm, lingering hug that left her feeling safe, and made her promise to set the security locks when he left, even standing outside the door until she had done so. He'd smiled and waved through the paned windows of the door and sauntered to his car. She'd watched until she could no longer see the taillights.

She allowed her mind to wander to the possibilities, here, in secret, where she did not have to hide her feelings from anyone. Chris Breuning was a strong man; someone she knew she could trust. But she deftly squelched any thoughts of the future, until these times when she was alone, where she could envision herself and Bill, Chris's grandfather, working in the gardens. Planting tulips and daisies, and pumpkins for Halloween. Travis in the sunlight on the back of the mare, whom he had already renamed Ginger for her red mane. The tall, strong form of Chris working in the barns, or getting ready for a shift, and making him lunch. God, she was hopeless! She had to laugh at herself.

The pup, now already twice the size of when he was first delivered to the farm, pounced around on her, playing with the ball she rolled for him, never exhausted. He jumped on the couch with her, licking her face and holding himself close to her, tilting his head and looking at her with curiosity as she cooed at him like a parent to a baby. When he started to whine, she brought him to the door and let him outside, in the back, where there was a tie down so he would not go so far from the house. She watched him saunter around the yard but did not step off the porch because of the rain.

He stopped suddenly and peered into the darkness as a growl emerged deep in his throat. She called him; he would growl at anything that moved, and she wanted to get him in before he woke Travis. He turned to look at her and began to run toward her, just as she felt a gloved hand across her face and a strong arm wrap itself around her torso. Oh, God, no, please not Hank, she thought.

But this was something far, far worse.

Matt and Claire sat quietly, watching a fire glow in the fireplace. Claire had teased Matt about starting one in the summer; he'd grinned, but then sobered. "I always dreamed of this." He said, awkwardly. "You and me, sittin' on the couch, watching the fire…"

Claire felt such contentment here, such peace. They talked, first, about the past, some things hurtful, others that made them smile.

"Claire, I know I was not the same after Jeremy died," Matt said. "I know I can't take it back."

She shook her head, sadly. "No, you can't. *We* can't, Matt. But, maybe, if all the stars out there align, and it stops raining, we can move beyond them." She smiled and he pulled her close.

She shared Eva's secrets, knowing that, if she could trust anyone, it was Matt. "I'll show you the trunk. It's where I found your letters, too."

He was thoughtful. "I was a lost soul the first year you left, Claire. Partying. 'Kept thinking *you*'d come to your senses, and really didn't figure out that it was me that had lost any senses I'd had in letting you go."

Claire, shrugged. "We were so young, then. And, I suppose I do have that Nielsen temper…."

He laughed and tickled her in the side until she cried out. "You have the looks, too, Red."

She rolled her eyes, "Oh, please, not that again! Hasn't time and a good bottle job fixed that redhead problem?"

"Bottle! I thought that was your natural color!" He ran his fingers through her tresses, teasingly searching for grays. "Hey, here's one…!"

She pulled away, playfully. "Ouch! Stop looking!" she slapped away his arm and they both laughed and cuddled up again.

"I think, in the last few months, you've added a grey hair or two to my head," Matt said, and snuggled in to kiss her on the neck, right under her ear, just the place he'd always remembered.

She caught her breath and held him tight, kissing and holding. This, this was what she'd been searching for. Simply, to come home.

They talked more about the journals. "What do you think Grandpa Tom knew? He must have forgiven her because they were so happy, at least, in later years. And Mom never suggested otherwise. They held hands, remember? You never really saw her without Grandpa by her side. He was just so good to her, Matt."

"Yeah, I do remember. I always thought it would be perfect to have a marriage like the Nielsen's."

"Me, too. I don't know, maybe he never knew what happened. I mean, people keep secrets, sometimes, especially those that are painful."

Matt shook his head. "I don't think she'd do that, Claire. She was just so open, and I can't see her keeping something like that from him."

"But she kept it from me, even when I would ask questions. And, she must have kept it from my mother…." Claire's voice trailed off, a puzzled frown furrowing her brow. "You know the one person who would know?"

They stared into each other's eyes. "Betty…" they both said in unison.

Chapter Twenty

The first thing Claire noticed as she pulled up next to Lyneah's car was that the door to the porch was swinging in the gusts of wind that were whipping around the yard. The storm was getting stronger, rain coming in torrents to crash on the car, making so much racket it overshadowed the sound of the thunder, no longer in the distance.

She took off her sandals and ran in bare feet to the door, grabbed the knob with her free hand, and twirled around as she closed it behind her. The porch was a mess; the rain had gushed through the windows and left the furnishings soaking wet, and several of the pots that Lyneah and she had filled with the flowers of summer, dahlias and impatiens, were tipped and broken across the floor. She gingerly stepped over the mud as she moved to go into the house door, which was also ajar.

"Lyneah?" she called as she slowly entered the house. "You here?"

Nothing but silence.

She felt a spasm of fear as she surveyed the room. The lasagna was still sitting on the stove where they'd left it, and the dishes were untouched on the countertop. Not like Lyneah to just leave things like that, and the house seemed too quiet.

She ran across the hardwood floor to the stairs, taking them two at a time, and rushed into Travis's room. He was curled up, asleep, and she felt a sickly fear coupled with relief that he was fine. Something just felt off.

She closed his door quietly so as not to awaken him and checked all the rooms before she headed back down the stairs.

Claire became aware of the scent of something nasty, unclean, before her conscious mind registered it. She stopped at the bottom of the stairs, cautiously looking around the main foyer, dim in the growing dusk but for the flashes of lightening. Suddenly, there was a flash of lightening and a loud crash of thunder, followed by the sound of a boom, and then, the lights went out.

She hovered at the edge of the stairs for a moment, letting her eyes adjust to the darkness. She could sense something in the room, but her mind did not register the menace until, with the next flash of lightening, she saw him standing, inches from her face, and she screamed.

The man was small and wiry, but Claire felt his strength when he grabbed her by the neck and pulled her toward him. He smelled strongly of old sweat, as though he had not bathed in months, and his face was gaunt, twisted into a rakish grin, made grotesque by the gaps empty of teeth and the strobes of lightning that flashed across his face.

"Hey, Red...." the man's voice was muffled, like he was holding something in his mouth while he spoke. She felt his breath on her face and she closed her eyes, and grimaced in distaste at the foul scent of his breath, decay and ugliness. "I 'been waitin' a long time to meet up with you..."

Claire tried to stay quiet as she struggled to get out of his grasp, but he was strong. The panic in her increased when his hand came up to her hair and grasped it in his hands and pull the mass to his face, facing her, and breathed deeply in, then out, his foul breath weaving through her hair and filling her nostrils.

"Wh-what do you want?" she whispered. "Where's Lyneah?"

He held her snuggly and reached around, running his hand along her back and squeezed her buttock. "She's down there," he gestured behind him with his head. "She with the Bossman."

Claire didn't know what to do; she struggled and squirmed to get out of his grasp. "What are you doing in my house?" She managed. "Let go of me!"

He held her fast. "I don't think so, Red," he whispered in her ear. "You smell fine. So fine..." He buried his face in her neck, and she felt the scratchy beard brush against her skin.

She heaved and pushed and tore away, but he was quick, unnaturally quick, and he grabbed her from behind and pulled her back, laughing. She kept fighting, clawing at his arms that were encircling her waist and chest.

"I knew you'd be spunky," he said near her ear. When his hand circled and squeezed her left breast roughly, she sucked in a breath, kicked her feet to the doorframe and pushed with all her strength, knocking them both to the ground.

The small man hit the banister before they both hit the ground. He never wavered and did not let go of her body; Claire felt quick pain in her left shoulder as she hit the ground hard. He rolled her atop him, then, thrashed from side to side, trying to get her turned over so he could be on top of her.

They battled for a long time, all the while he was holding her with his legs and arms and using his hands to touch her most intimate places. Claire couldn't figure out how he could hold her so strongly and violate her so personally at the same time. She contorted again, and then, he was on top of her, she face down on the hard floor, he sitting on her rump, pulling her hair back, causing her to cry in pain.

"Dumb bitch," he shrieked, twisting her arm with one hand and yanking on her head with the other. "You don't wanna make this so hard. You don't want me up there, doin' the same to that little boy all snuggled in his bed, now, do ya?"

Claire stopped struggling, and she squeezed tears back.

"Answer me." He demanded and knocked her head into the floor.

"No."

"Good." She could feel his hands reaching up under the skirt she had on, pulling at her panties. When she whimpered, he became rough, pushing his hands under the panties. "You like that, don't you..." his voice was excited, the lisp pronounced.

He let go of her hair at the same time he moved his hand from under her dress and started to work the belt and zipper of his pants. When she felt him relax, just enough, she heaved up and sent him off her. She ran, as fast as she could, for the door, and yanked it open, smashing through the screen door and falling into the wet grass of the lawn before heaving herself up again, and began to run toward the barn.

It was so dark. The rain blurred her vision as she ran, disorienting her. She could hear the stranger behind her, calling her names, telling her she didn't want to go down there, but she ignored him. She stumbled and fell in a hole the pup had dug in the yard, and her ankle caught, twisting around, and she could feel something pop.

She lay still for just a moment, wincing in pain, before picking herself up. There was a sharp clatter of thunder, and suddenly, the man was silent. She watched his form crumble, and turned toward the barn, where she saw another man, larger, all shrouded in black, holding a rifle in his arm, and the gun was aimed at her head.

"Claire, run!" She heard Lyneah's voice from somewhere in the barn, saw something hit the man, saw the large man turn toward the door and strike at something (someone?) with the gun, and she turned and headed down the path into the woods, toward the ruins of the old place.

She ran, and ran, blinded by the storm, fearing the man would overtake her, not knowing where to go. She stumbled, several times, and the sounds of gunshots and thunder meshed together; she could not recognize one from the other. The ground was uneven, and her twisted ankle burned with pain each time she hit ground, but she kept running.

She found herself running through wet, swampy pockets, and realized the river was high, abnormally high, and tried to move to higher ground. When she heard the crack of the rifle, and the sound of bullets whizzing past her head, she turned and headed further down the slope.

She hid, down deep in the vines and sumac that hung low over the river. The thistles tore at her skin and her ankle throbbed. She could hear sobbing above, and she tried frantically to figure out what to do.

"Where are you, Red?" a voice called

"Leave her alone!" Lyneah's voice was distraught. "Please— I don't know where your stuff is, and she wouldn't, either! Please, just let me go and get out of here! Talk to Hank, for God's sake..."

"'Might be a little late for that, sugar." The man's voice was smooth, like warm oil, and slithered across the space like a serpent. "Old Hank is in no shape to be talking to any, especially God."

Claire could hear their footsteps crashing through the trees. "No, my guess is that Hank's met his maker and never got past those pearly gates."

"What?" Lyneah sounded confused. "What are you saying?"

"You heard me..."

Claire felt around on the ground, hoping to find a rock, or a stick, something to use as a weapon. Maybe, if they passed her, she'd be able to startle the man enough to get Lyneah away. Maybe the two of them could subdue him.

"You hear me out there? You have to the count of ten to come out of where you're hiding or I'm gonna blow blondie's head off. You got that? One... Two... Three..." Claire heard Lyneah cry out as she hit the ground, and the click of the rifle.

"Okay, Okay! I'm coming. Please, wait-" Claire continued to feel around in the muck and mud, trying to find something to use. Please, God. She reached far to her left, and her hand encountered a something solid. A plank, or something, if she could just pull it out. She felt it give, slightly, and then hold fast.

She continued to yank on it, calling to the man. "I'm – I'm stuck, in the sumac," she lied. "Please, please just let me get out!"

The man was impatient. "You're trying my patience, Red." The accent was deep South and mixed with undertones of the French Quarter. "You don't wanna do that." She heard a sharp clap, and Lyneah cried out in pain.

She'd have to stop and accept this fate. She reached up the embankment, and began to climb, slipping and sliding along the wet surface, still groping for some type of weapon that was not there. Her fingers came across something metal, and she pulled it easily from the ground. Maybe, just maybe... Her fingers closed around the object, some sort of handle, and stuck it into her pocket.

Chris squinted at the heavy rains coming down on the windshield. He'd decided, after having a delicious dinner with Lyneah, Claire and Travis, that he would run into town, pick up a few things, and head home. His thoughts were on the blonde bombshell he'd just left; he'd become quite attached to her, and her boy.

The kid was smart, and direct, so direct that it was somewhat disconcerting to Chris, how inquisitive Travis was. Chris's grandfather, Bill, had also taken a liking to the two of them; Chris had watched with amusement when Bill took Travis down by the old barn, where they sat on two old five-gallon pails and whittled twigs into whistles.

Lyneah had been tainted, Chris knew she'd had a rough time of it, more than once. He took things slowly; she was like a frightened deer, always skittish, but curious, inching close, but not too close, only to inch away just when he thought he could reach her. Many women who'd come in when he was a cop in Chicago, had been where she'd been. Victims, who came in after a neighbor's 911 call and a visit by Chicago's finest, cops who stepped in and made the arrest, and brought the abuser down to the station to sober up. Unwilling to press charges.

Many unable to look Chris in the eye, with theirs swollen from the beating, or, in the heat of a July day in the city, finding anything to cover the bruises, coming into the station with coats on when it was 100 degrees in the shade. Heavy make-up and lipstick. Do you wanna press charges? Shake of the head, no. You wanna file an order for protection? Another shake of the head. 'Cause, you know, he's gonna be out of holding in seventy-two hours and free to come home and do this again. This time, no response, just a lost look of misery.

It had frustrated Chris; his people going out and stepping into a domestic, putting their lives out there, only to have no resolution. The victims had been programmed into dependency and were unwilling or unable to be self-reliant enough to leave and make it on their own. They found themselves and often, their children, at the mercy of a system that did not always work. The misery and self-doubt and pain had been engrained, but so had the *need*.

That's what Chris saw in them. Need. And the need for love and something to hold onto was overpowering. Countless times he'd heard it. 'Besides, he was just drunk; he's better when he's sober.' 'The kid needs a father, even a nasty ass drunk.'

Lyneah had the need, but she also had the guts to move ahead, and Chris admired that. That, and the fact that she was easy on the eyes and had a swift sense of humor. And a great kid.

It had never been in him to be attracted to a victim he'd worked with, but this woman, with her huge and knowing eyes, her quick wit, her spirit, and the long blonde tresses he wanted to run his hands through, was different. Chris imagined the two of them sitting on the porch, sipping lemonade and watching the fireflies dance. He sensed that Lyneah was the kind of woman who would find contentment in these simple things, the things that he had waited for all his life. His thoughts roamed, and he smiled at himself, shaking his head as he made his way to the checkout.

He was just pulling out of the Walmart parking lot, when a black and white pulled in next to him. Ben Lahr opened his window and waved, and Chris also hit the button to open the window. "Hey, Ben, how's it going tonight?"

"Quiet, for now, anyway." Was Ben's reply.

Chris could feel the cooling rain coming into the car and splashing across his face, dripping from his prominent nose. "Yeah, I guess the juvies don't like to get too wet..." He smiled.

Ben nodded and grinned back. "'Just wondering if we've heard anything new on Mr. Hank Beaudine? Seems to have disappeared."

Chris shook his head. "Piece-a work, that one. You on for the overnight?"

Ben nodded. "Took the shift for someone who had a wedding or something. Nice night for it, huh?"

The two chatted for a few more minutes. The storm kicked up, lightening flashing across the sky and the winds swirled debris across the parking lot. Empty cans, soggy sandwich wrappers and even a shopping cart went scurrying by the headlights of Ben's car.

"Jesus, looks like we're in from some trouble, tonight-" he said, just as the radio binged on. "10-70 in progress..."

Dispatch relayed the address, and Chris froze. "That's Lyneah's address!" He put the sedan in gear as he heard Ben identifying his unit. "10-76, Bravo-Charlie-10."

Chris bit his cheek, wishing he had his unit vehicle; the sedan was equipped with lights and radio, and he would be able to hear what was being relayed to the squad in front of him. Some sort of fire, and, most likely, since he'd just left Lyneah at her aunt's place, caused by the lightening that was continuing its coruscating dance across the night sky. In just minutes, they pulled into the drive, with the fire department following shortly behind.

The entire house was ablaze; Chris was amazed at how quickly the fire must have spread, noting that the natural gas tank on the back side of the house appeared to have exploded. "Holy shit," he heard Ben say next to him. "Looks more like a bomb than a lightning strike."

Chris watched, silently, as the fire department personnel began working on the blaze. Already, on the kitchen end of the structure, one could see the metal skeleton, the skirting warping out from the underbelly. Curtains were ablaze in the bedroom at the far end. Toys that were strewn across the lawn cast an eerie sight as they melted from the heat of the flame, while still glistening from the heavy rains.

The air was acrid from smoke. Chris stayed out of the way of those working to put out the fire, and started to slowly walk the perimeter, after first pulling an extra waterproof jacket and flashlight from his trunk. He also reached into the glovebox and pulled the Remington and its holster out, just in case.

Chapter Twenty-One

Matt drove his pickup slowly through the storm, wishing he'd not let Claire go ahead without him. He'd called Betty and told her they were coming and needed to hop in the shower. "You get ready and pick me up at the farm" Claire had said. "We can drop off my car..."

The sentence had held much promise, and the look in her eye said everything.

He'd reached to draw her face to his and kissed her with such hunger she'd looked dazed when he finally let her lips go, and she'd held him tight, whispering something naughty into his ear that made him smile. She'd kissed him again, said the three words that he'd waited a lifetime to hear, and ran out the door.

When he was ready, he'd headed down the gravel road that wound along the river, taking a short cut across the old field road, and ended up back-tracking when he found a spot where the river had flooded, washing out the road. He'd sworn loudly, as he'd navigated the truck around, feeling the backend slip into the ditch more than once. He'd thrown the truck into four-wheel drive and barely made it back on track, cursing himself for trying to take the shortcut.

When he navigated Eva's driveway, Matt paid little attention to the barn, and did not notice the door was wide open. The house was dark; where Matt's electricity had only flickered, it looked like the farm had lost its to the storm. Maybe a transformer had blown. He grabbed his cell phone from the console beside him, and jogged toward the house, felt his stomach do a little lurch when he noted that the door was hanging open.

When he saw the inside door open, he felt a surge of panic and took the steps in a giant leap, running into the house, calling. "Claire?" He could barely make out the room in the gloom and ran through the main floor. "Lyneah?" Silence. He tried not to panic; perhaps, the two had taken Travis down to the old cellar, as was common when a storm got to be as violent as the one tonight.

He made his way slowly through the house, around to the back porch, and opened the door to the basement. "You down there?" He called. No one answered. Still, he stepped gingerly down the stairs; the old cellar was rock solid, but the high-water table and constant rain of the season had left it smelling musty. No one there. Something wrong. He jogged back up the steps and quickly out through the door of the house, searching around the yard in a panic. He started down the slope toward the barn and tripped.

Claire emerged from the slope, slipping and sliding in the mud. "I'm here." She said unsteadily. "Please, let Lyneah go." Her voice quavered. "Please. I don't know who you are, or what you want, but if it's Hank you are looking for, he's not here."

The man was maybe in his thirties, very tall. Lyneah was kneeling on the ground, and even in the growing darkness, Claire could see the blood pouring from a wound on her head.

"Come here, Red." He gestured with his gun, and she felt sickness, and fear, so deep it nearly doubled her over.

She slowly walked toward them and began to cry. "What are you going to do?"

He gazed at her in silence. His eyes were dark, and hollow; devoid of feeling. He had long, dark hair, tied back, and a handsome face, but for the eyes, which were empty. A scar ran across his temple, and with each lightning strike it seemed to grow. Claire was so afraid, she feared her wobbling legs would give out and she would fall before him, and die right here, in the muddy meadow, where she'd run and played as a child.

She walked slowly forward until she was in front of his dark form, and he cocked his head and smiled at her, a dead smile, and held out the hand that was not holding the gun, and pulled her closer, using the tip of his boot to nudge at Lyneah. "Let's go."

Claire could see fear and pain mirrored in Lyneah's eyes, and she reached down to help her up. The Bossman yanked roughly on her arm, pulling her close to him. "Stay put." He commanded. "She can get up on her own."

Lyneah just sat. "Please, please, let her go. She doesn't know anything about any of this."

"And what is it she don't know, *Cheri*?" he responded.

"She doesn't know where your drugs are, or where your money is-" Lyneah looked up at him, pleading. "She doesn't know Hank."

"Get up." He ordered quietly. She complied, but the running and the cold and the battle with him made her stiff. She pushed her hands into the mud and heaved herself up, slowly.

"Two beautiful women. It's such a shame, really, that we will not have more time to get to know each other." His oily voice held no menace.

"I would have liked to know you. You are cousins, no?" His gloved hand slid up Claire's side and rested on her throat. "I see the resemblance, yes."

Neither woman answered the question. The rain began to dissipate, and the storm seemed to be passing. "Such beauty in cousins is hard to find. I would have enjoyed taking you." He sighed, then. "But I did not come here for that, although my late friend, Red, he could think of little else. He wanted to rip into you and devour your flesh..."

Claire could feel bile rise in her throat. "Who is your late friend?" She asked, hoping for time.

"The little man lying on your grandmother's lawn, Cher..." Another sigh. "Too bad he was such a junkie. He was good at tracking women who, hmm, shall we say *misbehaved...*"

Claire could only guess at the horrors behind that statement. "He's dead?"

"As a doornail." The man grinned again, his white teeth flashing, a grin that did not reflect in his eyes. "He's no longer useful to me, Claire," her name on his lips sent shivers down her spine. "He's damaged, much like his mother was when I found them together, in the gutter. You, on the other hand, could be very useful to me..."

He seemed to enjoy toying with her, and she thought that this is what a mouse feels like, when a cat has it within reach, but continues to play with it until the final moment when it clamps its teeth into the rodent's neck and bites, hard.

She could not look at Lyneah, who seemed paralyzed with fear. Instead, she let her eyes focus before her, feeling the man's body behind her, his hand closed loosely around her throat, seeing the meadow stretch out before her. Oh, Matt. I am so sorry.

The man turned to walk through the ruts back to the main trail to the house. As he did, he lost his footing, and in that moment, a scream ripped from Lyneah's mouth as she lunged at him as hard as she could. The man released his hold on Claire and grabbed Lyneah around her neck as all three of them tumbled down the embankment, arms and legs askew.

Claire felt the sharp brush cut into her skin, ripping her clothing and her face. She heard Lyneah fighting with the man as she tumbled, hearing her cousin's fear mingle with rage as she appeared to be wrestling over the gun. She tried to stand and move toward the two of them but kept sliding further down. Desperately, she grabbed onto the grass to heave herself up.

Finally, able to get her bearings, she felt a tiny triumph, a glimmer of hope, and she started toward them. She heard the report of the rifle at the same time she felt a searing heat rip through her, and she tumbled, falling backwards, hitting hard, and felt the ground give way under her.

Chapter Twenty-Two

The heat from the fire that engulfed Lyneah's home was tremendous, and it blistered the paint off the old shed, several yards away. Chris and Ben stepped away from the heat as one of the hoses was trained onto the shed, cooling the steaming lap siding, then turned back to the fire.

The shed door creaked loudly as Chris opened it by hand, and Ben shown his flashlight into the interior. Though nothing appeared out of place, Chris could smell the pervading odor of gasoline, and he shown his flashlight around, trying to place the source. The floor of the garage, made of old and patched concrete, was glistening. He heard Ben comment, just as it hit him. The fire was deliberately set.

Both men turned, moved quickly to the squad car. As Ben reached for the radio, they heard dispatch calling out the code. "All units, proceed West 280th, shots fired..." "That's the Nielsen place," Chris could hear his heart pounding in his ears. "Let's go." Ben already had lights flashing as Chris answered the call.

"What the hell?" Matt heard his own voice as he looked down at what he'd tripped over. The man was lying in a pool of blood, his throat slowly bleeding out where a bullet had blown through it. It took Matt aback, and he scrambled to his feet and began to run down to the barn, not knowing which direction to turn.

"Claire!" He could hear the panic in his voice, and his hands shook as he tried to make the 911 call. He dropped the phone twice, and finally connected; adrenaline coursed through his body as he answered the dispatcher's voice. "There's been a shooting, out at Eva Nielsen's place. West 280th, I can't remember the number—God, please, hurry! There are two women and a small child gone. I can't find them!"

Dispatch asked about shooting. "Yes, there's a man down. He's dead. No, I don't know the man. Yes, I believe that is the correct address. Please, hurry. We have to find them."

He stood, wet, on the knoll of the hill, holding the cell phone to his ear, and circled, looking everywhere, trying to find some trace, fear sickening him as he searched the grounds, praying that he would not find her lying in the grass. "Oh, God..." his voice shook, and he knelt and prayed. Please keep her safe.

He heard a shot in the distance and lifted his head toward the sound. Down by the old place. He stood and began to run down the old rutted path, his mind cleared of all but Claire. He could feel her small arms encircling him, like it was yesterday that he'd carried her along the path back to her mother.

                              ✥

Dazed, Claire felt she was in a tunnel, with no end anywhere. She felt completely enveloped, as in a box. The box smelled of must and earth and death. She could hear nothing, not above, nor below. She put her hand out, and felt something solid, rough, and slowly moved her fingers along it. Some sort of wall, made of wood, perhaps. Her fingers ran down the length of this wall, and she tried to push herself up from whatever she had landed on but felt pain in her side.

She gingerly moved her other arm and winced when she realized that it was nearly useless, likely broken from the fall. In the darkness, she let her good hand drop to her side, and it collided with something else, something encased in a sort of fabric. She felt cold. So cold. She tried to call out but could only muster a moan. Her hand brushed along the *thing* she was on top of, and she carefully turned her fingers to probe further.

Cloth, ragged and damp. Some sort of thick stick. As her fingers trailed along her side, she felt herself drifting. What is this? A round globe. Her mind did not register what her fingers were touching. As Claire lost blood from the wound to her side, she began to feel that she was not alone. Hearing nothing from the outside world, but here, in this cocoon, she felt something, or, someone. A voice, in her ear, but words that did not make sense. Jumbled, the words confused her.

She willed herself to stay conscious and focused on the globe. Solid. Her fingers shook as they probed. She could make out an orifice, half buried in the dirt.

She began to feel weak and began to drift again. Mama's voice, soothing her. "Shhh...." she felt the hot tears begin to glide down her cheeks. Another voice, inside her head, but words she did not know. She wanted so much to go to her mother and said so. "Mama, please, pick me up." Then, warmth.

Her mother's arms, and the arms of another, comforting and careful, holding her, caressing her forehead. "Stay awake, Claire," her mother demanded. "Matthew's coming!"

She tried, once again, to sit up, but she could not. She weakly clutched the globe, digging into the dirt with her fingers. Only then did she realize that it was not a globe, but the skull of a human. She unconsciously registered this fact, yet it did not shock her. All she really wanted was to sink into the arms she still felt around her and go to sleep. As she drifted toward the unconscious, she felt a warm, rough hand squeeze her own, closing it firmly around the skull, and held hers there firmly, until she drifted away.

Lyneah heard sirens and felt the crack of the rifle across her face. She fell to the ground; the man was standing over her, with the gun pointed at her forehead, but she could not move. She felt herself giving in. *Lord, bless me for I have sinned...* and she began to speak.

"Our Father, who art in heaven..." She heard the man click a bullet into the chamber and continued to pray. She thought of Travis, but, surprisingly, did not fear for him. *Chris will come. He will take care of my* boy. "Hallowed by thy name." her cheek throbbed, and she tasted blood in her mouth. When the shot came, she felt nothing but peace.

Matt took a long, flying leap and lunged at the man standing along the edge of the marshy embankment, and they both tumbled to the muddy ground as the weapon he'd been holding discharged. The man was large, and strong. He reeled back and punched Matt in the side of his head, and Matt felt the crunch of a signet ring crack against his eye socket. He grabbed the man's collar and neck with his hands, and squeezed, hard, trying to gain a grip to overtake, both men tumbling further down the embankment. They hit the water of the Cottonwood with force, and both felt the jarring cold as they plunged into the river.

Both men surfaced, still locked in a fighting stance. The larger man dragged Matt with him out of the water, and they continued to struggle, both trying to gain the upper hand. Finally, Matt broke free from the rumble, stepped back and aimed a punch at the other man's jaw. The blow caught the man across the cheekbone, and Matt felt something crack in his hand as the man went slack and dropped to the ground. Matt kneeled and grabbed the man, realizing he was shouting for Claire. "Where is she?"

Chris ran down the path as quickly as he could go, with Ben following on his heels. Officers of Brown County also followed, with flashlights and weapons drawn. As the procession approached the glen, Chris could see Matt kneeling over another man. Matt was pounding at the man, and Chris could make out the words. "Where is she? You bastard, where is she???"

The man did not answer. Chris called the procession to a halt and walked slowly toward the men. "Matt." Matt barely looked up, just continued to pound on the man. "Matt, that's enough."

He approached the two of them and shown his light around the area. "Is there anyone else?" He asked but got no response. "Fan out. Be careful. We have three missing; two women and a child." He felt his gut wrench as he thought about Lyneah and her son. He put his hand on Matt's shoulder. Matt stood and Chris turned the beaten man over to cuff him.

Chapter Twenty-Three

Early Spring, 1945

Christmas dawned bright and cold. Mom and Dad finally appeared, and we had Christmas dinner and opened gifts from under the tree. Mama commented on the ugly bruise on my face. Daniel stood close, watching, and I said that one of the heifers had acted up and I had hit my head on the stanchion post. She seemed to accept that explanation and did not ask about it again.

We lingered in the parlor over gifts that had been carefully picked and stored away. Mama had somehow been able to find a pair of Kayser stockings and had seemed so pleased when I opened the package. I wondered, everything in our world seemed to be rationed for the war effort, even our stockings.

"You're all grown up now, dear." She said as I opened a second box that held DuBarry leg makeup and a pencil for drawing the seam on my leg. I grinned and hugged her; it was so unlike her to embrace such frivolity, but it was kind and I felt a momentary stab of guilt as she squeezed me back.

Late in the afternoon, we sipped the home-made wine, made from dandelions and honey, brewed and aged over the summer, and listened to holiday music on the radio. It was quiet; Daniel, for once, did not have much to say, and we were all lost in our thoughts, missing Christmases past.

Dad noticed a car come into the drive, and we hovered near the window, as two policemen left the car and approached the house.

Mom opened the door before they were on the porch. "Good afternoon, ma'am." A tall, older officer said, removing his issued cap. "I am Sgt. Harry Jones, and this is Deputy Franklin. I wonder if we might have a word with your husband?"

"Certainly. Please, come in, it's so cold out here. What is this about?" Mama asked, nervously. She led them into the foyer, and, by that moment, Dad had also stood and approached the door. I sat stiffly on the sofa and felt Daniel seat himself next to me.

"Good afternoon, Sir." Sgt. Jones removed his glove and shook Dad's hand while the younger officer surveyed the room, taking in me, and Daniel, who was seated at my right. I sat, frozen. I felt Daniel creep closer to me on the sofa, and my insides turn.

"Sorry to disturb your Christmas celebration, but we've had an incident with one of the war prisoners out at the camp."

Both my parents looked concerned, and the knot in my insides grew as I felt Daniel's hand press, hard, around the back of my neck, warning me to stay quiet. "What sort of incident, Sgt.?" Dad asked. I could see he was anxious.

"One of the PWs seems to have disappeared. An Erich Gebhardt. Seems he disappeared sometime yesterday, and no one has seen him since. We were told he worked for you, here, Sir, and wondered if you'd seen him in the last few days?

Dad shook his head. "No, Sir, we have not seen Erich since last week, I believe." He looked at my mother, questioningly, as if to verify the dates. "What day did he last come for chores, Abigailee?"

"Last Friday," she replied. "Where could he have gone? Isn't the camp locked down and guarded?"

The deputy nodded. "It is, ma'am, but we've come to find that it's easy for fellows to sneak in and out from there."

The pressure on my neck tightened. Daniel was sending a clear warning and I kept my mouth shut and my head down, unconsciously lifting a trembling hand to touch the bruise on my face.

The deputy saw this. "You've got quite a shiner there, ma'am." He said to me. "'Looks like it's pretty painful."

I nodded, and Daniel responded, jovially. "She had a little match with one of the cows, didn't you, Eva?"

I nodded again. To the others in the room, the arm casually draped across my back would appear to be a show of affection, but the hand that squeezed the back of my neck was like a vice, and I dared say nothing.

The older man had a gentle smile for me. "Sometimes those cows can get worked up. I grew up on a farm, on the east side of Tracy. Used to love going out to feed calves in the morning."

I smiled, weakly, back at him, and did not meet the younger deputy's eyes. He was too suspicious, his gaze to inquiring.

As they spoke with my parents, it came out that Erich had been reported missing in the morning. They had spoken with the Officers, a tight-lipped group of older Nazi Germans who had shared very little, but for the fact that no one knew where he was. A young soldier had appeared to have been roughed up a bit; he'd been a friend of this Erich fellow, but he said he didn't know anything about where he'd gone.

The two officers made comments about how difficult it was to get any answers from the PWs; they liked to have control over their own and kept their own ranking system. Camp justice was often left to them, not the American guards that were overseeing the camp. Those guards were often 4-F, not qualified to go to service, but were available to guard the camps when there was such a shortage of healthy men.

"We haven't had a lot of trouble with this group; most of them are good men who are just serving their time and working over at the cannery. No one seems to know why he'd take off. We're searching the river and the woods, nearby. When we looked over his bunk, it appeared he left everything, so we're not sure if he intended to leave for good, or just wandered off and had trouble."

"Sgt. Jones, will you let us know? Erich was a good worker and seemed not to be a troublemaker. I find it hard to believe he would just leave." Dad said.

The Sgt. nodded. "We will. Thank you for your time and enjoy the rest of your Christmas." The gentlemen tipped their hats to us all and left.

I sat, numb. When it was time for chores, Daniel volunteered to do mine, a move that surprised all, and made me instantly wary. Daniel never volunteered for anything. Mama beamed at him, so happy that he was being so generous, and I felt sick as I made my way upstairs to lie down, having excused that the wine had made me lightheaded and I had a headache from the bruise.

Without snow, unusual for a Minnesota January, it was nearly impossible to track the escaped prisoner. Dogs were brought in but could not track beyond the river's edge. The Feds came to see us, to talk to each of us about Erich, and each time, I was in terror of being found out. Daniel had caught me alone, the week after Christmas, and warned me not to speak of what happened. Ever.

"He's a Nazi, Eva." He would say, his eyes narrowed and menacing. "If they know what you did, they could hang you for treason."

That was months ago. The investigation into Erich's disappearance was long; they assembled searches everywhere, dredging the open spots on the river, walking the woods and fields near the camp. Rumors swirled; perhaps he died and they'll find him in the woods; it was brutally cold this winter, and there was not a lot of snow. He's in the grass somewhere.

Old man Hanson had some clothes stolen on Christmas Eve when he was at the Lutheran church service; maybe the Nazi was headed North to Canada? Some rumors were about us, the Kellys. Did the Kellys help him escape? They say his English was nearly perfect. He worked on the farm even when the harvest was over, when most transferred to the cannery...

I keep my mouth shut, my head down.

It is April, just a few days after President Roosevelt's death. On this Saturday, while I swept the front room, I listened to the announcers, hearing the Bishop's words, praying for courage and sympathy, in the face of war, requesting that we the American people do not give up faith, even when faced with our leader's death. When he quoted President Roosevelt's words that we only need to fear, fear itself, I stopped to listen more closely. I am not sure I can muster the courage or will to believe that. I fear Daniel, and I fear being tried for treason.

A familiar police car came in the drive, and I felt sick, as two gentlemen emerge; Sgt. Jones, in his uniform, and another gentleman, in a black suit and tie, walking toward the house. I panicked and wanted to run and hide. The front door was open, to let in the fresh air of spring.

He removes his hat. "Good morning, ma'am. Is your pa around?"

I shake my head. "He's gone over to the Bakers to help with chores." My voice is shaky, and nervous. "Mr. Baker fell on the ice and broke his wrist..."

"All right, then." He smiled kindly, but his voice was reserved. "We would like to talk with you a little more about that PW that disappeared from around here a few months ago. You remember? This here's Detective George Brandt. He'd like to have a word with you and your folks."

"Mama's not here, today..."

Mr. Brandt stepped forward. He was tall, having to duck to get into the doorway. "That's fine - Ms. Kelly, isn't it? It's *you* we want to talk to..." His face drew a thin smile, but his eyes were unsmiling in a rather non-descript face. He had dark hair and thick glasses through which he squinted at me because of the bright sun filtering in through the glass.

He did not remove his hat, instead, moved so close I could smell his cologne, and towered over me. I felt myself physically shrinking back, and he took another step closer. "This won't take long." He looked around the parlor and I found my back against the wall, clutching the broom to my breast.

"Here, why don't you let me take that, Ms. Kelly." He held out a hand, gesturing for the broom, and I handed it over to him. He set it against the wall and gestured for me to sit down.

The spring breeze, coming in through the screen door, felt cool on my skin, and I shivered. He saw this. "No need to be afraid, Ms. Kelly," he said softly.

There followed an awkward silence; Sgt. Jones seemed uncomfortable and spoke up. "Detective Brandt, maybe we'd be better off waiting until this girl's parents are home before we talk with her."

"No, Harry, I'd hate to waste a trip when we can get this all cleared up right here." Brandt pulled a small notebook from his coat pocket and looked at some notes. "Now, Ms. Kelly, you are how old? Seventeen, right?"

"Yes."

"You go to school in New Ulm?"

"Yes."

"You know of an Erich Gebhardt, a PW from the internment camp, who came to work on this farm last August, correct?"

"Yes."

"What did you think of this young man?"

"What do you mean?"

"Well, did he scare you? Did you find him nice looking? How well did you get to know him when he was working for your family?"

I didn't know how to answer. "He was nice. He did not scare me."

"You are aware that he is a Nazi and an enemy of the United States, aren't you?" I stared at him; he stared back. "You have brothers, in the war, correct? In fact, you have one brother who is missing in Italy and presumed captured or killed by German Nazi soldiers since around April of 1944? How does that make you feel about how "nice" Mr. Gebhardt is?"

He went on further to talk in depth about what it means to be a traitor, and how traitors are punished in this country. "Did you, or anyone in your family, help this prisoner to escape?"

"No!"

"When was the last time you saw him, Ms. Kelly."

I told him it was before Christmas. He continued to ask questions, taking notes and pushing me to say things I was unprepared to deal with. He began to imply things, very deep and personal things, and Sgt. Jones stepped in, saying that it wasn't necessary to scare a young girl like that. It made me sick inside, knowing that the detective's words were not far from the truth, and I could not meet the Sergeant's eyes without feeling tremendous guilt.

Just as I felt I was going to break, I heard a voice at the door. "Hello-o, anyone home?" Rebekka, Betty's mother, stood at the door, carrying a satchel and a freshly baked pie.

I jumped up, opened the door and her eyes met mine, briefly, as she waltzed into the house, first setting the pie and satchel on the table, then throwing her arms around me and giving me a tight squeeze. "What's going on here, Harry?" she directed the question at Sgt. Jones, who looked about as relieved as I must have. "Where's your mother, Eva?"

"She's in town."

"What are you two gentlemen doing out here?" she asked pointedly.

"Mrs. Nielsen, we're still trying to figure out what happened with that PW that went missing in December." Sgt. Jones said.

"Oh, how terrible that all has been." She continued to hold her arm around my shoulder. "I suppose by now he's way off in Canada somewhere." As she released me, she patted me on the shoulder and handed me the satchel. "Here, Eva, will you take these to the kitchen? I brought some sandwiches and some lovely pears that I canned last fall."

The detective stood. "We're not done questioning Ms. Kelly."

"Oh, yes you are, Mr,?" Her voice was light, but I could hear a biting undertone.

"Detective Brandt, ma'am."

"Well, *Mr.* Brandt, I'm sure you're aware that you've probably scared that child half to death with these questions. Not to mention that it is inappropriate to ask these questions without her parents or an adult here. For heaven's sake, he's long gone; it is indecent of you to continue to harass this family. Perhaps you should focus on tracking him down, instead?"

There was a great deal of discussion while I stood nervously near the door of the kitchen. "Mr. Brandt," Rebekka finally said firmly, "Your efforts to capture a Nazi prisoner are commendable. Senator Garvey is a cousin of my husband." Rebekka's confident voice was smooth as honey. "In fact, the Garveys are having dinner with my family on Saturday. When I see him, I'll be sure to enlighten him on your efforts."

Brandt said nothing, just stared.

Jones held his hand up, "Now, Rebekka, you don't have to go and get all worked up about this; we're just tryin' to make sure we cover all possibilities..."

"Well, I think that this possibility is covered, Harry. Please tell Bonnie hello from me when you get home." Rebekka had somehow, with sheer force of will rather than physical touch, managed to hustle those two men out the door before they even had a chance to think.

After she shut the door, and watched them drive out, she turned to me. "Eva, what's going on here?" she demanded, approaching to grasp my shoulders. "People are talking all over town, all sorts of nonsense."

"Nothing-there's nothing going on," I heard a whine in my voice and didn't like it.

She stared deep in my eyes. "No matter how friendly our good German neighbors are, Eva, those people would not take too kindly to learning that someone in this neighborhood actually harbored a Nazi prisoner. For God's sake, some of these people lost their own sons in France, fighting for you."

"I know that, Mrs. Nielsen," I said. "I'm not stupid—"

The hands on my shoulders shook me. "This is not a game you're playing, so stop being petulant." She removed her hands and I folded my arms across my chest, shivering. "This is serious business, and I suspect there's more to it than what you're letting on."

"No, there isn't."

"Eva, those people wouldn't come out here and pay you that kind of visit without reason. Whether it's rumor or fact, they mean business."

I looked helplessly down, and felt tears start to form. "I know."

I stood there, sobbing quietly, and started to feel faint. "Lord, girl, you're white as a sheet," Rebekka's voice was concerned. "Come here, let's get you on the sofa." She led me there, and, as I went to sit down, her hand brushed my middle, and she stopped moving. I pulled away, but not before she had touched my belly again.

"Oh, my God." She stood over me as I sank further into the sofa. "Oh, my God," she repeated. "how late are you?"

"I don't know what you're talking about..."

"Oh, yes you do," her voice rose. "Lord, child, what were you thinking?"

I put my face in my hands and sobbed. She stood over me, waiting, watching, not comforting, but not menacing either. I felt a hand on my shoulder and a handkerchief was thrust into my face. "Here, dry your eyes, Eva." I sniffled into the kerchief and felt her sit next to me. "So, how late are you?"

"Three months." I replied.

Rebekka sighed. "Well, I guess that rules Thomas out." She stared out the window, silently. I stared with her, my eyes watching tiny particles of dust float in the beam of the sun coming through the window, catching glimpses of tiny rainbows of color at the end of the beams streaming through the prisms that were cut into the leaded glass.

"Whose is it?" her voice cut through my thoughts.

I said nothing. "It's that PW's, isn't it."

I remained silent, staring out the window. Taking my silence as assent, Rebekka let out a long, drawn breath. "Does your mama know?"

I shook my head, still staring out the window. "No." I said softly and began to cry again.

She waited for me to stop sobbing, sat next to me in silence, until the tears trickled away again. "Eva, my Thomas doesn't deserve this from you." Rebekka said, firmly. "But I don't particularly want to see you go to jail, or prison, or worse."

Mom's car pulled into the driveway, and Rebekka's eyes followed it until it stopped in front of the house. "You go on, now. Go clean yourself up. Your mama and I are going to have a talk." As I stood, she reached out and gripped my arm tightly. "Make no mistake about this. You have hurt my boy, and he's in Germany fighting for his life so you can be here and consort with the enemy." She glared at me. "I don't know if I can ever forgive you, and you'd better pray Tom comes home safe." Her voice caught, here. "But so help me, God, I don't want to see your life, or his life, ruined because of your stupidity."

She released my arm and walked out the front door to greet my mom.

That night, Mom and I drove, in deathly silence, to Rebekka's house. The evenings were still cold, and I shivered in my light jacket while the car heated. In the twilight, turning to go down the steep hill into town, my gaze lingered on the entrance to the camp. Mom sat, gripping the steering wheel so hard her knuckles were white, mouth held in a tight line, not once looking in my direction. Rebekka let us in, and there, they hatched a plan.

Rebekka had a rich aunt, she said, who lived in Hudson, and she would take me in until the baby was born. I would have to work for my living, as a companion, of sorts, until my time was near. She could make the arrangements within just a few days. I stared down at the table as the two of them spoke in hushed tones about what to do with me. Mama said very little, just sat in grim silence, nodding, and, on occasion, sniffling into her kerchief.

The plan was that I would graduate from school in May, as planned, hide the pregnancy and be on a bus for Hudson shortly thereafter. I was to tell no one, not Betty, not Dad, or Joe, or anyone. Rebekka had many connections in the area; she and her husband were contributors of various political and social organizations, and they knew a lot of people. She would get the investigation re-directed, away from me, and my family. She could make calls and get the investigators to stop snooping around my family, but we would have to act quickly and stay silent.

When we left, the uncertainty of my future was like a weight hanging from my shoulders. I was not healthy and strong as I'd been during my fall romance; I had been throwing up a lot, and had been in such a state of anxiety since Erich had left that my heart would pound inside me, sometimes, in the dead of night, as if it was going to pound a hole in my chest and I would split in two.

I couldn't stop feeling paranoid, watching over my shoulder for the investigators, watching, continuously, for Daniel and his cruelty. He loved to call me names, and berate me, keeping me afraid. Perhaps this would be the only way to escape the constant fear I had that I was being watched. I felt it, everywhere. I just didn't know if it was the authorities, or Daniel. Or Erich…

The world was abuzz with talk when Adolph Hitler and a woman, Eva Braun, died in some underground bunker. Apparently, no one knew that the two were lovers, and I laugh at the bitter irony that she and I share the same name and harbored a secret romance that was doomed to fail. I wonder what Erich is thinking right now. Is he happy at this news? Will he be able to go home?

The war, still, does not end. Perhaps the fight in Europe is ending, but it will not truly end until Japan is defeated, and our boys are home. My beloved Joseph, flying somewhere over the Pacific Islands, was shot down again. We know nothing of his condition; it is like going backward in time, the feelings I have inside, knowing he's injured, yet again, and not knowing much more. This time, though, I believe he will come home, and his time in this bloody battle is over.

I quietly graduated from high school in May. While my friends and classmates had parties and celebrations and cake, I went home that Friday evening and packed my things into the old suitcase that mom had in her closet. Somewhere along those few weeks, mama had found a confidante in her church, a church elder, who had persuaded her that he knew of a place, in Minneapolis, that took in girls such as myself. Mom, heavily involved in her new faith, was completely pulled in, and, before I knew it, I was on the greyhound, bound for a boarding house for women of ill-means.

When Rebekka found out, she had been confused, then angry. She had driven over and argued with my mother. You don't know anything about this place, she'd said. Eva will have a good, solid life at my aunt's home. But my mother, a stubborn Irish woman with a streak of pride and an even deeper streak of ire, would not budge. I knew she wanted nothing more than to punish me for my willful indiscretions, and in those last few weeks I was home, she could barely look me in the eye.

I felt so alone and frightened. We said nothing to my father, a sweet and frail old man, whose world had turned upside down at the loss of his son. I know not what she said, but I do know my mother made up a story about finding me a job in the 'Cities, and he did not question it.

I was for all practical purposes, banished to the house. The only freedoms I had were when I took Sasha out. I spent hours grooming and cleaning the horses up, brushing the long, winter coats from their flanks until each of them glistened. Betty came by one evening, and we sat on the porch, sipping soda and talking quietly. She was, by then, heavy with her child, and when she took her shoes off and set them on the table in front of her, her legs were swelling a bit. "I'm so tired of being so huge and my feet hurt all the time," she complained. "Mostly, though, I'm just so excited for the baby!"

"How is Jerry?" I asked.

"Near as I know, he's doing fine. I pray he'll be coming home soon, but I don't know. He's in Saipan, fixing B-52s and P-51s and P-38s, and I read all about it when he sends me letters. I swear, it seems like he's enjoying himself way too much out there! They've been hit with air raids a few times, and I'll be glad when he's home. Thank God, he's not infantry, like Tom..." Betty's voice trailed off.

"How is Tom, Betty?"

"I don't know, really. We worry every day. He has not written for a while. But each day we don't get a telegram or a letter is a good day." She replied to my inquiry. "Now that the evil little coward, Hitler, has killed himself, maybe he'll be able to come home. How's Joe? Still flying?"

"Oh, Betty, I suppose you haven't heard yet. Joe was shot down. He was flying escort. We don't know much about his condition, but, we, too, just wait and hope he is well. He's in a hospital in Australia. I've got to believe that this war with Japan will be over soon, and he'll be coming home, too."

We talked. About Shane, and his beauty. About Jerry's humor and penchant for storytelling. About Joe's quiet intellect that belied the prankster inside. And, about Tom.

"I'm sorry, Betty." I began, feeling tears begin to form. "I was so young. So foolish. Tom is a truly wonderful man, and he will make someone a wonderful husband, someday..."

"Yes, he will, Eva. But I had always hoped it would be you."

I shook my head, looking past Betty's round form, at the pastures beyond, where I could almost see Erich's blonde hair shimmering in the sun, and felt such sorrow. As tears flowed down my cheeks, Betty reached out and took my hand. "It will be all right, Eva. You'll see."

I shook my head again but said no more. I could not tell her of my traitorous behavior, any more than I could tell her of the child I carried inside of me. She had been my closest friend and confidante since we were children, but I was certain that would end if she knew the extent of my betrayal. I just clung to her hand and sobbed.

Chapter Twenty-Four

I live in is a three-story boarding house, just off the University campus, which had previously housed visiting scholars and doctors who were here on temporary assignments to the school. We each have our own room, but it is crowded. All of us are in various stages of our pregnancy, and only a handful are married. We come from many different backgrounds, and places.

One girl of about twenty, Wanda, a beautiful black woman with swaying hips and a wide, toothful smile, is due any time, and often complains about her back and the food. She says her mama is from the south and could cook up the best fried chicken and hoe cakes in the country. We are required to cook our own food and are assigned duties all over the house.

Edith Walker, a tall, waiflike woman who was nearing thirty, met her prince when she was a nurse in a London hospital. His name was Jonathan, and he was on a crew of American GIs who were ambulance carriers, a medic who drove ambulance caravans through the battle fields and delivered wounded patients to her hospital. He was, she said, a good man, and they had fallen in love and married quickly.

When, just a few short weeks after they wed, he went out to the field and never returned, she set out for his family home, hoping to escape the ravages of war and her cockney heritage, and bring their baby up right. But his family would not accept her, with her loud, boisterous accent and her rather brazen ways, and sent her packing. Her room is next to mine, and we often sit up late at night and talk; she smoking one cigarette after another, me sipping cool water and resting my feet. I like her; she is unlike anyone I've met before. We are due to have our babies around the same time.

We are assigned work, and sometimes that shifts, depending on our condition. We wash and fold bandages for the war effort, clean rooms and toilets at the university or at local businesses. Some work as secretaries or clerks, filing documents and typing correspondence for officials at the school. We all wait for the day when we have our babies.

Some of the women have decided to put their babies up for adoption, and the head mistress, a stately woman with thin lips and her hair tied into a neat bun, arranges meetings with an adoption service. There are hundreds of war babies to be had, and many will end up with good families, we are told. We are encouraged to sign papers and meet with the gentleman in the dark suit who comes in every Wednesday and tells us how much we and our babies will suffer if we do not do the right thing and give them to good homes.

Some of us, myself included, adamantly refuse to speak with the man, and are often conveniently absent at the 1:00 hour when he is set to arrive. Wanda, Edith and I walk to the park a few blocks away and sit in the sunshine. Here, in the bustle of the city, we do not stand out, and few people even glance our way. While I know not what I will do when my child is born, I do know that I will not give this piece of Erich away, no matter what I must endure to keep it.

We have regular visits with a physician, who takes us, one at a time, to a large pantry that has now been converted to a makeshift hospital room. There we are examined in a very clinical way, and, again, encouraged to do the right thing for the child and consider adoption. This, also, is the room in which the girls will deliver their babies, and after that, they are moved to the rooms once designated for servants, also in the lower level. After a week or so, they are sent home.

Edith takes the bus down to the VA hospital, and because she is married to a soldier killed in action, is eligible for some benefits. But the hospital is not well equipped for deliveries, and she will have her baby here. Once she has saved enough, she says she will go back to England. I feel for her, because this is not what she had planned, but she brushes it off.

The lies I tell become so intertwined with my real life that I sometimes cannot tell the difference. When Edith asks about my sweetheart, I talk about growing up with him, how he is the older brother of my best school friend, and that he is in Europe somewhere. The truth must never be shared. This makes it easy to lie and lead Edith to believe that my lover is not an enemy, but a heroic boy who protected me in my youth and loved me before he left. I show her the watch that Tom handed to me before he left and feel lightheaded.

"Does he know about your baby?" Edith sits with me in the courtyard, fanning herself in the summer humidity.

I shook my head. "No. I don't want anyone to know."

"Why not? He sounds like a good bloke." Edith. "He'd marry you."

I shook my head, again. "I can't think about that right now." My heart lurches. "He's got enough to deal with, Edith," referring to his soldier status. "Even with the war ended, he won't be home for a while, and I am not ready to share this with him."

She eyed me intently. "Your mum doesn't really want anything to do with you, does she?"

"No, not really. I've disappointed her."

"That baby's not Tom's, is it?" Edith was very astute. When I said nothing, she continued, "that's why your mum sent you here, instead of taking care of you, isn't it?" She shook her head in disgust. "No matter, Eva. You are a good kid and you're smart. You'll do all right. Even my mum, who cooks for the boarding school, would not turn me out into a place like this."

"It's better for me, here, Edith. People gossip."

"Do people know you're here? Your friends?"

"No. I think she has convinced them that I took a job as a nanny somewhere."

Resentment begins to burn inside of me, but it is coupled with guilt. I worry about my dad. Mom will not tell me much, but did say that Daniel took off, claiming he was getting a job as a roughneck on some oil rigs in Oklahoma. I don't know if I believe that but am relieved. At least he won't be there when I go home. If I go home.

My mother does not call often. I think she continues to want to punish me. Our conversations are short and without warmth, but, sometimes begrudgingly, she shares information when I ask for it.

Betty gave birth to a beautiful baby girl, whom she named Diana Eva Hamilton. I cling to the phone and feel tears behind my eyes as she describes the baby, who favors her mother's dark heritage. She tells me that Betty asks about me, and she thinks I'm working outstate. Mother is vague, but I'm certain that Rebekka and my mother have been doing their best to keep Betty from knowing the truth.

I await some word that, perhaps, Erich's body would have shown up somewhere. With the war in Europe fulfilled, this is a time that the PWs would be repatriated and sent back home. But I never ask, and the news of his escape has become back page news. Most people think he fled to Canada and is making his own way home.

I was called, overnight, to assist with Wanda's delivery. It was scary, and intense, and, in the end, Wanda's boy came screaming into the world. He has a head of curly, dark hair, and weighed nearly nine pounds when he was born. Wanda is so happy and will be leaving within a few days. She is hoping that her man, who is a cook on a ship in the Philippines, will be happy when he gets the news.

She and her mother, and three sisters, will be returning to her hometown in Mississippi soon. She says she came to this place because her mama had enough mouths to feed and Wanda was fired when her boss found out she was having a baby. But she is happy, and I am excited for her.

My little one kicks like crazy and moves inside of me all the time. I feel heavy and hot, and the humidity of summer sticks to me, making me cranky. After a long day in the laundry, my feet are nearly purple, and I spend most of my nights, now, on a chair in my room with my feet propped up on a pillow, trying to ease the tingling and swelling. The doctor says I need to be careful; my blood pressure is high, and the swelling indicate I may have some issues, so we monitor it closely. But the baby is moving and healthy, and that is what is most important to me.

Summer is passing by so quickly. No one comes to visit me from home, but Edith and I have become good friends, and she makes me laugh, especially when she cusses. Sometimes I can hear her in the room next to mine, and I giggle. "Bloody hell, I can't fit into these damned shoes, anymore, my feet are so big."

"I shoulda' made him keep his wanker in his pants." She clips from next door. "Even my arse is getting too big for me own bloomers!" At time she is angry; angry, I think, at her husband, the war, herself. "Stupid pikey; I must have been off my trolley to go and marry some American from the middle of nowhere."

A group of us goes to church every Sunday, making the seven-block trek on foot to the Presbyterian church on Nicollet. Here, some people stare at the group of young women, few older than twenty, who come hobbling in with their big bellies in hand-me-downs from previous residents of the home. Most just ignore us.

I take communion each Sunday, and hope that, somehow, I can atone for my sins and be forgiven. Edith refuses to go to church. When the head mistress, a woman we are required to refer to as Mrs. Nelson, even if I'm certain she has never been married and never leaves the home, comes knocking, I can hear Edith tell her to go to hell. I, myself, am too young, and too afraid to say such things, and am dressed and ready before she gets to my door.

I'm heavy, lightheaded, and uncomfortable. On this Sunday I just sit and listen to the radio in my room, with my feet propped. The news of the world is filled with excitement and promise. The U.S. has sent bombs to Japan that are of such devastating proportion, it's impossible to really understand how one can destroy an entire city. I do not hate the Japs, I just know that something had to be done to get them to stop the fight, when it has become obvious that they are not able to win. Victory is near, and we are all relieved and happy that our soldiers will soon be home.

I received a package from my mother yesterday, and it sits on my lap, waiting for me to open. I've found myself more and more angry with her; perhaps it is that imminent motherhood has brought out the lioness in me, but I'm resentful that she sent me to this place instead of following Rebekka's plan.

When I open the box, I find letters from my aunt, wishing me a happy birthday, and realize I'd missed it. There are cards from others, as well, and a photo of Betty's daughter, all smiles and plump cheeks. My Dad is not well, mother wrote. Joe is on his way back to the states, and due to arrive in Virginia, where he will stay for a while. She is vague; it seems his injuries are severe, but she will not elaborate. I only feel happiness that he is coming home.

Betty's letter is more detailed, mostly about the baby. She is waiting word for a final date, but Jerry is on his way back. She could not be more happy and is excited for him to meet their daughter. When he returns, they will be moving into a house just a few blocks from where she grew up and she and Rebekka have already been fixing it up, painting and decorating, while the baby lays on a blanket on the floor and coos. She is blissfully happy.

Tom is heavily involved in a repatriation commission in Europe and will not be returning for some time. He is well. He was injured in March or April, but it was, she says, nothing serious, some shrapnel in his leg. Is it selfish to feel a pang in my heart when I think of his inevitable return? I don't know if it is fear, guilt, or hope, but it is unsettling.

The heat of the August air woke me; these rooms of the upper floor are stifling, and the fan that circulates at the foot of the bed does nothing for me. Drenched from head to toe, I have a horrible headache and, when I tried to turn in the bed, I felt something gush between my legs. Sitting up too quickly, I was immediately nauseous and had to lie back down, calling for Edith, who rushes to my side just as I felt the first sharp pain in my abdomen, sharper and deeper than I could imagine and I let out a scream. It happened so quickly, and when she reaches the light switch, we are both horrified by the blood that stained the sheets.

I was so frightened. "Edith!" I shouted at her. "Run, get nurse!"

By this time, other girls are waking up and I could hear them moving around the hallway, and see lights switching on. Nurse took one look at the blood and ran to call the doctor. The pain ripping through me was horrible, as though I were going to be broken in half. I was moved to the surgical room in the cellar.

Throughout the night that turned into day, and then to night again, the nurses stuck me with needles. Morphine for the pain, they said. You are toxemic, Eva. Your body is full of poisons and the baby may be breech. I drifted, unaware of my whereabouts at times. Dreams of Shane and Erich and Danny. Sometimes I would moan, sometimes outright scream.

Outside the window, I could hear heavy noises, as if there is a carnival or a parade in the street. The nurses and other girls who assisted seemed so excited; something about the war and Japanese surrender. I didn't care, I just wanted to get the baby out of me before it could rip me in two.

More shouting in the streets. Someone comes running in with small flag shouting that the war is over. Perception did not hit me then; the contractions hit with remarkable speed, one on top of the other, and finally, the doctor comes.

The nurses ignored my protests and gave me another shot. I hear a voice screaming, "Erich… please, please help me…. Mama?" I fought to stay alert but was too weak. Just as I felt the darkness descend, but before it consumes me, I heard the cries of a baby, strong and piercing and angry.

I next woke to sunlight, in my room, alone. For just a moment I was disoriented, and then my first thoughts were for the baby. I tried to call out, but my throat felt scratchy and I could only whisper. When a nurse came in, I asked her where the baby was, but she just shushed me and said the doctor would be in soon. When she gave me yet another shot, I was too weak to protest and fell back into a deep sleep.

When I next woke, it was dark and there was a table lamp on in the corner. The headmistress was sitting next to the table, with a bible in her hands. She is clinical and cold, in telling me that the Doctor says your baby did not survive birth.

It is clearer now, and I know she can't be right. "I don't believe you!" I screamed at her. "You're a liar. What did you do with my baby?"

She quickly called in the nurse, but I fought like a mad woman and the needle did not hit its mark this time. With the help of restraints from some of the other girls, they were finally able to dose me. I lay on my side with my back to them and sob huge, heart-wrenching sobs until the drug carries me away.

I endured a horrific infection, growing weaker by the day, until they finally put me into hospital. There, they told me that the baby boy had been buried in Edina in a private cemetery, without a headstone. When I recovered, I was told, I could go and visit his grave.

The irony hits me at some point in those weeks in the hospital that my child was born and died on August 14, 1945, the day the war officially ended. Sometimes late at night my dream was so vivid I could swear Erich was next to me in the bed, and our golden-haired boy was nestled between us. Then I would wake and weep and pray that Erich, who must surely be in heaven, and our baby boy were watching from above.

My mother tried to visit me in the hospital, but I threw such a tantrum that she was asked to leave. My baby is gone; I will not return to my childhood home, no matter what I need to do.

Chapter Twenty-Five

Claire feels the soft caress of a loving hand stroking her hair. She sighs and snuggles into the warm embrace and hears a voice as sweet as honey whispering.

"Claire, honey, you must wake up now."

"No, Mom, not yet. Please? Just a few minutes longer."

The voice is still soft and sweet, but insistent. "Princess, it's time."

Grandma? Claire is confused and tries to turn her head to the sound of the voice, but can't quite muster the strength and it is irritating to her. She tries harder, but still can't budge. She opens sleepy eyes, but everything is blurred, and she has a hard time focusing. The light is bright, so brilliant, it makes her eyes hurt.

What finally comes into focus is her lovely mother, just as Claire had seen her last, standing at her left side, smiling. Her hair was flowing around her face, like spun satin, and she was haloed in the brilliance of cascades of color and light unlike anything Claire had ever seen.

Claire can *feel* the joy and love pouring out of her mother's body, and she is drawn to it. She wants nothing more than to be forever embraced within her mama's golden beauty, but she is not able to move. As she struggles, she is able to free just one arm and reaches as far as she can toward her mother but can't quite make it. She turns her head in frustration, and there, on her right, she sees Eva, also smiling down at her. Eva reaches out to touch Claire's face, trying to soothe her.

"Shhh, Princess." She whispers. "You must calm down and let them take care of you."

"Grandma," Claire whispers through cracked lips. "You look so beautiful." She turns her head back to her left, and there, beside her mother, stands her father, with an arm draped across her shoulder. They look so handsome together, so happy, that it takes Claire's breath away.

She begins to cry. "Daddy," she says between sniffles. "I've missed you so much." Edward nods and a shimmering smile comes across his face, filled with such sweet sorrow and love that Claire can feel her heart breaking.

She turns again to her Grandmother, who still stands next to her. The light that emanates from her parents casts a gleam on Eva, and she shimmers in its shadow.

"Claire, it's time to go back. You're needed."

"No, please. Daddy, please. I want to go with you." Claire pleads and sobs. "Mama, I love you so much."

Isabelle nods, and Claire sees the look that passes between her mother and her grandmother. "Princess, your mom and dad have always been with you. But your life is long, and you have such love waiting for you right outside the door. You must be strong."

Claire listens closely to the words but does not yet understand them. Suddenly, there, in the distance at the foot of the bed she is lying in, she sees Grandpa Tom, and another man, with golden hair. She can feel a faint glimmer of recognition, but then it fades. She tries hard to focus on her mom and dad, but they seem far away now.

She turns to her grandmother for assurance. Eva is changing before her eyes and suddenly the bed she lies in is in a field of wildflowers. Eva is young, and astonishingly beautiful, more so than Claire had ever realized. Eva looks into the distance, where the two men stand. Claire can feel her happiness cloaked around her in the field. Eva looks back at her and says, gently, "Claire, my time here is soon over. But yours is not. Go back and love again."

Blackness.

Matthew awoke with a start, feeling the cramp in his neck from sleeping in the hospital chair for a fifth night in a row. In the days since the incident, he had not left Claire's side. Even when her family and friends came, he would hover just outside the door, willing her to make a move. To do something, anything that would show she was going to make it.

The blast that had sent Claire into the muddy water had torn a hole through her side, leaving an open wound that had been difficult to repair. When she slid deep into the mud, surrounded by the water and the remains of the old beer keg she'd fallen into, the mud had seeped into the wound. The doctors had cleaned it out during surgery, a long process during which Claire flatlined twice, having lost so much blood. Battling an infection and weak from blood loss, it would be a long recovery, before Claire's body would muster enough energy to pull her from the cocoon, and Doc Johnson had warned Matt to be patient. She just needs time.

Matt's patience wore thin as the hours ticked slowly by. He replayed the life that he and Claire had lived, sometimes together, too often apart, and vowed that he would never let her leave his side again. As he shifted in the seat, he heard sound and saw the arc of light shine into the dimly lit room as Chris Breuning pushed a wheelchair bound Lyneah through the door. Her head was bandaged, and a neck brace circled her throat. "Hi," she spoke softly through swollen lips. "I couldn't sleep. How is she?" Lyneah put her hand over Matt's. "Any change?"

Matt shook his head, squeezed her hand, but his eyes never left Claire's face. "How are you doing?" he asked.

"Good," she whispered. "Face will be turning a bright purple before it's done, but Doc says I can go home tomorrow."

"She's strong, Matt. She'll pull through, it will just take some time." She continued. "There's nothing that will keep her from staying on this earth with you, after all the time wasted between you. Have faith." She squeezed his fingers slightly, then gestured to Chris, who was leaning against her chair. "Chris has been working on some things, and I think they would interest you."

Chris smiled at her, and Matt caught a glimpse of something that passed between them, an intimacy that exists between a man and a woman who feel connected, like a brief glimpse of what could become. He wondered what was going on between the two, smiling inwardly.

Claire will be happy, he thought to himself. "What have you found out?" he asked.

"Darius Troy," Matt heard the disdain in the detective's voice. "Drug Lord from Oklahoma, grew up in New Orleans. Seems Beaudine owed him money."

"The dead guy?"

"Still trying to figure out how he fit, but we think he worked for Troy. Name was Jimmy Frank. He's wanted on a number of felonies across Oklahoma, Indiana and Wisconsin, mostly drug related. What we know is that he lived in the same neighborhood as Troy, and his brother was a buddy of Troy's."

"Where's Beaudine?"

"Troy isn't talking but we're pretty sure he's dead." Chris gently stroked Lyneah's shoulder. "Feds are coming in to take over the case, because of the interstate drug business."

"What did you find out about the bones?"

"They're in Ramsey County. Forensic anthropologist was brought in from the University. They're pretty interested in those bones. No one's talking yet, but it looks like they belonged to a German who was in prison camp here in the 40s."

Something clicked and Matt suddenly turned to Lyneah. "Has Claire talked with you about the diaries she found?"

"Not really. Why?"

"She said Eva had known a prisoner who worked on the farm during the war, who disappeared from the camp."

"Yes, that was true. I remember Mom and Dad spoke of it, but briefly. I did a project in school about the camp, and they said that he had disappeared around Christmas, of '44, I think?" Lyneah pondered. "There was an investigation, but no one could find anything."

They talked quietly, Matt often glancing at Claire or caressing her arm. She looked so fragile in the bed, and it hurt Lyneah's heart to see her cousin like this. It was especially difficult because she also felt incredible guilt. She was filled with such levels of emotion it was almost overwhelming her. Her heart was so grateful for the men who had saved her life that day.

It had been like a dream, really. She would never forget the moment she gave in to death. With the gun pointed in her face, she had suddenly felt such a sense of peace, and she closed her eyes. But out of nowhere some primal force seemed to whip into the meadow from the shadows, like a strong wind, and she felt herself rolling, hard, into the man's legs. Almost as if someone had pushed her, and the man had slipped and pulled the trigger a second later, right into the ground where her head had been. He lost his footing and fell with a heave to the ground, grabbed her by the leg as she twisted to get away, and pulled her back, holding the gun in one hand and her in the other.

He wrestled with her, slamming her head with the butt of the gun, a crushing blow right into her cheek, and the pain had been unbearable. She'd fought back, screaming the entire time, taking hold of the rifle and pulling on it, twisting it, but he was so much stronger. He'd shouted back at her, "Where's my fuckin' money? Why are you making me do this?" When the monster put his hands around her throat, squeezing hard, she found herself floating, high above, and the pain in her broken cheekbone and bruised body seemed to wash away. She vaguely heard Matt calling for Claire as the man's fingers lost their grip on her neck.

Then suddenly, out of the mist, there he was. Lyneah heard him roar and bear down on Troy, jerking him off her with strong arms. The pain in her face came back, and while the men fought, she turned to her side and coughed blood. She felt grit in her mouth and smelled the blood, felt it rolling from her nose. When Matt, frantic, asked where Claire was, Lyneah could only point. "In the river," she had whispered between gritted teeth.

When the search team found Claire, she'd been nearly dead. As they pulled her out of the mud, she'd been clutching a skull, like a talisman, and even in near death, she clutched it close to her heart and they'd had to pry it out of her hands.

She had crashed down into an old steam tank, the kind that was used to ferment hops before the tanks were replaced with stainless steel. Inside the barrel, skeletal remains, nearly intact but for the force of impact.

When her body hit the top, iron spikes that had rusted away from years of erosion disintegrated into dust, and the planks had pealed like an onion, revealing the bones inside. The barrel appeared to have been buried on the banks of the river.

When the Cottonwood flows after a heavy winter, spring melts its crystal shards and pushes easterly, where it meets the Minnesota River, and, ultimately, contributes to the Mississippi River watershed. Years of wetland reductions destabilized the embankment, annual flooding through the valley causing erosion. The erosion crept further and further inland, until it eventually seeped into the barrel that had been buried with the bones of a young male encased inside it.

There were some who were speculating, but most agreed that the bones were likely those of a twenty-three year old German soldier who had disappeared from the encampment sometime in 1944 or '45. Any records had long since been destroyed; about the only information left was from the archives of the Brown County Journal. Chris said that Officer Lahr was over at the museum trying to find more information.

"They picked up a search warrant for a house that Troy was renting," Chris said. "an old farmhouse out by Swan Lake."

Claire heard the soft murmur of words before she became fully awake, like a sound that carries across the water on a foggy night, echoing in her head, making it feel like it was splitting in two. Her mouth was dry, so dry, and she tried to open it, to speak, but nothing came but a tiny sigh. She tried again. She willed her eyes to open, but her eyelids stuck together. As she grappled with the darkness, she felt a warm hand take hold of hers and another touch her cheek.

"... Claire, honey," Matt's voice softly enveloped her in the mist, becoming more insistent. "...Chris, pull the call light... waking..." More voices, stronger now.

She felt the presence of another in the room, and felt cool hands touch her forehead and then pick up her wrist. The cuff encircling her arm squeezed and a bright light came on. As her eyes open, the first thing she sees is Matt's face, close to hers, and there are tears falling. She feels their wetness, and she focuses, finally able to look closely at him.

"When..." she tried to say something.

"What, sweetie?" she feels Matt shaking next to her, and tries again, struggling to make out the words, which come out faintly and muffled, as though her mouth is full of cotton.

"When did you grow a beard?"

He cries. Openly. Puts his head down on the bed and sobs. And holds her hand so tightly it hurts, but not as much as the grains of sand in her eyes, so she doesn't mind. When he comes up for air, he grins the biggest grin she's ever seen, and says, "Why, do you like it? I'm thinking of keeping it."

She tries to shake her head, but it hurts too much, so she just closes her eyes again, and squeezes his hand back.

Hours later, after Lyneah has gone back to her room, taking Chris Breuning with her, she lies in clean sheets, her teeth brushed with the help of Sadie's sister and Matt, she feels very much alive. The shot they'd given her I.V. drip has made her feel less nauseous, and she begins to feel hungry. The ice chips and lemon sorbet has not given her much by way of nutrients, but she feels good.

When she learns details, she weeps.

A few days later, Betty and Uncle Jerry come by to visit her, bringing her flowers and some home-made chicken soup. Matt, at the urging of the hospital staff, had gone home for a much-needed shower and some sleep. Betty told her it had been like musical chairs for a while, first her, then Lyneah. Eva had been returned to the hospital, with an infection that the doctors think may be pneumonia.

When Claire asked Betty about the boy, Betty mulled for a while, then began. "Eva and I, and Tom and Eva's brothers, we all grew up together. Tom, your grandpa, was best friends with Eva's brother, Joe. When the war broke out, Joe was one of the first to enlist. But Tom had just been in a car accident and his number was postponed. It was all done by a board of locals who were selected to decide who was going to go, and when. It was a rough time for all of us who had brothers and boyfriends. Eva and I were just kids. It's hard to remember what it was like; it was so long ago." She squeezed Claire's hand, gently.

"Tom always had a fondness for Eva. But she was so much younger than he was. He went off to college, lived in the Cities for a while, and Eva and I just sort of grew up.

"When we went to war, everything changed. People just got, oh, I don't know, fatalistic. Girls married boys who were off to war, like me and Uncle Jerry." She smiled at the giant man who was sitting by the window. "Tom had just gotten back from living in the Cities, I think, because he wanted to be closer to home and didn't like living in the city. He really loved it here."

"Eva was an incredibly beautiful young thing, Claire. No boy in this town could ever really keep their eyes off her when she walked by, and what was so lovely about her was that she didn't know it. She didn't know how stunning she was, and she was just as beautiful inside as out. Tom saw it, though and I think the war gave him a chance he thought he'd never have because, when he came back to town, he set his cap for her."

"I found her journals. In an old trunk, after the fire." Claire spoke softly.

Betty nodded. "Jerry, honey, can you run down to the cafeteria and bring us some coffee?"

Jerry got up, said, "Sure," kissed his wife's cheek, patted Claire's hand, and left the room.

"Claire, your grandma is, and was, a complex creature. I knew she kept the journals. What have you read about?"

Claire was torn between wanting to protect her grandmother and wanting to know what Betty knew. "I read about the boy on the farm. And her being sent away..."

Betty nodded, slowly, and shifted to get more comfortable in her seat. "My mother loved Eva like a daughter, but for many years, there was a rift between them. I think she had something to do with Eva being sent away; you see, we had money, and so did my mother's family, and the plan had been to send Eva to go work for my aunt. I think it was really to get her away from the town; there was so much talk, especially when that German soldier disappeared."

"Of course, you know, Eva's mother was a callous woman, and a really religious fanatic. She didn't want to take any of the Nielsen charity, so she sent Eva to live in some group home in Minneapolis. I found out about it so much later. I'd moved to an apartment with a bunch of other gals in Sleepy Eye and was working at the cannery, working so many hours a week, and time had slipped by, so when I was next home, my mother said Eva was gone. Of course, I didn't know much at the time, but I could tell Mom was unhappy about it. It wasn't until years later that I knew what that was all about."

Jerry came in with the coffee, then left to run some errands. The two women talked for a long time. "What did Grandpa know?"

"Oh, I can't begin to really understand the inner workings of another couple's marriage, but I do know that Eva loved Tom with all her heart, all through their marriage. You knew that, too."

When Claire nodded in agreement, Betty continued. "When Tom came back from the war, he was hardened. You know, he always had that limp, after being injured in the Battle of the Bulge. Tom never really talked about what it was like, except to say that it was like being in a snowstorm in hell. But when Eva came home and they saw each other again, everything just seemed to wash away."

"I never thought that Eva would agree to come back here, but she did. She spent a lot of time hating Abigaile, her mother, but when Abigaile asked her to come back, she came back."

"I can't imagine what it was like for her, to lose the baby." Claire spoke softly. "How crushing it was for her. I always wondered why she only had one child."

"Oh, honey, Eva wanted more children. She truly did. But she had miscarriage after miscarriage. She kept trying but just couldn't carry a child and blamed herself. She had so much guilt and turmoil. When she finally was able to stay pregnant with your mom, she was on bedrest for months, and nearly died in childbirth. Tom said no more. No more trying. He couldn't bare the idea of losing her..." Betty's voice cracked and she reached into her purse for a tissue.

"No matter what happened, Tom and Eva loved each other so much. I actually think that the war, and the circumstances were what made their marriage so solid." She sniffed, as did Claire, and they both smiled through tears.

When Matt came into the room, he carried a box in one arm and a huge bouquet of summer flowers in the other. He had shaved but for a well-groomed goatee. He bent to kiss her, and Claire's fingers lingered on it.

"I like it," she said. "tickles when you kiss me." He grinned, kissed her again, and set the box on her cart. "I brought you something." He pulled out the journals and laid them on her lap.

She thanked him with tears in her eyes. "You just missed Betty and Jer." She said. "We talked for a long time. Thank you for bringing these to me."

Matt sat down in the chair previously occupied by Betty. "Eva's on another floor." His voice was concerned. "She's pretty sick, Claire."

Claire nodded. "I know."

Matt filled her in on what was happening with the case. "So far, no sign of Beaudine, but something tells me they won't find anything. People like that, they don't leave a trail." His voice was grim. "Chris told me that, when they searched the abandoned house, they found a bunch of stuff, stuff that had been stolen around the area, probably by that sidekick of Troy's, and also a lot of pictures."

"Pictures of what?"

Matt's jaw tightened. "Pictures of you."

Claire's jaw dropped. "Me?" she exclaimed, incredulous. "What kind of pictures?"

Emotions ran across Matt's face, and she could see he was angry. "All kinds, Claire."

"Oh, my God." Claire was horrified.

"Some of Lyneah, even of you and me, but mostly you..." his voice trailed off as his thoughts drifted. Matt was glad the little bastard was dead, or he'd have been tempted to do it himself.

Claire tried to hold back tears. He climbed into the hospital bed with her and held her close. "It's okay, baby. He's gone."

"Tell me everything, Matt." She said.

"I don't know, honey-"

She put her hand across his mouth. "Please. I'm fine."

The police had ordered the abandoned farmhouse sealed, and a Hazmat team had been brought in to clear it. The entire house was full of both raw materials and manufactured meth, all bagged and ready for distribution. "Chris says it's worth hundreds of thousands of dollars. Looked like there were a bunch of people living there, mostly immigrants. Some women. All junkies but a few. It was going to take weeks to clean up the mess."

They have not been able to positively i.d. the bones you found, there's no genetic material to compare, but the State Department is involved. I think they're hoping to reach out to German records, but, you know, it's a long shot."

"Hmm." Claire's furrowed brow showed her concern. "I asked Betty not to say anything about what we know about him, Matt. At least, not until we can finish reading the diaries. There may be something in them but I'm just not going to share it. Not even with Chris Breuning. These things were Eva's private things. I want her protected from this, even if she doesn't really know what's going on."

Matt nodded. He settled back into the chair while Claire adjusted the hospital bed, and together, they continued Eva's journey.

Chapter Twenty-Six

Tom crawled across the snow to the German soldier, who was no more than a boy, and touched his hand to the boy's neck. Earlier in the night, he'd swung the pickaxe hard to dig his foxhole as deep as he could in the snow and the frigid, frozen ground, first placing his wool blanket in the hole, not even a foot deep, but just long enough for his tall frame. The cold was brutal, worse than he'd ever known, worse, even, than any he could remember experiencing in Minnesota, and as soon as he settled, he could feel it creep under the standard issue coat that held no warmth.

The 101st had been pushed toward the Front, traveling northeasterly across the French border into Belgium, having left Camp in a hurry, with few supplies and even fewer weapons, believing that weapons would be replenished along the way. But increasing fog, swirling in with a cold front creeping in from the North Sea, had made it impossible for the Allied air forces to drop supplies for several days, and, without them, soldiers on the ground were helpless.

Moving through the countryside on the edge of Luxembourg territory, Tom had taken in the sights; tiny, picturesque villages, like the quaint town of Arlon, decorated for Christmas, where people walked along the streets, shopping, as though war was not just miles away. The snow, wet and heavy, fell on the convoy, leaving the men cold and even more miserable.

The sight of shoppers and Christmas lights made Tom long for home, and all he had taken for granted. The heat of a fire, electric lights, telephone lines that were not strung for miles only to be cut by the firing of German Panzers moving steadily eastward. Dry socks. One of Rebekka's home-cooked meals that wasn't a frozen K-ration out of a tin.

As Tom's convoy marched further along the highway, it became clear that the line between Belgium and Germany, Hitler's last stand, would be unlike anything he'd known. GIs, running east, away from the Front, equipment stuck in the mud, blown to pieces or just abandoned as Americans beat a hasty retreat.

Grown men, with haunted eyes and hollowed cheeks, some shell shocked, some silently weeping as they scrambled around the mud and the ruts and the equipment and watched their replacements, many of whom had never shaven a day in their life, in their clean coats and shiny boots, marching in columns on either side of the road leading to Germany. And certain death.

One of the kids, a piss-ant Private from Milwaukee, disdainfully pointed out that those "cowards" were running away like pussies. Tom wanted to punch him, but figured it wouldn't be worth it, and the kid wasn't long for this world, anyhow; he was too much of a loud mouth to figure out when to shut up, and, if an SS didn't put a bullet in him, Tom was sure one of his own would. Most of the replacements, though, just kept their heads down, or watched in shocked silence as their predecessors passed by.

Montgomery had sent the boys off to Camp Mourmelan after the shitshow in Eindhoven that had been Tom's first taste of combat. He'd joined the Paratroopers when he reached Georgia, and the training had been swift, because, rumor was that the replacement troops weren't keeping up with the dead, and it scared the hell out of every kid he trained with. He knew the car accident he'd been in had not been his friend, and there was more need in infantry than intelligence. And, at the age of twenty-four, he was the oldest draftee in his training battalion.

Tom as a young boy had been quiet, steadfast, preferring work to play. He'd sold newspapers for the Brown County Journal, swept floors at the hardware store. Shoveled snow for old Mrs. Engelkes and others down the block, saved his money. His world had been numbers. Statistics fascinated Tom, and he'd had a gift that helped him get many a job assisting with the bookwork for businesses in town, and, ultimately, a scholarship to the University.

Then the war took over, and he'd gotten into that accident, driving too fast one night on his way home from school in the dead of winter, and flipped the car. He was lucky to be alive, and the slight limp and ache in his leg were the only remnants. Not enough to keep him off the front.

The days of battle in Holland had taken their toll on Tom, and all the boys around him. The weeks of constant shootings, exhaustion, and sleeplessness, were disorienting. And blood. So much blood. You never got away from the blood; the sickly smell of it, mixed with gun powder and gasoline. It sank into your skin, and pretty soon you no longer noticed, and you no longer noticed the dirty beard building on your chin or the fact that you haven't bathed in weeks, because no one else has, either. Vanity escapes, even in the face of the nationals, the women, the children, who stare at you when your truck drives by their burned-out homes.

No one knew anymore who was running the show, Commander Bradley, or the Brit, Montgomery. Word had it that Eisenhower had relieved Bradley and handed his men over, but Tom knew only that not a one of 'em had been here. Watching the gunners take a pounding from the Wehrmacht tanks, or seen the fear in a young man's eyes when he's been hit by a bouncing betty and knows he'd be better off dead than to live a lifetime, without.

Tom had spent his life understanding numbers, statistics, strategy, and knew now that it meant not a God damned thing when you were lying just below the surface of an ice field and feared your nose was sticking too far out of your foxhole. While, miles away, Generals use that strategy, those numbers, to determine where you may lay your head for the last time.

At night, when he wasn't moving under cover of darkness, then, and only then, would he think of home. Of Eva, the girl, her pretty face, her soft, warm skin. Lying in the bitter cold, with nothing but bursts of rifle shots and then cold silence, he felt such an ache in his chest he thought it would burst. He would squeeze his eyes tight so as not to shed a tear and felt as if he were the only soul on the earth.

He remembered Uncle Sal talking, once, about what it had been like in the trenches during the Great War, and how he'd always had his buddies around him, even as some lay dying. Here, in the icy bed he'd made, Tom

Cottonwood Flowing

had never felt so alone. After days of exhausting movement and energy of battle, he would fight sleep, fearing he would freeze to death, but, when dawn would come, he would dread the awakening for another day of battle.

The September landing in Holland, taking the jump into the beautiful Holland countryside, had been unexpectedly serene. As he descended to the ground, Tom had seen for miles; lush, green rolling hills, and cows out to pasture. He'd had a soft landing in a field, near a grove of trees that was as thick as a jungle, and he and the other paratroopers had come together in formation, M-1s in hand, marching toward the single road across Holland into Germany, to take the bridges back.

Nearing Arnhem, the men could hear and see the destruction that the SS had wrought on the people, with their heavy panzer tanks, designed to 'doze through anything, and they'd done an all-out job of it there. The rubble was everywhere, along with litter of empty clips, dead horses, cows. Soldiers. The stench was horrible, and Tom held back the bile in his throat as he pushed past the dead, wanting only to get this show over with so he could go home. He realized quickly enough that his skills as a radio specialist were of much less use than his skills with a rifle.

The forest to battle was thick as a jungle at times, a battle in itself, and the lone highway across the border had been in shambles. Tom never reached the bridge. He didn't think about who he killed or what he was doing, he just did what he had to do to live. When they liberated the 100 or so British soldiers, starving and weak, orders came down to withdraw. Tom, weary and exhausted, was relieved.

The troopers were sent to Camp Mourmelon, to re-outfit. Tom had never tasted food as good as that at the mess hall, and did not balk at the horsemeat, which the cooks said were from old nags, but which tasted like the venison Tom and Joe would hunt in the fall back home, sweet and lean. Some of the boys complained, but few left any food behind. To sleep on a mattress rather than the ground, to sleep at all, really, had been like heaven.

It was at camp that Tom finally received letters from home. From Betty, whose husband, Jerry, was somewhere in the Pacific, working on airplane engines. From Rebekka, who wrote of ordinary life and how much he was missed, he received a photograph of himself and Eva, from the night of the dance. He sat staring at it for a long time, until he felt a tap on his shoulder.

"That your girl back home?" Tom turned to hear the voice of his buddy, Frank "Frankie" De Luca, standing over his shoulder, peering at the photograph. "She's a doll."

Tom casually slipped the photograph into his vest pocket and turned. "I thought you were getting a pass to Paris?" He smiled at the shorter man.

"Yes. You should get one, too. We'll get drunk on French wine and dance with the ladies..." Frankie was an Italian/Irishman brought up in New York City. He was small, and wiry, with the darkest eyes Tom had ever seen. Frankie was the prankster of the Company, and it never ceased to amaze Tom that someone didn't kick his little Italian ass.

"I don't know, Frankie," Tom said absently and continued to gather the letters together in his satchel. "It's pretty damned nice right here. I was thinking of catching up on some sleep and food before we go back to the Front. Maybe watch a couple shows..."

"Ah, yes, but there are no ladies, here, Tommy boy." Frankie grinned. "Go get your pass and let's get the hell out of here while we still can."

Tom listened to Frankie chatter while he continued to go through his mail. Stars and Stripes, another letter from Betty and cards from several friends back home. Absent, however, was any word from Eva. He looked up at Frankie. "Let's go."

The mess tent was full of boys ready to get some time away from the front. The CO lectured the men on the proper use of prophylactics and preventing disease, making it clear that anyone who came back with one could face court martial. General information, how to stay safe, alert. France had just been liberated in August, and there was still a general feeling of unease, but most of the men were elated to have the chance to get away from the battle if only for a few days.

The two men caught the last bus, loaded with GIs looking to let off some steam. The boys were jovial, telling jokes and whistling at the girls walking along the boulevard. City streets were crowded with people, French women, children playing in the streets, waving as the convoy of Amis drove by. Women, some well-dressed, riding bicycles along the walkways in high heels and long linen coats. It was Frankie's mission to find some nice French girl and get cozy before the next round of fighting, but, for every French girl on the streets, there were dozens of GIs looking for the same.

Everywhere you looked, there were American and British flags, draped over banisters and flat windows. There were few rooms left, but Frankie and Tom found their hotel on the riverfront, overlooking the Siene; a room just vacated by a couple of Brits going back to the front. The weather was chilly, and both men wore coats over their uniform shirts, and took a walk along the river front. Paris was, despite the length of the war, intact. There were still some restaurants with outdoor seating, so they grabbed a table outside of a little joint with a sign above the door that read, 'Cafe' Vivant.

A young woman with full lips and a dark, brooding look surveyed them from the doorway. She stood in tight trousers, with a sweater draped over her shoulders, shivering against the cold, smoking, her red lipstick staining the cigarette. There were several American and British GIs around other tables, but few natives. Since neither could read, nor speak French, but for a few words, Frankie pointed to the mugs at the next table, indicating that they wanted a drink. She did not move, just stood and continued smoking, looking bored.

Frankie leaned over to the next table, "Hey, you see the waitress around here?"

The flyboy gestured with his chin. "She's it. Looks like she's on a break." He laughed, easily. "Or maybe she just doesn't like you." He grinned at Frankie, then reached out to shake hands. "Name's Grayson. Grayson Butler."

Frankie took it. "Frank De Luca." He gestured across the table. "This here's Tom Nielsen. Where you from?"

"Little town in Tennessee, not far outa Memphis. You boys must be Yankees." His grin was lazy and he took a swig of the ale in his mug, wiping his lips with the back of his hand.

Frankie once again looked at the woman in the door, who'd finished her smoke and still had not moved. He cocked his head and raised his voice. "You gonna' serve us here, or what?"

The woman came over to the table and leaned close to Frankie, speaking rapidly in French. «Vous parlez français, non? Les Américains sont si stupides. Vous souhaitent certains pisse avec votre vin, monsieur? Peut-être un bol de merde qui va avec?"

Frankie leaned in close to the girl, close enough to feel her quickened breath, and appraised her, thoroughly, with eyebrows raised. "You sure are pretty when you're angry. Man could get lost in those lips."

She rolled her eyes. «Les hommes sont des salauds. Tout ce que vous pensez est votre robinet...»

Tom watched the interchange with amusement. "Tommy, she's sayin' she wants me. Baby, you want a little of this?" Frankie held his hands out. "I may be a short man, but I know how to please the ladies."

He gestured to Grayson but kept his eyes on the woman. "She got a name?"

The woman tossed her head and stated in perfect English. "*Her* name is Monique. What do you want?"

Tom laughed quietly at his friend's bemused look and said they'd both like a beer and the stew. She looked him over, nodded and walked back into the cafe, turning to give Frankie a scathing look.

"Tommy, I think I'm in love..." Frank said, only half joking.

"She's a foot taller than you, Frankie." Tom responded. "And way better looking. I think she's more woman than you can handle."

"Never underestimate the many talents of a short Italian, Tommy. When you're as small as I am, you gotta' make up for it by being better than everyone else. Keeps 'em coming back." Frankie watched as Monique returned with the meals. "Watch and learn, Tommy, my boy..."

Conversation turned. "How long have you been here?" Tom asked Grayson.

"'Forty-two. Came in over Algiers." Grayson took a long swig of ale, wiped the foam from his lips with the back of his hand. "Nice countryside over by Oran. Felt like home..."

Grayson's buddy, a burly kid with wild, red hair and days-old beard, chimed in with a distinct Scandinavian accent. "Yah, except for 'de damn Germans." He shook his head. "Stole everyt'ing from those people. Nothin' left but grass huts and oranges."

Another airman joined in. "I'll shoot myself with my own gun if I have to eat another fuckin' orange again. Gave me the shitters for weeks!"

"And those little French motorbikes..."

"Those damned caves underground, gave me the creeps..."

Tom turned to Grayson. "What do you fly?"

Cottonwood Flowing

"Bomber. B-25 Mitchell. These bastards are my crew." The all had a jolly laugh. Frankie had, by now, somehow found a seat at the crowded bar, and was being jostled about by the crowds of airmen, gunners, and infantry piling into the seating area, still relentlessly trying to engage Monique into conversation. It didn't look pretty.

"How was it out there, Captain?"

Grayson sighed, and pulled a cigarette from the standard issue pack in his jacket, holding the pack of Lucky Strikes out to Tom, who took one, and lit them both. He pulled deeply on the cigarette, then shrugged. "It was nothing. Desert. Dead Germans spread out all over the sand in pieces. Nothin' like flyin' in over the dunes and strafing a bunch of Nazis with their pants down."

Tom was silent, listening. These boys, good American kids, were laughing and joking about the best way to take another life, and it disturbed Tom. They described, in detail, each killing, with a surreal sense of pride. Tom wondered what it was that took good old farm kids and made them murderers. He also wondered when his day would come where he didn't feel sick each time he took aim at the enemy, some so young they looked like they could barely carry the weapons slung across their shoulders. Nope, it was not in him, not yet, this callous disregard for human life. Just the one driving force deep within him. Get home. Take aim, shoot, don't watch the death. Shoot again. Get home. He felt a sadness for these boys, and knew that, one day all too soon, his day would come.

The Germans had all but annihilated Algeria before the U.S. troops descended, laying waste to a dry but fertile landscape. Farther inland, the Sahara burned vast and magnificent, an intriguing mystery to the kids from the Midwest, who had only seen pictures of the great sand dunes and camels and palm trees. They exchanged stories into the evening.

Somehow, Frankie convinced Monique to accompany him along the river. Tom said his goodbyes to Grayson. "Good luck out there." Grayson nodded and watched him leave the bar and go out into the streets, still packed with people, mostly young girls in long coats and dresses, and GIs. The scent in the air was pungent, perfume, food, cigarette smoke, liquor, sweat.

Tom, lightheaded from the wine and spirits he had drunk, walked along behind them as they made their way along the boulevard, stopping here and there, Frankie calling out an occasional "Salut!" to the pretty girls and old Frenchmen in their tattered wool coats. Some of them waved and called back, others ignored the little American with the tall barmaid walking arm in arm. Monique knew several people at a little tavern a few streets from the river, and she, Frankie and Tommy sat there for several hours before stumbling to Monique's flat above the tavern.

The flat was tiny, sparsely furnished, and spotless. There was a small sofa against the street wall, and Tommy made his way to it, and sat heavily down, the wine sending the room spinning. He watched as Frankie and Monique kissed, she bending down slightly, watched Frankie's hand snake up her thigh, and wished his friend, "good luck" and a reminder to avoid a court-martial. Frankie laughed and continued to laugh as the door to one of the two tiny bedrooms closed behind him.

Tom lay his head on the pillow, the softest, sweetest pillow he'd felt on his head in a long time. It smelled of lilac and rose and he breathed deeply as his spinning mind drifted. Like Eva. He found himself drifting into a sweet dream as he pushed the sounds of Frankie and Monique's whispers and kisses out of his head.

Tom felt something small touch his face, and thought he'd imagined it. His head was splitting and he did not want to move, the alcohol now having run itself out. He felt another poke, under his eye, and opened one, startled to see a child of perhaps three, holding a doll of some sort, and peering intently at him, close enough to feel the breath from the child's body.

Tom closed the eye, and blinked rapidly, slowly clearing his vision. The child, a boy, with intense eyes and a furrowed frown on his forehead, did not move and continued to stare at Tom. The light coming in through the curtain above his head was blindingly brilliant, and as Tom sat up, the child pulled a few feet away, his eyes never leaving Tom's face.

"Hello," Tom said. The boy said nothing.

"Bonjour?" Tom said. Still, the boy was silent. He seemed curious, and stood, three feet away, cocked his head to the side, and pointed at Tom's head. "Chapeau."

Tom reached up to his head. "Chapeau?"

The boy nodded slowly, "Oui.." He reached behind the doll and pulled a beret from behind it. "Chapeau..." and he slid it onto his head, before pointing at the floor next to Tom's feet, which were still encased in his boots.

Tom looked down and saw his dress hat on the floor, and he picked it up, smiled, and gestured to put it on the boy's head. The boy hesitated only for a moment, then smiled back and ducked his head forward.

Just as the hat slid onto his head and over his eyes, a woman's voice called from the second bedroom, "Henri!" Both Tom and the boy jumped, and the hat skewed to one side of his head. He quickly turned and ran to his mother's side, chattering rapidly in French all the way. «Maman, Maman, il ya un homme étrange ici! Je porte son chapeau, vous voyez?»

The woman knelt and spoke to him in a quiet, stern voice. «N'ai-je pas vous dire de rester dans la salle jusqu'à ce que je me suis habillé? Maintenant, donner à l'homme son chapeau. Nous devons nous habiller pour l'église.» She sent disinterested glances Tom's way, then sent Henri back into the bedroom with an affectionate swat to his behind. "Trouver votre beau costume."

She stepped out of the room and closer to where Tom had slept. He ran his fingers through his hair and stood, wobbling from the alcohol induced vertigo.

She pursed her lips. "You are American?" she asked him.

Tom nodded slowly and extended his hand to her. "Yes, Ma'am." He said. "My name's Tom."

She ignored the hand. "What are you doing here?"

Tom felt rather foolish and dropped his hand to his side. "Monique, does she live here?"

"Yes. She is my sister." The woman sighed. "She brought you here, I suppose."

"Yes, ma'am. I'm sorry; I did not know she had others living here..."

"Yes. My son, Henri, and I live here. You met Monique at the tavern, yes?"

Tom nodded, still feeling lightheaded. "Listen, I'll be on my way soon. Just need a little water and a few minutes. I had a bit too much wine last night."

She nodded, and smiled, faintly. "You would like coffee, yes?" she asked.

Tom shook his head and smiled. "Oh, you don't need to trouble yourself."

"Please sit. I will make some coffee before you go."

"Is there a washroom, here?" he asked.

"Yes, through my bedroom door you will find a closet." She filled a coffee pot with water from a jug and pulled a can from the shelf above. "You can wash up there."

As she lit the stove, she called Henri to come to the table. The boy raced out of the room, and collided with Tom, still wearing the hat and now dressed haphazardly in a pair of knickers and a button shirt.

Tom laughed and put his hand on the boy's shoulders. "Hold on, Buddy! You're gonna' hurt yourself if you can't see where you're going." And he tipped the hat back to look down into the smiling blue eyes before Henri darted to the table, where his mother had placed crusty bread and some creamy cheese, and poured the boy a small cup of water. "*Manger*."

When Tom returned, the coffee was poured. She set out a bowl with sugar and sat across from him at the table. She was a petite, pretty woman, with slender arms and short, brown hair that curled around her ears. She seemed very young, although Tom could not guess her age. They sipped in silence but for chatter from Henri, who kept up a constant banter while he finished his breakfast.

When he left the table to play with his toys in the bedroom, Tom asked the woman what her name was. "I am Juliette. You are Tom. Who is your friend who is making love with my sister?"

Tom smiled; she had a wicked twinkle in her eye. "That's Frankie. He's in love with your sister... Coffee's good."

She smiled and poured another cup. "*Oui*. For a long time, we did not have coffee. Or sugar. The Germans, they took everything..." She paused and slid the sugar over to him. "*Everyone* is in love with Monique..."

"'Probably no one as short as Frankie." They shared a laugh, and talked a while of life, before the war, and now. Juliette and Monique had grown up near the German border, in a small village, until the German advance in '40. "My papa was killed, as was my brother." She said. Monique and I hid in the stable." Up in the *grenier*, she said, pointing upward with slender fingers.

Ah, loft." She nodded and smiled, shyly, showing small, even teeth.

"Oui." She nodded then fiddled with her cup and kerchief before continuing. "But then, Monique slipped out of the loft, to find food, and a German man, he come into the stable…" her voice trailed away, and she stood, putting the dishes away, wiping crumbs from the table into her hand. "Monique and I, we come to Paris, and she finds work at the tavern. I clean at the motel. But, the Germans kept coming, and then they took Paris, too."

Tom didn't say anything and then he heard Frankie and Monique stirring in the next room. Juliette went to her room to change, she said, to go to church; she and Henri try to go to pray every day. When Frankie emerged, he had a satisfied grin on his face.

Tom shook his head. "'Was wondering when you were going to show your ugly face."

Frankie's grin widened. Monique called from the bedroom. "Frankie, we go for pique-nique today, no?"

"Yes, my lovely, French girl, we go on 'pique-nique'." Juliette and Henri came into the room, dressed in light coats, with Henri still wearing Tom's hat. "Ah, you must be Juliette." Frankie bowed. "I am Francis. Francis J. DeLuca. And I'm going to marry your sister."

Juliette raised her eyebrows. "You are Italian."

"Well, ma'am, I'm from New York. Italian in my blood, but Brooklyn in my heart."

Monique came into the room, buttoning her pink blouse. "What is this, Brookline?"

"Brooklyn, my sweet. Brook-lin. Where you and I will make music together all night long…"

He pulled her face to his and kissed her. She just kissed him back and rolled her eyes when they finished. "Juliette, you come on pique-nique, also?"

"We'd better check in, Frankie."

"Sure, we'll go get cleaned up and come back."

Tom looked at Juliette. "Will you come along, Juliette?"

She hesitated. "I do not know. Henri…"

Tom held up his hand. "He'll be fine. He can come along with us." He smiled down at the boy, who solemnly took the hat off his head and handed it to him.

For the next few days, Frank and Tom accompanied Monique and Juliette, with young Henri, to various parts of the city. The October skies were often cloudy, and days cool, but the vibrant colors of the city's changing season were stunning. On the day it rained, a neighbor took care of Henri and the four adults toured the city, took photographs at the Eifel Tower, and ate lunch at the Cafe' de la Paix.

Tom learned that Monique was two years older than Juliette and took care of her and Henri. When Juliette, heavy with the child of the German soldier who found her in the loft that day, became sick, Monique worked two jobs, during the day at a factory, and at night, at the tavern. The sisters were afraid of the Germans who occupied their city and kept their heads down.

Juliette had given birth to Henri right in their apartment, overseen by a midwife who lived next door with four children of her own. It had been a tough birth. She lost a lot of blood, and it had taken months to recover. During that time, she said, Monique and the lady next door cared for her and for her newborn.

"Ginette is a good woman. Her husband was killed by those Germans; he was part of the Resistance, before we came here. I did not know him, but she weeps each time she speaks of him. His son, Adrien, who is thirteen, looks so much like the photograph she keeps in her room. He is an angry boy..." Juliette's voice trailed off.

They sat under a canopy in the park; a light mist was falling and he resisted the urge to wipe the dew as it settled on her nose. He listened to her speak in her heavily accented English, and, impulsively, he reached over and kissed her on the lips. She hesitated a moment, then kissed him back. When the pulled apart, she smiled at him, her face alight with pleasure. She said nothing of the kiss, but as they walked under her umbrella, he took her tiny hand in his.

Frankie and Monique had gone to the flat earlier, tiring of the rain and the walk, eager to shut out the world for a while. Without speaking, Tom and Juliette found themselves in the tiny hotel room, with its view of the Sienne, where they took off their wet coats and shoes, and sat by the window, watching the crowds below. Tom told her about what it was like in to live in Minnesota, and Eva, the girl he cared for back home, so far away; she spoke of the war, and her family and her love for her son, even though he was born of violence.

When she shivered from the dampness of her light dress, Tom gave her one of his shirts to wear and she hung her dress over a chair to dry, draped a blanket from his tiny bed around her shoulders. Tom took her legs from where they were curled underneath her, into his lap, rubbing her tiny, cold feet with his rough hands.

Neither intended it. War does things to a man of virtue, slowly seeping from him the future he fought for, giving him only the now. And when she adjusted her tiny form under the blanket, to move closer to his warmth, he claimed the moment and began making love to her with light kisses across her brow, then her mouth, the tiny curve of her arm, the softness of her firm breasts. Thoughts of Eva immediately leapt into his mind, and he tried to push them out. He felt himself comparing her soft curves and creamy flesh, to Juliette's thin frame. But, as he moved above Juliette and began to unbutton his shirt that she wore, he stopped comparing. She was beautiful, and tragic, and her caresses were disarming.

The union was sweet, and quiet, and when it was over, they lay together, naked, and when Tom slept, he dreamed of Eva, and lying next to her In this dream, he felt like he was home. He mumbled her name in his sleep, and Juliette reached up and soothed his cheek with her hand, and he relaxed. Juliette's heart hurt, but she knew, when the time came, she would be left behind.

An abrupt banging on the door awoke them both with a start. "Hey, Frankie! We gotta head back! We got orders."

Tom called. "Thanks, Hank. What time will the bus be here?"

The Private First Class recognized Tommy's voice. "The bus is already here, Sir." Tom sat up as did Juliette, and she covered her small form with the blanket while he stood in the moonlight. They hurriedly got dressed. She helped him pack his and Frankie's bags before heading to the apartment the two sisters shared. It was still dark, but the streets were not empty; G.I.s from all forces were making their way along the walkway to where the buses waited to take them back to camp.

Frankie and Monique were still asleep, and Tom walked quietly into the room to wake his friend; the lamp from the sitting room shown on the entwined couple, and Tom felt a pang of regret for both himself, and his friend. "Frankie. Frank, time to go."

Frankie was instantly awake. Monique stirred, then sat up, and Tom left the room quickly so they could dress. Tom could hear Frankie's voice, and heard Monique quietly weeping. "It's okay, baby, I'll be back. It's okay. I gotta go, honey…"

Tom turned to see Juliette staring at him from near the door where she'd walked in. He stood there awkwardly, then approached her and wrapped her in his arms. She stood apart, and put her arms around him, as if in a friendly embrace.

Her eyes misted, but she did not weep, just stood silently alongside him until she saw her sister and Frankie, who had only met four days before, leave the bedroom in such an embrace as to appear as one.

The last kiss was brief, hard. Tom told her to take care of herself, and of Henri. She nodded, and said, softly, "Please, Tom, live through this, and make your way home."

He nodded, and then they were gone.

Here, in this empty place of echoes, the cold biting into any exposed skin facing the sky, he could only wait, and pray, for death or salvation to come quickly. The sorrow of loss was permanently etched into his face, and the faces of the soldiers around him. He wondered where Frankie was, could he be the one crying for his mama? Tom heard the calling and he both cursed the kid who wouldn't shut up and felt such deep sadness that his chest ached from it.

Chapter Twenty-Seven

I have not had any desire to write in a long time. The pain of losing my baby in that ugly, cold place drives me to the edge of madness, and I sometimes wake, screaming in the night, in the little apartment I have rented downtown. Each day I grapple with the loss of my love and my hope, knowing that nearly all things that are important to me have been ripped away, leaving gaping scars that will not heal. I have lost Shane. I will never see Erich again. I have lost the only thing that I could keep of him. I now feel such burning hatred for the war, for my mother. For myself. I wonder, sometimes, if it was real.

There is so much I do not know. Times I feel such a yearning in my heart that I ache with it. Perhaps he got to Canada, or all the way home? Will he find me again? Then I realize that these are the dreams of a lost girl, and I know that, no matter how much I hope, or pray, that Erich is gone for good, and that Danny did something terrible to him that night, or that the Nazi officers caught him trying to slip back into camp and meted out justice for his traitorous risk. What I do know is that, if he were alive, he would stop at nothing to find me. Nothing. I believe this to be true, and nothing keeps me from these thoughts.

It took weeks to heal from the infection that put me in the hospital. The doctors said I may never be able to have children again. Too much damage to my body from the birth, and the lack of sterility in that damned house. During those weeks, I would lie awake and want to hunt down every person who put me there and kill them with my bare hands.

I received letters and gifts from friends back home, but I did not open them. My mother came again to see me, toward the end of my stay at the hospital. I told her that I would never, ever forgive her for what she had done to me. She sobbed and sniffled, but I did not back down. The other girls in the ward tried to look away and not appear to listen, but they heard the punishment that I bestowed upon my mother's shoulders, and she sat miserably and took it.

"What have you told people, Mother?" I demanded, bitterly. "How are you explaining this to your church friends?"

She sniffled. "I told them you'd been in an accident…"

"Ha! An accident! Some accident. Did you tell them you stuck me in that God forsaken den to hide me away? Did you? Did you tell them that I was a traitor and a sinner and was going to go to Hell for having a Nazi baby?" My voice was getting louder, and she tried to shush me.

I pushed her hand away from my arm. I did lower my voice, then, but continued. "Well, your prophecy came true. I was in Hell. And now you can live with that for the rest of your life. Just like I have to."

"You have no idea what it's like to lie there, in that God-forsaken place, feeling your life sucked away from you. Why didn't you send me to a place where I could get proper care? Why? Did you know they told me there will be no more children?"

My mother gasped, looked horrified, and my head fell back onto the pillow, my energy spent. I looked away. "Where is Dad? Have you poisoned him, too?"

"Your father is not well, Eva. He has suffered so." She fumbled with her kerchief and wiped her eyes. "He believes you to be working as a nanny for a Rebekka's family."

I looked back at her. "You mean you lied to him, too? What of *your* sins, Mother?"

"Eva, I'm only trying to protect him from the truth."

"What truth is that? Your truth, or mine? And Mother, what about Danny? He had something to do with this. You know he did."

"Now, Eva," she protested. "You know that is not true. Daniel would not do such a thing."

"Like he wouldn't steal or get drunk or start fights?"

"He's just hit hard times, Eva."

"You always spoiled him, mama, because of his hearing. But many people live without hearing, or arms or legs, and never turn mean like he did. And I know he killed Erich-"

"Don't you say it, girl!" she spat at me. "Don't you dare say that! If anything happened to that, that prisoner, it's because he deserved it. Why, he *forced* himself on you, my very daughter, and if Danny tried to save your honor, then he deserves some thanks for that!"

I stared, dumbfounded. "Are you serious? No one forced himself on me. For God's sake, you can't really believe that, can you? Does that help you feel better, to lie to yourself? Your precious daughter is no saint. I loved Erich. I still love Erich."

Her lips were thin. "You don't know what love is, Eva. You don't know the things people do to protect their loved ones."

I shook my head. "I can't believe this. You know as well as I do that Danny never loved anyone but himself. And you are no better. You put what people think far ahead of your family, and, soon, you will have nothing left." I stopped, my thoughts racing, and stared at her again. "What did you do, Mother? Did you- Did you help him hurt Erich?"

"I'm not going to sit here and listen to this-" She fumbled with her purse, and gloves, but made no move to leave.

"Go away, Mother. I have nothing left to say to you."

Over time I healed, at least physically, and set about starting anew. Jobs became scarce once the war was over, and soldiers and nurses started to come back from overseas, but I was able to get a job as an operator for Northwestern Bell. Rebekka and Betty came to see me, taking me to lunch at the St. Paul Hotel where we were treated like queens. It was so lovely to see them. Betty had for the first time, left her daughter with Jerry, who had returned in January, thankfully, without injury.

When I asked about Tom, Rebekka's eyes became shadowed, and Betty answered, saying Tom was recovering nicely back at home.

"He was injured in Germany," Betty glanced at her mother as she spoke. "his leg. The same one that he crushed in that accident in 1941. He's healing properly, but I think he will always have a limp. Doc Johnson told him that the leg would never be the same, because they weren't able to get him treatment when he needed it. I know it causes him pain, but he never says anything. You know how Tommy is; he just forges ahead."

Rebekka inquired about Joe. "Your mother told me that Joe will be in Saint Cloud at the hospital in a couple of weeks."

"Yes, Joe wrote me a letter. He's in Virginia now for rehabilitation. I plan to go see him as soon as I can."

We spoke of the town and whose marriages survived the war, whose did not. Over desserts of apple pie and rich, dark coffee, we had a lovely conversation, and when they dropped me at my apartment building, I felt such loneliness that tears came to my eyes. How I have missed Betty and the girls we used to be.

Chapter Twenty-Eight

On a crisp and sunny day in May, I drove to Saint Cloud, to finally see my brother again. He'd arrived there a little over a week before, and I could not contain my excitement as I parked the car. Because I had no information about which building he was in, I wandered into the main lobby, and was taken aback when they directed me to the psychiatric ward.

I felt my first pang of anxiety as I wandered down the halls toward the building where Joe was staying. Soldiers in wheelchairs lined the halls. Some looked at me, others did not, just staring at the floor. Nurses in white uniforms and caps handed out medicine. No one paid much attention to me.

The extent of injuries to these men was beyond my grasp. Men with missing arms, legs. Some with hollowed skulls and sunken eyes. I had been naïve in my excitement, and I was nervous as I stepped through the door of the psych ward. When the charge nurse, a grim looking woman with bad teeth and a long, narrow face, directed me to Joe, I had trouble spotting him.

I asked again, and she impatiently pointed, "there, don't you see?" and continued working on the charts in front of her. Joe had not known I was coming, but suddenly, there was a man wheeling himself toward me. A man I did not recognize, and I tried hard to contain my shock at the sight of him. The man who was coming toward me was terribly gaunt, with a patch over one eye and pure white hair.

He was unshaven and in a robe over hospital issued cotton pajamas, several sizes too large for his frail frame. His hands, pushing the wheels of the chair, were shaking. But the one eye that saw me twinkled with happiness as he reached where I was standing, dumbstruck.

"Chickadee," he said, his voice so familiar. "I'm so glad you're here." He reached with those hands to me, and I threw myself into his arms, sobbing quietly.

"Oh, Joe. I have missed you so." I cried into his shoulder.

"Me, too, Eva." He replied. His arms, though as thin as spindles, were still strong.

I wheeled him out to the grounds, and we strolled, feeling the pring sun on our backs. Calls of greeting came from several others, and Joe greeted each of them in kind. He seemed to be well-liked, a leader of sorts, and the men who were there seemed to regard him with affection.

I found a spot in the shade and we sat, Joe in his wheelchair and I on a bench. The breeze was warm, and I removed my hat to feel the sun on my head. We spent some time just catching up, and laughing, almost like old times.

I had packed a picnic basket with sandwiches, fruit and jars of lemonade. I'd even made Joe's favorite cookies, a soft sugar cookie made with sour cream. Joe barely ate anything, just picked at the foodstuff in his lap. At times, when we were between topics, he would sit and stare at nothing, and at one point, dozed off. Sleep, he said, was nothing but a nightmare, and he tried not to, at all costs. I asked him what he meant, and at first, he didn't appear to hear me.

When he spoke, his voice was strangely devoid of emotion, and he did not look at me. "Eva, I have been in hell." I waited, trying to be patient. The protracted silence was overwhelming, but, finally, the floodgates opened and he began to speak.

"I lost. I lost. I-I lost…" He seemed to have difficulty putting things into word. "I watched good men, good boys, fall. I looked the enemy in the eye, and I never missed. The water churned with the blood of the boys, and the Japs, and the natives. There was a beach where I put the wings down for the last time. It was covered with death. Children. Women holding tight to their little dark-haired babies. Young soldiers, with rags on their thin bodies and old guns that failed them."

"The stench seeped into my skin. Bodies, blackened from the sun, were strewn all along that beach...."

"I pulled my service revolver and ran toward the jungle. It was so thick, so hot. I ran, Eva. I ran away from my machine and kept running until I was deep in the jungle. I kept hearing the rounds, and the screams. My God, the screaming wakes me every night..." Joe's voice trailed away. I reached over and took his hand, but he seemed not to notice.

He spoke, and sometimes mumbled. The things he had seen were beyond what his mind could comprehend. He'd been the Ace, he said. Graduated top of his class and earned the title of Second Lieutenant before he ever saw battle. He was up for a medal, and he was sick with it, because he did not deserve it. It was nothing more than being in the wrong place at the right time, he said.

When he sat in the jungle that day, hearing the sounds and smelling the stench of rotting bodies and fuel and gun powder, Joe's spirit broke. When he heard someone running toward him, he panicked. And when he saw the young boy break through the heavy foliage, he shot, hitting the boy in the face. Joe sat, watching the boy die, and wept.

The days turn dark early in the South Pacific. He sat there, with the dead boy, until long after dark. The cries turned to moans, then the moans turned to silence. He crept out of the darkness and back to the beach, stumbling over a fallen GI whose body was grotesquely burned. It was pitch black, but he made his way back to the plane, a P-51 Mustang he'd christened, "Maggie" for the girl he left at the station in his hometown that day. The plane was a burned out shell, still hot and smoldering from the blast that had taken her from flight.

In the distance, he heard sounds of artillery. He felt the ground shake from the continuous torpedo assault and the strafe of gunnery fire that accompanied it. The dark of night did little to slow the assault, due in large part to the radar equipped TBMs, continuously hammering the islands with bombs of fire.

I wept as he told me the story, holding his cool, gnarled hand in mine, and listened, sometimes murmuring softly, "Oh, Joe..."

The horizon continued to light up throughout the night. Joe sat against a palm tree at the edge of the dense jungle foliage, brushing mosquitos away and waited. He never saw what hit him, but the next thing he remembers is waking up in a hospital bed with one eye and unable to speak, his jaw wired shut, and his broken mind screaming in agony.

Over the next few weeks, I drove to the Veteran's Hospital as often as time and my budget would allow. I would push Joe's wheelchair out over the grounds and sit in the sun. Even on the hot days, Joe is wrapped in a blanket. On the days it rained, we sat in the cafeteria and talked, sometimes with other soldiers. He seemed to gain strength more and more each visit, but he had trouble, sometimes, with breathing.

"The malaria got me, Evie," he said as he wheezed. "I spent months in Australia after they took me out of the field. There were hundreds of men there, many who had been airlifted from Bataan. They were like the walking dead, Eva." He said, absently wiping crumbs from the blanket. "If anyone deserves a medal, it would be one of those guys, stuck on that Godforsaken island with no food or water, slowly dying. They were so bitter."

I took a sip of the strong hospital coffee, suffused with sugar and cream. "I have heard stories on the radio and in the news about that. How horrible it must have been for those men, Joe."

He nodded. "They called the General, "Dugout Doug." Many of those men had very little good to say about him. Such a lack of respect." He picked at his plate. "They were left there for over two years, to rot in the stinking jungle, wiping their asses with their shirttails and shitting out more than they could ever eat."

Joe's face had a hard grimace, and a muscle twitched under the patch covering his absent eye. "The Filipino people, they had no chance against the Japs. They are kind, and subservient. But they have such faith and never gave up." He sighed. "They just weren't built to fight…"

I changed the subject. "Joe, tell me about the airplanes you flew over there. Remember, when I was a kid, you used to grill me every time I walked in your room."

He grinned then. "Ah, you remember, huh? I flew that Mustang on recon with the B-29s. Yeah, Maggie, she could fly. She'd get a little shaky at the higher speeds, but she was smooth and quiet on the lower end." Joe was staring out the window, watching the rain pour down on the ground below. "I dodged many-a Kamikaze with that beast. Bastards…"

I had to smile at that; it seemed that Joe was finally getting back to his old feisty self.

Joe smiled back, cocked his head. "Eva, what happened between you and Ma?"

I nearly choked on the water I had put to my lips. "Why? Has Mom said something?"

"No, see, that's the problem. She won't say a word about you." He looks puzzled. "Only thing she would say is that you never go home anymore. Did you know that Dad had a stroke?"

I shook my head, feeling suddenly sick. "No, no one told me. Is he all right, Joe?"

He shrugged. "I don't know. He doesn't come here often and never really says much. The war, losing Shane. It takes its toll on all of us. But, Evie, you're the only daughter she has. Talk to her."

I shook my head. "I can't. Not this time." I gathered the plates and utensils together, avoiding eye contact. "Please don't ask again."

"Did Danny have something to do with it?"

"Why do you ask that, Joe?"

"Because he was always a mean little bastard. And always wanted what he couldn't have, ever since he was a kid. He never figured out that the only thing holding him back was himself. He's disappeared, Mom's nearly mute when it comes to him, and you won't say a damned thing. I know he's a drunk, and I know she babied him all those years because of his ears. But what I don't know is what happened between you two."

He continued. "What of this man, Eva. The Nazi who worked on the farm."

My eyes widened. "What?"

"People talk." Joe shrugged. "It was in the newspaper. The radio. He worked for Pa. Tell me straight, Eva. Did he do something to hurt you? Is that what this is about?"

"Just let it go, Joe." There would never be a day that I would share the secrets. The betrayal of my heart. Love of a Nazi. The child borne and died of that love. The punishment I knew God was wreaking on my soul for loving the enemy. I was convinced Joe would never forgive me, any more than I could forgive myself.

I set my jaw and I shook my head, staring out over the grounds. "He would never hurt me, Joe. Never. If you're hearing that from Mother, she is lying to you."

"She says nothing, but Evie, I'm going home in a few weeks. I'd really like it if you would be there." He sighed. "Ma's throwing some God damned party, thinks I need to see all my old friends." He let out a bitter laugh. "Me with one eye, no legs and lungs that cough blood. Why the hell would I want to see anyone?"

I thought about that conversation some weeks later. With my work schedule, I had not made it back to the hospital to see him before he was discharged. Mom planned a party for that Saturday in July, roasting a young sow from the farrowing pen, slicing watermelon and making an endless array of salads. All the neighbors, friends and family attended. A bunch of Joe's friends, some of whom had returned from the war as heroes.

Eli Shutz, who had stood with Joe on the platform waiting to ship off to the war, was there with his wife, a girl he married and brought home from Iowa, and their two young sons. Eli had returned to the States with a Medal of Honor and a leg full of shrapnel, but he never lost his boyish good nature, and seemed happy to be back on the family farm.

The Hamiltons were there, and the Nielsens. Betty set her plump little girl onto Joe's lap, and he held her a long time, holding her hand and bouncing her on his knee. Betty told Joe that Tom was doing well, that he'd been injured in Germany but was happy to be alive, and he was intending to stop out to see Joe soon.

Maggie Gunderson came to the picnic, looking beautiful and voluptuous and sporting a brilliant diamond ring. She'd become engaged to Jonathan Shank after he returned home, a fact that surprised us all, considering they had hated each other in high school. Maggie had always seemed to have her sights set on Joe, but it seemed she and Jonathan had started talking after he returned to New Ulm where she still worked at the grocery store. Jonathan appeared in the store often, always on Maggie's shift.

They'd talk at her checkout counter, or he'd find her stocking the canned goods, or wrapping meats. Her uncle owned the store, and he'd roll his eyes and walk the other way when he saw Jonathan coming, but he had a twinkle in his eye. A girl like Margaret could do worse than to attract the attention of a good kid like Jonathan, who was tall and resembled Van Johnson.

I received a letter from Maggie after, and she said it had pained her so much to see Joe in that wheelchair, but she had so enjoyed spending time with him that day. The summer had been muggy and hot, but that day, the breeze had been cool, keeping the mosquitoes at bay, and the crowd that gathered had been so delighted that Joe, the golden boy whom everyone adored, had come home in one piece.

As the day went by, families and older neighbors drifted on, until there was just a small group of Joe's friends, sitting around a fire in the backyard and drinking frosty mugs of homemade cider beer. They talked and laughed way into the night. No one really mentioned the war, or Joe's eyepatch, or the fact that he was unable to walk.

Several of the boys set up a ramp so Joe could wheel in and out of the house and into the make-shift bedroom that had once been Mom's sitting room. It had been a beautiful day, and long after Mom and Dad retired to bed, Joe and his buddies stayed around the fire, until the last few had left.

Joe sat there for a long time, until the last embers of the fire went out. Somewhere in the predawn hours, when the sun was beginning to cast a glow in the east but the moon was still in the horizon, Joe wheeled himself into the tool shed, where he had earlier hidden a small box of shells and the old Winchester Dad kept there for coyotes and the occasional skunk that ventured onto the farm. With almost superhuman strength, he pushed a heavy box of tools in front of the door, struggling to pull the old wooden crate across the room, and spread out on the floor an old tarp that used to cover the firewood next to the outhouse.

He pulled himself out of the wheelchair, carefully placing himself on the tarp so as not to leave a mess for Ma or Pa, or, God forbid, his little sister to clean up. Loading one shell into the chamber, Joseph Kelly rigged the trigger with a lever made of twine and a wooden stick, placed the gun under his chin, and fired.

I got the call that Sunday afternoon. I had skipped the party, even after receiving letters from Mother and Joe, even Betty. Instead, I'd spent Saturday with friends; we'd packed sandwiches and gone to Como Park to bask in the beautiful day, walk through the gardens and the zoo, and try to escape the guilt I felt for choosing not to attend Joe's coming home event.

I'd slept restlessly; had nightmares of blood frothing pink in the Cottonwood River and woke with a start in a cold sweat just before dawn. I went to church and then to lunch and a matinee. It was late when I returned home, and the telephone was ringing when I walked through the door.

"Eva." My mother's normally strong voice, now weak with pain and swimming in tears. "Please. Come home."

I felt fear grip me, making my breath catch in my chest. "Mom, is it Dad?"

"No." I heard her sob, and I knew.

"No, Mom. Please. No…" I slid down to the floor, dropped the telephone and wept.

Why is it that all the men I loved in my heart and soul were taken from me? My beloved Shane. Erich. My beautiful baby boy. Now Joe. I stood in the cemetery over the casket that held Joe's body, shaking, feeling the heat through my smart linen suit. My mother knelt by the casket, sobbing and wailing.

Dad, unable to walk anymore, in a wheelchair that was provided by the local Red Cross, just staring at the ground. Danny, the only brother I had left, was nowhere to be found. When the bagpipes played Amazing Grace, I had a vision of Joe and his pals, walking the Oktoberfest parade in full Scottish kilts and regalia, trying to play the bagpipes but only making wretched whining noises. How we'd teased him. I wiped a tear with my gloved hand.

Across the casket my eyes met the impassive eyes of Rebekkah. Betty stood next to her, holding her hand and wiping her eyes with a kerchief. As my eyes traveled throughout the group, I felt the weight of the oppressive heat, and the malignant stares of the community who had gathered to say good-bye to Joe, ever curious. Some hostile.

The Benediction was read. Jerry, Jonathan and Eli were among the soldiers who stood at attention, firing their weapons into the horizon. I felt the salute in my bones, heard the haunting melody as taps were played. Felt the sweat slowly slide down my back and the sickness inside that was threatening to overtake me. It was too much for me.

I turned to leave, stumbling as I tried to disentangle from the mourning crowd. I began to feel light-headed and put a gloved hand to my head. I felt the ground give way, and a strong arm reach me as I began to fall. Just before I fainted, my eyes caught those of the man who grabbed me before I hit the ground.

When I came to, I was lying in my old room. I felt a pang of nostalgia as so many memories came flooding back to me. It was as though I had never left it. I lie there, feeling the air of the box fan that was in the window, and cried for a long time. Eventually, I tied my hair into a braid, pulled on an old dress from the back of the closet, and went to find Sasha.

I rode Sasha bareback, along the meadow road and out to the old place, feeling the hot July air on my face, and Sasha's supple back against my skin. How I had missed this, the way she and I would be connected, flying like the wind. We were both rusty, she and I, but as soon as she felt the subtle shift of my leg, she cut loose, running fast and furious to the meadow, knowing the trail by heart, trusting her instincts.

We rode for a long time, meandering by the river, then into the clearing. My heart, barely 19 years old, felt old and broken, and I wept for a long time, laying across Sasha's back, who stood with such patience. The sky began to turn dark, bringing with it much needed rain, and I turned the mare to head back home, leaving the meadow and following the ridge of oak trees along the trail.

Suddenly there was a man standing, on the edge of the clearing by the oak trees, his hat shielding his face. Startled, Sasha reared beneath me, and I felt myself sliding from her back. I fell to the ground, felt pain in my shoulder, and lay stunned for a moment. I could hear Sasha's nervous whinny, but she did not leave my side.

When I opened my eyes, two polished black shoes came into view. I sat up and saw Detective Brandt who had interrogated me so many months earlier, stop a few feet from me. Sasha snorted and pranced around me, and he did not step any closer.

"I'm sorry, Ms. Kelly. I didn't mean to startle the horse." He said. But the words were not convincing of sincerity.

"Don't you know better than to sneak up on a rider like that?" I demanded, sullenly, wincing at the throbbing of my head. "What do you want? Why are you on my property?"

He didn't answer right away, just stood there, chewing on a long piece of grass. "Well, now, Ms. Kelly, I hear you lost your brother. Killed himself, didn't he?"

I stared at him, wincing at the abrasive words, then repeated. "Why are you here?"

"I thought it was about time we had a little chat, since you were back in town and all. You were, where, staying with an aunt?" He asked, kneeling to offer a hand to help me stand, which I ignored. "I admit I was confused about you disappearing after we last talked. But Ms. Nielsen, she insisted that you didn't know anything about that Nazi soldier that disappeared last year."

I stood and attempted to brush mud and grass from my legs and dress, noting how his eyes lazily traveled the length of my body, the dress now soaked from the rain and clinging to me like a second skin, before his cold eyes met mine.

"I don't know where he went, Mr. Brandt. But I'm sure if you wanted to talk to me, you could have phoned and asked me to come to the station so Sgt. Jones could ask questions as well."

"Oh, I don't see a need for all that. Better that you and me just have a nice, quiet little talk where no one can bother us."

I felt a pang of fear but held it in check. "I don't think so, Detective. I have nothing new to add to the story, and I'm, frankly, not interested in standing in the rain out here with you. So, if you'll excuse me-"

I felt his hand grip my arm, and he stood close to me, so close that the water from the brim of his hat dripped to my face. "You aren't listening to me, Eva." He said. "I want you to tell me everything."

I wrenched my arm away. "There's nothing more to tell. You have obviously been listening to small town gossip. Erich worked for my father. That is all. You know more about what happened that night than I do."

The rain was pouring down on us now, and I pulled closer to Sasha's side. "You must have gotten nowhere with your digging if you're out here in the rain talking to the one person who has been gone since that whole affair."

He cocked his head. "Interesting word. Was it an affair or just some little fling with the enemy? Sedition is a dangerous charge, Eva. Your whole family could suffer if it came out that they were untruthful about helping the enemy escape."

"You know my mother and father did no such thing!"

"I do not know that. I do know that he was a prisoner who was befriended by your family, and then he was gone."

"Please, leave my family alone. They are innocent."

"Ah, yes, Eva. But are you?"

The rain stopped, suddenly. In the eerie silence, I heard a voice. "Eva. Are you all right?"

Startled, I turned my head toward the path, and my eyes met those of the man who had saved me from hitting the ground when I fainted. "Tom."

Tom approached, his eyes never leaving my face. "I saw you ride out. Your mother was worried when it started to rain." He stopped near me and touched my arm protectively.

I was so relieved to see him, I nearly fell against him, but steadied myself. "I am fine. Thank you. I was just going to head back to the farm when I ran into this gentleman."

They eyed each other squarely. Then Brandt smiled and tipped his hat. "Well, Ms. Kelly, now that you're in capable hands, I'll take my leave. Mind, you come down to the station so we can finish this discussion now, y'hear?"

He left, not saying anything more, walking along the fence that would lead him to the road. I closed my eyes and laid my head on Sasha's shoulder. Tom's hand dropped to his side, and we were silent. I could not know why Brandt chose to just drop the subject and leave, but I was so relieved. I did not know what secrets Tom knew, or what lies he had been told, but I felt such sorrow for the young girl I had been when he had last touched my face.

Oh, Tom. What have I done? The words are in my head, but I do not say them aloud. Instead, I tell him he looks well, thank him for coming to my rescue, at the church, and in the meadow, and I grasped Sasha's mane to pull myself to her back. Tom's dark face, leaner than before, scarred from the war, is unreadable. He let me go.

Chapter Twenty-Nine

Some secrets between a man and his wife are never revealed to the outside world. Eva and Tom loved beyond all guilt and shame and lived a life of absolute dedication. They were madly in love. Tom held onto his grieving wife each time she miscarried, as she clung to him and wept huge, haunting tears. He prayed, keeping a vigil by his wife's side, when the doctors said that the baby was a miracle, but she would not be able to have another.

When Tom was diagnosed with cancer, Eva took care of him, nursing him, soothing him as he endured chemotherapy and radiation treatments that left him spent. She watched her beloved Tom waste away slowly and hated the cancer that was eating him up inside. Eva lay beside her husband in his last days, in the bed they had shared for over forty years and held him as he took his last breath.

The FBI and the local Sheriff's office began an investigation into the death of Erich Gerhardt, identifying his remains by the remnants of the soldier's PW suit that had been issued at his capture. The forensics lab noted he had been badly beaten, and that his death was likely due to a heavy blow to the head. The death certificate indicated homicide as the cause of death.

Although Claire knew of Eva's secrets, as did Matt and Betty, and, to some extent, Lyneah and her Detective, no one, not even Chris, divulged them to the authorities. The conclusion was that someone, likely Daniel

Kelly, had killed the German man and dumped his body into an old wooden fermentation tank from the brewing company. Although no records existed, it was believed that Kelly had stolen the tank, or taken it from the brewery grounds, during a time of remodel and growth for the brewery following the end of Prohibition.

The barrel was buried near the banks of the river. Over time, wetland drainage has caused the Cottonwood river watershed to change course. With periods of drought and then torrential flooding in the valley, the river slowly eroded the soil around the barrel, causing it to become part of the marshy riverbank, slowly heaving upward each spring during thaw.

During the investigation, it became clear that Daniel Kelly had not been well liked in the community. He'd had an abrasive personality and had struggled to keep a job. It had been no surprise to anyone the level of violence that he was capable of. They interviewed some of the older folks in town, those whose names came up as acquaintances or friends of the family, including Betty and Jerry. Both confirmed what the others implied, that Daniel was bad seed, and there had been suspicion in the town from the very beginning that he had something to do with it.

Chris Breuning tried to locate the cold case file, but no archives remained, and the Feds divulged little, only that they'd traced Daniel Kelly to an oil rigging outfit in Oklahoma. Kelly was in a memory care facility in Oklahoma City, and unable to communicate. He'd had a wife and son. His wife died in 1983. The son, also named Daniel, lived in Oklahoma with his wife, and two of their three children. The FBI was sending an agent from their field office to connect with the Kelly clan.

After Lyneah's recovery, she and Chris had dinner with Betty and Jerry one evening toward the end of August, when the world began to change and the slightest hint of summer's end was in the air. They sat on the deck, watching Jerry grill steaks while the sun set, and Betty spoke.

"You know, Eva came to stay and work on the farm after her Dad passed away. She and Tom got married and lived with Abigaile all those years. I know it was difficult for Eva to take care of her toward the end. They never had a good relationship." She took a sip of her wine. "Eva and Tom wanted kids right away, and every time she tried and miscarried, it seemed Abigaile had something to say. She was a very unhappy, superstitious old woman, and she would make these little comments to Eva about reaping what you sow and God's punishment."

Betty paused, then said, "After Abigaile died, Eva hired a private investigator to find Daniel."

Lyneah stared at her mother. "Really? What happened?"

"Nothing, really. They traced him to Oklahoma, just where the FBI said he was, and she sent him a letter about their mother's death. When he responded, all he wanted to know is how he was going to get his half of the estate. Tom and Eva sold land that Abigaile and Bill had purchased south of the river and paid him off, got him to sign something about his inheritance."

"It was difficult for her to deal with Danny. He started calling the house I think in the late 90s, looking for more money. He wouldn't let up, calling all the time. Tom and Eva hired a lawyer in town, you know, Dave Carlson's dad. It turned out that Danny had a real gambling problem, first on the horses, then casinos. He had blown through the money from the estate really quickly, and wouldn't leave Eva alone until Ed Carlson stepped in." She paused. "I think Ed knew what had happened between Daniel and Eva and he was able to persuade Daniel to stop going after her."

"Wow, Mom. That is so sad. I had no idea."

"You know, she kept that stuff to herself. But it was hard, especially after she lost Isabelle and Claire, bless her heart, was such a strong willed and hurt little bird. She had her hands full without having to deal with him, too."

"You think he killed the POW?" Chris asked.

"There is no doubt in my mind." She stood up as Jerry approached with a platter of steaming steaks and shrimp skewers. "No doubt whatsoever.

Claire made her way uphill through the Stations of the Way of the Cross, an homage to the last moments of Christ's life. The day was beautiful, and she was reflective as she stopped to observe each depiction, with statues imported from Germany encased in brick and glass. She knew Eva's time was near; the nursing home had called and said it was time to meet and discuss hospice options. Claire felt the burden of the decision as a heavy weight on her heart, but at 90, Eva had lived a full and rich life.

The painful circumstances that surrounded Eva's firstborn also weighed heavily on Claire. Suspicion about the circumstances of the birth, and death, of the child began to form in her mind. Perched on a bench near the chapel, she pulled a file out of her bag and paged through it.

Eva had said she'd heard the strong cries of a baby before she passed out, but Claire had done some research and found no birth or death certificate for the child. Throughout the years, and the more and more sporadic entries in the journals, Eva, herself, had questioned whether the child had died at birth. During the '40s, there was a significant increase in pregnancies among young women whose lovers were shipping off to war. Baby brokers sprung up all over the United States, and a black market for babies, places where young mothers could drop their infants and return to the factory Monday morning, were a growing populous. Claire contacted a colleague at the U of Minnesota, a former classmate, who gave her information about the home where Eva had been incarcerated until her baby was born.

"Frankly, Claire, there were a lot of suspicions about the place, but in the '40s there were no laws protecting young mothers from these places. Nothing was in place to prosecute the people who made a living selling those kids. Even when those laws went into place, the home was long dissolved. There are no records."

Claire's friend sighed. "I wish I could tell you more but there's nothing. I'm sorry. You could check the City of Edina for death or cemetery records to see what they have."

Claire's research in Edina also yielded few clues, most notably, that the "private" cemetery was a plot that was in the corner of the old St. Patrick's Cathedral cemetery. Claire and Matt got a list and map for "baby does" and walked among the mostly unmarked graves. Claire placed daisies on as many graves as she could and wept with frustration and sadness. Eva would never know what happened to her son.

They buried Eva on a crisp September morning, next to her beloved Tom.

Obligation forced Claire to return to Champaigne to fulfill her contract at the University. She and Matt visited each other as often as possible. They quietly married in the old farmhouse on the weekend before Christmas, sharing the ceremony with only their closest friends and family. Claire could feel the flutter of the child inside her as she said her vows, and Matt had tears in his eyes as he kissed his new bride.

The diaries ended. Years later, Eva's last entry were words for her granddaughter.

How does this story end? With forgiveness. Your grandfather and I had such a life and cherished every moment. War stripped us of our boys, but it also set us free to embrace all that our lives had to offer and not waste a moment.

We lost your mother, but she has always been with us. I know you feel her, Claire. I do, too. Every day, I know she is near us, watching over you. Life flows by, just as the Cottonwood flows through the valley. Don't waste a moment of it.

Epilogue

"Matt? Can you change Shane, honey? The bag is on the counter and I need to run to the bathroom again." Claire reached down and blew raspberries on her son's neck, listening to his giggle in her ear. Run may be pushing it; she stood heavily, feeling the weight of the daughter she carried pull on her aching back.

Matt walked into the living room with the bag, carrying a sandwich. "You okay?" he asked her.

She made a face as he reached down and helped her stand. "My bladder is the size of a pea and my back is killing me." She grumbled. "And my feet look like balloons."

"Hey, I love your feet!" Matt said, kissing her before he sat down with the boy. "Even when they're purple...."

He yelped as she aimed one of those toes into his side. "Very funny..." she threw at him as she hobbled to the bathroom.

Matt called to his wife through the door. "Lyneah called; said she needs us to bring an extra roaster for the picnic."

"Did she say when she expected Nate to arrive?"

"She wasn't sure, but sometime around 1:00." Claire heard her husband chatting with their son and grinned at her image in the mirror as she put finishing touches on her makeup.

Today was the day she would finally meet Daniel Kelly's grandson, Nate, who was driving from Oklahoma. Nate had been serving overseas when Erich's remains were found. Over the last several months, Claire and Nate had corresponded via email and facebook, making plans to get together when Nate returned to the States. Lyneah was hosting a picnic at the farm, like the annual bashes that Tom and Eva had held there. There was so much to know, and so much to share.

Today was just the beginning.

CPSIA information can be obtained
at www.ICGtesting.com
Printed in the USA
LVHW031545180521
687783LV00001B/106

9 781684 707935